INVERCLYDE LIBRARIES

Published in 2012 by FeedARead.com Publishing –
Arts Council funded

A CIP catalogue record for this title is available from
the British Library.

Dedicated to my parents

Acknowledgements

I owe a great debt of gratitude to the many people who have supported me on this journey. A huge thank you to Ron Woods who has been so generous with his talent and time in helping to shape my story. To my friends in the Writers' Workshop, thank you too. I couldn't have done it without my husband Bob and children, Rhona and Callum, for their belief in me, their patience and for being such superb sounding boards. I am also very grateful to all my relatives and friends who have provided me with gems of information to add a sparkle to the story. To Natasha Footman for that last touch of polish. To Phillip Woolford for reading the final manuscript. Last but not least, to my mother who was my personal and the best story teller.

………Where is God, my maker who giveth

songs in the night….

Job 35:10

Chapter 1

London
April 2005
6.45 a.m.

The alarm clock in the bedroom jangled like a fire station's alert to an emergency. It was the only way to rouse Nick from his sleep. As my mother once said, if the sky fell on him he'd pull it over him like a blanket and go back to sleep. I was already in the *en suite* bathroom having got up fifteen minutes earlier. I heard him yawn and popped my head into the bedroom, already quite light with the half-opened curtain, to see him stretching his arms over his head, his hands tightly clasped, his face looking like a pimple being squeezed.

'Morning, darling. You remember I've got an early ethics meeting this morning?'

'Good morning, sweetheart!' Nick replied in the middle of another yawn as he wriggled to sit up. 'No, I haven't forgotten.' I turned back to the sink and heard a small groan from the bedroom. '*Ohh*, it'd be nice not to have to go in to work this morning. Instead, sit on the beach.'

I knew he was thinking of Pulau Tioman, an island off the east coast of Malaysia, where we were the previous summer. I pictured him in bed admiring his tanned lean body; he was always boasting that he hadn't put on an ounce since he was twenty one. I had to concede he didn't look too bad for his fifty-seven years. Aside from his greying sideburns and the sparse crown he'd maintained his youthful look, which I put down to his happy disposition.

'We could give up working here and, say, set up a clinic in one of the villages in Malaysia.....or maybe in the outer Hebrides.'

I spun back to the door again and pulled my toothbrush out of my mouth which was frothing like the head of a glass of beer.

'No way. I'm not going to that cold end of earth, no matter how beautiful.'

'*Och*, why not? It'll be great!'

'It's fine for a break, a get-away from the manic race, but not to live and work there. Not on your Nelly!'

I returned to the sink. I knew he was exhausted and demoralised by the cuts in the hospital. 'Shortfalls, bloody shortfalls,' he'd said, 'that's all I hear these days.' The morale on his ward was at an all time low – the staff were waiting to find out where the sharp edge of the axe was going to fall. The anxiety and dread of worse to come hung over them like a layer of oil spill. Then the Hospital Trust delivered the greatest blow. Thirty staff across the trust - doctors and nurses- were to be made redundant. In his own department, the nursing staff was already down by two. As Lead Consultant in Paediatrics he, along with other consultants, had confronted the Chief Executive but to no avail and now it was a case of waiting to see who was next to go. The senior nurses from his unit had approached him for his support. He'd seen the anxiety in their eyes. They'd been told that they would have to apply for their own jobs as the five sisters' posts were to be reduced to three. He felt most sorry for Mary who'd been Sister in his ward for as long as he'd been there. He now saw a woman, demoralised and desperately frightened of losing her job, and ironically, because of her seniority and experience. He hated what the Trust was doing to the good people he worked with and his being powerless to change the situation. He also knew he didn't have the stomach for the brutality and heartlessness that came with the axing of the staff. No wonder he was thinking of a change.

A few minutes later I heard him walking downstairs to make coffee. The morning arrangement we had for the bathroom suited me; it meant that I didn't have to hear the sound of tap water running while he brushed his teeth, a sound that still grated on my nerves.

I applied the plum-coloured lipstick, puffed up my hair after rubbing on some of the hair gel I'd pinched from my daughter, Emma, then headed for the stairs. I stood for a moment by the landing to listen for sounds in Emma's and her sister, Sarah's, bedrooms. The corridor was awash with the morning sun pouring in through the clear glass window at the end, creating sparkling reflections on the two large framed water colour paintings of petrified rocks and bamboos. I listened. There wasn't a sound. Emma, the older of the two girls, had been over-excited like a toddler on a sugar rush the night before. 'Can't sleep, Mum, *sooo* excited about my birthday party!' she'd said, clasping her hands under her chin and doing a pirouette, her face glowing with happiness. The two girls were lucky they could sleep a little longer; they could pole-vault from their bed to school which was the City of London Girls' School. From our balcony we could just see the top of its roof behind St. Giles' church.

Our decision to buy the town house in the Barbican was the best decision. An oasis set right in the middle of London city, it was fifteen minutes' walk to Bart's Hospital for Nick and forty minutes or so for me to walk to the Middlesex Hospital via the raw meat-smelling Smithfield's. Alternatively, I could take the less odorous route by No. 25 bus from Cheapside. This morning, I would take the bus because there was much to do including picking up the birthday cake that I had ordered from Selfridges.

Emma's door flung open wide and she stood grinning in the doorway, fully dressed in her uniform.

'Morning, Mum! I'm seventeen today! I can start driving lessons! *Yay!*' She rushed towards me and threw her arms round me.

'Happy birthday, darling.' As I hugged her I thought how easy it was to love her. Such a good natured girl without a trace of the Chiang temper in her, unlike me. In appearance she had a look of her own – dark brown eyes that only just hinted at the Chinese in her, and rich deep brown hair that was straight and glossy. She had no hang-ups about her looks or her race. I remember when she was about ten, she couldn't wait to tell me what had happened in school when I got home.

'This girl in Year Five called me 'Paki', Mummy!' she said, her eyes wide open. 'And I'm not even that.'

'So, what did you say?' I asked.

'I said she was ignorant to her face and walked away.'

'Good,' I said. She then promptly forgot about the incident. I was proud and relieved; long before she was born I was afraid that Nick's and my offspring would attract teasing and bullying. Emma had shown me my fears were unfounded and it seemed that Sarah was following in her footsteps. Apart from her jet black hair in contrast to Emma's and the fact that she loved her sleep like Nick, they were very similar.

They had complained when there was no box in the forms for them to tick where they had to fill in their ethnicity.

'There's *White*, *Chinese, mixed,* different mixes but not one for White and Chinese. Shall I put *Anglo-Chinese*? White? But we are not *white* white, are we, Mum?' they used to moan.

'No, you're not. You're the best mix of the lot,' I would say.

'*Ooh,* I'm so excited. Seventeen! This party is just going to be the best! Zoe has just texted me to wish me a happy birthday and so has Ella. They both said they were so looking forward to the party.' Emma had been planning the celebration of her birthday since after the Christmas decorations were taken down and put away. It was not going to be a large party, just a few good friends. The final number was sixteen, and we were going to have a meal at Joe Brown's Café in Soho. The grown ups – our good friends Vicky and Colin, Nick and I - would eat in *Luigi's* restaurant nearby, so as not to cramp their style.

'Make sure you clear your rooms a little before Mrs Kingsley comes,' I said.

'But Mum, that's why she is here, to clean!'

'Just reorganise your mess anyway, so it doesn't look too bad. Is Sarah not up yet?'

'No, she said not to wake her. Her alarm's set and she'll catch up with me.'

I took a last look in the mirror in the hall. I was pleased with the new tailored black silk suit which contrasted well with my red stilettos. I ran my fingers through my black hair once more then picked up my handbag and briefcase.

'I'm off now and don't you be late for school!' I called out as I opened the front door.

'No, we won't! Bye Mum! See you tonight and don't forget, it's at Joe Brown's Café!' Emma shouted back.

7.42 a.m.

As I pushed open the heavy door from the lift area onto the Podium level above the street, the buzz of the city hit me like the rush of air into a vacuum. I loved it - hurrying footsteps on the tiled floor and the sound of the morning traffic below. I felt alive and ready to meet the onslaught of the day starting with the Ethical Committee meeting with Prof. Jones in the chair, a ward round and then outpatients' clinic in the afternoon. The morning sunshine added a lift to my steps as I made my way across London Wall and down Wood Street to the corner newsagents on Cheapside.

'Good morning,' I said as I paid for my *Times* over the counter, behind which the solemn-faced Mrs Rawal was sitting. She made no attempt to engage with me when she took the coins from me. As I walked away, I heard her greet the man behind me.

'Good morning, sir,' she said in a high-pitched voice. 'Very nice morning today.'

I bought my papers there nearly every day, and yet, Mrs Rawal was reluctant to acknowledge me. Years ago I would have taken offence, taken it to be a snub on account of my colour, but not now. As I walked out of the shop, my thoughts went back to what Nick had said earlier about working in Malaysia. *No, I wasn't ready for that.* Maybe in two or three years' time when the children were older. Or, at least after I'd finished the book that I was writing with Rob Jones. My life was full, and I was enjoying it. Involuntarily, I inhaled deeply. There was too much to do. Although sometimes I felt as if I was a traveller and hadn't set down roots anywhere, I was much more content and happier than I'd been for a long time. But, did I feel part of the community that I lived in? I knew my next-door neighbours whom I got on well with. Apart from that I was too busy. Besides, everyone else was the same.

The suited city workers, scurrying like ants out on a hunt for food and water, were rushing around me as I hurried across Cheapside towards the bus stop. Three yards from the bus stop, I noticed a fresh bunch of flowers at the base of the lamp-post where a black taxi-driver had been killed by a group of white youths.

11.05a.m.

The telephone on Angela's desk rang. Angela, who'd changed out of her motorbike leather outfit and now looked like a model out of some glossy magazine, picked up the phone and put on her plummy voice.

'Good morning, Dr. Chiang's secretary,' she said. A long pause, then, 'I'll put her on.' She placed her hand over the mouthpiece and turned to look at me. 'It's long distance. Malaysia.'

Something in her voice, or was it the look in her eyes, immediately alerted me that there was something wrong. I was aware that my pulse was racing. I wondered which one of my sisters it could be. It could not be my father; to him, long distance calls were too expensive for social chats. I quickly worked out that it would be about five o'clock in the evening in Malaysia. Knowing my sisters

14

wouldn't call me at work it had to be urgent. I lifted the handset on my desk.

'Hello.'

'Chiew, it's Mei Lin,' her voice quivered. 'Papa had a heart attack this morning.'

'Oh, no! Oh, God! Where is he? How did it happen? How is Mother?'

'He's in the General Hospital... he's in a coma.' I felt as if a cold hand was slowly clawing out my heart. 'Ma is very calm. In shock.'

'Give me the number of the doctor's hand phone, the doctor looking after Papa.'

'I'll get it for you and ring you back.'

'I'll come home right away. Get me the number quickly.'

I came off the phone shaken and realized I was crying as I pictured my father lying still, eyes closed. I wiped away my tears. Angela looked at me without saying a word. She handed me her box of tissues across my desk.

'My father collapsed not long ago and is in hospital now,' I said.

'I'm so sorry,' said Angela. 'Is there anything I can do?'

For a few moments I was flustered. Emma's party. Nick. I had to tell him. Someone to cover for me, while I was gone. I would need to speak to Keith, my opposite number, immediately. An overpowering sense of dread and fear came over me.

'Yes, will you get me the first available flight to Kuala Lumpur?'

'Yes, of course. I'll do that right away.'

I picked up the phone again and started to dial. A few seconds later, 'Nick, Father just had an M.I. I'm waiting to speak to the attending doctor...I have to go home...Angela's seeing to it for me...I'm O.K... yes...yes. I'll talk to you later.' I replaced the receiver.

Something niggled me, irritating me like food stuck between my teeth. Was it something I had seen, something someone had said to me or something I had read?

I had never felt more helpless and useless in my entire life than when I was waiting to speak to the doctor looking after my father. There I was, working in a leading cardiology department in London, while my own father was lying in a coma six thousand miles away in a hospital which might not be equipped to cope with the situation. I wanted to scream at the irony of it. I kept looking at the clock, willing Mei Lin to ring. Suddenly I realised what was niggling me. It came like a kick from a horse.

It was the dream I had several weeks earlier.

It is not any old bed; the bed frame is white metal, one I recognise as a hospital bed, similar to the ones I'd seen in the hospital in Batu Pahat as a child. The man lying in it is an old man. His face is serene, his eyes are shut. I recognise him. It is Father. There's a strange silence, almost eerie, there's no one else around apart from me. It's as if we were suspended in milky white space. I'm sitting at the bedside, holding his left hand. The gesture itself is weird, for I'm conscious I had never held his hand before as an adult. His thin hand feels cold in mine while I'm burning with questions which I can't bring myself to ask him. Suddenly he opens his eyes. He looks at peace. He turns to face me; his eyes which have lost their fire are beseeching me- to do what, I'm not sure. Then he says, 'It is alright. Everything is fine.'

I burst into tears.

I had woken up sobbing and felt warm tears running down my cheek.

An icy cold trickle went down my spine. I had a crushing sense of having been there before, that I was re-enacting a scene that had happened a long time ago. It had to do with my brother Yao. Suddenly the urgency to get to my father became overwhelming. *Hang in there, Papa. Wait for me, please don't die! Please God, don't take him away yet. I need to tell him that I'm sorry, that I love him.*

I was gripped with fear of the worst to come. I had to do something quickly, had to speak to the doctor. As I was about to pick up the phone to call Mei Lin, the phone rang. I picked it up.

'Chiew …' Before Mei Lin could say another word I knew that Father had gone.

It wasn't meant to be like this. Father wasn't meant to die without first clearing misunderstandings between us. I thought I had time, time to talk to him, to have a face- to-face confession on my part. I wanted to tell him that I was sorry. And now it was too late. A small consolation was that I did talk to him on the phone the day before he died. He was in a good mood, happy because his brother Tian was visiting him and Mother. He had brushed aside Mother's concern about his stomach-ache. '*Ahh*, nothing to worry about. Just indigestion. I ate too much onion, that's all. Mother cooked her special pig trotters in soya sauce. The pain is gone now,' he had said. Pig trotters were a rare treat; both of them were careful about their diet and Mother loved her vegetables. Every morning before sunrise they would take a long walk finishing in some food court for breakfast before taking the bus home.

Father had always been a healthy man apart from the time he broke his arm when he was struck by a motorbike and thrown off his bike in a hit-and-run accident on his way home from work. A fractured left ulna, which was not aligned properly, left him unable to bring his rice bowl to his mouth so he couldn't use chopsticks and bowl to eat. It had broken his heart as this was a part of Chinese-ness which he was particular that we children should keep, and now he had to resign himself to using a spoon and fork with a plate, the new way of eating, the Malayanised way.

'Go see a doctor if it troubles you again. No, go and see David tomorrow morning, first thing, to have a test,' I had said.

The next day when I rang my former classmate and doctor friend, David Tan, he assured me that Father's ECG was fine. Should I have insisted on a more thorough investigation? Should I have seen that heart attack coming?

I felt I had failed. I couldn't believe that I would no longer see him or hear his voice.

'I'm so sorry I can't go with you,' Nick said softly as he squeezed my hand.

'It's okay. I'll be alright.' I squeezed his hand back.

All I really wanted to do was to bury myself in him, feel his strong arms round me and hear him say it was all a dream, that Father was alive and well. But as time slowly ticked away, the fact of my father's death became more and more concrete. Mei Lin had said that the funeral would be delayed until I arrived. I knew this trip was about more than just rushing home to bury my father; it was a journey I had to make by myself to find some peace.

Nick put his hand to my face. I was aware that my eyes were puffy but I hadn't done with crying yet. The tears rolled down my cheeks. I was glad that the MAS business lounge we were sitting in was quiet; half a dozen or so men and women reading in the large arm chairs.

'I'm so sorry to have to do this to Emma,' I said.

'Don't you worry, she's fine. The party will go on as planned and she'll manage. Besides, Vicky and Colin will be there if she needs anything. So don't worry. You've got enough to think about. Remember, she's like you; she'll be alright,' said Nick.

'You think she'll deal with it, the fact that her *Koon Koon* died on her birthday?'

'She will.'

'And Sarah?'

'She's good. She had a little cry with me and said she wished she could go with you.'

18

I nodded. 'Yes, she said the same to me.' Sarah had hugged me tightly when she came home from school and found me sitting on my bedroom floor sobbing, clutching my wooden Japanese doll that Father bought me a lifetime ago. My clothes were folded on the bed ready to put into the open suitcase.

'Mum! What's wrong?' She threw herself down beside me and held me as if I was a little child.

'*Koon Koon* died this morning.'

We simply held each other as we cried. Emma came in not long after; her cheerfulness cut short by my news.

'I hope *Koon Koon* didn't suffer too much. Do you think he did?' she asked through her tears.

I shook my head. 'I don't think so.'

When I told her that I was flying at ten that night and that her father was taking me to the airport she quickly said, 'Don't worry about me and Sarah, I mean *Sarah and me.* We'll manage. I'm just sorry that you won't see *Koon Koon* any more.'

Although I wished they and Nick could come with me I knew that it was a journey I had to make by myself. There were too many things to sort out in my head without having to worry about how they were coping when we got back to Batu Pahat. A snapshot of my father and the two girls popped up in my mind: he was holding a brush in his hand poised over a sheet of paper and telling the girls how he would paint them each a picture. Within minutes he had painted a caricature of them while their little jaws dropped. I regretted that Emma and Sarah didn't get to know their grandfather better because of the physical distance, but then, I didn't know my father all that well myself. When was the last time we had a long heart-to-heart talk? I couldn't remember. It was easier to talk to him on the phone; he was always happy to hear me and we would talk about what we had done, but nothing that went deeper than the surface of our day–to-day routine. As long as I knew he and Mother were alright I was happy and then it was 'good-bye' from me.

I looked at my watch. 'I should make my way to Departures now.'

Normally Nick would say we had plenty of time and not to hurry but this time he didn't argue. He picked up my hand luggage, stood up and waited for me.

'Ring me as soon as you arrive,' he said when we got to the departure gate. There was a short queue of passengers, some repacking their bottles of lotion into clear plastic bags. A security man waved a clutch of the bags at a group joining the queue. I turned to Nick and held him close.

'Thank you, darling, for everything. I'll ring as soon as I arrive,' I said. For the first time I was not self-conscious about holding him in public as I clung to him. 'You take care of yourself and the girls.'

His face wore the look that said how much he hated being apart from me. 'Love you very much, sweetheart. Give Mum a big hug from me.'

As I settled into the leather seat by the window a smiling air stewardess came up to me.

'Ma'am, can I get you a glass of champagne?' she asked.

'Yes, please,' I replied. I wanted to sink into oblivion, to blot out the pain. I was exhausted and the hum of the plane's engine was sure to lull me into a stupor as it usually did. A glass of champagne would simply hasten the process. I took the glass handed to me, swallowed the champagne and waited for its effect, my soft blanket pulled up to my chin. I told the stewardess I didn't want any food and I didn't want to be disturbed. I closed my eyes expecting to drift into quiet emptiness. But sleep played hide-and-seek with me. Long after the meal had been served then cleared and the lights had been dimmed away, I was still wide awake. My frustration grew as I saw that the other passengers looked as if they were fast asleep. The same stewardess came round to check that we were comfortable, but it did nothing for the rage that was whipping up inside me. Fury at the fact that I could not help my father. That I didn't phone sooner and then perhaps I would have been able to do something, to intervene and prevent his death. While I had been waiting to phone the doctor he had been preoccupied with resuscitating Father.

I tried to blank out everything from my mind but Father's face came into view again. He had an unfortunate face; my mother described it as a black thunderstorm. But when he smiled it was like a burst of sunshine and clear blue sky through the black clouds and his top single gold-capped tooth would show. To my brother, Yao, who would giggle whenever he described it, the corners of Father's mouth curled downwards like a shark's mouth. His look had been enough to scare away a friend of mine who came to visit when we were little. 'I'm scared of your father,' she said. 'He looks so fierce, as if he's going to scold me.'

I was sure he wasn't always like that – quiet and sullen. How did we drift apart? And how did the rift between us fill with so much silent anger?

Chapter 2

'Your papa loves you so much. Loves you the most.' Mother always started this story like this, one that she told me several times when I was a teenager. 'That time when he found a mosquito bite on your leg, when you were no more than one, *wah,* you would think I'd bitten you myself, the way he ranted at me. "*Aiyahh,* why did you let that happen?" he demanded to know as he gently rubbed tiger balm on the spot.'

I had never tired of listening to it and loved listening to it, probably because my father never ever verbalized his love for me, which was the Chinese way. Neither did my mother. Yet, I never doubted that they loved me.

I was born in 1951, the year of the Tiger. It was well past midnight when my mother went into labour. Father had rushed out on a bike he had borrowed from the next-door neighbour to fetch the midwife from the other side of town. The streets were deserted, the silence of the night punctured only by the sound of the wheels of hawkers' stalls crunching on the road. In the distance a stray dog was howling. As Father pedalled furiously, sweat streaming down his body in spite of a thin singlet and shorts, he noticed the full moon in its full glory. *An auspicious sign,* he thought. So happy and preoccupied was he that he didn't even grumble about the stench coming from the blocked monsoon drains that he had cycled past. He was soon to be a father.

Meanwhile, upstairs in the back room of No. 22 Hakka Street, my mother was panting in agony as the waves of contractions hit her. For once she didn't care what my paternal grandmother thought of her as she screamed with each contraction. In the airless room, Grandmother sat quietly on the stool next to her bed. She laid out the towels and a basin of water on Father's desk by the window, ready for the midwife. Now and again, she took a wet cloth in her hand to wipe Mother's forehead.

I emerged, yelling without ceremony, when the cockerels would have crowed. By now most of the household were awake. Downstairs, Father, who had earlier been drinking coffee with Uncle Heng before dozing off on the camp bed, leapt up at the announcement of my arrival. He ran upstairs into the bedroom; his jaw dropped when he saw me in my grandmother's arm.

'Tiger daughter,' said my grandmother, her face had softened a little at the sight of me. She gave me to my mother. Then, not looking at her she continued, 'Well, there's time enough for you to produce a son.'

Father took me in his arms and gazed in wonder. 'I know what I'm going to call her,' he said, 'I'm going to name her *Chiew*.' *Chiew* is the transliteration from Chinese for autumn. The full moon he saw earlier had put him in mind of the Autumn Harvest Festival, on the fifteenth day of the eight lunar month, when the moon is supposed to be at its fullest and brightest. '*Chiew* is perfect. Look at her. Look at her eyes. She's bright, like the moon.'

'No, you can't!' cried my grandmother. 'You can't give her the same name as your uncle's, it's disrespectful. No, you can't. What would your grandmother say?'

I don't remember much of my paternal grandmother and never met my grandfather. Grandfather Chiang Chun Hong died not long after the Japanese Occupation ended in 1945. In 1915, at the age of fifteen, he came with the tide of immigrants from China to the British colony of Malaya. He had left his home in the province of Kwantung, which was ravaged by poverty and famine. On his journey by boat, he met and became friends with Ah Heng who was a little older than him. They were bound by a determination to survive and a strong sense of kinship as both were Hakka. The word Hakka means 'Guest People', a euphemism for a displaced people who became wanderers in China for thousands of years and Hakka people regard one another as 'our own people'. So the two young men stuck together on their

23

hazardous journey. The bewildering new landscape that greeted them held out the promise of a better future, for here was a land brimming with an abundance of natural resources. Many of their fellow countrymen had already made their mark by developing better methods for the mining of tin and pioneering plantation agriculture of sugar, tapioca, gambier, spices, tea and coffee. And yet, more labour was required by the British government, not just to tap the resources, but also to build roads and railways to make access easier between the ports, mines and plantations. The eager hungry migrant workers were welcomed while the natives, the Malays, continued with their fishing and small-scale agriculture.

Chun Hong and Ah Heng quickly adjusted to the heat and humidity in their new country as they worked at anything and everything initially including mining for their bowl of rice and some money to send home to their family in China.

'Hunger sharpens your mind,' said Uncle Heng when I was old enough to ask him questions about where he and Grandfather came from. 'It steels your will and you would be amazed at how we put up with the tough physical work, long hours and the heat.' He recalled the days in China when food was scarce. 'You didn't dare drop your chopsticks. If you did, and you bent down to get them, the food on the table would be gone by the time you've picked them up.'

Heng had trained as a cloth cutter in his village in China while my grandfather Chun came from a family of tailors. Once they had saved some money they decided to set up their own business. They liked Batu Pahat with its wide streets laid out like a fish's skeleton, its mouth touching the river's edge, its tail bordered by the foot of blue-green hills, and the shophouses built in a style reminiscent of their homeland. Best of all, there was an air of prosperity and the promise of a better future for them. They were right.

Chun Hong was the more business-minded of the two and on his suggestion they bought their first Singer sewing machine, rented a tiny space in a shop and started to make shirts. Heng would cut while Grandfather stitched the pieces together. Then one day Grandfather said, 'Big Brother Heng, I think it is time to expand.'

'Expand? *Wahh*, that is ambitious,' was Heng's response.

'But this is what we came here for - make a fortune, send money home, make our future here.'

'What have you in mind?' asked Heng.

'I have seen a shop on Hakka Street. Number twenty- two. It is the ideal location, we will be amongst our own people and the rent is also reasonable. Think - there will be more space. We can employ help with the sewing while you measure and cut,' said Chun.

In a town which was predominantly Hokkien Chinese - the native Malays lived in *kampongs* (villages) dotted outside town - Hakka Street was home from home. The official name of this side street was Jalan Ibrahim but because the residents here were predominantly Hakka people, it became popularly known as Hakka Street. It was also appropriately referred to as 'Haberdashery Street' for it was the place to find whatever was needed for sewing, from needles to nylon, buttons and bows, satins and cotton and when the synthetic fabrics such as Dacron were invented, they quickly found their way into the shops here first. The street throbbed with buying and selling while the hot air was suffused with delicious aromas from the stalls of hawkers offering Hakka beef balls and noodles. In the shade, brown wizened trishaw pullers hungry for a fare waited to pounce on shoppers laden with their bags.

'You are the brains, I am only the worker,' said Heng.

'I have a good feeling about this,' said Grandfather.

The two men who had become like brothers now became partners in the new venture. While Chun would work at the sewing machine stitching the pieces together, Heng's flare for cutting the cloth to suit the shape and build of his customers soon attracted more customers. By the age of thirty, Grandfather was able to buy the entire shophouse while Heng was content to work and have his share of the profits. By now my father Jung was already three, with an older sister and two younger brothers and sister. Such was the bond and friendship between the two friends that Heng, who never married, became 'Uncle' to Chun's children and continued to live in the same shophouse until a short while before he died.

As a little girl, I had seen Uncle Heng burning joss sticks at Grandfather's shrine; he would nod with a sad look in his eyes, as if he was agreeing with something Grandfather was saying. I was always fascinated by Grandfather's sepia photograph on the wall that had been lightly blackened by the smoke from the burning joss sticks. He had a moon face and wore John Lennon spectacles which made him look more Japanese than Chinese to me. There was a hint of a smile that drew me to him. I was taught to show my respect for him from a very early age; as soon as I was able to clasp the joss sticks between my tiny hands I was told to say prayers to Grandfather. Mother, standing by me, looking down at me and fussing, would say to Father, 'Look at her. She has so much to say. What could she be saying?' I would look up to Grandfather, my lips moving as I offered my silent prayers. Perhaps it was Grandfather's kind eyes that compelled me to open up freely to him. Whatever it was, I was held up as an example of how to venerate our grandfather to my sisters, brother and cousins, which was perhaps the only virtue I had as far as my grandmother was concerned.

Uncle Heng's face was thin with a black mole on his chin. I used to stare at the mole and count the hairs that sprouted from it; to me, it looked like a bomb with its fuse hanging freely. Unlike Grandfather who was an extrovert, he was more of a listener although he did tell me stories, stories about my Grandfather and their time together. I loved his tales about their escapades and about their homeland, which vicariously became mine, as I romanticised about the great country with the richness of its ancient culture and colourful history. Although he missed his family and home, he was only able to return to China twice, in the sixties, to see his elderly parents. In those days when diplomatic relations between communist China and Malaysia were non-existent, the only grounds for going to China was either ill health, presumably to find treatment or die there, or to see aged parents.

Grandmother Kwee was a second-generation Malayan Chinese whose family were farmers in Bukit Pasir, a village about five miles from Batu Pahat. She was considered a good match for Grandfather as she was an excellent homemaker and good at sewing. Like all grandmothers, she always wore a blue top with a Mandarin collar and black pantaloons. Her hair was pulled back into a bun and fixed with a gold and jade hairpin. Neither Grandmother nor her mother had had their feet bound, unlike the old Hokkien woman who owned the jewellery shop at No.18 and hobbled in doll-sized embroidered shoes. When I once asked my grandmother why she didn't have feet like the Hokkien old lady, her reply was, 'Hakka women are tough hardworking women. We have no use for tiny feet. How could we walk fast or work fast?'

Grandmother made the best rice wine; friends and relatives praised its taste and fineness, saying it was indisputably the best outside China. Mother could attest to that for she had had much of it during her confinement when her staple diet consisted of chicken cooked in equal quantities of rice wine, chopped ginger and sesame oil for its restorative properties. Grandmother shared her secret with Mother, reminding her that making it was illegal.

'Make sure the glutinous rice is clean, pick out any bits that should not be there then wash thoroughly,' she said as she swirled the rice and water in a large earthenware jar. 'Now mix in the yeast.' She crumbled her special preparation of yeast and sugar on to the rice before mixing it in the rice with her bare hands. Satisfied that she had mixed them thoroughly, she then placed a muslin cloth over the jar followed by the wooden lid. On top of the lid she carefully placed a pair of scissors – 'to keep the devil away' so it didn't spoil the fermentation process. Then she hid the jar in a corner of her bedroom, securely wedged between any mischievous spirits and the law, until the aroma of fermentation filled the room.

On the pillars on either side of the shop, the town's best mason had carved *Chiang Fah San* in both English and Chinese characters, the name that Grandfather Chun had given his new shop.

Tax on buildings was based on the width of the building; hence shophouses, usually two-stories high, were narrow and very deep. On the right-hand side of the shop floor, there was a long wooden worktop made to Heng's specifications, it was here where, with his measuring tape, chalk and scissors, he performed his magic on the fabric that passed through his hands. Whatever the weave, whether it was cotton, linen or silk, he was able to transform it to mould like a second skin around any male physique.

On the left of the shop, five or six Singer sewing machines lined the wall like desks in a classroom. At the back was a soft-top table with an iron filled with smouldering charcoal. The iron stood on a metal coil next to a bowl of tapioca starch which looked like white custard. Uncle Heng would let me play with the starch; I would stand on a stool and stir the white mixture with a metal spatula as I watched him measure and mark out shapes with coloured chalk on the fabric before cutting it.

'Why do you do that?' I asked as he spread the starch thinly on a piece of fabric.

'To make them stick together and stiffen the piece. This becomes the collar.' He put the piece round his neck. 'It needs to stand up like that so whoever wears this collar can hold his head high.'

Occasionally Uncle Heng would let me look into his drawers of buttons and spools of thread that matched the colours of the fabric in the shop, all neatly laid out in boxes. When everyone was working, the shop would turn into a musical workshop with the sewing machines chugging like the sound of several distant trains, the slapping of the fabric against the work surface and the clinking of the hammer against the chisel on a wood block to cut buttonholes.

A wall with a wide door to the right separated the shop from the living area behind. Tall glass-fronted cabinets lined this wall to display a wide selection of fabric in muted shades of blue, grey, green, brown and white for shirts and trousers. The living area was a large hall with three round marble-topped dining tables and stools where the family and workers ate. Immediately to the left were an air-well and the wooden stairs. The air-well, with a sliding zinc roof, provided a through-draught to keep the building cool as well as dry the washing on bamboo poles. When the afternoon rain beat down on the zinc roof it felt like we were inside a drum.

The stairs led up to the five bedrooms for Grandfather's family and Uncle Heng. The end room facing the top of the stairs was to be my parents' room. A large landing separated it from the rest of the bedrooms that ran along a wide corridor. In the middle of the landing were a small low wicker table and two chairs facing the large window above the air-well. It was here in the wooden floor of the landing that three holes were made by bullets from a Japanese soldier's rifle. These holes became the children's spy-holes. When I was older they were useful when unwelcome male visitors called for me at the bottom of the stairs. The holes were also a test of my own strength in resisting the urge to sweep the floor when my Third Aunt and her family were eating at their table immediately below. How often I wanted to do just that, to sprinkle dust on their food, out of revenge because of Third Aunt's spitefulness.

The large window overlooking the air-well was my favourite spot for learning. I would sit on the sill memorising aloud, '*six times six is thirty six, seven sixes forty two…*' in between peeping at the boy next door through a gap in the wall. Nearby Mei Lin would also be into her book, my cousin Chung Lin ironing as she listened to some story on the radio while Mother was pedalling away at her sewing machine in her room.

There was no ceiling between the high pitched roof and the tops of the walls of the rooms along the corridor. On one side of the ridge was a large skylight. If you could look through the skylight into the house it would be like looking at the various rooms of a doll's house with the roof taken off. Sometimes we children would stand on a stool placed carefully on a table to look over into the next room when we were playing hide-and–seek or if we were just feeling curious and daring. During the day, when there was no breeze, it would get very hot and sometimes suffocatingly so. Often I would sit and watch the column of sunshine from the skylight, mesmerized by the twinkling dust particles rising heavenward, my earliest verification that hot air rises.

Downstairs, beyond the hall and through a door on the left, was the kitchen where clay stoves stood in a row on a concrete worktop below which the firewood was stored. Stocking up the firewood was a constant source of anxiety for me as it was often my job to split the wood in the back alley and I was terribly self-conscious of the boy next door watching me.

On the wall was a row of woks corresponding to the number of stoves. When Grandfather was alive and in charge of his business, a large black wok hung on the wall, large enough to fit two turkeys, large enough to cook for his family of six sons and two daughters and the six or so workers. Grandmother was in charge of the cooking with the help of her cook and a young girl who was bought to be betrothed to her first son. After Grandfather died, cracks in the family fabric appeared; the number of woks also increased. It became two, then three and then four in a row on the wall. By the time the largest and oldest wok broke the family had become irretrievably divided.

Chapter 3

In 1931, my grandfather Chun Hong returned to his village in China in a hurry and in a rage. One of his brothers, in a moment of opium-induced mindlessness, had sold his eleven-year-old son, Kau, to fuel his habit. Chun Hong wanted to revoke the sale but in effect, he bought back his brother's son and then brought him back to Batu Pahat. But Kau hadn't come willingly. Angry and confused with all that was happening to him, he found it difficult to adjust to his new family including a girl and four boys: Kui, Jung then aged four, Soong, Keow and Kok. He tried to run away several times but was brought back each time. In the end, seeing how unhappy he was, Chun Hong arranged for him to work and live in a village near Senggarang where he was taught to sew.

Chun Hong had started sending money back to another of his brothers to pay for his son, Toong, to go to school in the same village. He decided that Jung should attend school to learn both Chinese and English.

'A good education is what he needs,' he explained to his wife, Kwee. 'He needs to learn English. It will be an advantage. There is a demand for English-speaking personnel in the many workplaces that are coming up like the European companies and government departments. He could be a clerk. *Ah*, even if he does not get to work in these places it will be useful to speak English – the British are everywhere.'

So Jung and later his four younger brothers were sent off in the morning to the Chinese boys' school off the main street in town, where they were taught Mandarin (as the Chinese National Language it was the unifying factor amongst the diverse dialect groups). In the afternoon, it was to the mission school some twenty minutes' walk to the top end of town to learn English. Jung was due to attend the boys' High School, an English-medium school. But he never got the chance to start his education there.

On 7th December 1941, Japan bombed Pearl Harbour and the next day swiftly invaded Malaya from the northeast coast. The Japanese soldiers overran the country with the force of an army charged with the divine right to displace and replace the *white imperialists*. The British, preoccupied with war in Europe, were ill prepared for the onslaught; they retreated south to Singapore where their main base was. With the speed of light the Japanese army reached Johore Bahru, the southernmost point of the peninsula, directly across the straits from Singapore. Then, contrary to all expectations, they attacked the island from the northwest while all the time the British had been expecting them to come from the north east where their defences were ready and waiting. Caught off guard, the British and their Australian allies were easily overpowered forcing their capitulation in February 1942.

On the day the warning came that the Japanese soldiers were approaching Batu Pahat, Chun Hong hurriedly gathered his family and workers upstairs, locking the door to the corridor behind them. All the windows were shut and in the dark mosquitoes buzzed around them as they crouched on the floor of the second room along the corridor.

'Everyone keep very quiet,' whispered Chun Hong barely able to control his shaking voice. As silence descended and the room got warmer, their bodies became drenched in sweat. Fear mingled with the smell of their own odour hung heavily over them. Kwee, with baby Tian in one arm, pulled the other boys, Keow and Kok, close to her with her other arm. The older children, Kui, Jung and Soong, huddled with Chun Hong and Heng. 'We have to keep still,' Chun Hong said when one of the younger boys started waving his hand to swipe at the mosquitoes.

In the deathly silence, both in and outside the house, Chun Hong could feel his heart pounding. There was nothing he or any one else could do. They waited and waited wondering how it was going to end. Then suddenly they heard the sound of boots pounding through the shop and voices shouting in a foreign language. Shots rang out. The children threw their hands up to cover their ears as they squeezed their eyes shut. Baby Tian screamed and Kwee squeezed him tightly to her chest to silence him.

The shooting stopped and a man shouted in Hokkien, 'Come out and surrender. Come and pay respect to the Japanese Emperor.'

For a long time no one moved, then Chun Hong nodded to Heng, to the workers and then to Kwee. Kwee nodded back, tears streaming down her cheeks. They got up and herded the children towards the stairs. Chun Hong felt as if his heart would jump out of his chest, convinced that they were going to be shot as he approached the top of the stairs and looked down. At the bottom of the stairs were three soldiers waving their rifles and shouting and a non-uniformed man without a rifle. He could hear banging and the sounds of things being thrown around in the shop. The man without a gun translated, 'Get down quickly and kneel!'

Chun Hong led the group down the stairs as quickly as he could and when they had got to the bottom, he said, 'Quickly, kneel, everybody. And bow.'

There was more shouting from one of the soldiers and then the translator bellowed, 'Every one out to the street!'

They stood up slowly and followed Chun Hong through the shop and out to the street. There they found all their neighbours, all looking as bewildered and frightened as themselves, gathered in the middle of the street surrounded by more soldiers. Hanging over them all was their knowledge of the recent rampage and rape of their homeland, China. No one dared speak above the sound of crying. Suddenly a voice through a loud hailer rang out in Japanese, followed by another in Hokkien.

'The Japanese Emperor is now your ruler.'

The warning was issued: any one resisting the Japanese would be killed. The message was clear: the Japanese, not the British, were now in command.

The High School that Jung was to have attended became the base of the Japanese army. Although the people of Batu Pahat were left much to themselves, many witnessed some of the atrocities committed against the Chinese by the Japanese soldiers. Stories were told of pregnant women's bellies being cut open with bayonets like splitting a watermelon, babies being thrown up in the air to then impale on the soldiers' bayonets.

Bowing or kowtowing to the soldiers was essential to staying alive. No anti-Japanese talk was permitted and the residents quickly learnt to keep their mouths shut while others who were strongly anti-Japanese went into the jungle to wage guerrilla warfare on the enemy. Chinese Communist Party sympathisers were harshly treated or killed. In one fell swoop, the Japanese wiped out these enemies by systematically rounding up and killing thousands of Chinese men in Singapore immediately after Occupation. Furthermore, they took advantage of the distrust between the Malays and Chinese and sought to fan the smouldering anti-Chinese feelings among the Malays, encouraging the Malays to fight the Chinese resistance groups.

Food was scarce and rationing was imposed. The staple diet was a watery gruel made with rice and sweet potato. To this day, amongst the older Malaysians and Singaporeans, the sweet potato and its leaves have become synonymous with the Japanese Occupation which ended in August 1945 after the bombing of Hiroshima and Nagasaki.

Chun Hong was lucky that his shophouse was intact apart from the three bullet holes in the floorboard. His stock of fabric had dwindled but he and Heng worked hard to revive the family business and restore it to its former status.

For a long time Jung could not forgive the Japanese for depriving him of his education. Things would have been so different for him if he had continued in school for just a couple more years; he would have been better qualified for a white- collar job. As jobs were scarce in the post-Occupation period, he had no choice but to learn the tailoring business from his father.

Heng looked up as he finished cutting the fabric on his work counter and saw Kau walking onto the five-footway, his face tense, shoulders stiff and slightly hunched, like someone ready for combat. He stepped over the threshold and into the shop casting a quick sharp look around as if assessing the worth of the merchandise in the shop. Immediately behind him was a woman carrying a toddler across her hip and holding the hand of the smaller of two older children. Heng assumed the woman was his wife.

Looking directly at Heng, Kau called out in a loud clear voice, 'Where is my father?'

Jung and his mother were both in the shop; he had been working at his sewing machine while his mother, behind him, was sewing a button on a shirt. Both looked up in surprise. Kau ignored Jung but to his mother he grunted, 'Mother.'

'You've come, that's good. Your father is resting at the back,' said Heng. Kau marched past him into the hall where Chun Hong had been taking his afternoon nap in his favourite rattan chair by the air-well.

'I have come as you asked. What do you want?' Kau said.

'*Ah*, son, sit down.' Chun Hong signalled to the woman behind Kau and pointed to two stools, 'Come, sit.'

'This is my wife, Siew Ping,' said Kau.

'*Ah*, good, good,' said Chun Hong. He brightened when he saw the children and said to the older boy, 'Are you not going to greet your grandfather?'

The boy and the girl latched themselves to their mother and turned away; Siew Ping saying nothing to encourage them.

Chun Hong turned to the toddler. 'How old is this little one now?'

'Almost one,' replied Siew Ping as she sat down. Her face was unsmiling as if she had been scolded. She pushed the hair off the child's forehead.

'So, what do you want?' said Kau as he sat down.

'I have been thinking. You should come back home. Why don't you come back and live here?'

'What for?'

'Take care of the business. And you wouldn't have to worry about paying rent as you have been.' He nodded at the children. 'And you have a growing family.'

'Who says I've been worried? I've been doing alright.' Kau's eyes hardened. His gaunt face was set taut like stretched hide.

'You are family,' said Chun Hong keeping his voice calm. 'Your brothers are too young. Jung is only nineteen. Besides, you are the eldest. It is only right that you run the business alongside me.'

Nobody knew for sure why Grandfather felt so strongly about Kau, not even Uncle Heng. What was so special about him? Children, especially girls, were sold to feed the rest of the family. After all, Grandfather had already bought a three-year old girl named Fong. This came about when Grandmother Kwee told him about her friend's plight, how she couldn't afford to feed all her seven children. Grandfather thought that they could help her by 'buying' Fong to help in the house and to be betrothed to Jung who had just started going to school. Fong's mother readily and gratefully accepted a dowry of four hundred dollars.

On the surface, this abominable practice was a sensible solution to an economic problem for both families concerned. The girl would help in her new home, a much cheaper way of getting home-help, while at the same time she would be helping out her own stricken family. Selling a son, on the other hand, was unheard of and would have been considered more shameful and disgraceful than selling a daughter. Was it shame that motivated my grandfather, the shame of selling a son? Would he have rushed to do the same if Kau had been a girl?

Two days after Chun Hong had asked him to come home, Kau and his family arrived at the front of the shop in three trishaws- his wife and children in one, he and his bags in the second and the rest of their belongings in the third. They stormed into the house and took over the second largest room overlooking the air-well, which had been Heng's room.

'It is alright, I can sleep in the camp bed in the corridor. A single man like me can sleep anywhere,' he said when Chun Hong apologised.

'No, you will not do that. You will have one of the boys' rooms. Take Tian and Yew's. They can share Jung's room.'

Under Grandmother's supervision, meals in the Chiang household used to be a sumptuous affair; several dishes of fish, king prawns, pork, chicken and duck with the best mushrooms and vegetables were served in huge portions to both family and workers. There would be at least two sittings at the three marble-topped tables. After Siew Ping took over the catering, more vegetables appeared in place of the meat and fish while the portions became smaller. When Grandfather Chun Hong first noticed this he said nothing until finally, during the sixth meal of vegetables, tofu and white bait he spoke out as he put down his bowl of rice and chopsticks on the table.

'*Ah*, Siew Ping, is there a shortage of fish and meat in the market?' he asked quietly. She was seated at the largest table with him, Grandmother, Uncle Heng, Jung and his brothers.

'No. Why do you ask?' said Siew Ping, putting her bowl down as she glared at Grandfather.

'We seem to be eating more vegetables than fish or meat.'

'If you want more fish you have to give me more housekeeping,' Siew Ping's voice was curt and loud.

'I like sweet potato leaves. After all, it was what kept us alive during the Japanese Occupation. But we seem to be eating lot of it lately. I haven't heard that prices of fish and meat have gone up. And I generally get to hear about these things.'

'Well, Mother can take over the shopping if you prefer. She can even take over the cooking,' Siew Ping almost spat the words out, stood up and, taking her bowl, walked away into the kitchen.

By the time Kau and his family moved into the shophouse, Fong had grown into a lovely girl of seventeen, a delight in Chun Hong and Kwee's eyes especially as both Fong and Jung had become good friends. For no obvious reason, Siew Ping turned on Fong and would hit her for the slightest mistakes she made always making sure no one saw her do it. When Jung found out he was furious.

'Why? Why did she hit you?' he asked.

'Little things. Sometimes I forget to boil water, or just late to do it,' Fong said as she slowly pushed up her sleeves to show him the black-and-blue patches on her arms caused by pinching and often slapping.

'How long has she been doing this to you?'

'Nearly every day… when no one is looking.'

'I will have a word with Mother.'

'No. No, don't. It will be worse, please, don't.'

Ignoring her, Jung stormed off to complain to his mother.

'It was a sad day when they moved in, but there was nothing I could do,' said Kwee, sighing deeply. 'It was your father's wish, as you know.'

'But why has Fong got to suffer and put up with these beatings from her? What has she done to deserve it? It will get worse. You know it won't stop. In that case I don't want her to stay here. Maybe she ought to move out!' said Jung.

'No matter what I say to your sister-in-law, she will continue to do it and without us witnessing it,' said Kwee.

'We have to stop it, Mother. It cannot go on!'

'As long as Fong is in this house, it will go on. That is the sort of woman your sister-in-law is.' Kwee was not going to confess that she herself was also a target of her daughter-in-law's sharp tongue and rudeness. Or that she suspected Siew Ping of stealing from her.

'Then Fong has to go.'

'What do you mean?'

'I don't want to marry her and have her live here. Set her free, Mother, find another home for her,' said Jung and left the room before his mother could answer.

On the day that Fong left to be married to someone else she looked happy. Siew Ping could only cast her a very dark look. Jung saw it and was relieved that Fong no longer had to take anymore of her bullying.

By now my father, Jung, realised that although he was his father's first-born son he was powerless. Because Kau was older, by eleven years, my grandfather had placed him at the top of the hierarchy of brothers. Kau became First Brother and Jung was relegated to Second Brother.

Chapter 4

1948

The weather had been hot and dry for days before Chun Hong decided to visit his old friend who owned a farm in the little village of Parit Raja, about thirteen miles from Batu Pahat. The sky was blue when he set off in the morning by bus. By the time he arrived at the farm it had turned an angry black and then the rain came in torrents followed by thunder and lightning. The monsoon drains in Batu Pahat had filled up and were threatening to spill over while in the partially cleared jungle around Parit Raja, rivulets had formed and the exposed laterite tracks turned into red rivers.

The rain continued to pour and after he had been with his friend and his family for a few hours, he said, 'It is rude of me to get up and go so soon after eating such a delicious lunch, but I cannot stay any longer. I must go home. Kwee will worry.'

'She would worry more if she knew you were trying to go home in this downpour. Look at it,' said his friend, looking out of the window at the sheets of rain beating mercilessly down on the trees beyond his fifty yards of clearing. 'It is like the gods are furious and have opened the heavens' dam.' The pelting rain had turned the ground into a huge frothing puddle.

Chun Hong agreed to wait until the rain had eased a little, by which time it was late in the afternoon. At the sight of the first gap of blue in the sky he made up his mind to take his leave. Declining his friend's invitation to stay for the night, he set off along the red muddy track. But he didn't get far. Half way along the track between the house and the road where he would get a bus, he lost his footing in the mud and caught his leg on a tree trunk that had fallen across the track. From the pain that shot through him he knew he had done more than sprain his leg muscle. He shouted for his friend but to no avail; he was too far from the house to be heard. He pulled himself up and dragged his injured left leg, determined to get back to his friend's house. The rain started again and by the time he reached the front door he was a shivering wet heap.

His friend quickly went to fetch a bonesetter from the village to attend to him. In the meantime Kwee was sent for. She rushed to the farm with Heng and Jung to find Chun Hong, propped up in bed wearing his friend's pyjamas with his left leg in a splint. He looked tired but his eyes lit up when he saw Kwee.

'You didn't have to go this far to get out of work. You only had to ask and I would have given you time off,' said Heng forcing a smile.

'Such bad luck,' said Chun Hong shaking his head as Kwee sat down on the edge of the bed.

'I told you not to come, but no, you would not listen,' said Kwee fighting back her tears. She touched his arm. 'You feel hot.'

'I've done it now. No use scolding me,' said Chun Hong. 'I will be back on my feet soon.' He tapped the splint. 'It's only a small fracture, a bit painful but that's all. I am not so easy to get rid of.'

'You stay put for now. You must not move yet,' said Chun Hong's friend.

'Do not worry about the business, Father. Take as long as you need here,' said Jung. 'Uncle Heng and I will make sure everything is alright.'

Kwee stayed behind with Chun Hong on the farm while Heng and Jung returned to Batu Pahat. The next day Chun Hong's breathing became rapid and shallow as his temperature soared. The herbal brew that Kwee made for him had no effect. As his body started to burn he became delirious. When he was eventually taken to the General Hospital in Batu Pahat, the doctor said there was not much else they could do. Chun Hong died a few days later with Kwee by his side. He was forty-eight.

Grandfather's funeral took place at the grand building of Chinese Commerce on the main street of Jalan Rahmat. In the parlour where his coffin stood, a large photograph of him was placed at the head of it on a table with food offerings. Kwee sat to Chun Hong's right while Kau, as the eldest son, sat to his left. The other sons and daughters and Heng, wearing black with a sackcloth over their heads, sat closest to the coffin while one son-in-law, in white, and the grandchildren, in blue robes, were seated behind them. Every so often one of them got up to burn paper 'gold' to ensure that Chun Hong was well provided for on his journey. Masses of flowers and wreaths with messages of condolences in beautiful calligraphy were lined against a wall. A group of nuns, with shaven heads and robed in grey, chanted periodically in between burning incense and joss sticks. In the midst of the wailing and chanting, and the playing of mahjong and cards, four cooks turned out a large selection of dishes for those who had come to pay their respects including relatives, friends, business associates and members of the Hakka Association. The continuous vigil lasted five days.

While the others sobbed loudly, Kwee, grieving silently, knew that her life would no longer be the same. She had never known her husband to be ill in all their time together, not even during the Occupation when food was scarce; he had always been strong. She had been shocked when she saw his changed appearance on arriving at the farm. Panic and worry had set in then but she refused to let it show. That evening after Heng and Jung had left the farm and they were alone, he'd started to talk.

'The business is doing well, very sound. You will be alright, Heng will make sure of that…'

'What are you talking about?' Kwee asked.

'Listen to me. You must make sure the boys finish their education. The boys must continue going to school. Keow is almost finished. Maybe … maybe at last our sons can do something different, if they want. Do not get me wrong, the tailoring business has been good, but it is right to give them the choice... Tian is the most academic one. You... Heng and Jung will make sure you are alright.'

'Say no more. Rest, sleep now.'

Now, faced with a future without Chun Hong, she could not ignore the fear that had crept into her heart.

Immediately after Chun Hong's funeral when the mourners had only just removed their sackcloth, Kau called the four older brothers -Jung, Soong, Keow and Kok- to the shop leaving the others in the hall. The shop was closed; the shutter boards across the front of the shop had been left in place since the day Chun Hong died and now only the main door, a piece of white cloth hanging across it, was ajar to let the afternoon light in.

Not waiting to sit down, Kau stood in front of Heng's worktop and spoke in a firm voice, 'I am in charge of the business now, so that means you work for me.' He looked directly at Jung and Soong standing by the sewing machines. 'You will get a wage as before. You two,' he said turning to the younger two, Keow and Kok, 'you will stop going to school. Go out and work.'

'But why? I am almost coming to my last year,' said Keow who was sixteen. Both he and Kok, who was fifteen, had just re-started attending the High School after the interruption of the Occupation. 'Besides, Father was keen for us to carry on in school.'

'I'm not paying your fees, that's why. Anyway, what good is that education? You learn a few English words and you think that will give you your bowl of rice? You can go out and earn your own living now,' replied Kau curtly.

'Mother can pay.'

'Then you ask her,' said Kau.

'Mother is not in the best of health. You know her asthma can flare up. We cannot upset her with this, not so soon after Father's death,' said Jung.

'Second Brother, what am I going to do?' Kok grabbed Jung's arm, looking bewildered, tears started to well up in his eyes.

'We will think of something,' said Jung, patting Kok's hand at the same time. 'How much are you paying us?'

'As before and count yourself lucky.'

'Why?' Jung frowned in surprise. He pointed to the stack of unstitched trousers on the worktop. 'Business is picking up and I have been working harder than ever, you can't deny that.'

'The outgoings are more than before.'

'But not that much more.'

Ignoring Jung, Kau continued, 'Uncle Heng will stay on doing as before.'

Soong, scowling, stood up suddenly. 'I have no intention of working here,' he spat. 'I have already found a job elsewhere,' With that he marched into the hall.

'You do whatever you want,' Kau called after him, his face showing no sign of what he thought of his departure. Turning back to the boys he said, 'As I said, I am in charge.'

The two sisters – Kui, who was eldest of all except Kau, and Lan, fourth in line- had no share or say in the matter of the business. They would be married off and become the responsibility of their husbands. Kui was already married to a haberdasher eight years older than her and lived in the small town of Senggarang. She had started a hairdressing business at the back of her husband's shop and in between cutting and perming hair she produced three children.

Lan was afflicted with haemorrhoids as a toddler and when Grandmother Kwee consulted a diviner in the temple on the street next to Hakka Street, she was told that the child's trouble was the result of a clash of spirits within the family. Perhaps he was not far wrong, but which spirits he didn't say. The solution, he said, was to give her away, which Kwee did, giving Lan to a herbalist on the main street

44

to be betrothed to his son. Lan grew up as part of the herbalist's family but she always came back to No. 22 to see her biological family and always seemed very content. Her square mouth, permanently open and showing her teeth like two crooked rows of corn on a cob, always gave the impression she was smiling and therefore happy.

Following that first meeting after Chun Hong's funeral, Jung and his three younger brothers had no choice but to accept what Kau had laid down on the table. He continued to work in the shop along with Heng and Kwee.

Soong packed a bag and after a brief explanation to Kwee that he knew someone who could give him work in Singapore he left home. Kwee, worried that what he said was just a ruse, had pleaded with him not to go. She was afraid because he had spoken in the past about joining the jungle fighters, constantly railing against the British, 'The damn red-haired devils! We should get rid of them! See what they did to our motherland, plundered it and now they think they can do the same here.' Kwee was afraid that with his father gone this was his chance to do what he wanted.

The jungle fighters were originally the communist Chinese who had retreated into the jungle to wage warfare on the Japanese during the Occupation. Post-Occupation, their target became the British; they attacked and killed European plantation managers, disrupted the return to normality and intimidated the locals. The most rife and intense activities had been in the state of Johore where Batu Pahat is. To many, including the residents of Batu Pahat, the fight between communism and colonialism was a nuisance. Their main concern was survival; under the red-haired devils' rule life had not been too bad. Most simply wanted a peaceful life after their horrific experience under the Japanese army. Ideology took second place to survival.

No one knew for sure where Soong had gone; he didn't make any contact but when he didn't come home for the Chinese New Year celebration Kwee was sure that he had gone into the jungle. She and the family listened out for news of the activities of the terrorists always wondering if he was involved and right in the thick of it. Then less than a year later he reappeared in Hakka Street, looking leaner and browner. He said nothing to Kwee or his brothers about where he had been and resumed life in No. 22 as if nothing had happened.

He then married the young woman who had been betrothed to him since she was five. She became 'Third Sister-in-law' to the siblings. Kwee, overjoyed at his safe return, gave up her room - the one at the front - to the new couple and moved into the next room which she shared with Tian and Yew. Not long after the wedding, a small wok appeared on the wall in the kitchen next to the large black one.

Kwee would have found a way of ensuring that Keow and Kok finished their schooling but Keow, not wishing to be a burden on his mother decided that he wouldn't continue. After much searching, he eventually found work in a bicycle repair shop at the top of Jalan Rahmat. He wasn't enthralled by the prospect - punctured rubber tyres, chains and grease - but after a while discovered that he was good with his hands and fascinated by the mechanics. The boss was so pleased with his progress that he rewarded him with a pay rise not long after he had started. Keow was thrilled as he had his eyes on one of the imported *Raleigh* bikes which were prized items but still too expensive for him. He dreamt of owning one but until then he had to part walk, part run to work and back home again, not pleasant on a hot day which was nearly everyday.

Kok, following his older brother's example, gave up school without grumbling and became an apprentice electrician. He was fortunate as the owner of electrical appliance shop at the end of Hakka Street offered to take him on. He took to it like a bird to flying, not regretting giving up school although he always resented the fact that it was not his choice.

There was no way Kwee was going to deprive her two youngest sons of their schooling, especially not after what Chun Hong had said. And he was right about Tian; he was not only better than the others at school, he actually loved it. Kwee continued to pay for his primary education in *Cheng Siew* Chinese School, until 1953 and when it was time to leave and start his secondary school. Tian was excited as he had wanted to go to High School. This was a government-run secondary school where the medium was English and he was so looking forward to the new venture. But when it came time to register for admission he was turned down because he was unable to produce his birth certificate. This vital piece of paper, which was proof of his legal status and hence eligibility for the government-run school, had been lost during the Occupation. Kwee, keeping her promise to Chun Hong, agreed to send him to the alternative school - the privately-run Charlton English School - costing her ten dollars a month, a lot more than she would've had to pay had he gone to High School.

Eight years old Yew continued at *Cheng Siew* School and would go on to follow in Tian's footsteps.

One evening Kwee asked Jung to accompany her on her walk after dinner. They strolled along the riverbank admiring the sunset as they watched a small group of hawkers setting up their stalls for supper. A cool breeze swept past.

'Son,' said Kwee, 'I think it's about time we found you a wife.'

Jung, looking straight ahead, did not respond right away. Then, he nodded.

'If you say so, Mother.'

Chapter 5

The British had thought that the destruction of the bridge in Pontian would seriously impede the advance of the Japanese army towards the south when in fact it was a mere inconvenience for the invaders who trampled through the village with great ease.

Pontian, situated on the west coast of Johore was where Cho Shao Li and his wife Ying, lived with their children and where he had built a tailoring business. Shao had made his fortune as a tailor in the town of Pekan Baru, on the island of Sumatra, Indonesia where he married Ying who was born and bred there. After Lian and her brother Weng were born, he decided that he should take his family back to his home in China but on the way there, while travelling through Singapore, the Japanese had invaded China forcing him to change his plans. They settled instead in Pontian, a thriving fishing village, and the year before the Japanese came, their third child, a son, was born.

The wooden bridge spanned less than a hundred feet across the river; the banks of which were the local children's playground, where Lian and her friends would wade in bare feet, squeezing the warm mud between their toes like brown toothpaste as they waited for tiny crabs to peek out of the mud. When the bomb went off on the bridge, Lian, then aged eleven, thought the world had come to an end. The noise was so loud, it shuddered through her entire being as she and her family huddled together in their wooden shophouse. She thought they were all going to die.

On the day after the Japanese army had stormed into the village, soldiers came marching down the main street, a wide and dry laterite path, to make their presence known. Lian was with her mother, Ying, and baby brother Poh in the shop while Shao and Weng were behind the shop hiding their stock of fabric and food. Two soldiers carrying rifles sauntered into the shop. They looked around and then eyed both Ying and Lian up and down. Ying, carrying Poh across her hip, was terrified. She bowed low and when she looked up one of the soldiers had come forward and stroked the baby's cheek. The other had his eyes fixed on Lian who was frozen to the spot about three paces from her, just out of her reach. He moved towards Lian, an evil smile playing on his lips. Instinctively Ying pinched Poh's thigh. He let out a high pitched scream, so loud that the soldier who had been looking at Lian spun round in disdain. It produced the desired effect: Lian snapped out of her fright and rushed to Ying's side as she rocked the baby pretending to pacify him. The other soldier shouted something and then they both turned around and walked out of the shop leaving Ying gasping with relief.

When Shao heard what had happened, he said to Lian, 'You must always stay close to us. Never, never go far from us.' He went to shut the door and, turning to Ying, he spoke in a hushed voice, 'We have to leave quickly, while there is still light. I know of a house in a very remote part of the jungle. I know the family who live there. We must go there to hide. It is so remote the Japanese wouldn't think of going there. Quick, we must pack.'

Grabbing as much food and water as they could carry, and some clothes, they slipped out of the shop through the back door and headed into the jungle, constantly checking that there were no soldiers around. The jungle was lush, thick with tall and straight trees, their leaves forming an umbrella above them but the thick undergrowth made walking difficult. The green womb-like cocoon of the dense vegetation imparted a sense of protection from evil in spite of the monotonous buzz of insects, the unceasing bird songs and occasionally the cries of monkeys. Shao led the way, beating the matted undergrowth with his *parang* that he normally used on the grass behind the shophouse. Swatting mosquitoes and flies with their hands in the steamy heat, they slowly made their way through the jungle, their bodies drenched in sweat. Sometimes it seemed to Lian as if her father didn't know where they were going. They had to keep quiet, which made them concentrate on where they were stepping. Even baby Poh was good throughout and didn't cry with Shao and Ying taking turns to carry him.

As Lian trudged behind her father she wondered if he would ever find the hut. She sensed that he was becoming desperate and then suddenly her mother spotted it. She pointed to it, a large wooden hut partially hidden with cut branches and twigs. Shao also saw it at the same time and became excited; his breathing became heavier and faster. He ran up to the door and started banging on it with his fist. Ying caught up with him and stood beside him holding baby Poh. When he paused to listen, there was no sound or movement inside the hut. He thumped it again and again until the door was eventually opened, very slowly. A man's head appeared in the gap but before Shao could open his mouth, the frightened looking man pointed at Poh.

'Go away!' he hissed. 'You cannot stay here. Your baby will give us away. Go!'

Lian could see his face. It was contorted with fear and shiny with sweat, his eyes opened wide and she could see several more faces behind him all looking terrified, as if her father had delivered death to their doorstep. The man slammed the door in Shao's face and Shao banged on the door again.

'Please let us in!' he called. 'I promise we will keep the baby quiet! Look, he is not crying. Please!'

After a long while he stopped, his arms slumped by his side and he pressed his head against the door. Ying gently put her hand on his shoulder.

'If I were to die,' she said softly, 'I would rather die in my own home. Come, let us go home.'

Shao lifted his head and looked at Ying, then nodded before he turned to lead his family back the way they came. They returned to a dim moonlit village, shrouded in deathly silence; there was no lit kerosene lamps in any of the houses that they could see, no sound of children playing or of hawkers' woks clanging on the street. Instead upturned stools, tables, baskets and urns were strewn on the ground as if a tornado had passed through. Luckily their shop had been left intact.

The next morning, the villagers slowly ventured out of their houses to pick up the pieces. Shao did the same and he wanted to find out what was happening as well. After he had been talking to the neighbours on the five-foot way, he came back into the shop looking pale and shaken.

'What is the matter?' asked Ying.

Shao's voice trembled when he spoke.

'I just heard that the Japanese soldiers found the hut in the jungle, the one we tried to get into. Every single person in it.... all thirty of them were killed...the soldiers chopped their heads off.'

The fortunes of many including those of Ying's parents were lost during the Occupation. They had owned a huge fruit plantation where they grew papayas, durians and rambutans near the river in Pekan Baru. Lian used to visit them on the plantation when she was little and was fascinated by the strong smells and the huge amounts of fruit heaped high in baskets during harvest. She would watch the workers carry the heavy baskets to the jetty in front of her grandparents' house and then load them into their *sampan* to be taken to the town. Then, as a treat, her grandmother's cook would prepare a delicious *eight-jewel* rice for her, served in a gilt-edged bowl. When her grandparents went into hiding the house and the land were plundered, and on their return they lost their claim to their property. In the same foul stroke that the Japanese had dealt on her grandparents, they had also devastated her dreams.

Lian had had an ambition: she wanted to go to school and learn and then become a teacher. From an early age whenever her father took her out for a walk she would pick out and learnt many complicated Chinese characters on scrolls outside people's houses and shops, words like 'fortune', 'prosperity', 'peace' and 'protection'. Or she would try to read her father's newspaper with him. By the

51

time the Occupation ended her mother considered her too old, at fourteen, to be going to school. Lian was fair and tall for her age and to her mother's mind, it wasn't right for her to be playing at school. Instead she was to help in the house and to work in the tobacco factory where she earned a dollar a day rolling cigarettes. In between working at the factory and helping at home she had to queue for rice rations, sometimes dragging her two brothers to stand in the queue with her. Often, this was a good thing for she was given ration cards by those who didn't want to wait or just took pity on them, thus increasing her entitlement from two *katis* of rice to four.

Lian's best friend, May, also worked in the same factory and they would walk together to and from work. When May told her that her parents wanted to find her a husband, Lian was aghast at the thought of someone marrying so young and especially at the fact that May was agreeable. Her own mother had been trying to find her a husband with the help of a professional matchmaker ever since she was thirteen and she hated it. Each time the matchmaker turned up with someone in mind, Lian would protest, 'I am still young, too young to get married. No, I am not interested.'

'*Aiyahh*, if you carry on like this you will end up a spinster,' said her mother in utter exasperation.

'Tell the matchmaker to go away. She is a busybody.'

'That is her job.'

'She can go and find somebody else a husband.'

The matchmaker went away empty-handed again.

When Ying next broached the subject Lian bravely said, 'If I must marry, there is someone I might consider.'

'Who is this person?' asked Lian's mother.

Lian told her and to her surprise, Ying didn't object but instead informed the matchmaker who promptly set about making enquiries and then approaching the parents of the man. Excited at the prospect of marrying the man she liked, she couldn't wait to hear from the matchmaker.

When the matchmaker returned a few days later and saw Ying as she stepped into the shop, she shook her head. 'Not good news,' she said.

'Why?' asked Ying.

'The young man's parents regard the match unequal,' said the matchmaker, putting on a dejected look.

Ying and Shao were stunned, as was Lian. Lian was confused; she and the young man worked in the same factory, so where was the inequality? They had got on well, besides she was sure that he liked her in return.

'But we work together,' Lian blurted out before her mother could stop her.

'The young man's father owns the factory,' explained the matchmaker. 'His father wanted him to learn about the business so he sent him to work in the factory.'

'I shouldn't have let you talk me into getting the matchmaker to consult with that family,' said Ying, mortified.

Her father was livid as he looked out of the shop from the sewing machine, peering above his spectacles and puffing furiously on his cheroot before taking it out of his mouth.

'We may not be rich but our daughter is worth more than the gold their money can buy!' He shoved the cheroot back into his mouth and drew on it again. 'Who do they think they are?' he muttered as he resumed sewing. Unlike Lian's mother, he was in no hurry to see his daughter married.

The matchmaker returned again some weeks later in the hope that Lian was still willing to consider marriage as she had someone she considered suitable in mind.

'Ma, I don't want to marry, I am not ready,' Lian said, still smarting from the rejection.

'If you wait any longer nobody will want you,' wailed her mother. 'This other young man is from a good family. They have a tailoring business. His mother is widowed and there are six brothers and two sisters. Six brothers is good. They can protect you.'

'You can see him,' said Lian, 'but I am not going to marry him.'

A week later the young man, Jung, and his mother Kwee arrived in Pontian to meet Lian's parents. Lian hid in the kitchen with May, the two of them giggling endlessly as she pressed her face to the slit in the wooden panels of the wall dividing the kitchen from the shop, eager to see the man who had so bravely come to be spurned. May by now was betrothed; the match to Lian's mind was like that of a phoenix to a crow, the man being the crow, but she could see that May was happy. She looked through the slit and saw Jung. Smart in his white short-sleeved shirt and khaki trousers he seemed at ease sitting on the stool in the shop with her parents. His face was slim, his eyes bright but it was when he smiled, in response to something the matchmaker had said, that she thought he didn't look too bad.

'He is too short! People will laugh at me,' Lian said later when Ying asked what she thought.

'*Aiyahh*, how can you be so fussy? What does it matter that he is shorter than you?' replied her mother. 'He's hardworking. If he can support you and if he is good to you, that is what matters.'

Again, Lian refused, still adamant that she was too young although she was now eighteen. But she knew that her mother was getting impatient with her and that she couldn't delay much longer. Besides, continuing to work in the factory had become awkward for her.

Less than a year after that first meeting my parents married. Lian was nineteen and Jung twenty-two. The dowry from Jung to Lian was four hundred dollars and with that Lian bought two eighteen-carat gold necklaces, half a dozen bangles and a pair of jade earrings as part of her trousseau. She had already made a few frocks, skirts and blouses for herself. By way of announcement of their marriage, the remaining money was spent on gifts of cakes and roast pork to her relatives and friends.

On the morning of the wedding, Lian put on the white satin dress that, much to her annoyance, Jung's elder sister Kui had obtained for her. When they had first met after the agreement of the match, Kui took one look at Lian.

'You are very slim,' she said, 'size thirty-four. I should have no trouble getting your gown in Batu Pahat. Let me take some measurements to be sure. We can hire this gown I saw in a shop the other day. Pity I cannot do your hair for you.'

Out of deference to her, Lian didn't object to her choosing her gown with a matching veil but she got to choose her bouquet of white orchids and her shoes.

Jung and Keow arrived in a taxi, a highly polished blue *Mercedes Benz* hired for the occasion, with the door handles decorated with red bows and a great pompom of red silk cloth adorning the bonnet. Jung, smiling broadly, looked very smart in his hired cream-coloured suit, brown leather shoes and neatly *Brylcreemed* hair. As he stepped out of the car a cheer went up from the neighbours and friends who had gathered on the five-foot way outside Shao's shop. When Lian walked out of the shophouse to an even louder cheer she felt nervous even though May as her bridesmaid was by her side, but when Jung took her hand she felt reassured; his warm hand was firm. She saw her family getting into a second taxi and thought that it was the first time she had seen them so smartly dressed and looking so happy although earlier her father had shed a few tears. Her mother was smiling and there was no doubt that she was pleased that at last her daughter was getting married.

It was the first time that Lian had travelled out of Pontian since her father brought them here. Driving along the narrow dusty tarmac road edged by a shallow ravine of bare laterite, they weaved their way through miles of palm oil and rubber plantations dotted with a few *kampongs* of attap-roofed houses on stilts. They would have travelled in silence most of the way if it were not for the loquaciousness of the Hokkien driver who boasted about the new air-conditioning in his car and pointed out things of interest as he deftly swerved to avoid suicidal chicken flying out on to the road, potholes in the road or fast-moving taxis coming from the opposite direction. Keow sitting in the front passenger seat had been slightly unnerved by the near-misses. Almost an hour later as blue green hills came into view against a clear blue sky, Jung pointed to the left.

'We are approaching Batu Pahat, see those hills there,' he said as the driver slowed down. 'They are beautiful when the morning mist is just hanging over them at dawn. Keow and I used to walk up them when we were boys.'

'And here is the start of the town,' said Keow. They had arrived at the large roundabout with the largest Angsana tree around for miles. 'The main street starts here and ends at the river edge.'

Lian looked out of the window and saw the new landscape before her. She suddenly felt very anxious and nervous. It struck her that this was a one-way journey into the future with a man she hardly knew despite the few meetings after she had agreed to the match. Leaving behind her own family, she was now marrying into this huge family most of whom she hadn't even met. She knew there was no turning back.

Chapter 6

To Lian, marrying into the Chiang family was like walking blindfolded towards the edge of a cliff. With her mother's words about Jung's six brothers ringing in her ears, *They can protect you,* she didn't derive any comfort or reassurance but wondered how right her mother would be.

No.22 was closed for the auspicious occasion of the marriage of Jung and Lian. The shutter boards were in place leaving only the two central door panels ajar with a sash of red cloth hanging across the top of the entrance.

As Lian stepped out of the bridal taxi outside the shop, she noticed immediately Jung's handiwork, the red paper cut-out Chinese character - *Double Happiness* - stuck on the door panels. It was one of many characters that she had picked out and committed to memory a long time ago with her father's help. The left and right halves of it were symmetrical and symbolised the conjoining of two persons in marital bliss. There was no one waiting for her on the five-foot way outside the shop which was in contrast to what she had just experienced outside the home she'd left and she felt a sense of apprehension until she heard a little boy's voice shouting, 'They are here, they are here!' Immediately it was followed by a lot of commotion as a horde of people, giggling children and grown-ups came rushing out of the shop to surround them.

'Second Brother,' called out one of Jung's brothers. It was Tian, who turned to smile at her and behind him was Yew. The two boys became shy and quickly greeted her, 'Second Sister-in-law'.

Lian smiled and then felt as if she was being carried on a wave into the shop then into the hall with Jung grabbing her hand. Relief came over her when she saw Kui's smiling face and then her mother-in-law standing next to her wearing a beautifully-made blue silk top and a pair of black pantaloons, her black hair neatly combed back in a chignon fastened with two jade hairpins that matched her jade earrings. She smiled at Lian but said nothing. Lian smiled back at her and felt her stomach somersault when she glimpsed at the other faces watching her. Before she knew it Kui was organising her and Jung, guiding them towards Chun Hong's shrine where the scent of burning joss sticks pervaded.

'Here, you must pay your respects to our father,' said Kui handing Jung and Lian a bunch of joss sticks each.

The bride and groom, holding the joss sticks in both hands and facing the shrine, bowed. Then they were turned to face the elders who by now were seated in a line like idols arranged in a temple for the tea ceremony.

'Come, come and stand here,' Kui fussed like a mother hen. 'Here is the tea for you to serve,' she pointed to the tray that her sister Lan was holding next to her. It was neatly laid out with a china teapot and cups. Lan was smiling, her square mouth even wider than usual.

'Here, Jung, you pour the tea and Lian, you serve the tea to Mother,' said Kui.

Lian waited for Jung to pour the tea and then with both hands picked up the cup and bowed as she offered it to Kwee. Kwee smiled, accepted the tea and drank it, a sign of acceptance into the Chiang family. This was repeated for each of the elders. In her nervousness Lian couldn't remember who was who as she was led from one to next. When she came to Kau he smiled and nodded as she handed him the cup of tea. Every one including Kau and his wife Siew Ping seemed happy and gracious during the ceremony, watched by the younger members of the family, Lian's family, bridesmaid May and friends. Standing back from the crowd in the air well, Kok, Tian and Yew made fun of Jung's shiny *Brylcreemed* hair and suit and the fact that he could not stop grinning.

After the ceremony and a sumptuous meal in a restaurant, Kui led Jung and Lian with May by her side upstairs into the bridal bedroom which was Jung's room at the top of the stairs. He had taken great care to decorate it; the wooden wall facing the stairs was covered with pink floral wallpaper while the other three brick walls were white washed. A framed picture of a landscape hung side by side with a calendar on the papered wall. The beige patterned linoleum on the floor was new as were the white lace curtains across the window and the door. A red satin bedspread covered the bed against the wall opposite the wooden wall. Next to the bed, in front of the window, was a wooden desk, the top of which was covered with presents: neatly arranged of bundles of plain and patterned cloth, blankets, two flasks and a set of enamel wash basins. On the floor under the desk were a newly varnished wooden stool and a new enamel chamber pot. A large new wardrobe stood in the corner next to the desk.

'I hope you like this' said Jung as he waved his hand around the room.

Lian nodded, feeling a warmth rushing to her cheeks as she tried to take in her new surroundings, the room she was to share with her husband.

'He fussed so much over the room,' said Kui. '*Aiyahh*, everything had to be perfect. Took so long to cut out these characters.' She pointed to the Double Happiness on the front of the wardrobe then patted the bed. 'Sit here,' she said. 'Friends and neighbours will want to come and see you.' Turning to Jung, 'You can go downstairs and see to other guests. I will come with you.' With that she turned round and left the room walking behind Jung. May pulled out the stool from under the desk and sat down facing Lian. They looked at each other and then broke into a laugh.

'I wonder who will come and see me,' said Lian. Just as she said that Tian's face appeared at the door.

'Second Sister-in-law,' said Tian, leaning to one side to pull away from Yew who was dragging on his arm. He turned and whispered to him, 'Come and greet her. She won't bite you.'

Lian smiled. 'Come in, I won't bite, I have just eaten,' she said with a chuckle.

Yew slowly pushed into view at the door. 'Second Sister-in-law,' he said half looking down at the floor.

'Good boy. What are your names.'

'Mine is Yew and his is Tian,' said Yew. 'Have you come from far away? That was a nice car you came in.'

They heard footsteps coming up the stairs and a woman's voice approaching the door. Tian pushed Yew away from the door to make way for the woman.

'Ah, there you are. Congratulations. I am Ai Chien. I live two doors away,' said the woman with a broad smile showing off a fine set of teeth. Her voice was loud but her open face was kind. Lian liked her instantly.

'Thank you. My name is Lian and this is May,' said Lian. She could hear more footsteps and voices coming up the stairs.

'*Wah*, Jung has certainly done a good job,' said Ai Chien as she scanned the room, one hand on her hip. 'Your mother-in-law told me how excited he was about doing this room up. Listen, I am as good as next door. You can call on me any time. I must go now. Got to cook or there will be an uprising. Don't forget. Come and see me,' she said and then turned towards the stairs to make room for others behind her.

After about an hour or so of being welcomed and viewed by dozens of well-wishers, Lian and May were finally left alone.

'Did I tell you about the story of some groom's mother who waited at the foot of the bridal bed the morning after the wedding night?' asked May, patting her glistening face with a handkerchief.

'No,' said Lian raising her brow. 'Why?'

May's face broke into a smile. 'So that she could get proof of the bride's virginity,' she said.

'No!' said Lian.

'I wonder if your mother-in-law is planning to do the same,' said May and the two women covered their mouths to smother their laughter.

Later that night Lian cried but her tears sprang from a fear of the unknown, an unknown future she hadn't the slightest sense of security or certainty about, and her doubts about how she was going to fit into her new family. She slowly recalled the faces but not the names of the elders she had served tea to. There had been no hint of objection or animosity; each one a showcase of charm, graciousness and politeness. They had smiled and said words of welcome and encouragement. She put her misgivings down to the fact that she missed her own family whom she saw little of throughout the day. When she was saying goodbye to her parents she had fought back her tears and put on a smile for them and her brothers, not knowing when she would see them again. It was only when her father lost his control and started to cry that she too let the tears roll. She knew she had to be brave; lying beside Jung in their matrimonial bed she felt terrified and very alone. The only witness to her misery as she sobbed into her pillow was a lizard that had been hiding behind the framed picture on the wall earlier as it ventured out to seek its prey.

It was not living with her new husband that overwhelmed Lian but the women in the household. She knew her first duty was to make sure that her mother-in-law was happy with her, before she even thought of Jung's happiness or her own. According to May, Kwee was courteous which was more than could be said of many. She was not a very talkative woman and Lian learnt to go with her mood, to talk when Kwee wanted to talk or otherwise simply listen when they were sitting side by side sewing buttons in the shop or hall.

She had hoped that she would see more of Kui for moral support and to learn from her. But her hope was quickly squashed when she found out that Kui lived a fair distance away and her visits were not to be as frequent as she would like. She found her to be warm and genuine in spite of her bossiness; she had a big heart and an equally big laugh so that you heard her before you saw her when she came home to visit. The younger sister, Lan, was as welcoming and friendly but she didn't live in the house either. And so naturally Lian turned to Jung's sisters-in-law, Kau and Soong's wives, hoping that being in the same position as in-laws they would accept, if not embrace, her.

The face of Kau's wife, Siew Ping, changed very quickly from a smiling to a scowling one. She ignored Lian when Lian greeted her in the hall the morning after the wedding.

'I will show you where your things are,' Siew Ping said curtly as she walked to the kitchen.

Lian followed. In the kitchen, Siew Ping pointed to a new stove placed next to the largest one on the worktop.

'This is yours and that's your wok.' A new un-blackened iron wok hung on the wall above the stove. 'I cook for your First Brother, Mother, Uncle Heng and the workers. You and Third Sister-in-law cook for yourselves. I will show you where the market is later.'

Her Third Sister-in-law, Yin Li, was even less helpful. Lian found that she would look to the side or obliquely but never at her whenever Lian spoke to her which was not often. Yin Li was loyal to her husband Soong. For reasons known only to Jung and Soong, the two brothers didn't speak to one another. No one asked why, no one spoke about it. It was just there, woven into the tapestry of the Chiang family. Consequently Yin Li refrained from speaking to Jung and Lian. Initially she would speak to Lian, more out of curiosity than anything else, but as time went by she stopped and it became obvious that Yin Li thought she was above Lian for she had found favour in their mother-in-law's eyes, having just given her a grandson.

One day not long after she had moved in, Lian was cooking alongside her mother-in-law Kwee and Yin Li in the kitchen which had become very hot and humid with all the stoves lit. She became hot, started perspiring and wiping her forehead with her forearm. Yin Li looked at Lian, her pale face turned on a hollow smile.

'*Aiyahh,* I am so unlucky,' she said, 'I don't sweat so people think I don't work hard. You sweat a little and people think you have done more than your share of work,' she said.

Lian was stumped; conscious of her mother-in-law's presence she merely smiled back at her and said, 'Yes, I am very lucky. Sometimes I just stand there and sweat so people will think I am working.'

Yin Li said nothing and still wearing the hollow smile she walked away into the hall, her head tilted high.

It was to the neighbours that Lian turned for friendship. She wasn't slow to strike up a conversation with strangers and very soon made friends with the neighbours and other shopkeepers in Hakka Street on her way to the market. Ai Chien was one of them. Lian didn't forget the invitation she had made to her on her wedding day and decided to take it up. In spite of the age difference they got on very well. She had been apprehensive initially when she found out that Ai Chien and her husband owned the lucrative tailoring business two shops away and that she was in fact very much the boss who held the purse strings.

'How are you managing?' she asked Lian one day in the alley way when they were taking a breather after cooking.

'I wish there was more work for Jung. His First Brother is not giving him enough. Uncle Heng has taught him to measure and cut and he can do it well but his brother will not let him do it.'

'What about you?'

'I help with sewing the buttons and ironing, but it's not enough. I can sew but there is not enough work for us.'

'If you want work I can find you some. We can always do with another pair of hands in the shop,' said Ai Chien.

At the time Lian didn't realise how indebted she would be to her new friend for this or when she would need to take up her offer. The day came not long after I was born, when Kau called another meeting of the brothers.

63

'There are going to be changes. Jung, you and you, Soong, will pay me rent for your room. Twenty dollars each,' he said.

'What?' said Jung, standing up to look at his younger brothers for their reactions. Their eyes had widened and their mouths opened to protest but nothing came out. He turned to Kau. 'This is our home. Father made clear it was ours to share, us sons.'

'Your father is dead and I am in charge now,' said Kau.

'It's not right, not fair!' said Soong, his pale face now red. He had been content with working in the new tailor's shop in Jalan Rahmat while his wife kept home and looked after their two year old son, Kin.

'Twenty dollars each and there is the cost of water and electricity which will be split between us.'

'The bills, yes, but not rent. It is our right to live here,' said Jung.

'Big Brother, what about me and Kok?' asked Keow.

Before Kau could answer, raising his voice Jung asked, 'What about Mother and the boys?' He was thinking of the two youngest brothers, Tian and Yew, who were twelve and seven respectively. 'And what about Uncle Heng?'

Looking at Keow and Kok, Kau said, 'You pay rent too. Uncle Heng will carry on. Jung can continue working here, if you want, and your Mother too. You will be paid piecemeal. Tian and Yew can stay with her here. I just will not be feeding them.'

'How can you do this?' asked Jung glaring at Kau in disbelief.

'I can do what I like. Take it or leave, all of you.' Kau's stern face didn't twitch, his voice still firm.

'Why are you doing this? What have we done to you? Father was always good to you and now you treat us like this?' said Jung. He felt his voice shaking, the pulse in his temple pounding.

'*Ahh!*' Kau screwed his cold eyes and waved his hand. 'As I said before, take it or leave.'

In the privacy of their room Jung told Lian what Kau had said.

'He's got us by our testicles,' said Jung slamming the desk. 'How dare he!'

'He knows we can't go anywhere. We are stuck here,' said Lian. Her heart dropped like a gunny sack of sugar. They had discussed moving out and renting a room somewhere. Having to pay for the rent of their room and the bills now meant that they wouldn't be able to save. She felt as if she had stepped into quick sand with nothing around to grab on to, her dream of moving out evaporating before her eyes.

'No, we are not.' Jung's eyes suddenly lit up. 'I have an idea. We can get our share of the house and business and move out. I've had enough of his bullying.'

Chapter 7

My grandmother Kwee already had four grandchildren before I came along. The first three grandchildren were First Uncle Kau's children. The oldest of them was Hock, a boy of ten, who together with his brother, Sek aged five, became the terrors of the neighbourhood. They were bad-mouthed, rude and, at their mother's instigation, stole firewood from the neighbours when they thought no one was looking. Their unruliness and badness didn't endear them to Grandmother who already felt that these children including the middle child Chung Lin, a girl of seven, didn't count as her own flesh and blood, just as Kau himself didn't regard her as his mother. None of the children went to school because they hated it which suited Kau as he thought education was a waste of money.

The fourth grandchild was Kin who was one. When he was born to Soong and Yin Li, Grandmother rejoiced. At last, a real grandson. She announced the birth by sending out gifts of roast pork and cakes to relatives and friends. Yin Li's self-importance was highly inflated by this gesture and she would not let anyone, especially my mother, forget it.

Grandmother's expectations must have been very high when my mother Lian was pregnant with me. When I was born, the celebration was muted in contrast to that for Kin. No roast pork, just cakes were sent out. This didn't dampen my parents' joy at my arrival although my mother's sense of worth might have been dented. For my father, it was the best thing that had ever happened to him, the best fortune he had had in a long time. It didn't matter to him that I wasn't a boy. He couldn't stop smiling for days, overjoyed at becoming a father. With fatherhood came a heightened sense of responsibility which added to the pressure of providing for his new family.

My mother had by now started to do some work for Ai Chien's husband in their shop two doors away. Although not regular, it gave her two or three dollars for every pair of trousers she machined together earning her about ten dollars a week if she was lucky. But First Uncle's demand for rent for their room and sharing the payment of water and electricity bills could not have come at a worse time for by now my mother was pregnant again. Father became determined to move out of No. 22.

Jung thought that an evening stroll with his mother would be a good time to talk to her about his wish for the family business to be shared out between the brothers. The night air was considerably cooler with a breeze hinting at promise of rain, a welcome change from the earlier oven-like heat under the relentless sun. A gentle stroll away from the shophouse was the most certain way of getting away from eavesdroppers. He and Lian had noticed that Yin Li, either on her way downstairs or going upstairs, had a habit of slowing down when she got to the landing, which was next to their room, and pausing for a bit longer than was necessary. When either Jung or Lian caught her in the act an innocent look would come over her face, instantly replaced by one of guilt and she would hurry away.

There were already many others who were enjoying the cool air, strolling casually while some headed towards the food hawkers who had started cooking. In the lallang grass by the river's edge, the crickets were chit-chatting like a classroom of children.

'*Mak*, I think it is better if we split up the business, we each take our share and go our own way,' said Jung.

Kwee's response was quick and definite.

'No, you cannot,' she said. 'No, you cannot move out. What would I do if you moved out? It would be shameful, the family splitting up like that. No, you cannot go. I will not allow it.'

Her face became flushed and her breathing became noticeably faster but Jung didn't think it was from the walking. They had only just arrived at the river's edge where they could hear the sound of crickets.

'*Mak*, there is no shame in that. Besides, the neighbours know what First Brother is like. They were just saying the other day that they didn't understand how we cope with him. You can come with us. You, Tian and Yew,' said Jung.

'No shame? How can you say that? Your father would not want that, breaking up the family and the business. No, that is not the way to go about it.'

'But Keow and Kok are planning to move out. Keow is doing well but he wants to go to Singapore to see what he can do there. I know Kok will move out soon. He told me the other day about going somewhere like Muar. He too is fed up with First Brother's attitude. They definitely could use their share.'

'That is different. They have to go and get work where they can find it. As the oldest you have the responsibility of seeing that your father's legacy is kept intact, not to split up the family business and home the way you want.'

'But *Mak*, First brother has already frittered away so much of the business.' Jung wanted to say more, that the business was not brisk as before and that Kau seemed determined to waste it; the stock had halved compared to how it was in his father's days. Three of the sewing machines lay idle. He wanted to take his share before it came to nothing. He wanted to tell her there was going to be an additional mouth to feed when the new baby arrived but he could see that his mother was getting agitated and not wishing to upset her any more he didn't push the matter further. Her asthmatic attacks had become more frequent and he didn't want to risk another one.

'That may be,' said Kwee, 'but at least we are together now as a family. Where would I be if you go?' There was a hint of panic in her voice.

'As I said, you can come with us,' Jung said gently.

68

'No, you cannot split up the business. Not while I am alive.'

Jung resigned himself to the fact that he had no choice but to continue to work under Kau, at least until he could find something better.

The baby walker -a special purchase Father made for me his first-born- was made of bamboo and rattan. He had saved long for it and was pleased. It became my personal wheels, my key to freedom as I discovered the power of my tiny feet touching the cool concrete floor. Enthralled, I glided here and there like a skater on ice, zigzagging across the hall, charging into the stools neatly stored under the dining tables without hurting myself. At first Father was thrilled that I took to it as easily as sliding down a water chute.

'Look, see how good she is,' he said to my mother, beaming with pride.

'A waste of money,' muttered Grandmother in her corner with her sewing in her hands, not looking up. 'It is going to cause more trouble than it is worth.'

My first few days in the walker went without incident. Emboldened and eager to explore, I raced around, first in the hall and then I ventured into the shop floor.

'Get her out of here,' shouted First Uncle, frowning. He was working at one of the sewing machines while Uncle Heng was, as usual, cutting fabric at the work counter.

'Now, go away, go to your mother,' coaxed Father getting up from his sewing machine behind First Uncle's to direct me back to the hall.

I did as I was told and went to my mother. After a while, I decided to return to Father. I glided up to him again and banged against the side of his sewing machine as I skidded to a standstill.

'Get her out of here!' Father now shouted to Mother who rushed to take me away then returned to cleaning the vegetables in the kitchen.

A little while later when Mother was not looking, I headed towards Father again. When I slammed into the side of his machine again, he shot up from his stool, grabbed me out of the walker and walked into the hall where Mother had come in from the kitchen looking aghast. He put me down on the floor next to her, charged back to the shop and returned carrying my walker, walked past me and Mother and through to the kitchen. His face was distorted with fury.

'What are you doing?' Mother called out behind him but he didn't answer.

She hurried to catch up but by the time she got to him he had already taken the axe from under the stove and laid the first strike on my walker. Mother couldn't stop him. He struck again and again until the walker was a heap of tinder ready for the stove.

That was the first time Mother witnessed Father's temper and realised the depth of his frustration at his position.

Every year a roadside opera was staged as an offering to the gods in the temple on the street behind Hakka Street. On stage the singers with heavily painted faces in traditional Chinese costumes swung their arms in long sleeves as they emoted in high pitch voices while the audience, eating and drinking, watched the drama being acted out. Jung and Lian had found a quiet spot to stand at the back of the crowd to watch the performance. Halfway through the show, Lian suddenly felt wetness trickling down the inside of her legs.

'But it is not due yet, not for another two weeks,' she cried out, panic-stricken.

'We must get you to the hospital quickly,' said Jung who started looking desperately for a trishaw. He found one; they jumped into it with the trishaw puller game for the challenge of getting to the hospital in record time.

My sister, Mei Lin, was tiny when she was born. 'Not much bigger than the size of a new-born kitten,' was how my mother would describe her, 'looking so very helpless and frail.'

When she arrived home two days later carrying Mei Lin in her arms, Uncle Heng stopped his cutting and rushed up to my parents and sister to greet them.

'Congratulations! *Wah*, how fortunate, another child,' he said.

I was with Grandmother in the hall. When I heard my mother I ran out to her, eager to see my new baby sister. As Mother and I walked together into the hall, Grandmother came up to us. We stopped so she could see the baby. She pulled back the cloth from the baby's face to look at her.

'Another girl,' she said without any joy in her voice.

Mother couldn't bring herself to say anything. Third Aunt was lingering as usual, wiping the dining table over and over again so she could stay to see and hear what was going on.

'*Mak*, girl or boy, it is the same. Still our child,' said Father.

'How can a daughter keep or continue your name?'

'There are enough boys now, you have enough grandsons to carry on our good name.' He guided Mother upstairs and when they got on to the landing they heard Third Aunt saying to Grandmother in her sugary voice,

'It is a blessing that Second Sister-in-law didn't have any problems during labour. I wouldn't have been standing out there to watch the opera, not so late in the pregnancy. At least the baby is well.'

Later they overheard her saying to my First Aunt, 'One son is worth more than two daughters.'

As soon as Lian was able to leave the baby with Kwee she went back to work for Ai Chien's husband. It provided not just a small additional income but also respite as she enjoyed the banter with Ai Chien and her seven men machinists.

One morning after they had just started sewing one of the men asked, 'Did you hear about Ah Kong's son?'

'No, what about him?' said one of the others.

'He won the lottery yesterday.'

At that, everyone including Lian stopped working. Even Ai Chien who had been leaning against her husband's worktop with one hand on her hip straightened up to listen.

'*Wahh*, is that so? How much did he win? Big one?'

'Big one, enough to stop work, lucky man.'

'What does he work in?'

'He paints those posters in Rex cinema.'

Lian felt a surge of excitement.

'Has he left his job yet?' she asked, her heart now racing.

She had seen Jung's drawings and paintings which he kept hidden in the desk drawer. They were drawings of animals, portraits and cartoons which he did when he was younger and he had mentioned once that he enjoyed drawing and painting.

'Not yet. Can't find a replacement is what I heard.'

Lian lifted the presser foot off the cloth she had been stitching, pulled the cloth out from under it and pushed to one side. She turned to Ai Chien.

'I have to go and tell Jung about this. I will explain when I come back,' she said and rushed home to look for Jung.

She found him at his sewing machine in the shop and dragged him away to the hall out of Kau's earshot.

'What is the matter?' asked Jung.

'Jung, there is a job,' Lian took a deep breath, 'in the cinema in the main street. It is just the sort of thing you can do, drawing and painting. You know the posters that we see up on the boards outside the cinema? The man who has been doing it won the lottery and he is going to give the job up. You must go and apply for this job. Quick, there is no time to waste,' said Lian.

Jung's eyes widened. 'How do you know?' he asked.

'From one of Ai Chien's workers.'

'You go and make some excuse to First Brother. I'm going right away,' he said. He quickly dusted the thread ends and lint off his shorts and then slipped out of the house

72

through the backdoor and ran along the main road, Jalan Rahmat, until he got to the cinema.

Rex Cinema was situated about half way along the main road, diagonally opposite the post office and about fifteen minutes' walk from the shophouse. A square boxy building in contrast to the traditional shophouses, it was the latest edifice in town owned by the two famous Shaw brothers from Hong Kong for showing their own Chinese films as well as Malay and Hindi films made in Malaya and imports from Hollywood. It stood well back from the street. Two large twelve by eight feet billboards stood to the right to advertise the films that were playing and ones that were 'coming soon' to the pedestrians, cyclists and motorists passing by. It was posters for these boards and the many smaller ones strategically dotted around - in the marketplace and by the hospital on the outskirts - which the resident painter would paint.

Lian held Mei Lin in her arms and waited in the backdoor, every so often peering out down the alley in the hope of seeing Jung. It had been a long time since he had gone which she hoped was a good sign. She had been considering pawning one of her gold necklaces before she went to work that morning. Mei Lin at five months hadn't put on as much weight as she should have. Lian felt a stab of guilt. She knew she couldn't continue to give her five month old baby more of the tapioca paste; she needed something more nutritious than that but milk powder was too expensive. She looked up again and then she saw Jung. He was out of breath as he hastened towards Lian.

'How did it go?' asked Lian, steeling herself for disappointment and half not believing that it could be possible that Jung would get the job.

Jung inhaled deeply and smiled, his eyes wide open as if he didn't believe his luck.

'I start tomorrow,' he said.

Chapter 8

The paintings that Jung produced were usually stunning snapshots of action such as a sword fight scene from the film *The Warrior*, courtesy of the Shaw Brothers. He would do the designing and painting in the large workshop backstage behind the big screen; the entire floor was his new worktop with a faint hint of turpentine blotting the air, and paintbrushes his new tools. The wall directly opposite the back of the screen had several large windows to afford the brightest daylight when he worked. Against the wall, huge tins of paint of various colours and rolls of canvas and paper and jars of cleaned brushes of all sizes were neatly arranged ready for his use. This was the outlet for his talent and his bottled-up feelings as he applied paint on canvas or paper creating whatever came to his mind; it was also where he was happiest, where he could express himself away from noise. The backstage workshop was his haven.

The films that were shown were either Cantonese or Hokkien ones made in Hong Kong or Taiwan, and Malay ones made in Malaya. In the main it was the Hollywood-made films that pulled the crowds. And it was these American films that allowed Jung to put his education to use, translating the English synopses into Mandarin for local consumption. And he was equally able to translate them into Malay as he was fluent in Malay, which was just as well as most of the other staff who were either Malay or Indian hardly spoke English or Chinese, although their manager was Chinese.

His mother Kwee was ambivalent about his new job. On the one hand she was happy that he had a sure income but on the other she was afraid that it would augment his wish to move out of the house. Others, like Heng and Ai Chien, on seeing how happy he and Lian were and knowing what it meant to them were delighted for him. For Heng, he

74

right away realised that Jung's good luck was also his as his absence from the shop meant that the air would be lighter as Kau would have less reason to create tension.

When Jung told Kau about his new job, Kau's face remained expressionless, not a muscle twitched.

'Good. I have less responsibility now, no need to worry about keeping you in work,' he said. 'Finish off what you were doing and you are clear to go.'

Jung's starting salary of eighty dollars a month and perks such as free entry to the cinema were a great boost to his self-confidence. It meant that Lian could buy a little more fish and some meat for the family meals although she herself preferred vegetables. He could also take her out to the movies which became a favourite pastime for Lian when she could tear herself away from her work and leave Kwee to look after the children. Sometimes he would stop to buy banana fritters or peanuts on his way home as a treat for us. Such small changes in their lives didn't go unnoticed by Kau's wife, Siew Ping.

It was about a year after Jung had been working at Rex when Lian noticed that he was in a decidedly good mood when he came home. She had cooked and laid the dinner on the table so that as soon as he'd had his bath he could eat. If there was one thing that Lian had learnt about Jung it was that he was a stickler for punctuality and didn't like being kept waiting. He came to the table smelling of fresh *Brylcreem* in his washed hair. As he sat down he leaned forward to take a deep breath to inhale the aromas from the dishes set before him. There were the usual fried *ikan kuning* fish, sweet potato leaves and braised tofu. He noticed the small plate of king prawns cooked with chilli and soya sauce placed immediately in front of him as he picked up his bowl of rice and chopsticks.

'This looks good,' he said. 'Not had prawns like this in a long time.'

'They were slightly cheaper this morning, there was a good catch I was told. Knowing how much you like prawns I bought them. Here,' said Lian as she put a prawn that she had just shelled in Jung's bowl.

'*Mmm*, tastes delicious, very sweet,' said Jung licking his lips.

Lian thought Jung was unusually talkative. Whatever the reason for his good mood she wasn't complaining. My sister and I were behaving impeccably, eating quietly as we did which was how Jung liked it. After dinner, he took us upstairs to play with us while Lian cleared the table and washed up.

When Lian came to join us in the room, we were on the floor next to the sarong hammock that Mei Lin slept in; we were playing 'house' with the set of wooden bed, table and two chairs that Jung had made and painted blue for us. He got up quickly, walked to his desk, pulled out a drawer and took out a small brown paper package.

'This belongs to you,' he said as he handed it to Lian.

Lian took it, gave Jung a look, and then looked down at the package.

'What is this?' she said.

'Open it.'

Lian undid the wrapping and then let out a gasp.

'How did you know?' she asked.

'I guessed.... and then I looked into your box.'

'I didn't expect to see it for a long time.' Lian carefully lifted the gold necklace that was part of her dowry out of the wrapping. 'When did you redeem it?'

'This morning, on the way to work. I hope you won't have to do this again.'

Jung would walk home for lunch during his half-hour break and to save time he thought a bike would be useful so he saved hard for one which he'd seen in the shop where Keow worked and whose boss had promised him a discount. When he eventually paid for the brand new *Raleigh* bike he couldn't cycle home fast enough to show it to Lian and his mother. Arriving back at the shop, he parked it on five-foot.

Heng noticed it first, told Kwee about it and they both joined him to admire the gleaming bike which Jung was now gently stroking, first the shiny chromium handlebars then the bell, before flicking off an invisible fleck of dust off the leather saddle.

'*Wah*, very nice indeed,' said Heng nodding his approval.

'This is real leather. Smell it,' said Jung caressing the saddle.

'I can see it is,' said Heng. 'This will definitely make it so much easier for you to come home for lunch. Save you a lot of time.'

'Not to mention your browning under the sun at that time of the day. See he how brown he has got,' said Kwee pushing up Jung's sleeve to make her point, revealing a clear band of paler skin in contrast to the rest of his chestnut-coloured arm.

Lian who had heard them came out with me and Mei Lin, walking past Kau who was sitting at his sewing machine and deliberately ignoring all that was happening on the five-foot way.

'Papa's new bicycle,' I said as I ran on to the five-foot way.

'Yes, you can ring the bell, like this,' said Jung as he proceeded to show me and watch the delight on my face when I made it ring.

After we'd seen enough of Jung's prize, we went back into the house. Kwee and Heng returned to their work while Lian and Jung ushered me into the hall. There in the hall were my two aunts, sitting at the large dining table. They were obviously in conference but stopped talking when they saw us. Siew Ping was breastfeeding her new baby boy while Yin Li was stringing long beans from a basket. Lian, Mei Lin and I went ahead of Jung up the stairs. When we got to the top, the two women start talking again.

'All this flaunting! *Ha*, just as well he didn't finish his English education. If he had he might have got the top job, then imagine how it would have gone to his head,' said Siew Ping looking at her baby to make sure it was sucking.

'*Aiyahh,* what is there to boast about?' said Yin Li. 'He is only working for someone else, not as if he is his own boss. Besides, English is the red-haired devils' language. My Soong said it was traitorous speaking their language.'

'As long as he pays his rent. Can't live here for nothing,' replied Siew Ping. 'The price of rice has gone up again.' Then raising her voice even more she called out to her daughter in the kitchen, 'Chung Lin, come here. You are supposed to sweep the floor and where are your lazy brothers? What is all that noise outside?'

Chung Lin came running in, wiping her wet hands on her skirt.

'What?' she said, her face drooping when she stopped in front of her mother. 'I will sweep as soon as I've finished the dishes. Hock and Sek are out at the back arguing with someone again. They should help here.'

'Leave them. They will take care of themselves. Make sure you wash all the dirty nappies when you've done sweeping, and hurry,' Siew Ping shouted as she pulled her baby from her breast. Just then Hock came charging into the house, his face turned to the back, shouting at someone in the alley,

'…….. your mother's smelly cunt! Pig face!'

'Mind your language!' said Siew Ping when he came into the hall. 'What was all that about?'

'That pig face boy from the goldsmith's shop accused me of cheating at the card game. So I punched him.' Hock, twelve years of age, was almost as tall as his mother and bore a striking resemblance to his father. He rubbed his chin.

'Then?'

Hock hesitated. 'We got into a fight. Then his mother came out shouting at me. I wasn't going to stand for it.'

'Too right. I don't interfere in your quarrels,' said Siew Ping as a smug look appeared on her face.

Of my cousins, only Third Aunty and Uncle's two children didn't acknowledge let alone speak to my parents thus upholding their family tradition. My siblings and I were taught to always acknowledge our elders and consequently we always did, regardless of whether my uncle and aunt responded or not. The two children got on with us children although Kin the elder of the two considered himself far more intelligent than any one of us that he would only speak to us if he couldn't help it.

Third Uncle Soong was a stranger to me. He had a bulbous nose - the family stamp - that my father and all his brothers and sisters had. As children my sisters and I used to make fun of their noses calling it the *jambu* nose, after the local three-lobed cone-shaped fruit. Soong was pale-skinned as if he had been kept out of the sun and always wore a well-pressed white shirt and a pair of striped trousers that looked more like pyjama trousers. He and I had never had an exchange of more than a few words in all the time we lived in the same house, although I would always acknowledge him whenever our paths crossed. 'Third Uncle,' I would say. He would respond with an '*Mmm*', sometimes with his hand over his mouth.

Perhaps this indifference to me, and my siblings, was not surprising since he and Father didn't speak to each other. They were oceans apart. You could feel the icy tension between them and it was not just between them; Soong didn't speak to his other brothers either although the divide didn't seem as wide. When the brothers had to walk pass each other you would think that they were invisible to each other. Soong would put his hand over his mouth as if the air around the brother was contaminated and he didn't want to inhale it. He always did that especially when he was walking past the rubbish bins in the back alley, his trousers flapping around his legs. And he'd take a different route to avoid walking under any woman's underwear hanging on the bamboo poles across the lane, which became a joke amongst the females in the household apart from his wife.

I got on well with all of Kau's five children –Hock, Chung Lin, Sek, Lee and Fah. I played with them and admired Hock for the things he could do like making kites and flying them. For some reason they were respectful towards my parents and were never ever rude to them as far as I could remember. They had no reason to be nasty to any one of us children either. I, however, was terrified of their father Kau as were my siblings.

The one clue that Kau was not my father's biological brother was that he didn't have the *jambu* nose. His was well chiselled, more pointed. In fact he was a good-looking man although I don't remember ever seeing him smile let alone laugh. He had a habit of flicking his left little fingernail - which he kept very long - with his thumbnail. Sometimes I would hear his flicking before I saw him and would quickly turn and walk away from it.

I was always afraid of him and would try to get out of his way whenever I saw him coming. Obsessed with saving water and electricity, not for ecological reasons but to save money, because he was mean, he made our lives difficult and unpleasant in the process.

Water rationing was a constant source of anguish, whether the cause was due to drought or burst pipes; it meant queuing at the water mains at the end of the street to fill our buckets which we then had to carry home. What we could carry and store in buckets in the air-well area was mostly reserved for cooking and boiling for drinking which meant that we had to restrict washing ourselves. Fortunately for us, Ai Chien, who had a huge storage tank installed above her bathroom and had plenty to spare, would invite my family to go to hers to have a bath.

There was no such storage tank in our kitchen or bathroom. Instead there was the original concrete tank built into the wall and on the floor, and which was shared between the kitchen and bathroom. It looked like an aquarium and came up to about three feet high. A tap from the mains pipe running along the wall above it fed water directly into it. On the kitchen side of the tank, near the bottom was an outlet with a tap from which we could get the stored water. The water, when there was any, was always cold so that we always drew our breath in before we poured it over us when washing ourselves in the bathroom.

When there was no rationing Kau would sometimes put a padlock on the tap, located at the bottom half of the tank, to stop us using water. I remember the time when I was squatting in front of the tank in the kitchen and playing with the tap, turning it on and then turning it off again. I didn't hear Kau flicking his nail as he came up behind me.

'What are you doing?' he snapped at me and then he pinched me hard on my thigh.

I was so shocked and frightened that I couldn't scream even though I was in pain. I jumped up and ran to my mother who was upstairs ironing on the landing.

'First Uncle pinched me,' I said and still trying not to cry, lifted up my skirt to show her the growing redness on my thigh.

Mother looked horrified. 'What did you do?'

'I was only washing my hands.'

'Don't play with water again and stay clear of your uncle,' she said as she rubbed my thigh. I knew she was angry with him.

This experience, together with the dread of carrying buckets of water from the street's mains tap, was how a healthy respect for water and hate for its wastage were instilled in me at a very early age.

My grandmother was troubled with asthma for years and she would only consult a herbalist for treatment as she was suspicious of western medicine. I remember witnessing one of her attacks. I was walking past her bedroom when I heard a loud frightening sound of someone sucking in air. I looked into her room and there she was, sitting on the edge of her bed, hunched over, and struggling to breathe, making a wheezing noise. My mother was standing by her, panicking but trying to help and not achieving much. Grandmother looked frightened, her eyes wide open, and each time she gasped, pushing her head back as she did, it was as if it was her last one.

The next thing I heard was my father and Uncle Kok running up the stairs into the room. They lifted Grandmother and carried her to the clinic that had recently opened six doors away, run by two doctors - a husband and wife team- who had trained in Australia. After a long while there she recovered.

Grandmother was adamant about not using western medicine. Once she was better she sought the advice of a diviner in the temple on the next street next to ours. She was 'prescribed' the most unbelievable and bizarre treatment which we witnessed her taking.

She sat at the large dining table. My cousins, my sisters and I sat with her while the adults stood behind us. It was as if we were waiting for a show to commence.

'I want to see what *Poh Poh* is going to do!' we children cried. 'What is happening?'

'Are you sure you're going to do it, *Mak*?' asked one of the adults.

Someone placed a large bowl in the middle of the table.

'*Eeeee,* what is that?' More squeals from us children as we pointed to the bowl.

In the bowl were several tiny hairless and pink-skinned baby mice, their eyes shut. Next to it was another bowl filled with pickled cabbage leaves. A pair of chopsticks was placed next to a plate in front of Grandmother, ready for her to use.

'What are you going to do, *Poh Poh*?' we asked.

Grandmother didn't answer but slowly proceeded to pick up a cabbage leaf with her fingers and spread it out on the plate in front of her as if she was doing a magic trick for us. She paused briefly. Then she picked up one of the mice and placed it in the edge of the leaf and slowly rolled it up in the leaf like rolling tobacco. She paused again for a moment before picking up her chopsticks, studied the rolled up cabbage and then picked it up and brought it to her mouth. At that point I looked away.

Chapter 9

1955 was the season for daughters. Baby girls popped up like mushrooms in the neighbourhood of Hakka Street.

Across the road from No.22 were several haberdashery shops. Wei, the eldest child of five children and still unmarried, helped run one of the shops that her parents owned. She was about three years younger than Lian and every morning when Lian was on her way to the market she would see Wei helping her brothers open the shop. They greeted each other and very quickly they became good friends. Wei confided in Lian about her worry that she might end up a spinster in spite of her parents' efforts to find her a suitable match.

Then to the surprise of everyone in the street who knew the family, Wei's middle-aged mother gave birth to another daughter. Even more shocking to the neighbours was the whiteness of the baby's skin and hair, and instead of dark brown eyes they were pale with eyelashes that were almost white. She was later affectionately referred to as the 'red-haired' child as she was more like a white person than an Oriental. Despite the bewildering aberrations, and stares from curious neighbours and shoppers on the five-foot way when the baby was out with her parents, she grew up as one of us although she rarely came out into the sun to play.

Two shops to the left of No.22, Ai Chien who could proudly boast that she already had three sons –ten, eight and seven years old- as well as a daughter who was my age, now had another baby girl. But she was delighted with her as she now felt the baby's gender didn't matter; she had after all more than done her duty with the first three sons.

One more baby girl was born to the shop next to Ai Chien's, another to the shop three doors away to our right and two more across the road. These babies were to become mine and my sisters' friends and playmates.

Even my Third Aunt Yin Li who had been trying to have another baby for several years finally became pregnant, her round belly protruding from her thin frame like a plump berry stuck on a twig. The birth of her daughter noticeably damped down her cockiness about her son. She said nothing about her baby when she came home with her from the hospital in a trishaw.

Grandmother met her in the hall and also said little. Her tongue was stilled by the knowledge that baby girls were arriving with a vengeance around her.

As if on a fixed course to annoy my grandmother, as well as keeping up with the other mothers, Lian gave birth to my sister Mei Chin. By now Lian was no longer sensitive about what Kwee or anyone else might say although she secretly wanted a son.

In 1957, the same year that Malaya gained independence from the British, Lian's fourth daughter was born. Both she and Jung were disappointed; by now they had great hopes and were convinced that the odds were in their favour, that the baby would be a boy.

A few days later I sensed that something unusual was happening. The house was busy as usual with everyone going about their daily business but Lian was jumpy and became impatient with me. She had wrapped the baby in a pretty floral cloth. Jung was home instead of being at work. He told me that we were going to take a trip to visit see my Aunt Kui in Senggarang. Then he and I walked with Lian carrying the baby to the taxi stand which was about ten minutes' walk away, next to Charlton Kindergarten. My other two sisters, Mei Lin and Mei Chin, were left behind in Grandmother's care.

All the way to Senggarang in the taxi we were quiet. Lian's face was sad as she kept looking at the baby while Jung's face was solemn, his eyebrows pulled together. When we arrived at my aunt's shop, she came out to greet us on the five-foot way.

'Come, come inside. Let me have the baby,' said Kui as she took the baby from Mother. We followed her into the shop where her husband was serving a customer. We greeted him.

'*Ah*, you have arrived. Go in and sit down,' he said, pointing to the back of the shop. He was a tall thin man with a long face.

We walked on to the back, into the hall. I sensed that Lian was not happy; she would normally be very cheerful when we visited a relative's house. She couldn't take her eyes off her baby which was still in my aunt's arms.

'Sit down,' said Kui pointing to the stools around the dining table. Lian and Jung sat down. I stood by Lian, wondering what was happening. It didn't feel like a normal visit at all although the house smelled of perming lotion coming from the small area in the hall that Kui called her hairdressing salon – two special chairs facing two large mirrors on the wall and lots of roller and hairbrushes on a large trolley.

Aunt Kui had a big voice and always had a big smile on her face; she would fuss about us children when we visited, buying us treats from the sweet shop nearby. But this morning it was different; she didn't buy me sweets and there was no sign of her children; she seemed to concentrate solely on the baby.

'What time are they coming?' said Jung looking at his watch.

Kui looked up at the clock on the wall. 'Not long now. Baby is clean and fed, that's good.' She handed the baby back to Mother and went to make coffee.

We sat and waited. Lian and Jung didn't say much.

'What are we waiting for, ma?'

'Never you mind. Sit here quietly,' said Lian patting the stool next to her.

Kui came back carrying two cups of coffee which she put on the table.

'I think that is them now,' she said. She had seen someone coming into the shop and then we heard voices.

'They are here.' Her voice was subdued, there was no smile on her face.

Her husband walked into the hall followed by a man and a woman. They were Malay; the woman was wearing the traditional *baju* – a colourful tunic over a batik sarong and a pretty headscarf while the man was in a shirt and trousers. They smiled shyly and then their eyes were immediately drawn to the baby in Lian's arms.

Jung stood up and said something to the man. They shook hands and then sat down and carried on speaking in Malay. The woman moved closer to look at the baby, she smiled at Lian and then her eyes turned to fix on the baby. I stared at the woman, watching her every move. There was a look of eagerness as she stroked my sister's hand.

'Ma, why are you crying?' I said looking up into her face.

'You go and wait over there,' said my aunt, gently pulling me away from my mother. I would not move; I pulled away from her hand on my shoulder.

'What's happening, Ma? Is the woman going to take baby away?' I asked. Lian nodded as her tears then came flooding.

'No, don't let her! Don't let her take my sister away!' I screamed as I threw my arms across the baby. I burst into tears myself, my arms tightly folded around my baby sister and not allowing the Malay woman near her.

'I will look after her. I will be good. Do not let her take my sister away,' I pleaded.

Lian turned to Jung, her eyes appealing to him to understand.

'I can't do it,' she said, shaking her head. 'I can't.'

That was enough for my father.

'I can't do it either,' he said.

In a moment of desperation my parents had decided that if they had to give their child away, a Malay family would be the best choice as they were known to dote on Chinese children. In the end my baby sister Mei Choon was saved from being taken away from us. When we got home with her safely wrapped in Lian's arms, Grandmother Kwee accepted the change of plans without saying a word.

By now I was almost six, Mei Lin five and Mei Chin four. When the three of us stood side by side, our black hair cut short in a bob with a pelmet of a fringe across our forehead and wearing pretty frocks made with remnants of fabric from Wei, she would chuckle and call us her *do-re-me*. With Mei Choon, she simply extended the notes to *do-re-me-fah*. She was proud of us although she never ever said so. We just knew.

My sisters and I have a strong bond and I daresay the bond between Mei Choon and me has always been particularly special.

A few weeks after that meeting, the three of us, *do-re-me*, were playing in our parents' room, sitting on the cool linoleum-covered floor. Lying on a mat in the centre of the bed was Mei Choon who had been fast asleep. Lian had warned us not to wake her up. Now her eyes were wide open and she was gurgling happily. I got up from the floor and climbed up on to the bed to sit next to her. Mei Lin and Mei Chin followed. We *coo*-ed at her and stroked her cheek as we tried to make her laugh.

'Look at this soft part,' said Mei Lin, gently stroking the top of Mei Choon's head.

'Be careful,' I said but I was more bothered by the way Mei Choon was dressed. A large piece of cotton cloth was wound round her body and arms like a cigar and tied with a piece of string. Her doll-like legs were free to kick and she was smiling in response to the noises we were making.

'I don't like this,' I said as I started to undo the knot of the string and then proceeded to remove the string, loosen the cloth wrap and cautiously pulled her arms out. 'There, she is free and happier now. See how she is waving her arms.' I felt freer and more comfortable myself.

'Ma will be cross,' said Mei Lin looking at me with a worried face. Lian was either cooking or washing clothes in the kitchen.

I shrugged. I had promised to look after my baby sister, just as I had promised my mother that I would when I begged her not to give her away. Mei Choon became my responsibility which for me included making sure she was comfortable.

We then heard Lian coming upstairs and into the room. She smiled when she saw us on the bed.

'Did Mei Choon cry at all?' she asked walking over to us but before we could answer, she said, 'Who has undone the knot again?'

'I did, Ma,' I said.'She looked so uncomfortable, she wanted to wave her arms like she is doing now.'

Mei Choon was smiling and kicking as if she agreed.

'No, you mustn't do it again.' Lian wrapped the cloth round Mei Choon and then tied the knot again.

'Why are you doing that?' I asked.

'This is to stop her becoming nosey and touching things that do not concern her when she grows up.'

'Did you tie us like that too?' asked Mei Lin.

'Obviously I didn't do it enough,' Lian replied.

When Jung announced that he was sending me to school Grandmother Kwee was shocked.

'Why educate girls? They only get married off into someone else's family to bring up a new family. You are wasting your money.'

'The world is changing. We have to give our daughter the same opportunity as boys. It will open doors for her. Who knows? Maybe work as a secretary in some big business instead of cooking or washing for someone else. I have registered her in Charlton Kindergarten,' said Jung.

Charlton Kindergarten was part of the school that was owned and run by an Indian man who was also the headmaster and whom I remember shouting at me to stop talking when he came into my classroom on one of his impromptu inspections.

'What? An English school, instead of a Chinese school? What will she become?' asked Kwee, the corners of her mouth curled down.

'That is tantamount to being a traitor!' said Soong when grandmother told him later. 'She should go to a Chinese school. She should be learning about China and all things Chinese. Not the imperialists' language and ways. *Ahh,* but it is his business, not mine.'

Soong had conveniently forgotten that he himself had been educated in English. His strong allegiance to China and his admiration and support for Chairman Mao had clouded his view. He was in no doubt about how his son should be educated. Like many of the children in the neighbourhood, Kin was put into a Chinese boys' school, which was located in the centre of town, not far from the girls' school.

'Going to an English school doesn't mean she can't learn Mandarin at the same time. I have to do what I think is best,' said Jung, trying to persuade Kwee who was not convinced of the wisdom of his decision.

Although Jung disappointed his mother by sending me to Charlton Kindergarten, fortunately his Uncle Wong, who was my grandfather Chun Hong's cousin, approved.

Wong came from China and had started up his own sawmill business in Kluang shortly after Chun Hong had built his. He was one of the elders that Lian and Jung had served tea to during their wedding ceremony. He regularly visited Kwee and Heng to catch up and exchange news and it was on one of these visits that he found out Jung's intention concerning my future.

He sat in the shop and drank coffee with Kwee while Heng carried on cutting his cloth and Kau stitching some cut pieces at the sewing machine. He had just started to take a sip when Kwee told him,

'Jung is going to send his first daughter to an English school.'

Wong didn't answer right away. He took another slow sip from his cup then gently placed it on the table.

'That is the way to go,' he said looking directly at Kwee. 'I am sure of that.'

Kwee was somewhat surprised at his response.

'Look,' he said, 'there are English newspapers next to Mandarin ones. The good jobs, the top jobs, are taken by people with English. Even the *Tengku* sends his children to England to study. If it is good enough for the Malay princes it is good enough for us.' Wong nodded to himself as if to emphasise his point, then sat up straight in his chair. 'Good, that is good. That is what I would want for my grandchildren.'

'I thought a Chinese school would be the way to go,' said Kwee, but she didn't seem so sure of herself now. By virtue of being the oldest in the Chiang family and a highly successful businessman in the community, Wong was much respected by all in the family including Kau.

'You can always learn Mandarin and all things Chinese at night classes,' said Wong, then leaned forward to Kwee. 'I am sure Chun Hong would agree.'

'Study hard or you will end up being a night-soil carrier,' was Lian's refrain after I had started school. 'Even then, you need to be able to read the house numbers and addresses.'

'*Eeee*, smelly!' Mei Lin and I would screw up our noses and laugh and then pretended to vomit. 'Who wants to do that?' we said, then quickly burrowed our heads into our books, banishing from our mind the picture of the man who came every night to empty the latrines.

We didn't need much encouragement to study. My first English language book opened with the first page showing two separate drawings of a man and a pan with the words *A man, a pan* under them respectively. On the second, the man and the pan were now together with the words *A man and a pan.*

A man, a pan... a man and a pan... a pan and a man...this is a man... this is a pan became the rhyme to

91

recite for a long time. After school I would sit with Mei Lin and Mei Chin on the lino floor in the bedroom with my book resting against my bent knees and I would read aloud, my finger pointing to each of the words. Then my sisters would imitate me.

Although Jung and Lian's room was bulging with the addition of us four children, the matter of moving out of No. 22 was never discussed again for Kwee's sake. The three of us older girls slept on the floor, lying side by side on a straw mat like fish neatly laid out to dry in the sun, while the baby slept in the sarong hammock.

The more pressing matter was to ensure that the school fees were met as Mei Lin was now in line to attend school. I was soon to move up to the main English primary school located on the far side of town which meant that I would need taxi fares as well as school fees.

At the end of each month when Jung came home with his pay, after he had eaten his dinner, he would sit at his desk to count his notes. He would place the notes neatly in a pile and count them like a bank cashier. When it was done he would start again.

'Your notes won't multiply if you keep counting them, you know,' said Lian whenever he did that.

'It feels good handling this,' Jung would reply with a sad smile. 'It will be gone in a blink. I just want to touch it while I can.' Then he would put aside my school fees and hand the rest to Lian and hurried to wash his hands.

When the opportunity came up for Jung to make some money on the side, he couldn't resist. He was to be a middleman for the local four-digit lottery run by some syndicate in town. His job would be to collect from punters their lucky four-digit numbers and the money, anything from twenty cents to a dollar per throw. In return he would receive five percent of his punters' winnings. In the first few weeks after he took on the job, he was lucky as some of his punters did win and he consequently made some money too. This extra money was just the breathing space that both he and Lian needed. But he also knew the risk he was taking.

Chapter 10

The playground for the children living in our row of shops was the concrete alley that separated our street from the one behind that ran parallel to Hakka Street. As soon as the sun had crossed to the other side of the river and the shade hit the alley we would run out to play.

'Don't run, not right away after your dinner!' my mother would be shouting. 'Your rice will drop into your appendix and then you will know all about it!'

Fortunately for us, immediately behind No. 22 and the adjacent five shops was a gap of open land that hadn't been built on yet and was left to waste. Here was our real playground where we made mud-cakes, kicked a ball, skipped a rope and played catch or hide-and-seek around the stacks of firewood.

These stacks were landmarks and belonged to different families including mine. They weren't labelled but we knew which belonged to whom. They weren't heaps, haphazardly thrown together, but instead were skilfully arranged as in works of art. The uniformly cut sticks, each about eighteen inches long were laid side by side like pencils on the ground till an area as wide as it was long was covered. Then another layer was laid at ninety degrees to it and so on until the pile was four feet high and was completely stable. Several piles like that were built and then carefully covered with a waterproof sheet weighed down by a rock or brick. Initially no one worried about the firewood being stolen until my cousins Hock and Sek came on the scene. They would pull out loose sticks of wood without disturbing the pile or, worse, toppling it. Sometimes, audaciously, they would simply take off the top layers without making it too obvious that some had been removed.

There was a work-hut with a rusted corrugated tin roof built against the wall that belonged to an old grumpy carpenter who would shout and chase us away whenever any one of us children went near him. He was brown and shrivelled, like a cuttlefish that had been left out too long to dry in the sun. He never seemed to make anything but was always planing or sawing planks of wood, muttering as he worked and shouting at us when we tried to hide in his hut.

On the far side of our playground, by the monsoon drain that ran along the street was a hibiscus tree. Nobody knew how it got there, who planted it or when. To me it was the most incongruous thing in the area but it fascinated me because of its tenacity, growing in spite of the poor soil it was standing in, its trunk twisting as if it was struggling to grow. But it grew, increasing in height and girth and then it stopped. Its bark was pale and silvery. Unlike the leafy trees I had seen in pictures, there weren't many leaves on the branches but there was always a flower, red and trumpet-shaped; it was almost as if it was making a plea not to chop it down by its offering of a flower, assuring us that there was life and potential.

Sometimes I would climb it when no one was looking, especially the old woman from three doors away, who called me a tomboy. My sisters, cousins and I would hang our paper folding of lanterns and boats on the branches or sometimes the lucky one of us would get to sit wedged between the branches to umpire a badminton match played on the relatively flat patch that was just large enough for a doubles game, away from the stacks of firewood, and bordered by the wall of the end shop. The net would be strung up between the tree and a post with imaginary lines for the court.

The concrete alley sometimes served as a singles badminton court where playing meant avoiding stepping on the hens that might be roaming around. Those of us who were learning to cycle and who were too impatient to wait till the shops closed so that we could cycle on the street, would weave between the hens and the turkeys let out from No. 34. Sometimes we would just chase the turkeys until they turned around squawking angrily, to peck at us. Other times we would just gather round and watch a man work his magic with coloured dough.

This man came regularly, pushing his bicycle laden with his stool, an umbrella and a large wooden box. As soon as we caught sight of him we would stop doing whatever we were doing and wait for him to set his stool down in the shade, open his box and then lay out the balls of dough made up in the colours of the rainbow. Sometimes he wore a straw hat but he never spoke, not before he began and not while he was making his models. He never told us what he was intending to make, he just sat down, made himself comfortable and then set to work. He would begin by taking a thin bamboo stick the length of a chopstick and then pinch a small knob of dough to go on the end of the stick. Not knowing what he was going to make added to the excitement of watching him work as he very swiftly added bits of red, yellow or green dough depending on what he was creating. Then, before our eyes, a cockerel, dog or a dragon would materialise at the end of the stick to gasps of wonder and delight from us. We would buy them from him; he would take the money and give us change and still not say a word to us. When he had made and sold a few he would pack up and move on.

Apart from the many falls, scrapes and cuts sustained here in this playground it was nosebleeds that stood out for me. The first one involved Mei Lin. She was making mud cakes with her friends and playing at buying and selling. She wanted to show me the cakes she had made. I was standing by the hibiscus tree watching the boys play badminton. As she tried to avoid the players by staying close to the wall, one of the boys reached out to get the shuttlecock just as she was walking past, smacking her right on the nose with his racket. Mei Lin bled instantly giving us all a fright. My cousin Chung Lin who was nearby rushed over to her and quickly placed her hand on Mei Lin's nose and rushed her home to Mother.

One evening while waiting for dinner, I decided to play hopscotch and marked out the squares with a piece of chalk on the concrete lane and started hopping about all by myself on my neatly drawn squares when a friend Swee from two doors away came up directly behind me and started to mimic me.

'Don't do that,' I said.

Swee ignored me and continued to hop behind me.

'Go away,' I said.

'Can I not play?'

'No. I want to play by myself. It's my game.' Swee stepped aside but as soon as my back was turned she hopped behind me again. I hopped again and turned around to face her.

'Go away, I want to play by myself.'

She ignored me again and when I turned away from her she hopped right back behind me. I took one more hop and swung round with my right arm out. I hit her face. She screamed; her hand shot up to cover her nose. I saw blood trickling down her chin before she turned away to run home to her mother. I didn't know who was more frightened. The thought of facing my father terrified me.

I flew into the house and in the kitchen, blurted out to Lian what had happened.

'What did you do that for?' she said. She was in the middle of cooking dinner and couldn't deal with me. 'Now go upstairs.'

I knew that meant that my father would deal with me. He was still in the bathroom. I ran past Kau and his family as they sat eating their dinner, and then past Soong and his children eating at the smaller table. They looked up at me as I whizzed by; they knew I had done something wrong. I darted upstairs to the landing and hid under the table. I didn't have long to wait.

Father came out of the bathroom, up the stairs and then into his room, rubbing his hair dry with his towel as he walked. My heart was pounding so hard I thought it was going to leap out of my chest. Then the inevitable happened. I heard Swee's mother shouting, at first from the hall and then she was at the bottom of the stairs yelling, yelling at the top of her voice.

'*Wahh,* what sort of daughter have you got, Jung? A tiger of a daughter, so wild, so fierce. See what she did to my daughter! Hit her nose, luckily it is not broken. See how much she bled. *Wahh,* what kind of girl is your daughter?'

For Father who prided himself on bringing up his children properly this tirade was simply too much to bear. He was in the middle of combing his hair; I could smell the *Brylcreem.* He came out of the room, his comb still in his hand. His face was now red with anger. He walked to the top of the stairs. His voice boomed out sending shivers through me.

'I am sorry,' he said, his face sterner than I'd seen for a long time. 'Is your daughter alright now? I will deal with mine.' There was no mistaking he meant what he said.

Swee's mother seemed to be pacified by that and walked away but still complaining loud enough for all to hear. I knew the worst was to come.

'Where are you?' Father called out. He was standing by the door to his room, his face slowly turned towards where I was curled up under the table.

I felt another shiver go through my body. I had no choice. I came out of my hiding place and slowly walked past him, not daring to look at his face this time, and went into the room. He followed me in shutting the door behind him. Then I saw him take the belt that was hanging behind the door.

'Papa, I won't do it again,' I said, my voice trembling as he stepped towards me. I ran to the foot of the bed and tried to squeeze into the space between it and the small cupboard. I threw my arms over my head and squeezed my eyes tightly shut. Then I felt the burning sting when he lashed out and hit me. Above my screams and crying, I was aware of my mother banging on the door and her shouting to Father to open the door.

The next morning when Father and I were getting ready for kindergarten and Lian was attending to my sisters, he turned to inspect me as he always did to make sure that I was properly dressed. It was then that he noticed the weal at the top of my right arm where the belt had struck.

'Come here,' he said gently. He pointed to the sleeve of my white blouse. 'Pull your sleeve down.'

He didn't look angry. I tugged down my sleeve, then picked up my bag and waited until he was ready. After we said good bye to my mother and sisters we went downstairs, he got his bike from the hall and we walked out through the shop where Heng was dusting his worktop.

'*Ah*, off to school then?' he said.

'Yes, Uncle Heng,' I said, looking up at his smiling face. I smiled back at him.

When we got out on to the street, Father took my hand in his left hand as he pushed his bike alongside us. His hand felt strong yet soft and warm. I was relieved that he wasn't angry with me anymore. It was a long walk to Charlton Kindergarten but neither of us spoke.

I was sitting on the floor in our room reading a book with Mei Lin when he came home from work that afternoon.

'Papa,' we both greeted him as he walked in.

'*Hmmm,*' he responded which I thought was a good sign, a sign that he was definitely no longer angry with me.

I stole a look at his face – it was flushed and moist with sweat - then quickly returned to my book to show Mei Lin what I had learnt at kindergarten.

When Father came home from work he would normally sit in his chair to cool down a bit before his bath. But that day he came straight away to us.

'Here, this is for you two,' he said.

We looked up at him. He was holding out a book to me. I took it.

'Thank you, Papa,' I said as Mei Lin tried to grab it from me.

On the cover of the book was a picture of a beautiful girl asleep in the forest with three little fairies looking down on her. *Sleeping Beauty*.

'Look at this,' I said to Mei Lin as I turned the pages. 'Papa, this is a good book.'

'Good,' he said.

When I looked up at him his face was soft and hinting at a smile.

Chapter 11

The grown-ups were talking about a big day that was approaching. Jung told us children that he was going to take us to see the fireworks on the evening of that big day which was going to be the mark of a new beginning for our country.

Two days before the day, Jung who didn't like hanging around in or outside the shop especially when Kau was there, found himself sitting with Heng on the five-foot way enjoying the cool air. The shop had not long been closed and Kau had disappeared out of the house.

The dim amber street lights were on and the hawkers had set up their stalls diagonally opposite them at the corner of the street; their bright gas lamps lighting up their cooking and drawing hungry customers like ants to a bowl of sugar. A short queue had already formed for fried *kwayteow* and Hokkien *mee* as the hawkers stir-fried, clanging the woks over the wood fire with masterful strokes and the aromas of fried garlic and chilli tickled the senses.

Heng had placed a low stool between himself and Jung for their coffee cups and a bowl of melon seeds. He picked up a handful of the seeds and then put one between his teeth to crack it while Jung sipped his coffee. Nearby, some children were hiding behind the pillars in their game of hide-and-seek.

'It has been a long time coming, this independence,' said Jung. 'So much talk of it by the British and now finally it is going to happen.'

'Is it going to be better though?' said Heng.

'At least that is what the communists, the jungle fighters, want - get rid of the red-haired devils. They might stop their fighting now. The thing is, it was just a matter of time when the British left, so all that fighting and killing from the jungle has been pointless,' said Jung.

Heng nodded, chewing as he did and then when he'd swallowed he said, 'At least under the British government we know where we stand. It hasn't been bad, they've been fair; at least I think they are when it comes to jobs. They allow Chinese into the Civil service. Chinese, Malay or Indian get the same treatment if they have the qualifications.'

'Yes, but in the new scheme, the Malays are insisting that the four-to-one Malays to non-Malays is maintained in the Civil service after independence, which is so unfair.' Jung reached out to the bowl of seeds and then changed his mind.

'It is not fair at all,' said Heng. 'It has taken me all this time to get my citizenship and I have lived here nearly all my life. I have more right to citizenship than that.. *that* man from Indonesia who just came here two years ago. Just because he has the right name and skin colour.' He was referring to one of the customers he was talking to earlier in the day.

'Thankfully, Lian and I have been successful getting ours. One problem less,' said Jung. 'The deal with the independence is that all born in Malaya will be given citizenship but in return, *this is the condition*, the Malay language becomes compulsory in all schools whatever the medium is.'

'A sure way to push everybody else out,' said Heng as he looked up into the distance. He shook his head and then took a deep breath before picking up some more melon seeds. '*Aiyahh*, their language is easy and we have learnt it, so that's not a problem.'

'Except, what use is the language outside Malaya?' said Jung.

'The question is whether we can ever be united – all the different groups. Look at the communist Chinese. They are still there fighting out of the jungle. When will that end?' he said.

'I suppose that as long as it continues, we Chinese have to accept some responsibility for the division between us,' said Jung. He took another sip of the coffee.

Ai Chien's husband, Lam, came out of his shop and walked up to the two men, his arms folded behind his back as he always did.

'Come and have coffee with us, Lam. We were just talking about the new era that is coming,' said Heng.

'Why not? A cup before I go for my walk,' said Lam unfolding his arms. His ritual of a brisk evening walk round the block before his supper of fried *kwayteow* was well known.

'I will get a cup. Take this,' said Jung pointing to his seat and then he went inside the shop.

Lam sat down and let out a sigh.

'*Ahh*, this is all very exciting, this next step. The Alliance seems to be working. As long as the Chinese party stands up for our rights within this alliance we should get a fair deal,' he said.

The Alliance was made up of the three newly formed parties - United Malay National Organisation (UMNO), Malayan Chinese Association (MCA) and Malayan Indian Congress (MIC) with Tungku Abdul Rahman, the leader of UMNO, as the new Prime Minister.

'You think so?' said Heng, his brow started to knit. 'We live side by side but we don't blend. We get on but we keep each other at a distance. That is happening at the top as well, in the government. We have parties representing each of the racial groups. Sure it seems right, but it's actually divisive, it's as good as saying we are separate entities although we work together. We each want different things, we all want to protect our separate interests. Can't be right. We have to wait and see. Have you got your citizenship yet?'

'Yes. I suppose you automatically got yours?' Lam coughed, cleared his chest, walked to the drain, spat into it, and then sat down again.

'You would think so, but no, I had to apply for it. To think we helped build this country..' said Heng shaking his head as if he didn't understand.

Jung returned with a cup of coffee in one hand and a stool in the other. He placed the stool next to Lam's and handed him the cup.

'At least all our children will automatically be citizens,' said Lam.

'Yes, in return the Malays get help with education, bursaries, and they also get plots of land and anything, anything that will help them like permits, licences,' said Jung, his voice raising. 'How can that be fair exchange?'

Looking at Jung who had sat down, Heng said, 'When your father and I arrived in this country it was peaceful. All shades of skin colours. I had never seen skin as black as charcoal, but so what? We did what we had to do and there was enough work for everyone. Sure, there were skirmishes between the Malays and Chinese but nothing serious. They felt we were marginalizing them but it was only because we were desperate and hardworking, and we grabbed what work there was. They want everything on a plate handed to them.'

Jung nodded. 'It is more or less the same where I work. We do our work because we have to. We share a joke, a laugh and even eat together; we don't talk about our racial differences... *Ahh*, it is alright, we get on but I just can't get over the unfair deal.'

'I wonder what our new Prime Minister is going to be like,' said Lam.

'He seems fair, says we are all equal as long as we want to live here,' said Jung.

'Which is refreshing,' said Lam.

'If he keeps his word,' said Heng.

Just then an old woman waddled up to them under the weight of a bamboo yoke across her shoulder balancing a pot at one end and a basket at the other end. She set her load down on the five-foot way, took a deep breath and called out, 'Anyone for a bowl of my sweet mung bean soup?' She

104

bent her hunched body to lift the lid of the pot releasing the aroma of coconut cream in the steaming soup.

'Yes, one for me,' said Heng as he stood up and dug into his pocket for some coins. A few minutes later more men from the other shops joined them for a bowl of the soup and to discuss the new era that was just round the corner.

At midnight 30th August, 1957, the British flag was lowered and in its place the new Malayan flag was raised signifying the Malayan peninsula's sovereign status.

The next day, shops and all other businesses were closed for the celebration of independence, *Merdeka*. Only the food hawkers continued to trade and they were kept busy. Spirits were high in the town and there was an air of expectancy that had not been experienced before. People, young and old, turned out in droves, pouring out of the *kampongs* by bus, bikes or trishaws into the town centre to watch the procession through the main street of Jalan Rahmat. The floats, in dazzling colours, displayed the different aspects of the multi-culture of the new united society – singing and dancing to traditional music rolled out on the drums and cymbals or plucked on stringed instruments performed by women and men dressed in brightly coloured costumes. Onlookers cheered as they passed by; children straddled across their fathers' shoulders clapped in delight, while strangers shook hands and congratulated one another, acknowledging and welcoming the new dawn.

They had come dressed in their best traditional costumes and it was the women who stole the show. The Malay ladies dressed in their figure-hugging *kebayas* or *baju kurong* of fine batik while the Indian ladies put on their even more vibrantly coloured silk saris. Chinese women turned out in their *cheongsams* or *samfoos* and the children looking awe-struck wore their best or newest more western-style outfits.

105

In our house, everyone was also caught up in the celebratory mood. Only Grandmother Kwee noticed Kau's absence.

'Where is your father?' she asked his son Hock. 'Is he not coming to watch the procession?'

'I don't know. I saw him going out the back door earlier and haven't seen him since,' he replied. Hock was anxious to get away as his mother Siew Ping would not stop grumbling.

'Come on,' he shouted to his brother Sek as they both charged out of the house leaving Chung Lin to attend to her younger sisters.

Soong grabbed Kin's hand as he waited for his wife and daughter.

'I suppose we should celebrate getting rid of the red-haired imperialists,' he muttered to himself and then cupped his hand over his mouth and nose when Kok coughed as he walked past him, looking for a place to polish the shoes he was carrying in his hands.

'Has any one seen my accordion?' shouted Keow from the top of the stairs to no one in particular. 'I've just searched the cupboard in my old room and I can't find it.'

'You've not even been home one day and you're searching for your accordion,' Kwee called back. 'You haven't got time for that now. It's safe in my room. We're about to go, are you coming?'

'That's a relief. Yes, I'm coming,' said Keow. He had been working in Singapore for some time.

'Tian, that's enough combing. You'll go bald at the rate you go,' said Kwee shaking her head at Tian who was still poised, re-shaping his quiff, in front of the mirror hanging on the wall in the air-well. 'Where is Uncle Heng?' she added.

'I'm right here and ready,' said Heng coming out from the kitchen.

'Good, let's go then before we miss it.'

'*Hmmm*, never thought I would live to see this day,' said Heng, 'and I'm not going to miss the procession.'

106

'Come on then, you two,' Kwee called out to Tian and Yew who eventually rushed to her side.

I pulled Mei Lin's hand to hurry her along and then took Uncle Heng's hand while Mother and Father gathered Mei Chin and Mei Choon and caught up with us along the five-foot way which was as busy as a station platform. When we got to the main street, Father lifted Mei Chin onto his shoulders as he pointed to the pretty girl dancers waving their fans and moving gracefully on one of the floats. He then picked up me and Mei Lin in turns.

After the procession had finished and the sun was gathering in its last rays, we joined the wave of pedestrians to make our way to the Stadium situated off the main road about half a mile from home. Overwhelmed by the horde of people pressing in around us, I clung tightly to Uncle Heng's hand as we walked. Although Father had wanted Grandmother to get into a trishaw, there wasn't one free for hire. So we walked slowly; Mother carried Mei Choon in her arms, Father took Mei Chin's hand while Grandmother took Mei Lin's soaking up the atmosphere while others rushed ahead to look for the best vantage points for the fireworks display.

We could hear more music in the air as we approached the entrance to the Stadium; some bands were playing Malay music to accompany the dancers in one corner, while Indian and Chinese music came from other parts of the stadium. Apart from that, all we could see around us were bodies like penguins gathering to keep warm until we came to a clearing where a red, green and yellow lion was dancing to the thunderous sounds of drums. It leapt about, bowing and shaking its head as it told its own story.

It was the fireworks that thrilled me most - the loud bangs and whistling, the explosion of colours against the dark sky like giant fistfuls of sequins thrown high up to the sky, *whooshing* and *wheee*-ing as they went. We *oooh*-ed and *aaah*-ed as the sparkling sequins - red, yellow, green, blue and pink - swirled and made stunning patterns above

107

us. Standing next to my father, I watched, spellbound, my mouth open and thinking how magical and beautiful it was. I turned to look at Father's face. He was smiling, entranced, lost in the dazzling beauty of the colours in the sky. I felt happy.

A few days after the *Merdeka* celebrations Grandmother died. She had a sudden attack of asthma and struggled to breathe. Immediately she was rushed to the hospital where she was treated in the accident and emergency department and later admitted to the ward.

She was in a 'third class' ward where the food was correspondingly basic but shared the same smell of disinfectant of the 'first class' ward which cost more money. The white metal bedstead was high; the thin mattress was covered with rust-stained white sheets. On her second night there, whilst in her sleep she slipped and fell from her bed onto the hard concrete floor. The night nurse found her unconscious, her head in a pool of blood. She died the next day.

A hush came over the household when the news of her death was announced. For once the children, including me, were subdued. But I felt no sense of loss, no sadness, perhaps more due to my youth than the distance between us.

Even in death Grandmother still seemed to reach out to me as if to say that she still didn't like me. I couldn't forget how when I was younger I had stood in front of her with my arms reaching up wanting her to pick me up. When my cousin Kin rushed up to her she pushed me aside as if I was a stool standing in her way; she bent down to pick him up instead of me.

I even felt her unremitting disapproval during her funeral, a noisy affair in the Chamber of Commerce side parlour. The wailing and crying that were the mourners' filial duty, the monotonous clanging of cymbals to accompany the nuns' chanting, the chatter amongst those who had come to pay their respect, and the clashing of ladles and woks coming from the makeshift kitchen churning out meals for everyone there - they all came together to make a great send-off for Grandmother.

My parents, uncles and aunties, including the distantly related ones many of whom I had never met before, were dressed in white or black sackcloth. I noticed Father looking very sombre and his eyes were dry. I had caught him crying alone in his room the morning that Grandmother died. He didn't know I was there standing in the doorway. It was the only time I ever saw him cry. He was sitting at his desk, his head in his hands, and he was sobbing; his shoulders were shuddering but the sobs were muffled as if he didn't want anyone to hear him. I was afraid to disturb him so I quietly turned and walked away.

Grandmother's wooden coffin was huge. I thought it was large enough for two people and that it would make a fantastic doll's house, the lid with the graceful curved ridges as its roof. A large framed photograph of her stood at the end of the coffin facing outward for all to see. My sisters and I, along with our cousins - over twenty of us - were dressed in blue. We sat on straw mats on the floor by the side of the coffin, feeling either bewildered or indifferent and tired from the two days of mourning and keeping watch. The rest of the family were crying loudly especially Siew Ping who was wailing, lamenting how unjust that Grandmother had been taken away from us so soon, her head hidden under the sackcloth hood. I was sitting behind her; I wanted to see her face and leant forward to peer up into her hood. Her eyes were shut, her mouth open and wailing but her face was dry - no tears - which puzzled me. Bored and curious to know what was happening elsewhere in the funeral parlour, I whispered into my mother's ear.

'I need to go to the toilet,' I said.

Mother nodded. 'Be careful how you go,' she said.

I scrambled up and weaved my way through the relatives seated around. As I walked past the head of the coffin, I stopped to take a last look at Grandmother's black and white photograph. In the picture she was wearing a mandarin-collar blouse and she looked like she always did, her hair combed back from her forehead and wearing her favourite jade earrings. She was not smiling. Her eyes stared straight out of the photo.

I fixed on the eyes and suddenly they became alive and engaged with me. I gasped. I took a step to the left; the eyes turned to the left. I moved to the right, they followed me again. A shudder shot through me; I panicked and ran back to my mother's side.

The only time that I thought that Grandmother showed any sign of being interested in me was when I came home from the cinema one night with Father and Mei Lin. Earlier, as our treat he had allowed Mei Lin and me to join him in the cinema to watch a film. I sat with Mei Lin on my right and to her right was Father. To my left was an empty seat. When the lights dimmed, I turned to the back to look at the small square projection window in the wall and counted down to the moment the huge screen came alive.

Not long after the film had started I suddenly felt a large warm hand sliding up my left thigh. I froze. I had earlier noticed a man in the seat next to the empty seat but paid him no attention. Shock and fright immobilized me. The hand moved higher up my thigh. Then I jumped up. At the very same instant the man stood up and disappeared in the dark before I could say anything to Father. By the time Father ran out of the cinema after the man, he had long gone. In his fury at not being able to apprehend him, Father took us home.

'That son of a tortoise! If I had got him…,' shouted Father after telling Mother and Grandmother what had happened.

Mother groaned. She bent down, held my shoulders and searched my face.

'Are you alright?' she said.

I nodded.

Then I heard my grandmother say in a voice I had not heard before, 'Son of a tortoise.' And then taking my hand, she said softly, 'Let me look at you.'

Grandmother's photo was placed beside Grandfather's at the shrine after the funeral. For a long time I avoided looking directly at her eyes whenever I had to pray to them. Now with her gone, there was nothing to hold my father back from demanding his share of the family business.

Chapter 12

Jung and his brothers observed the custom of a hundred days of mourning for their mother by wearing a small square of black cloth pinned to their sleeves. Accordingly, he refrained from broaching the subject of the family business so when he received a message from Chun Hong's nephew in China, he was furious.

'Didn't he receive the news of Mother's passing? Or is he so obsessed with his own well-being that he's ignored the fact that I'm in mourning?' he said throwing the letter down on his desk.

'What does he want this time?' asked Lian who was cleaning Mei Choon on the bed.

The responsibility for sending him money had passed down to Jung after Chun Hong died and although he tried his hardest to send whenever he could, it was pulling him apart trying to keep up what his father had started.

'A camera, no less!' said Jung sitting down in his chair by the door where there was a gentle stream of breeze which did nothing to cool him down. His face was flushed. He wiped the beads of perspiration from his forehead with the back of his hand. 'Does he think I'm made of money? We may not be in a communist country but I'm not rich, doesn't he know that or does he think I am loaded, that I'm growing money?'

'We've just sent money, and it wasn't that long ago.'

'That's all he does. Want, want, want. First a bicycle, then a radio and now a camera! I want too but I have to do without. I could do with an electric fan here,' Jung forced a laugh. 'I don't have a camera. I'd like one myself. How can I send him one? Where do I get the money from?' he was speaking more to himself than to Lian who by now had finished cleaning Mei Choon.

'You can only do what you can,' she said, lifting up Mei Choon. 'I'm going to see what the girls are up to.'

The responsibility for his two youngest brothers had also fallen on Jung and Lian. Although Kwee had left some money for the boys, Jung knew it wasn't going to be enough when they realised that Kau and Siew Ping would not help and were deliberately throwing out what food was left before Tian and Yew came home from school. There were school fees for Tian who was doing very well in his third year at the secondary Charlton English School. Knowing that he also enjoyed his studies, Jung was determined to ensure that he would finish his education and thus fulfil his promise to his mother. Yew, a year behind, had become restless and lost interest in his school work.

'Look, you have to work hard at your studies,' Jung confronted him when he saw how bad his grades were. 'These grades aren't as good as what you normally produce. You'd better work harder or else you will just fail and then what?'

Yew pulled a face and his shoulders dropped. 'I don't want to study anymore.'

'What? Why not?'

'Don't like it. I want to go and work, like you.'

'You don't want to end up like me. You can do much better. I wish I had finished school but it wasn't to be. If I could go back to school again….you must think carefully about what you want to do. Don't waste your opportunity.'

Yew shook his head, his face still glum.

'I've decided to stop school. Besides, that will mean you don't have to worry about my fees. I'll look for a job, any job,' he said.

'But what can you do?'

'I'll do anything.' Yew's eyes brightened. 'Maybe even help you in the cinema.'

'*Hmmm,* I don't know. If you're really sure about not continuing with school…'

'I am,' said Yew, his face slowly breaking into a smile as he realised that Jung was coming round to his way of thinking.

On the day after the hundred days of mourning, Jung and Lian laid on a table of offerings to Kwee at her shrine – a whole steamed chicken, roast pork belly, dumplings and buns. Gold paper folded into the shape of an ingot was also burned to ensure that Kwee wouldn't be destitute in the other world. The squares of black cloth were removed from everyone's sleeves and burned as well.

The next day, Jung went to see Uncle Wong.

'Uncle Wong, you've seen how the business is dwindling and before it disappears altogether I want First Brother to divide what is left between us brothers. I need my share, I have all these responsibilities and expenses. What the other brothers want to do is up to them, but I want what Father built for us. It pains me to see how First brother has allowed it to fizzle to this,' said Jung.

Uncle Wong had listened intently; he shook his head, then rubbed his chin.

'Of course I've noticed it,' he said. 'To think your father built it from nothing. Kau is distracted. Do you know the reason?'

'We have our suspicions, that's all.'

'Is that so?' said Uncle Wong. He rubbed his chin again as his brow creased. 'I can see the business evaporating and disappearing. Yes, we must do something about it. I will talk to him and convince him to divide the business now or get it back to how it was.' A note of irritation crept into his voice, 'What is he playing at?'

'I have no idea but whatever he is up to, I think he will listen to you,' said Jung.

Wong wasted no time and came to the shop the next evening, in time to catch Kau before he could slip out.

Lian made a big pot of coffee and carried it with four cups to where Wong was sitting with Jung by one of the sewing machines. Kau was tidying up while Heng was clearing his worktop. Knowing that she could not sit in on the discussions, she left the men to it. The children were ready for bed and were reading or playing on the floor in the bedroom. Anxious and unable to concentrate on much else she decided to wash the clothes.

Chung Lin was in the kitchen, squatting next to a basin of washing. Her mother Siew Ping, almost at full term of her pregnancy and looking like she was ready to burst, was upstairs, resting in her bedroom.

'Second Aunty, you're going to wash too?' she said as she lifted up a shirt onto the washing board and then started rubbing it hard.

'Yes, the children are ready for bed,' said Lian. She put down her basket of clothes next to Chung Lin's basin and took down her basin hanging on the wall by the water tank. 'Have you finished with this?' She lifted the hosepipe that was dangling into Chung Lin's basin.

'Yes. Is Second Uncle working tonight?' said Chung Lin; her eyes were bright in spite of the extra work she had to do, working late into the night.

'No, he's not needed tonight. He's in the shop with Uncle Wong. They're drinking coffee with your father and Uncle Heng. Is your mother feeling any better? I noticed she didn't eat much earlier.'

'Her legs are a bit swollen.' Chung Lin picked up the shirt and wrung it out before putting it into another basin of clean water. 'What about you? Mother's baby should be arriving soon. When is yours?'

'Not for a long while yet,' said Lian.

Lian then heard the shutter boards going up in the shop. Heng came into the kitchen with his cup. He said nothing, his face revealed nothing as he scooped some water from the tank to rinse his cup and then turned and walked back into the shop. Lian wanted to ask but held back, her ears strained to the shop but she couldn't make out what the men were saying. Trying not to appear anxious in front of Chung Lin she continued chatting.

115

Just as the two of them were putting away the basins and buckets, Lian heard footsteps on the stairs. She knew the discussion was over and that it was Jung going upstairs. She dried her hands quickly and ran upstairs into their room.

The three older girls were fast asleep on the floor while Mei Choon was wriggling in her hammock. Jung was too excited to sit down. He was smiling, looking like a boy excited with a new toy.

'I didn't think it would be so easy,' he said. 'First Brother has agreed to give me a thousand dollars.' He waited for Lian's reaction. She stopped rocking the hammock.

'Really?' said Lian, her face broke into a smile.

Jung lowered his voice. 'One thousand dollars and no more, he said. I can't believe it was so easy. He was *actually* reasonable, agreed with what Uncle Wong said all the time. *Ha*, maybe he is not so bad after all.'

'That's your share, what about the others?'

'They can have theirs whenever they want.'

'When will he give us the money?'

'He said by next week.'

'Do you believe he will keep his word?'

'He as good as promised in front of Uncle Wong.'

Lian and Jung looked at each other, each feeling the rush of fresh air into their chest as the weight of the last few years' worries lifted.

The next morning Jung woke up to a sense of hope and anticipation; his head soon filled with thoughts of how he could use the money. He felt a spike of excitement as he got ready for work thinking that change, big change, was on its way. Later as he pushed his bike through the shop, Kau stopped him by the sewing machines.

'I've been thinking about what I said last night,' Kau said to him. 'I can't give it all in cash.'

'But you've already agreed to it.'

'I agreed, but I can't give all in cash. You can have half in cash and the other half in fabric.'

'What am I to do with the fabric?' said Jung. He could feel blood rushing to his head.

'As I said, I can only give you half in cash. It's the best I can do.'

'I have to discuss this with Lian.'

Jung parked and locked his bike on the five-foot way and then rushed back upstairs to Lian.

'That son of a tortoise! He's going back on his word,' he almost shouted to Lian who was surprised to see him. 'Now he's only going to give us half in cash, the other half in fabric.' Looking like he was going to explode, he repeated what Kau had said.

'I thought it was too good to be true,' said Lian. As the news sank in, the picture of the house, the lovely wooden house off Jalan Mohammed Akil that had been on her mind all night, that she and Jung had set their hearts on, began to fade. They had walked past the tin-roofed wooden house numerous times during their evening walks and had even dared to dream that maybe one day they would live there.

'What are we going to do? That son of a tortoise. I should have known better. All my dreams of what I could do with the money. Gone. Just like that!' Jung threw his hands up in the air.

They fell silent as they racked their brains for what they should do. Suddenly Lian grabbed his hand.

'Take the money and the fabric, but tell him you want a sewing machine as well. Take the newest looking one. I know which one I would like.'

Jung raised his eyebrow.

'I can use the sewing machine to work here,' said Lian pointing to the spot where she knew it would stand, against the wooden wall.

The Singer sewing machine that Lian chose hadn't long been installed in hers and Jung's room when Siew Ping, who had been feeling unwell and then suddenly bled between her legs, was rushed to hospital in an ambulance. Chung Lin

117

stayed by her side all the way while Hock and Sek went to search for their father.

Kau had left Heng in charge of the business again and gone out without saying where he was going. It was Hock who found him - how, he wouldn't say - but by the time the two of them got to the hospital, several hours later, Siew Ping had already given birth to a baby boy. The doctors told them that there had been serious complications during the birth and that she had lost a lot of blood; she was now unconscious.

Siew Ping never regained consciousness and died a day later without ever seeing her son.

The funeral was modest – no nuns to chant, minimum refreshments and a brief wake.

It was obvious that Kau had plans which he was not ready to divulge to anyone, not even to his older children especially Chung Lin as he left all responsibilities of the children to her including the newborn baby.

Without notice to Jung or any of the other brothers, Kau started clearing one half of the shop floor with Hock and Sek's help and once that was done, Mr Ting, a shoemaker, moved in.

Not only were Jung and Lian now bound to the shophouse with responsibilities for Tian and Yew as well as their own children, but the house seemed to have shrunk even more, becoming more like a train platform during rush hour. As the back door was seldom shut let alone locked during the day, neighbours could walk through the house using it as a shortcut to Hakka Street and then on to the market or the coffee shop. The other shopkeepers from either side would come into the shop during a lull in business for a gossip, talk politics and moan about the government or share a cup of coffee bought from the Hainanese coffee shop at the end of the street.

When Mr Ting took over half the shop floor, the sewing machines were lined against the back wall to make room for his shelves and racks against the side wall and a large low square table for himself and his son Leng to make shoes. His speciality was men's leather shoes and football boots. They bore no brand name; the quality of his handmade shoes was his trademark and the fact that he was busy with orders was testament to the popularity of his handiwork.

Going through the shop now meant walking through an infusion of the smells of leather, polish and the special shoe glue that he concocted using white spirit and rubber. On the low table were a variety of tools – pincers, nails and metal studs, sand paper blocks, waxed thread, needles, awl and hooks, iron shoe stands and wooden lasts, and gleaming knives that were held like pistols and cut leather with the ease of slicing lard. The shoe-making area extended to the air-well which now housed another work table with the same equipment and where Mr Ting's three workers would produce the shoes. As if that was not enough, a set of shelves were erected in the hall to store an assortment of sheets of leather.

To the children, this was a fascinating addition, opening our eyes to a whole new experience. My sisters and I loved watching the men craft the shoes. We would sit on the stairs, heads between the posts of the balustrade and completely awe-struck at how deft they were in cutting the leather, the stitching, the hammering and shaping of the pieces together to form the shoes, first the right then the left shoe. But we were only allowed to watch and never to touch the equipment.

To my parents, Mr Ting and his team of workers were an invasion, an imposition and yet another reason why they should move out, but how could they? They were trapped by their responsibilities. They had no choice but to stay on.

Chapter 13

A few weeks after Siew Ping's funeral, Lian and Ai Chien were exchanging news in the back alley after dinner when the subject got round to Kau.

'There's got to be a woman somewhere,' said Lian.

Ai Chien leant forward conspiratorially and lowered her voice. 'Mr Ang in No. 17 told me he saw him with a woman. She was a bit younger and not all that pretty. He thought that he had seen her working in one of the coffee bars. I asked him how he knew that since he insisted that he didn't visit such places himself.'

Batu Pahat was situated close to the bridge that linked the north-south trunk road, and was an attractive place for travellers and itinerant salesmen to rest as it boasted good and inexpensive food. Over time several coffee shops, with 'bar girls' serving, had sprouted up near the road alongside the traditional Hainanese coffee shops. But those with the bar girls soon became tarred with a bad reputation when it became known that some of the girls did more than serve coffee.

'Really?' Lian's eyes opened wide, sparkling with curiosity. 'I wonder what is really going on.' She nodded then as if she was beginning to understand. 'So are you saying she is one of those bar girls?'

'What woman would take another woman's husband?'

'It's more than a fleeting relationship. It's been going on for a long time.'

'I wonder what kind of woman she is, mesmerised by him and blind to his faults?'

'Or maybe he's a totally different person when he's with her,' said Lian.

'Is she stopping him from seeing the children? And what kind of a father is he, leaving his own children like that to fend for themselves?' Ai Chien put one hand on her hip as if she was ready to confront Kau himself and tell him what she thought of him.

'He doesn't stay away completely; he's here during the day working with Heng, so he sees the children.'

'So pitiful, so sad for Chung Lin. She must be fifteen?'

Lian remembered the day of Siew Ping's funeral. While everyone was getting ready for the funeral procession in the hall, Chung Lin, in a sackcloth and carrying her new-born baby brother, walked up to Lian; her eyes were swollen and red. She looked lost.

'Second Aunty, will you help me?' she'd said. 'I don't know what I should do.'

'Yes, of course I will,' Lian had replied, her eyes welling up. 'We will all help you.'

She knew she would be lying if she told her that Kau would be around to help share the burden of bringing up her two sisters and four brothers. He had left the baby to Chung Lin from the moment he picked them up from the hospital. Lian had had to show her what to do for the baby; she bought her a tin of milk powder and showed her how to make up the feed. Kau had shown no remorse for not being there for Siew Ping in her last few hours. No one said a word about his callous indifference although many suspected that there was another woman involved.

'Nearly sixteen,' said Lian, looking at Ai Chien. 'Not much of a life, is it? At least her big brother Hock has matured a little. He's been subdued since his mother died. He's doing fine, working with Mr Ting, learning to make shoes. Good to have a skill, that's what Jung told him. Sek's gone to do an apprenticeship with his Uncle Kok.'

She paused for a moment to watch two small girls laughing and playing hopscotch together as a boy on a man-size bike, frantically ringing his bell, wobbled past the girls and just avoided a turkey that was fixed on picking at the ground.

121

'As for the younger ones,' she continued, 'there's no hope of school for them. Luckily they will listen to Chung Lin and do as they are told.'

Ai Chien shook her head and sighed. 'And she has to look after them all,' she said.

'Yes, cook and wash for all the sisters and brothers and look after the baby as well,' said Lian.

Jung had just applied a coat of polish on the chromium handle bars of his bike in the back alley when Hock came out of the back door cradling his baby brother in his arms. He stood near Jung and watched him polish the bike as he rocked Fook, swinging from side to side, to get him to sleep.

'You finished work then?' said Jung, looking at Fook and then at Hock.

'Yes.' There was a long pause before he continued, 'Second Uncle, I want to tell you what I saw the other day.'

Jung looked at him blankly as he picked up his cloth to polish. 'What other day?' He started rubbing the handlebar.

Hock remained silent for a while as if unsure what he wanted to say. 'The day my mother died.' He looked at Fook in his arms, his eyes were shut. Hock stopped rocking and looked at Jung. He took a deep breath and then said, 'I found my father with a woman in one of the coffee bars.'

Jung continued to rub trying not to look or sound shocked. 'So, he was just drinking coffee with a woman?'

The news had confirmed his suspicion —what other business would Kau have outside of the shop?- but hearing it from his son outraged him.

'No, they weren't just drinking. They were holding hands and they seemed to be unaware of others around them.' Hock looked embarrassed but his voice didn't conceal his anger. 'The worst thing is he didn't even look worried or concerned when I told him that Mother was rushed to hospital. He was more concerned that he had to leave the woman.'

Jung stopped what he was doing and looked at Hock. 'Your father knows what he is doing. I'm sure there's nothing to worry about.'

'I hate what he is doing, leaving us like this. Where is he when he is not here?' Hock realised his voice had become louder and he looked at Fook to see if he had woken him but he hadn't stirred. In a quieter voice he continued, 'Like now, where is he? With that woman when he should be here with his baby?'

A little girl ran past chasing a turkey and clucking at it hoping it would answer her back. Jung straightened his back and glanced at Lian collecting her washing from the bamboo poles straddled across the alley. He felt helpless, not knowing how best to respond; he could see that Hock's face was taut. 'You are doing a good job,' he said, giving him a smile of reassurance, 'looking after your brother as you do.' Then he leaned towards him. 'But you can't say anything to your father. If he wants you to know, he'll tell you.'

'I just wish that he would tell us soon. We're like orphans, no mother, no father...'

'You are doing well. You will be alright. Your father has not abandoned you,' said Jung quickly, hoping that he was not wrong and at the same time suppressing his fury at Kau.

Lian and Chung Lin sat at the large dining table after they had finished clearing up after lunch while Fook was sound asleep upstairs. They were taking a moment to get their breath back after their usual busy morning. For Lian, the heat seemed to sap her energy more than the weight she was carrying; she couldn't wait for the baby to arrive.

'I wish I could go out to work and earn some money,' said Chung Lin staring into space, her voice soft with a hint of melancholy. 'There's no chance for me to go out and learn to do something. I never got the chance when my mother was alive and now it looks like I am doomed, tied down to bringing up my own baby brother.... and my father doesn't care.'

Lian looked at her and saw a tear roll down her cheek. She took a deep breath and then expelled it with the anger she felt rising within at the thought of Kau's selfishness.

'Of course you're not doomed, don't say that. You have your future ahead of you.'

'I don't know anything, have no skill. You have, you can sew. I can't even thread a needle,' said Chung Lin looking miserable.

'That's because you never had to and nobody showed you. We are around to help out and Fook will grow up soon,' said Lian.

'Yes, when I am old and shrivelled up. Then nobody will want me.'

'Don't talk like that. You were saying you want to earn some money. You can, you don't have to go out to work. You can bring it home. I'm thinking that there're lots of people who want their clothes washed, you know, men who work and have no wives to do it for them. Go round the shops and ask who wants their washing done. I'll show you what to do with it,' said Lian.

A look of horror came over Chung Lin's face as she wiped her tear away. 'You mean I just go into the shops and ask?'

'There's no shame in that. Start with that shop on the main road, the electrical appliance shop. The boss is nice and there're a couple of single men there who look like possibilities. And if they say yes, then say that each piece will cost twenty to thirty cents. A shirt for twenty cents and thirty cents for trousers? I think that is reasonable,' said Lian as she watched Chung Lin starting to chew her fingernail. She was almost as tall as Lian and with her long black hair pushed behind her ears, Lian thought she was pretty in a plain sort of way, not like her brothers who definitely had their father's features. 'Well?' she said, 'think you can do it?'

Chung Lin took her finger out of her mouth and a look of determination appeared. 'I can do it. I will go first thing tomorrow.'

'No time like now....I would go now if I were you. I can keep an eye on Fook,' offered Lian.

'Thank you! I'll go now,' said Chung Lin.

'Go.'

Half an hour later, she returned bubbling with excitement and waving a bag of dirty clothes. 'Look, Second Aunty, you were right. I've got six pieces here, two pairs of trousers and four shirts. I can't believe it. The man agreed to my price. There're two workers there, it's the older one.'

'*Wah,* that's good,' said Lian smiling, delighted to see the smile and look of surprise on Chung Lin's face. 'So, how much will that come to?'

'I've already worked that out. It'll be one dollar and forty cents!'

'Good. Now I will show you what to do with the clothes,' said Lian.

They went into the kitchen where Lian proceeded to teach her how to boil the white shirts with soda added to the water, then adding indigo to the final rinse to whiten the cloth before starching them and hanging them to dry out in the alley.

The next morning after both of them had been to the market and when the clothes were dry, Lian showed her how to iron the shirts and trousers and the right way to fold them.

'There, you do the next one,' said Lian stepping away from the table on the landing. She watched as Chung Lin carefully pressed the collar of the shirt first and then the sleeves. When she had finished the entire garment, she put the iron on the ring and then carefully laid out the shirt, did up the buttons and smoothed out the folds. Satisfied she looked at Lian for her verdict.

'Very good,' said Lian. 'It's so smooth a fly would skid if it tried to walk on it.' They both laughed.

When Chung Lin came home in the afternoon after delivering the clean clothes she went straight to Lian in her room.

'The man wants me to collect some more washing in two days' time,' said Chung Lin, smiling.

'That's good. Your first regular customer. Well done,' said Lian.

'Here, Second Aunty,' said Chung Lin holding out her hand to Lian.

'What is it?'

'This is for the money you gave me for our groceries this morning. Fifty cents,' said Chung Lin.

'Are you sure about that? What about tomorrow?'

'I have enough for tomorrow and Fook's milk powder will last for a while. First thing tomorrow morning I will go round to the other shops.'

Lian held out her palm so Chung Lin could place the coins in it. 'You know you can ask me if you are short,' she said.

'Yes, thank you,' Chung Lin nodded, then looking at the remaining coins in her other hand she smiled. 'I'd better put this away safely.'

The Singer sewing machine that Yew had helped Jung to install in his and Lian's room stood near the door during the day and when night came it was pushed out to the landing to clear the floor space for the children to sleep on. Lian was sure something good would come of it, besides it being more tangible and useful as part of the share that Kau could afford. Jung had cleaned it inside out for her, making sure it was in perfect working order, and then polished it until it shone like new. He had even managed to retrieve the pair of scissors that were his and put them in the drawer for Lian.

'Ai Chien said I could bring the work home and do it here,' said Lian.

'That's good. That means you can also keep an eye on the children at home,' he said. 'And no rushing about,' he added, looking at her huge belly.

'It'll be a lot easier, but what are we to do with the fabric?' asked Lian rubbing the small of her back as she surveyed the rolls of fabric standing in the corner of the room. 'I've already picked out the best cotton ones; I can use them for the girls' dresses but that lot is for men's trousers.'

'Kui has offered to take it and sell in her shop,' said Jung.

Lian's face lit up. 'That's a good idea. The sooner she takes them, the better. We need all the room we can get here.'

It was a warm sunny morning. Jung couldn't sit or stand still; he paced the floor, walking between the hall and kitchen and then back again and into the shop. The shop was busy with several customers browsing the shoes that Mr Ting had neatly displayed on his shelves and racks, while on the other half of the shop, Heng was measuring a man for trousers. Kau had his head down at his sewing machine, machining away, one of the rare times he spent in the shop.

Jung was oblivious to what was happening in the shop; his mind was fixed on what was developing upstairs in his and Lian's room. All he could think of was how the midwife and Lian were progressing, his ear straining to hear the sound of a baby's cry. He turned around in the shop and restarted his walk back to the hall.

Heng had just finished the measurements and written them in his ledger; he smiled at Jung. 'You're wearing down the floor, Jung,' he said softly. To his customer he explained that Jung's wife was in labour, '*Isterinya bakal melahirkan anak.*'

'*Ahh, tahniah,*' said the Malay man, smiling broadly at Jung as he congratulated him.

Jung nodded. '*Terima kaseh,*' he said and smiled back at him then turned to Heng. 'I've never had to wait this long before. I hope everything's alright.' Suddenly gripped by fear, he marched into the hall and stopped at the bottom of the stairs to look up. There was no movement or sound from the room. In the air-well, Hock was carefully tracing

127

out the shape of a sole on a piece of leather under the watchful eye of Leng, already an experienced shoemaker despite being only twenty three. They both looked up at Jung and then smiled at each other; they'd lost count of the number of times Jung had walked past them. Jung started cracking his knuckles and then walked to the kitchen again.

By the time he walked back into the shop again, Heng's customer had left and Heng was about to start on his next task of cutting. 'The baby won't come any sooner with you pacing up and down. Here, drink this coffee,' he said as he pushed a cup of black coffee towards Jung who took it more out of something to do than thirst. Heng set down his own cup on a side table by his worktop and proceeded to spread out the piece of cloth that was lying by the edge of the top.

'I know,' said Jung. 'I don't care whether it's a boy or a girl, as long as it's alright.'

'So what if it is another girl? Your four treasures do you proud. You can't complain,' said Heng.

'I know.'

Jung stepped away when a man who had been browsing wanted to feel the fabric on the worktop. As he did so, he heard a baby's cry and then seconds later Chung Lin charged into the shop.

'Second Uncle, Second Uncle! It's a boy!' she shouted.

'Really?' Jung's eyes widened, his smile suddenly bigger than his face. '*Wah*, really? Can I go up now?'

'Yes,' Chung Lin nodded, her face radiant with excitement.

Jung didn't waste another second; he dashed past her and bounded up the stairs, two steps at a time, his heart thumping with joy at the thought of seeing his son.

Chapter 14

Jung named his long-awaited son *Yao* which means 'brilliance'; his arrival had lit up his world. He thought it was better than winning the lottery. When Yao's brown eyes fixed on his that first time he held him in his arms, he felt he was the luckiest man alive. And when Yao's tiny hand clasped round his finger, all his worries melted away. Yao was perfectly formed; everyone who saw him said what a beautiful baby he was with his unusually large round eyes, inquisitive and bright. Jung was so proud, he insisted that red eggs were given out to all friends and relatives to announce his good fortune, the birth of his son. He was sure that had his mother been alive she would have splashed out on more –perhaps cakes and roast pork as well. As far as Lian was concerned, just seeing Jung's permanent grin and the happiness shining through his eyes for days made the wait for Yao's arrival worthwhile, blurring everything else especially the memory of her late mother-in-law's disappointment.

It didn't matter to Jung that he had one more mouth to feed. Neither did it matter that there were more school fees to pay; Mei Lin had just started her first year and I was now in Standard Two, of the primary Tengku Mariam School in Jalan Lim Poon which was on the outskirts of the town. We both needed not only the school fees but also school uniforms and books, and to get to school we needed to travel by taxi. He felt that he could take on all of the responsibilities and that somehow it would all work out, they would get by. He was just very sorry that his mother was not around to see her grandson Yao. Like Jung, Lian also regretted it but only momentarily felt cheated of the satisfaction of presenting her mother-in-law with a baby boy after four girls. And now that she had produced a son, the contraceptive pill could not come fast enough.

Lian had it all planned; as before, she would continue to work from home for Ai Chien. The knowledge that there was still some savings from the money that Kau had given Jung afforded her a sense of security. Tian and Yew would share their meals with them and Tian would help with looking after the children after school and homework. When one of Mr Ting's workers left and he agreed to take on Yew as an apprentice, it meant that Yew would not depend entirely on Jung and Lian for pocket money.

Lunch had just finished; Lian put the bowls of left-over food in the cupboard and started to wipe the table. She wanted to get back to her sewing as quickly as possible as well as get away from Yin Li and Soong who were still eating at their table with their two children. She was still annoyed with Yin Li for deliberately stirring the embers in her stove next to Lian's where her mackerel was frying; it'd whipped up the ashes causing some of it to settle on the wok. She had felt like sprinkling a handful of water into the hot oil so that it would spit at Yin Li but instead, not wishing to start an argument, she had quietly covered her wok while Yin Li put on her I-didn't-do-anything-wrong look and continued as if nothing had happened. As she hurriedly wiped the table she could hear the banter between Heng and Mr Ting in the shop interspersed with the tapping sound of Mr Ting hammering heels onto soles and Heng's clipping scissors while in the air-well Leng and Hock were concentrating on stitching soles to leather uppers as Yew watched studiously.

A few moments later from the corner of her eyes she saw movement in the doorway between the shop and hall. Normally it would not have interested her but this time she looked up to see two men marching into the hall, one Chinese the other Malay, smartly dressed in crisp shirts and trousers. They stopped at the table where Soong was still eating.

'Is Mr Chiang Jung Po here?' asked the Chinese man in Hokkien, directing his question at Soong. His tone was curt and he had an air of authority.

130

Soong stared up at the man with his mouth too full of food to speak, he pointed with his chopsticks at Lian. Without another word the two strangers stepped over to Lian.

'We are looking for Chiang Jung Po. Can you tell us where he is?' the Chinese man asked.

Puzzled by the sudden intrusion of these strange men, Lian did not respond right away. She pulled herself up to her full height to face the man who had spoken. His face was blank but she had a feeling that something was wrong.

'Who are you?' she said.

'*Polis,* 'said the Malay man.

Lian stared at him and then at the Chinese man as she felt a rush of panic. 'He's at the back. What do you want him for?' she asked the Chinese man.

He didn't answer but instead walked past her through the kitchen with the other man following. Lian dropped her cloth and rushed to follow them out to the alley where Jung was polishing his beloved bicycle. He was concentrating so hard on buffing the chrome handle bars that he didn't hear them approach and only looked up when Lian called out to him.

'These men have come to see you,' she shouted from behind the men.

Before Jung could speak the Chinese man said, 'We are police. We have reason to believe that you are involved in illicit gambling.'

The colour of Jung's face drained from it as it changed from bewilderment to terror. Turning to the men he dropped the cloth he was holding. His eyes darted from them to Lian and then to the men again. He said nothing. He could not lie. He had no defence. He couldn't deny the charge, neither could he run away. Looking dazed, he stood there not knowing what to say.

'You have to come with us to the police station,' said the Chinese man stretching his hand out to Jung.

Automatically Jung moved with them and as the two men led him back into the house, Lian followed behind trying to grab Jung's arm.

'No, you can't take him. This can't be right,' she shouted.

At that Jung snapped out of his daze and shock and he turned to call over his shoulder. 'Go and get Keow,' he said.

In the hall they came face to face with Heng who had become curious when he saw the men entering the hall and now came in to see what was going on. Yew was standing next to him, his mouth open and eyes wide.

'What is happening?' asked Heng.

Neither of the two policemen answered; they kept walking with Jung in between them forcing Heng and Yew to step aside and let them through.

'They're taking him to the police station,' said Lian, tears ran down her cheeks as she stared at Jung being led away.

Lian felt she was in a scene from a street opera, performed for all to see; she hated the fact that Jung's arrest was so public, carried out in front of the family, their workers and customers. She felt so badly for Jung who was completely stunned but there was no time to worry about the shame of what was happening. She knew she had to act fast.

She sent Yew to get Keow and Kok. Kok came first, rushing to Lian's side in her room while Yew went back out to find Keow who had come back to Batu Pahat to work in the same bicycle shop not long after Kwee died.

'Second Sister-in-law, don't worry, we'll do everything we can to help Second Brother. We'll wait for Keow to come home so we can decide what to do,' said Kok as he took a deep breath to calm himself.

'What does all this mean? Prison for Jung?' asked Lian sitting in Jung's chair and trying hard not to cry.

'Kok is right,' said Heng, standing in the doorway. 'Let's wait for Keow. It might just be a fine and that will be that.' His face did not betray the worry that he felt.

'Why him? It's not as if he is cheating or stealing? It's not as if he is the head of the syndicate. This gambling goes on everywhere. Why him?' said Lian.

She got up and walked to the hammock, her heart pounding, her spirit shattered and scattered into space. When she looked at Mei Choon sleeping soundly in the hammock her tears started to roll down her cheeks and then she turned to look at Yao on the bed, fast asleep with his thumb in his mouth. Yao was only five months old.

'What's going to happen to us?' she whispered.

'It is obvious that Jung is being used as a scapegoat. The government can't stop us gambling but it has to be seen to enforce its own law. Jung is unlucky,' said Heng, shaking his grey head.

'But how did the police find out that Jung is involved? Who told them?' asked Lian.

Before anyone could answer Keow appeared, breathless from the cycling.

'Second Sister-in-law, don't you worry,' he said. 'I stopped at the police station on the way back and the man who was here earlier, he's a detective, he said we should get a lawyer.'

'A lawyer? How am I going to afford one? And what will he do?' asked Lian, her voice rising.

'He can defend Second Brother, fight for him,' said Keow.

'How am I going to get one?'

'The detective gave me a couple of names,' said Keow. 'I'll get on to them.'

In a small air-conditioned room that had been partitioned off a photographer's shop in Jalan Rahmat, Lian and Keow sat facing the man behind his desk. Bespectacled and in his thirties, Mr Yong sitting with his back very straight looked at Lian, his face solemn.

'I will do what I can,' he explained in Hokkien, 'but I'm afraid the police have got the dockets they found in his pocket when they arrested him.'

'But someone could have put them in his pocket,' said Lian leaning forward.

The lawyer shook his head. 'Doesn't work like that. They found it there and that is enough for them,' he said, his mouth then set into a thin line.

Lian turned to look at Keow and then back to the lawyer. 'So what happens now?'

'The case will go before a judge and he will decide.'

'How do you think it will go?' asked Keow.

'We better not pre-judge the outcome,' said Mr Yong. 'I will inform you as soon as I can, I will try to get his case up as early as possible.'

A few weeks later Lian and Keow sat at the back of the court room in the town of Muar, an hour's drive from Batu Pahat in Mr Yong's car. On the wood-panelled wall facing her was a large photograph of the King, the *Yang di-Pertuan Agong*, his image overseeing the proceedings conducted in English. Not understanding a word, Lian watched intently, her eyes fixed in turn on the faces of the Malay judge, the prosecutor and Mr Yong in their black gowns when they spoke. She felt as if she was watching a silent street opera. She watched Jung closely. When the solemn-faced judge finally addressed him she saw his face turning white as he listened and then he turned to her looking petrified. She gasped and let out a cry. She knew the worst had happened. Her heart sank like a block of concrete into her stomach. She saw the panic and fear in his eyes as he was led out of courtroom. She felt then that the sky had collapsed and blacked out her world. Beside her Keow's face turned pale.

In the corridor outside the courtroom, Lian grabbed Mr Yong's arm and asked, 'What is going to happen to him?'

Mr Yong explained, 'Just as I suspected the dockets with four digits and amounts of money written next to them were all the incriminating evidence they needed.' He shook his head. 'If they hadn't been in his pocket there would have been no evidence.' He paused for a moment and then continued. 'The fine is a thousand dollars... or a one-year jail sentence.'

Lian let out a cry like an animal caught in a trap. She stared at the lawyer and then turned to Keow. A few moments passed before she said in a calm voice, 'We have to find the money to pay the fine.'

Keow nodded, his face was grave. Mr Yong who had looked sorry was now bending down to shuffle his papers into his briefcase on the floor with one hand while clutching his gown with the other. He straightened up and looked at Lian then nodded without saying a word.

'But what if we can't raise the entire sum?' Lian asked him.

'The sentence will be reduced proportionately depending on how much you can raise,' replied the lawyer.

'We will get the money one way or another,' said Lian suppressing the tears as she thought of what and how she was going to tell the children about their father not coming home for a long time. She couldn't bear the thought of how Jung was going to cope with being in prison as she marshalled all her strength and courage to face what was to come.

'Yes, Second Sister-in-law, don't worry, we will,' said Keow as they walked towards Mr Yong's Volvo, parked outside in the shade of a frangipani tree.

Lian had counted on the money from the sale of their fabric in Kui's shop. But the money never materialised. Kui's excuse was that her husband couldn't keep track of what belonged to whom and the money somehow got spent. It went against Jung's grain to agree to Lian borrowing money; she could see how much it was hurting him but it didn't stop her doing it. She had to stuff her own pride into her pocket and turn to her friends Ai Chien and Wei who were only too willing to help.

Not waiting for Lian to ask, Heng offered a sizeable loan from his savings. Still maintaining Jung was a scapegoat, he said, 'Jung is just a small fry. Why don't they go catch the big ones, the bookies? *Ha,* I wouldn't be surprised if they're taking money under the table. Maybe if Jung had been quick and slipped some money to the police when they were here, it wouldn't have come to this. Bad luck.'

Until now Lian hadn't troubled her parents with any of her problems; she had no choice now but to turn to them about Jung's impending incarceration. Acutely ashamed, she made them promise not to tell her friends especially May. Between them all and the two brothers, Keow and Kok, she raised enough money to pay the lawyer's fees of three hundred dollars and almost three-quarters of the fine. Jung's prison sentence was commuted to three months.

It seemed to Lian that all the neighbours knew about Jung's misfortune and either out of curiosity or genuine concern they each enquired after him and the children.

'Are you coping?' they asked, looking pityingly at her. She lied that she was fine and managing to get by.

Her mother Ying's words - *The brothers will help you-* when she found out about Jung's six brothers came back to her but she never for a moment thought her prediction would be tested out this way. The brothers fell into two camps. Keow and Kok had stood by her side; the youngest two, Tian and Yew, were also keen in their support by way of helping out with minding the children and doing any chores that Lian needed them to do, but Kau and Soong had shown no sign of sympathy. The only interest that Kau showed was when Lian overheard him talking to Mr Ting in the shop,

'I told him it would come to no good, this lottery business. He was stubborn and would not listen. Now he's in jail, he might think differently.'

Mr Ting neither agreed nor disagreed but carried on stretching the piece of leather he had over the last on his lap.

Lian suppressed her anger, resisting the urge to confront him knowing that it would achieve nothing.

One afternoon a few days later, Mei Chin came running up the stairs to where she was sewing in her room.

'Ma,' Mei Chin called out, tears running down her cheeks.

'What's the matter? What happened?' asked Lian, turning from the sewing machine and reaching out to her.

'First Uncle pinched me,' she said, then pointed, 'here.'

On seeing a red mark on her thigh, Lian jumped up from her seat not stopping to find out the reason for Kau's dastardly act. 'Stay here,' she said and stormed downstairs into the shop to confront him.

She should have been scared as she recalled the night that Kau had threatened his own wife Siew Ping, waving a cleaver at her in the hall. He had been drinking, his face was flushed and his eyes red. She and Jung had heard Siew Ping screaming.

'I should cut off your testicles!' she had shouted at Kau.

The whole household had been wakened. From the top of the stairs Lian saw him slap Siew Ping and then he flew into the kitchen to return with a cleaver in his hand, his face ugly with fury.

'I'll chop your head off first!' he shouted as he advanced towards Siew Ping.

Jung had run downstairs and positioned himself next to Siew Ping putting his arm out in front of her.

'Big Brother, whatever the problem is I'm sure you don't need this,' he'd said.

No one had said a word, not even Kwee; there was absolute silence as everyone watched from a safe distance. Lian had been terrified, afraid that Kau might charge at Jung instead. Then, as if the fire in him had suddenly been extinguished, Kau slammed the cleaver on the table and dropped onto the stool to everyone's surprise.

With the scene still replaying in her mind, Lian rushed into the shop where Kau had just walked from the hall towards his sewing machine. Mr Ting and Leng were seated at their worktable immersed in their handiwork. Before Kau could sit down, Lian charged straight up to him. As tall as he, she stood in front of him her face level with his and stared into his cold eyes. The smell of stale cigarette hit her nose. She felt no fear as she stood facing Kau now. In a firm voice and not caring what others around her thought, she said,

'I've had enough of your bullying. You bullied your brother and now you are bullying my children. You pinched Mei Chin, she's only three. What kind of man are you?'

Lian realised that she had never said so much to Kau before. She noticed his shoulders stiffened, his eyes hard, his nostrils flared. She heard him flick his little finger nail. She half expected him to hit out at her.

'What are you talking about? Pinched her? Who pinched her? She's making up stories,' he said glaring back at her.

Not wavering, Lian continued, 'She hasn't got it in her to make up stories. You are the one making up stories. You touch any of my children again and I won't be responsible for my actions.'

Not wanting to give him a chance to speak again, she turned and walked into the hall, past Yin Li who couldn't retract her outstretched ears fast enough and was looking sheepish.

Back in the safety of her room, when she was rubbing Mei Chin's leg, Lian noticed that her own hands were shaking.

Each of Jung's younger four brothers took turns to accompany Lian when she went to visit him in prison near Johore Bahru, about seventy eight miles south of Batu Pahat. It took two hours by taxi to get there and Lian could only afford to visit every other weekend. Each time she saw him he looked thinner.

138

'Are you not eating?' Lian asked.

Jung nodded, not looking at Lian, as if he had more important things to deal with than the question of eating.

She worried about how he passed the time of day. The drawing pad and colour pencils were vital to him and it was thanks to the kindly warden who allowed him to have them. The bare walls of his cell seemed to have sucked away some of his vitality and withered any vestige of an inclination to talk; he was more reticent than ever. Lian was sure that if the brothers had not been there with her, he would have stayed clammed up. But he always asked about the children, was always anxious about them and worried in case they weren't studying as hard as they should. And Lian would go through each of the children, updating him on their progress. He worried about how he was going to pay back money he owed.

One day looking past Keow and Lian, he said, 'I wonder how the police knew about me. I've been thinking. There are so many people doing exactly the same thing as I was, but why me?'

'I too have been wondering,' said Lian.

'It's not as if you have enemies,' said Keow.

'I wonder if it could be someone at work...last month when I won a few dollars myself I mentioned it at work. Even bought them a treat. Maybe someone is jealous, but who?' said Jung staring at nothing in particular in front of him.

'You'd better be careful next time, what you say to anybody,' said Lian.

The huge debts jangling over Lian's head was a constant reminder that until she repaid them, she too was imprisoned. Without Jung's income, she couldn't even begin to think about repaying. With only what she was earning from working for Ai Chien's husband, and that was not always reliable, she knew she had to find another way of making some money. She was very grateful for the kindness and generosity of Ai Chien and Wei who constantly brought gifts of food but she felt she would rather pay her way. As

139

she lay in bed finding it impossible to sleep, she suddenly remembered one evening long before the trouble with Jung started, when we were celebrating the fifteenth day of the eighth lunar month, the Mid-Autumn Festival. The sky had been clear and the moon at its fullest. Many residents of the street had come out to sit on the five-foot way to enjoy tea, melon seeds, pomelos and mooncake laid out on the tables while the children were out on the street parading and showing off their lanterns of different shapes, sizes and colour. Wei had come to sit with her and noticed the frocks that my sisters and I were wearing. Wei had admired her handiwork.

'They are pretty. I think that if you made more they would sell well,' she had said.

'You are flattering me,' Lian had replied, as she offered her another piece of mooncake.

'I am serious. There aren't many good children's dresses about and I am sure they will be snapped up. You should make them and sell them in my parents' shop.'

Lian had looked at her to see if she was joking, but Wei was serious as she had said. 'You are really serious. You really think people will want to buy my dresses?'

Wei nodded. 'It's worth a try. There're lots of remnant pieces, you are welcome to them.'

Lian had liked the idea then but she had enough to do with work from Ai Chien. Now the urgency of another source of income weighed on her and with the sewing machine right in her room ready for her use, she decided to turn the idea into a reality. The next morning she went to see Wei in her shop. Wei's mother, Mrs Tong, was feeding her youngest daughter Moi by the glass counter.

'How are you coping? You've lost weight, you're looking thin,' said Mrs Tong as she scooped up another spoonful of rice and chicken. Moi, chomping away and shading her eyes with her hand, looked up at Lian.

'I'm doing fine. The children are fine, that's the main thing,' Lian replied. 'Moi, you are growing up fast.'

Moi looked down quickly but gave a shy smile.

140

The thought of medical expenses suddenly crossed Lian's mind as she looked at Moi. Her skin had taken on a pinkish hue; her short hair was still straw-coloured as were her eyelashes which did little to hide the darting grey eyes. Lian couldn't help thinking that the child would not be thriving so well had her parents been less well off. She was glad that none of her own children was ill having just seen the packed waiting room in Australian Clinic opposite Mrs Tong's shop. The heat had taken its toll; business was roaring for the husband-and-wife team of doctors there. At three dollars a consultation, she couldn't afford this extra expense. So many people were complaining of fever and cough after the long spell of drought and heat but the clear blue sky showed no sign of relenting, no hint of rain, no imminent respite. She shuddered at the possibility of another water ration.

'You are doing a good job, I can see. *Aiyahh*, such bad luck. If there is anything we can do to help, you must let us know,' said Mrs Tong, her eyes starting to well up as she shoved another spoonful into Moi's open mouth.

'That is why I am here.' Lian turned to Wei, 'Some time ago you said I could use the remnants to make children's dresses. Can I take you up on that now?' said Lian.

'Of course you're more than welcome to the fabric. Here, take what you want,' said Wei as she led Lian to a box at the back of the shop. 'Go through this and take what you need. I'm glad you can do something with them.'

Feeling the pieces of cotton, lace and chiffon in her hands, Lian's brain had already gone into overdrive thinking of what she could do with them, what she could create that would shout 'buy me'. It seemed such a long time since she had felt such a sense of excitement oozing through her, not just at the thought of experimenting, of trying out new ideas, but also that people might like them enough to want to buy them. She couldn't wait to take the pieces of fabric back to her room so she could start to work on them. She looked up at Wei.

'Thank you, Wei,' she said, 'I think I can do something with them.'

Chapter 15

I felt very special in the new dress that my mother had made for me. The fabric was pale blue cotton with little pink and white flowers. It had a full gathered skirt with two plain blue pockets that looked like flower petals big enough to fit my hands, and puff sleeves. I did a twirl in front of my mother and sisters and then looked in the mirror on the wardrobe door to admire it myself.

'You look lovely,' said Mother sitting at her sewing machine and looking at me.

'I'd like another one just like that so when this is old and worn I can wear the new one,' I said. Mother smiled.

'Yes, you look nice,' said Mei Lin lifting up my skirt, then turning to Mother and chugging at her arm, 'Ma, am I going to have one exactly like that?'

'If you are good. This dress is for your big sister winning a prize at school.'

'I'll win a prize too. I know I will. I got all my sums right today. My teacher said I was clever,' said Mei Lin. 'I can show you my exercise book.'

'Good, then you can have two dresses.'

'Ma, who will take me to my prize-giving?' I asked. It had always been my father who had taken me.

'Your Uncle Kok. You will be taking the bus, like when we go to see *Chia Chia*,' said Mother.

'I like going to see *Chia Chia*,' said Mei Lin.

Mei Lin and I loved going to see our maternal grandmother whom we called *Chia Chia*; it was always an adventure travelling by bus to Pontian through the plantations and jungle. We would imagine being attacked by tigers and lions; we would fight them off with our bare hands saving everyone in the bus. It was not only an adventure but also a novelty as we didn't go to see our grandparents that often. When we asked her, Mother's reason was always that she was too busy, but during the time Father was away they would often come to see us and I always loved seeing them. Grandfather Shao was relatively tall for a Chinese, his face was kind with a pair of dark-rimmed glasses perched low on his nose and he was never without a cheroot or cigar hanging between his lips. Grandmother Ying was an older version of my mother – lovely smiling eyes, prominent cheek-bones and an hour-glass figure hidden under her 'grandmother garb'. Although her hair was combed back and tied in a bun at the nape it didn't make her look stern. She exuded warmth and I loved her touch especially when she became blind a few years later. Her fingers would gently trace every contour of my face as she smiled, as if she liked what her fingertips were telling her. And then she would ask, 'Are you wearing a pretty dress?'

When prize-giving day came, I was like a butterfly that could not stop fluttering and couldn't wait to go to school. Uncle Kok and I went by bus as planned and when we got to the school, I was thrilled to see all the other children and their parents. I waved and called out to them. Although I didn't mind Uncle Kok taking me I wished then that my father had been home to take me. I thought that he would be proud of me; I wanted him to be there when the teacher, standing on the stage in front of all my school friends and the parents, announced my name and the prize I had been awarded '....for General Proficiency'. I thought of him being in a place far away all by himself and I felt sad for him, sad that he missed my big moment.

The next day while Mother was sewing I sat down at his desk to write. Normally I would sit at the table outside on the landing when Chung Lin and Mother were not using it for their ironing. At the right hand corner of the desktop were a bamboo holder with pencils and pens, a large note pad, an English-Chinese dictionary and a pile of magazines with a round stone on top, all neatly arranged just as Father had left them.

'What are you doing?' asked Mother.

'Writing to papa,' I answered; I had my exercise book opened to a clean page.

'Good,' Mother sounded surprised. 'What are you going to say?'

'I'm going to say I hope he comes home quickly. Ma, will you tell Papa that I won a prize?'

'Of course,' said Mother, 'but can't you tell him in your letter?'

'I can but it is too long for me to write.'

When I had finished writing I cut out the page I had written on, folded it twice and then cut another which I folded into an envelope. I ran downstairs to Uncle Heng to ask for some of his starch to stick down the edge of the folds of my envelope and then put my letter in it before sealing it. Excited, I then ran back upstairs to Mother.

'Ma, this is for Papa when you go to visit him.'

I wanted him to know that I hadn't forgotten him but was thinking of him. My sisters missed him too; Yao was too young to understand. Some evenings, instead of playing, Mei Lin and I would stand under the hibiscus tree and talk about him. Some nights we would cry together and then Mother would cry with us before going to sleep. We all missed him terribly but I didn't really know or understand the depth of Mother's anxiety and worry.

One afternoon a long time after Father was taken from us. Mei Lin and I had just finished our homework when Mother came to check on us.

'Now I would like you to go and get some groceries for me,' she said. 'Tell Uncle Ong I want a kati of sugar, a tin of milk powder, he knows which brand I want, and ten katis of rice, he knows which variety I want but if he asks just tell him that it is the usual. He will deliver the rice but you bring home the sugar and milk powder. And give him this.' She handed me the small dog-eared note book that we always used when we shopped at Uncle Ong's.

Ong who was also Hakka was not my uncle; it was just our way of addressing our elders. A bald middle-aged man with a pot belly, he was the owner of the dry grocery shop on the main road. Although he seldom spoke when he was serving his customers, waddling between the gunny sacks of rice, sugar, pulses and dried mushrooms as he picked, weighed and wrapped up the various items, he was not unapproachable. Occasionally he would open one of the huge tins of biscuits he kept stacked behind the counter and let me and Mei Lin dip our hands in to take one each.

With the notebook in my hand Mei Lin and I walked out of our back door and along the alley. Before we got to the shop we passed the backdoor of the kitchen of the Indian restaurant. We could smell the delicious spices of the curries simmering inside. Next to it was the backdoor of the grocery shop. We pushed it open and went in. The shop was quiet and we could hear Indian music wafting in from the five-foot way. The awning partially blocked the bright sunshine so it was a bit cooler in the shop. We caught a whiff of *satay* from the Malay man barbequing skewers of beef over the charcoal in his grill on the five-foot way. Uncle Ong was sitting like Buddha, one leg resting across his other leg and fanning himself. He turned when he heard us, his face expressionless, and stood up.

'Uncle Ong, my mother said she would like a tin of milk powder for my baby brother, one kati of sugar and ten katis of rice. And here is the notebook.'

I held out the notebook to him. He took it from me, put it on the desk and then pulled a paper bag off a bunch hanging from the ceiling and proceeded to scoop sugar from a sack, weighed the bag with a steelyard which he balanced by adding more sugar to the bag. Next he brought down a tin of *Cow and Gate* milk powder from the shelf and then deftly flicked the beads of the abacus on the desk. He picked up the notebook and wrote in it before handing it back to me.

'Here you are. Tell your mother I will deliver the rice later,' he said as he handed the notebook, bag of sugar and tin to me.

We lingered ever so briefly wondering if he would offer us a biscuit and then to our delight he did.

'Go on, take one,' he said, his face still expressionless as he opened a tin and held it in front of us.

Mei Lin carried the tin of milk powder while I had the bag of sugar as we walked back the way we came; we mimicked Uncle Ong, waddling as we made our way home. When we got upstairs Mei Chin and Mei Choon were on the landing engrossed in folding paper to make a ball. Yao was still fast asleep in the hammock.

'Look, I've almost got it right,' said Mei Chin excitedly, holding up her folded paper to us.

'I'll show you how it is done,' said Mei Lin handing the tin of milk powder to me and went to join them. I turned into our room. Mother was at her sewing machine; she stopped pedalling when she saw our faces at the door.

'Here you are, Ma. Sugar and milk powder,' I said as I walked to the desk and put my bag of sugar down next to milk powder.

'Did Uncle Ong say he would bring the rice?' asked Mother.

'Yes,' I said and saw her face relax. 'Is there anything else you want me to do?'

'No, nothing else,' she said and I hurried out of the room to where the girls were still playing.

After we had finished folding four paper balls we looked for something else to do. We started to sing and dance; we clapped and jumped about and then started laughing loudly. Mother was sweeping up the thread ends and bits of fabric on the floor.

'Be quiet, I don't want you to wake Yao up,' she called out to us.

'Yes, Ma,' we answered and piped down a little but very soon started laughing loudly again.

'Did you not hear me?' she said, her voice rising.

I was the nearest to her; she was squatting on the floor with the feather duster in her hand still sweeping. Without any warning she struck out at my leg hitting me with the feather end of the duster. I jumped as I pulled away. A sudden silence fell on us. Mother didn't hurt me but I was

147

shocked by the sound of a suppressed cry coming from her. I swung round to see her in tears and right away felt ashamed of myself.

'I'm sorry, Ma,' I said.

Mei Lin shrank back and sat down quietly on the floor looking worried. Mei Choon did the same, looking puzzled. Only Mei Chin remained standing, a hand went up to her mouth. We watched Mother drop her duster and cover her face with her hands as the sobs came rushing. Then timidly Mei Chin walked to her and put her arms round her shoulders.

'Don't cry, Ma.'

But Mother couldn't stop. She had never hit me or any of my sisters before. It was only then that I began to realise the burden of worry she had been carrying in my father's absence.

In Father's absence I also grew to appreciate my uncles who stood by us.

Uncle Keow was my favourite uncle and he in turn treated my sisters, brother and me like we were special to him. On him the Chiang *jambu* nose was the most prominent, but when he smiled the nose blurred and all I saw was the kindness and the generosity in him. He was eager to teach us Mandarin.

'You should speak the Chinese national language,' he said, 'it will stand you in good stead anywhere you go. With both English and Mandarin, you will be well equipped.'

He not only patiently taught us Mandarin songs, singing to us as he played his accordion, he also showed us how to polish our only pair of leather shoes that Father had earlier bought us for Chinese New Year. His own leather shoes were always shiny to match the crisp shirt and well pressed trousers he would change into after work before taking us girls for a walk in town. More often than not he would buy us treats of steamed lotus dumplings for supper.

148

After him, Uncle Kok was the fun one who preferred polo-shirts to starched cotton shirts. The best looking of the brothers, he had a happy face and was never short of girlfriends. It was he who taught Mei Lin and me to dance. On the landing we would watch him swing his hips, doing the *cha-cha,* to the sounds of *Tea For Two* drifting from Father's record player in his room.

'This way,' he said as he swayed his hip to the left and putting his right foot forward, 'then this way. One and two and three, four,' and he was off, carried by the music.

We watched closely. I tried to imitate him, jerking my hip left to right and left again but I couldn't achieve the smooth moves that seemed to come so easily to him. Mei Lin and I would giggle throughout as we wriggled about like upturned caterpillars and then fell down laughing.

Uncle Tian was the academic one of the brothers, eager to learn anything and everything. After school he taught himself to play the flute and the guitar and made lovely music in his room where he couldn't disturb others. He even knitted a night cap with a bobble which made him look like a Chinese *Wee Willie Winky* in his night shirt and shorts showing off his skinny brown legs. My mother, sisters and I saw him like this one morning, bleary-eyed, after he had got out from under the mosquito net over his camp bed and was walking down the corridor.

We giggled, hands over our mouths, pointing at his night cap.

'Crazy,' said Mother, shaking her head and smiling. 'Your brain must be cooking under that thing.'

Uncle Tian simply shrugged, gave a half smile and continued downstairs.

He was good at drawing and painting. On the landing near the window where he could get the best light, but well away from Chung Lin's ironing table, he would set up his drawing board improvising with a large piece of ply-wood on a table, lay out his pencils, charcoal sticks and rubber and then proceed to draw anything from cars to a portrait of J.F.Kennedy.

Mildly obsessed with having the best quiff but not quite aspiring to look like Elvis Presley, he would spend a long time combing, moulding and re-moulding his tuft of hair to get the curry-puff shape just right. Apart from this, he was easy going and didn't think it beneath him to teach me to cook his favourite three-jewel fried rice with egg, shrimps and string beans when I was given the responsibility to cook for the family later.

Uncle Yew was what my Mother called 'biddable'. He was helpful and hardworking, charged with the task of keeping an eye on me especially after that first time I fell into a drain. I had a propensity to falling into drains like a nail is drawn to a magnet. The very first time I fell into one was when I was four. It was on a morning I'd decided to go exploring without telling my parents. I had managed to sneak out of the shop sauntering along the five-foot way, peering into the other shops and watching men set up their food stalls on the roadside. Somehow three shops away I found myself standing in the drain, my head and shoulders were just above it. I became frightened as I wasn't sure how I would get out. Then I looked up and saw a strange pink-skinned man with blue marble eyes and yellow hair. He bent down and reached to pick me up. As my mother said afterwards, luckily it hadn't rained or the drain would have been filled with water. Since then Uncle Yew had had to keep an eye on me but that didn't necessarily stop me falling into drains again.

Easy-going and care-free, Yew had a funny laugh; his head would nod continuously and his eyes disappear when he laughed. He would now help with the shopping and chores like taking Father's bike out from the hall in the morning and then bringing it back in again after the shop closed. Sometimes, even though the bike was clean and shiny he would still polish it knowing how much Father treasured it. He knew he had made the right choice taking up the apprenticeship with Mr Ting when he realised how much he liked the feeling of satisfaction when he saw the finished shoes after he had polished them.

Mother gave the first dress she made to Moi before she made two more to sell in Mrs Tong's shop. For more than two weeks after she had handed them to Wei she heard nothing. She was so pleased with what she had created and had hoped that they would be snapped up but as time went by with no sign or sound of a sale she became despondent and wondered if the whole idea was a mistake.

'But they are so lovely, Second Aunty. If I had a little girl I would buy one. I like the red one with the flower across the shoulder strap, it's so pretty,' said Chung Lin. 'How did you make the flower look so good?'

'I like it too,' I said.

'And me,' said Mei Lin.

But Mother was at the point of giving up.

Another week had passed when we heard a commotion as Wei rushed in through the shop. At the bottom of the stairs even before she kicked off her sandals, she called out to Mother who she knew would be sewing in her room. 'Lian, I've good news!'

Mother jumped out of her seat and rushed to the top of the stairs. 'Tell me, quickly,' she said, searching Wei's face when she got to the landing.

Wei was beaming. 'That dress has been sold. Sold to a woman who wants a bigger one for her older daughter. I told her you could make one.'

Mother was uplifted by the good news and seemed to draw new strength from it. She threw herself, mind and soul, into her new venture. Each dress that she made was unique and each one was one that my sisters and I would have liked for ourselves.

It was the morning of the day my father was coming home. I had played with Yao while Mother was getting ready to go and fetch Father, then I watched her pick Yao up and carry him downstairs. I followed them. Uncle Kok was standing in the hall waiting to take her and Yao to Father.

'Won't be long before Papa is home,' she said turning to me and my sisters. 'You be good.'

151

'I'll watch them,' said Chung Lin, holding on to Mei Choon's hand. Then they were off to the taxi stand.

The morning sun was warm on my face as I walked through the playground to the hibiscus tree. All around me I could hear the sound of the day beginning on the street beyond the tree - the crunching of the wheels of a hawker's stall on his way to the market and the rattling of a bus while cyclists zoomed past. The night before I had noticed a bud just on the edge of unfurling its petals on the hibiscus tree and making sure that First Uncle couldn't see me I had taken a can of water to pour at the base of the tree. Now I was eager to see what the bud had done. I was thrilled to see that in the early sunlight the bud had opened, showing off its delicate red petals like a frilly chiffon skirt. I reached up and gently cupped the flower in my hands. As I studied and admired its intricate design and symmetry, my emotions were jumbled and tossed like *rojak*. I was excited about my father coming home and yet nervous. It was not knowing how he was going to react to me that filled me with anxiety. His face - would it be sullen or happy? Would he be happy to see me, or would he be angry with me? There was no reason for him to be angry. I wanted to hide and yet I couldn't wait to see him. It had been so long since I last saw him. I wanted to show him what I had learnt at school; I wanted to tell him that I was the class monitor.

'Come, Chiew, let's play red seeds!' It was Mei Lin calling to me from the back door.

'Coming,' I shouted back as I slowly released the flower and ran back into the hall where Mei Lin was showing Mei Chin what to do with the dozen or so shiny saga seeds already scattered on the marble top of the dining table. I joined them in the game but I found myself either staring at the grey streaks in the marble or looking out to the shop when it was their turn to play.

It was Mei Lin's turn. She drew an imaginary line between two seeds with her finger and then flicked one seed to strike the other. Upon hitting the target seed she picked it up, adding to her winnings and carried on with the rest of the seeds. After a couple of successful strikes she stopped and looked at me, annoyed.

'What are you looking at?' she asked, frowning at me.

I'd kept looking out into the shop, expecting to see Mother coming in with Father. Every time someone moved in the shop I thought it was them. Uncle Heng and First Uncle were going about their business as usual –sweeping the floor and dusting the tops and the glass cabinets. In the kitchen, Third Aunty and Chung Lin were busy preparing lunch, moving between the kitchen and hall.

'Papa should be here soon,' I said.

'I know,' said Mei Lin and then she continued with the game. To me, it seemed neither of my sisters worried about Father coming home. When I eventually heard Mother's voice in the shop, I became even more apprehensive. Leaving my sisters, I walked to the large fish tank in the air-well and pretended to be interested in the fish. My heart started to race as I listened for Father. Mei Lin and Mei Chin ran out into the shop to meet them. I heard them call out, 'Papa! Papa!' Third Aunty and Chung Lin had also come into the hall. Then I heard Chung Lin greet Father while Third Aunty carried on as if he was invisible.

'Second Brother.' Uncle Yew had put down his piece of leather and stood up when he saw Father.

'Second Uncle,' said Hock standing up but looking unsure as to how he should greet him.

I turned to see Father nod; he was holding Yao in his arms. '*Hmmm*' he said as he kicked off his sandals at the bottom of the stairs. Then he saw me. Our eyes met.

'Papa,' I greeted him. His face was thinner; the corners of his mouth were turned down.

'*Hmmm.*' He paused as he continued to look at me. Then he said, 'Your handwriting was terrible. You need to work on it.'

'Yes, Papa,' I said and then looked down at the floor before turning to look at the fish again as I heard him go upstairs with Mother behind him.

Chapter 16

Going to school was like being let loose in a fairground without any adults to restrain me. I was eager to try everything and play with anything that I could reach. In class I was like a sponge soaking up every bit of learning that was around me. We were taught in English by teachers who were Indian, Chinese and Malay who had trained in Britain and occasionally a teacher from the American Peace Corp.

The headmistress of my primary school, Mrs Singh, was a beautiful and elegant Indian lady who wore the most gorgeous saris that would send me into daydreams whenever I saw her walk past the classroom. And those daydreams were squeezed in between my escapes to the worlds of *Secret Seven, Peter Pan, Alice in Wonderland, David Copperfield,* and *Little Women.* Once in school, we children left behind our mother tongues and spoke English and Malay, the latter being a compulsory second language. We got on well with one another; youth was either blind or indifferent to racial differences. We were all equal in our maroon pleated pinafores over our white blouses, white socks and white plimsolls. The only time in school when the Malays and non-Malays were split up was for the Malay language period when the Malays were taught Jawi, an Arabic-derived script, while the non-Malays were taught the Romanised version.

The school field was bounded on one side by the exposed scar of red and orange laterite at the side of the foothill out of which it had been carved, the mimosa and grass which would later overrun it hadn't yet taken over. In the rainy season our cries and laughter during recess would alternate with the croaking of the frogs in the surrounding lush virgin jungle; we'd shout our heads off.

'*Yeee,* don't go there, got big ants!'

'Where got?'

'There, *lah*!'

'You can't catch me!'

'Hey, stop shouting, you so *bising lah*.'

'*Alamak,* you so slow! Quick, she will catch you!'

'Why you do that?'

'What? I no do that.'

At times our chatter and exuberance simply drowned the frogs' cries completely.

School started at seven o'clock in the morning and finished at one in the afternoon to allow another school to use the premises. Getting ready for school each day was carried out in semi-darkness with military precision and absolute quiet as we didn't want to disturb the others who were still fast asleep. At five o'clock, Mother would get up before my sisters, Mei Lin, Mei Chin and I to make congee. Then she would come back upstairs to wake us up and shining a torch she would lead us tip-toeing past Uncle Yew and Hock in their camp beds lined end-to-end in the hall. After we had washed and changed into our uniform she would serve us little bowls of the congee with a dash of soya sauce or pickled radish. Sometimes she would boil an egg for us to share. Under the amber glow from the ceiling lamp we would stand at the table in the kitchen to eat as she watched and waited for the kettle to boil on the wood fire to fill up her flasks that were kept in her room. By quarter past six when we were all ready she would lead us through the shop weaving our way between Uncle Heng's worktop and First Uncle and Sek in their camp beds, then unlocked the door to let us wait on the five-foot way for our taxi to come and pick us up. The taxi, a black Austin Ten, was owned and driven by a lovely man although I often wished he had a modern Japanese car instead of an old-fashioned one.

Mother never stepped into my school, partly because she had so much work to do at home but mostly because she couldn't speak English although we discovered later that she understood a lot as she had assimilated a reasonable amount from what she heard as we practised aloud for our homework. The revelation came one day when Mei Lin and I wanted pocket money but didn't dare ask her. Somehow we felt we could say it aloud in English which we did.

'Give me five cents, Ma,' we said not thinking she would understand and yet hoping she would.

'*I no gif you fi cen*,' she said.

She smiled when she saw our dropped jaws and widened eyes.

Then in Hakka she said, 'What do you want the five cents for?'

We knew then we could never be sure she didn't know what we were talking about in English.

The advantages of my mother not being directly involved with school became clear to me when I got into trouble with my teachers. When I was in my final year of primary school, I had trouble with the only male teacher who taught Malay and whom my classmates and I didn't like as we felt that he couldn't stand us either. This mutual dislike and the resulting friction were particularly intense between him and a small group of four of us which included my best friend, Soo Yin. It had been going on from the first day he started; he looked at us as if he couldn't stand the sight of us when he walked into the classroom. Our class, Standard Six A, had a reputation of being very lively and energetic and we sensed that he was always waiting to pounce, waiting for the opportunity to punish us.

There had just been a great upheaval in the classroom as the Malays girls in our class moved out to another room while the non-Malays from the other classes came to join us and we had just settled into our seats when the teacher, *Enche* Mat, entered the classroom with his books in one arm. We slowly hauled ourselves up from our seats and grudgingly squeezed the words out of our mouths.

'*Selamat pagi che gu.*'

He stopped in front of the class, his chest stuck out as he glared at us, the white of his eyes showing. '*Selamat pagi,*' he responded.

We glared back and sat down.

He then walked to the teacher's desk near the window, put his books down and turned to glare at us again before he turned to the blackboard. He picked up a piece of white chalk and started to write on the board. He was a tall man and he was wearing a white shirt with a tie and well-pressed trousers. We stared at his back. I was sitting in the front row. A few of us in that row started making faces and giggling as we looked at each other, wondering how we could ruffle him. When he whipped round to look at us, we looked serious and pretended we were reading what he was writing. He returned to writing on the board. I started to roll up a piece of paper into a small but firm stick about the length of the piece of chalk he was holding, what I considered would be a reasonable missile. I hooked it onto a rubber band that someone handed me and I had wound round my index finger and thumb to ready as my catapult. *Enche* Mat was to be my target. I took aim at his trousers and fired. It hit the target. *Enche* Mat spun round.

'*Siapa champak itu?*' he shouted, his eyes bulged.

I was scared then. No one said a word. Before we knew it he had picked out my group and we were marched to Mrs Singh's office. Our class teacher, Miss Yeo, was duly informed.

Outside Mrs Singh's office we waited in silence with our heads hanging down until Miss Yeo came out of the office. Disappointment was written all over her face.

'Chiew, you wait here,' she said, 'the rest of you go in.'

I was going to be punished separately and more severely. I'd seen the yard-long ruler on her desk before, the one that she used to hit the children. I strained to hear what was going on inside her office but was unable to make out what was being said. Then I heard the strike of the ruler on someone's palm; a pause and then again and again. I was sure my punishment would be worse. I was mortified and remorseful. Eventually, my friends filed out looking sheepish and I was told to go in. I stood, shamefaced, before

Mrs Singh and Miss Yeo who were both standing behind the desk.

'Is there anything you would like to say, Miss Yeo?' asked Mrs Singh.

Miss Yeo shook her head and then, not looking at me, said, 'I'm very disappointed.'

In the music period before all this had happened, Miss Yeo had sung to us. Her velvety voice had moved us as she sang, *'Blow the wind southerly, southerly, southerly. Blow the wind south ov'er the bonnie blue sea'*. And I'd been blown away to the distant land where the song originated. Now she didn't look happy at all.

Mrs Singh in her elegant sari turned to me.

'What have you to say for yourself?' she asked. 'You've set a bad example to your classmates as the Head Prefect. What am I going to do with you?'

'I am very sorry,' I said meekly and I meant it. I waited to be told to stretch my hand out.

'Now, I expect you to behave and set a good example. I don't want to have to see you like this again.'

I steeled myself and waited for the ruler, my palm tingling as if it knew it deserved what was to come. I took in a big breath.

'You may go back to your class,' said Mrs Singh waving her hand towards the door.

I couldn't believe my good luck and how good my friends were for not telling on me. Not only had I escaped punishment from Mrs Singh but my parents weren't informed about my bad behaviour either. The beating from Mrs Singh would have been a tickle compared to what my father would have meted out to me for that aberration.

I was responsible for my sisters in school, making sure they had the right books at the start of each New Year and that they had their vouchers for free meals which were for the poor students. Mei Lin was a year behind me while Mei Chin was four years behind. Mei Lin was the quiet studious one who was good at Arithmetic, winning prizes for it almost every year. She was the wizard with adding and subtracting pounds, shillings and pence. Mei Chin was the prettiest of us sisters; taking after Mother, her features were delicate and she was tall, slim and athletic. She excelled in sports particularly netball and was chosen for the school team when she was in Standard Six. I was butter-fingers compared to her, so much so that when my netball-playing friends saw me coming they would walk away to spare me the embarrassment of turning me down in case I asked to join them.

The downside of school was seeing how other people lived, the comparison with them and the envy that came with it. I often wished that I lived in a proper house like some of my friends', equipped with mod cons like fridges, gas cookers and later on televisions. On the taxi run the driver would try to pack as many children as possible in the back seat and neatly arranged our school bags in the boot. Across town and especially on the outskirts; I would see houses that I dreamt of one day living in with my family. A few of the children lived in Taman Indah, a new estate with rows of single-storey terrace houses, that had grown up about two miles from town. Here, each house had a front porch, a garden and a fence with an iron gate. How I envied the people who lived in them. Although I would have preferred a white wooden gate and a neat English cottage, I wouldn't have minded an attap-roofed house on stilts that my Malay friends lived in, with chicken running around and underneath. To have a small room that was my own where I could bring my friends would have been heaven. Nevertheless, my friends did come to visit me, seemingly oblivious to the crowdedness and busy-ness of the shophouse. And they didn't mind when I had to take my little brother Yao along, straddled across my hip, when I went to visit the friends who lived in town.

Everyone in my close group of friends had rich parents. They had birthday parties with cakes, sweets and games. I was lucky to have two boiled eggs coloured red, which was the old Chinese custom and something Mother always did for us. I thought I had the biggest celebration when my eleventh birthday coincided with the first day of the Lunar New Year. I felt as if the whole town was celebrating with me. Best of all was the fact that my uncles Keow, Kok and Tian were home. Although they weren't obliged to give us children lucky money in red packets as they weren't married, I knew that Keow and Kok would and I couldn't wait to see my Aunt Kui and Lan either when they would come to pay their respects to Grandfather and Grandmother. This was the one time in the year when the kitchen was the busiest with Mother, Third Aunt and Chung Lin preparing and cooking dishes for the feast on New Year's Eve.

A few weeks earlier Mother had made sweet glutinous rice pudding that she steamed for hours until it turned a toffee colour and was very sticky. This was offered to the kitchen gods on New Year's Eve; legend has it that it sticks the mouth of the Kitchen God to prevent him telling tales in Heaven about the household's past year. Mother sometimes joked that Father must've had a good dose of it too which was why his lips needed prising with a lever to get anything out of him. On the same day she also cooked chicken, sea-bass, prawns, roast pork, snow peas, pig's trotters in rice wine and my favourite stuffed bean curd, a Hakka dish which was my mother's speciality.

After the feast, the much anticipated firecrackers were set off at midnight to chase away evil spirits. As far as I was concerned it was to herald my birthday.

I woke up early the next day and then woke my sisters and Yao up so I didn't have to wait too long to receive my red packet from my father. After a hurried breakfast we offered prayers and food to Grandfather and Grandmother at their shrine; Mother had laid out a whole steamed chicken, a pyramid of oranges and another of buns. We then rushed upstairs into Father and Mother's room where they were waiting for us. Father sitting in his chair had the red packets in one hand. Eagerly we stood in a line before him with me at the head. In turn we clasped our hands

160

together and greeted him and Mother, wishing them a prosperous and happy new year before Father handed us a red packet each. Once that was done we ran into our room to find out how much we had received, excited at the prospect of receiving more over the three days of celebration and especially when we visited our maternal grandparents who were always generous with their red packets.

My friends and I had planned that they should come to me first to start our visitation marathon which was the tradition; we would go from house to house to simply wish each other 'Happy New Year' and eat whatever was offered. Mother always made sure we had a good selection to offer - melon seeds, ground nuts, boiled sweets, pineapple tarts and bottles of *Fraser & Neave* orange - all laid out on the table on the landing. When my friends arrived Soo Yin wished me 'Happy Birthday' and handed me a red and silvery packet of cookies that her mother had given her to give to me for my birthday. I was surprised. These were no ordinary cookies, not the locally made ones; they were imported from England. I was overjoyed about them - something I had never had before - but more especially because someone else had bothered about me. It made up for the fact that I only had three new dresses-one for each of the first three days of the new year-compared to the fifteen new dresses that my friends had for the entire fifteen days of celebration.

While school was my other-world, my paradise, my father's workshop became even more of a sanctuary for him. He was lucky in that he still had his old job at the cinema to go back to when he came out of prison. He fell back into his old work routine quickly, sometimes staying back a little longer than he needed to, to paint which gave him a chance to reflect, to escape from the tedium and futility of making polite conversation, to recover from the harshness of prison life and recompose himself. He didn't talk much about his time in jail, what he felt or thought of it to my mother. Even his workmates accepted that and they respected it. But he carried the belief that someone amongst his workmates must

161

have informed on him to the police and he became very cautious. He had suspected the security man Avatar, the day- and night-watchman who slept outside the cinema in his camp bed. This had upset him as he had thought he could trust him and that they were friends. He didn't confront him, not without any proof; he merely became guarded towards him.

To Lian's mind, the day that he came home from prison marked the beginning of the change she saw in Jung. He had never been a patient man and was also meticulous verging on perfectionist. With a hefty dose of anger thrown in, the mixture was bound to be explosive. The one good thing about not having privacy in the shophouse was that I never heard or saw them row. That was because Lian hated *acting out a scene*, as she called it, in front of the rest of the household. She would keep quiet, letting my father grumble and mutter until he was spent. At least, to her relief, he had the decency to do it quietly although to her consternation he became grumpier than usual. And I started to notice the change in his attitude to her too. One day while Mother was engrossed in working at her sewing machine surrounded by pieces of fabric on the floor he walked into the room and tripped on the fabric.

'You stupid woman! Are you trying to kill me?' he cursed as he kicked the fabric towards the sewing machine. His face was flushed and his brow tightly knitted.

'I didn't realise it had spread out so far,' Mother said softly as she got up and gathered up the pieces of fabric.

'You're stupid,' Father hissed as he started re-arranging the things on his desk.

This sort of thing was to become a regular occurrence.

Tian's hard work and studies paid off when he was accepted by the Malayan Teachers' College in Penang in 1961. He was ecstatic, grinning like a monkey with a bunch of bananas in his hand when he charged into the hall and stopped next to Father at the dining table where we were eating lunch.

'Second Brother, I got accepted! I am going to the teachers' college!' He was waving his letter of acceptance in the air, not a hair out of place in his perfect quiff, 'I'm in, I'm in!'

Father's face broke into a big smile. 'Well done,' he said. Tian's achievement was his and my mother's pride and joy, the one thing that lifted him out of his misery, the first ray of light in a long dark season, knowing that Tian's future was secure. He would work for the government after his two years of training paid for by them. Tian was the last of his responsibilities; Keow was happy in his new job in Singapore working as a quality control manager in a bicycle factory while Kok was chasing a beautiful woman he had fallen for while working in Muar.

We were all excited for Tian and cheered. The commotion drew in Uncle Heng, Yew and Hock who were equally pleased. I was particularly proud, proud of the fact that at last one of my relatives, one of my favourite uncles, was going into a profession that was highly regarded. I could boast that my uncle was a teacher and hold my head up high. As the grown-ups started talking about how far away Penang was I realised I was going to miss him. He had taught me to cycle, patiently holding on to the saddle while I balanced myself on a borrowed bike out on the street in the evenings. I was going to miss seeing him draw and paint on the landing, his guitar-playing, his enthusiasm about the books he had read and our cooking sessions. Just a few months earlier he had shown me how to stir-fry *pak choy*.

This brought back a less happy memory. While we were getting ready to fry – the fire was just right and the wok hot enough- First Uncle came into the kitchen from the alley. We saw him scoop a handful of salt from the jar on the worktop and saw him go out. We looked at each other with a question mark on our faces and returned to the wok. Suddenly we heard a loud commotion in the alley. I rushed out to look, leaving Tian with a ladle in one hand and a

163

bottle of cooking oil in the other. I stood and peered out of the back door and turned to where the noise had come from. There to the left, a stray bitch and dog were in coitus watched by a couple of giggling boys and then I saw Kau do the most wicked and unforgiveable thing. He sprinkled the salt onto the dog's penis. The dog shrieked and yelped pitifully as it jerked itself out of the bitch. I turned away, angry with First Uncle, sorry for the dog and at the same time relieved that Tian didn't see it with me.

In a way, Tian's move to Penang was mine and my sisters' liberation. We moved out of our parents' room into the room he vacated, in between Uncle Soong's and Uncle Heng's. Mother said that we would have their bed when she and Father got a new one but we didn't mind a bit sleeping on the straw mat on the floor.

'It's a lot cooler like that,' we told her as we jumped up and down with grins all over our faces.

We inherited the book case with Tian's books including *Reader's Digest* and all the *Beano* and *Dandy* comics covered in a hint of moth-ball, his collection of abstract oil paintings and large charcoal portraits of Elizabeth Taylor and J.F.Kennedy to which I was to add from my own efforts later.

At dawn during the weekends I could hear the sound of hawkers' stalls rattling along the road to the market or the scraping of the street by the Indian road sweeper. Sometimes from out in the corridor where my cousin Kin slept in his camp bed I could hear the muffled patriotic communist anthem from his radio tuned to Radio China. During the day when I was studying or daydreaming, the sun would beam down on me through the skylight. It didn't matter that the room got hot and sometimes stuffy. Here my sisters and I danced, play-acted or mimicked the Teochew opera with our arms pushed through the legs of our pyjama trousers pretending they were the long sleeves of the costumes as we waved our arms in exaggerated gesticulation and squealed out some drama. At night when I lay on the floor to go to sleep I could sometimes see the moon peering through the skylight and I marvelled at the majesty of the universe. Best of all I could read until as late as I wanted and even after Mother had insisted on lights out I would continue under my blanket with my torch. This room was my space; I felt grown up.

Chapter 17

In 1960, the year before Tian moved to Penang, the government declared that the communist insurgency was no longer a threat and the state of Emergency over. In the year that he started teachers' training, moves were made to create an expanded Malaya to include Singapore, North Borneo, Brunei and Sarawak with its citizen loyal to the nation and not their ethnic group. By the time Tian graduated in 1963, this idea had become a reality and the Federation of Malaysia was born.

To the children in my neighbourhood, a much more important and significant event took place when Ai Chien installed her black and white television on the landing of her shophouse, probably the first one in Hakka Street. My sisters, brother and I were invited to watch whenever we liked and it was usually in the afternoon, after homework had been cleared. Ai Chien's eldest son, affectionately named Big Dog, was in charge of the switching on and off and the selection of programmes. *Zorro*, *Mr Ed the Talking Horse* and *I love Lucy* quickly became the favourites.

I got on well with Big Dog, his brothers Big Head and Little Dog, and sister, Li Sui. The boys attended the Chinese High School where Big Dog was making preparations to go the University of Taiwan. Sometimes I helped them with their English homework which was part of their third language studies. Li Sui who had attended the Chinese primary school was now studying in the same school as me and we often met for a chat on the five-foot way when the shops were closed.

The secondary school that we and my sisters attended was the Temenggong Ibrahim Girls' School or TIGS, a grammar school, situated off the large roundabout with the largest Angsana tree I had ever set eyes on at the top of the town, about a mile away from home. Mei Lin had to

166

walk to school, although sometimes she would save her lunch money for the bus fare home.

'Too hot to walk, Ma,' she explained to Mother when she was asked why she didn't have lunch, 'besides, I couldn't wait to get home to read my book.' She would eat the cold left-overs from lunch at the same time as she immersed herself in her story book or dash to our room, throw her bag down and get on with her homework before she dived back into her book.

I had the good luck to cycle to school. I started at TIGS in 1964 and a year later Father and Mother bought me a bike which was the best thing that happened to me. In the relative cool of the morning air I would meet up with Soo Yin who lived in one of the shop houses on Jalan Ismail - her father owned the optician's shop. The problem with her was that she struggled to get out of bed and usually needed the cane from her mother to wake her up and as a result I always had to wait for her which annoyed me. But once she got her bike out on to the street I would forgive her and we would race up Jalan Rahmat to join up with the other girls who cycled to school. We looked like the Tour De France in full swing. In our pinafore dresses, now bottle green instead of maroon, we were like a green and white river snaking from side to side as we pedalled uphill towards the Angsana tree.

Mei Chin and Mei Choon were still going to Tengku Mariam School by taxi and both still enjoyed going there. Like Mei Chin, Mei Choon also was blessed with dainty features like Mother's whereas Mei Lin and I bore a closer resemblance to Father, mercifully with a smaller Chiang nose. Whenever Mei Choon smiled a dimple on her left cheek would appear and the left corner of her mouth would lift just so slightly higher than the other as if she was teasing. Both of them had Mother's vivaciousness and grace although Mei Choon, surprisingly, was a chatterbox for one in her position as the second youngest. She also had Father's flair for drawing and painting and was seldom without her drawing pad nearby. If she was not twirling or leaping around she was drawing or painting.

Father took a special interest in how she got on with her art, and whenever she was drawing or painting on the landing, taking over from Uncle Tian, he would stand by her and watch, nodding with approval as she mixed her colours to achieve the right shade or tone. She once asked to see where he worked which delighted him and to keep her quiet I took her to the cinema one afternoon after school.

'*Wah*, Papa!' she said, her jaw dropped, her eyes sparkled and her button nose screwed up at the smell of paint and turpentine, 'so many brushes, and paint and paper!'

Father gave a half smile. He was working on a poster and we had arrived just as he was finishing it off with a few strokes of calligraphy beside the face of a fierce-looking tiger.

'*Wah*, papa, this is so good. You're so clever!' she looked at Father with eyes that were about to pop out.

'You can do it too, just need to make the eyes come alive,' he said, stepping back to look at the eyes, tilting his head one way and then the other.

'Papa, will you show me how?' Mei Choon stared at the eyes of the tiger. Father's face broke into a full smile.

Ai Chien once commented jokingly to Mother, 'If you had a coffee shop, you wouldn't need to employ anyone to help you serve, you've got your four daughters to help you.'

Mother had smiled and answered her, 'If I had a coffee shop, I would have other plans for my girls.'

'Pity my sons are so useless, they are not good enough for your daughters,' said Ai Chien.

That had got Mother ruffled as she knew that Ai Chien's son, Little Dog, had taken a fancy to Mei Lin although she was also sure that Mei Lin was completely indifferent to him. She didn't know about Big Head blaring out *Hey Jude* on his LP player in their front room upstairs just for me, so I could listen to it on the five-foot way below. He knew I loved *The Beatles*.

Yao grew into a lovable boy. He was the little brother I was proud to take with me to my friend's house so that Mother could get on with her work. There was a special bond between us, the eldest and the youngest. Not a bit shy, he would rush up to anyone and smile widely showing off his white teeth, as if he was glad to see them. His eyes, more rounded than almond-shaped, sparkled with curiosity and he was not slow to ask questions. Even at this very early age we could see that he was meticulous like Father. One day he had somehow managed to catch a mosquito between his fingers holding it by its legs so that its wings were vibrating furiously. He brought it closer to his ear to listen to it.

'Look, Ma, see how it's flapping its wings. That's what is making the buzzing noise,' he said.

On other occasions we would find him playing with the Singer sewing machine to see how it worked or asking Father what the dynamo on his bike did. When he was almost four years old he moved to join us in our room, carrying his small pile of clothes and worrying more about his army of soldiers, which were matchsticks in a box, than the other toys. When he started school he excelled, leap-frogging from Year One to Year Three as he was way ahead of the rest of his class.

While Father and his two youngest children bonded well I became more and more distant from him.

'You two are so alike, that is the trouble,' said Mother. That was her explanation for why we clashed so badly. She said that both of us were headstrong and bad-tempered, impatient and fastidious.

And he was fussy about his things. One day I heard him grumbling in his room.

'Where is my brush, the one that I always have here?' He sounded angry as he pointed to the exact spot on his desk.

'I don't know,' said Mother.

Earlier I had dusted the room including his desk. Feeling responsible I went and stood in the doorway.

'What are you looking for, Papa?'

'My brush, the calligraphy brush.' He looked through his half a dozen or so brushes neatly laid side by side in order of size again and then went through the pencils and ruler in the pot. He was scowling. 'Did you move it?'

'I moved them all to dust the top and put them back,' I said wondering to myself how I could have mislaid one brush.

'It is not here.'

I bent down on to the floor to look under the table.

'Can't see it here,' I said as I straightened up.

'Don't touch my things here next time.'

There was nothing else I could do but walk out of the room as I muttered, 'I won't bother tidying your room again.'

'Did you hear that?' he raised his voice at Mother. 'You see, that's how disrespectful she has become and it's all your fault.'

***

It is dark. The water has started rising around us. There are shouts, 'Flood! Flood!' I feel the weight of concern for my family's safety. They are near me. I have to do something to save them. The water is still rising and rising fast. I reach for my bed, I can use it as a raft. I help Mother up and make sure she is sitting in the middle of the bed, secure, and then one by one I help my sisters and my brother up. Once we all are up on the bed I feel happy and relieved. The water continues to rise. I look at my family huddled in the middle of the bed. A deep sense of satisfaction comes over me knowing we are all safe.

My alarm clock woke me up at five forty-five a.m. I woke my sisters and Yao. Mei Choon was now in Standard Two. She'd joined Tengku Mariam School the year after I left to start at TIGS. Yao was in Standard One in Montfort Boys' School. Like the *Pied Piper* I led the way shining the torch as we trundled down the corridor then down the stairs. Just as we reached the bottom, the hall light came on. First Uncle appeared in front of us standing by the entrance to the hall. I was surprised and was afraid that he was going to scold me for waking him up.

'Did you not hear your mother and father fighting last night?' he said.

'No,' I answered.

I detected not concern, but glee, in his tone. My heart sank. I had obviously gone to sleep early and slept through the row. I became anxious as I was sure it had to have been a bad row for him to want to make sure I knew about it. I was aware of their muffled arguments which always upset me and I hated it when Father called Mother stupid.

'Your mother left home. Went somewhere, didn't say where.' He waited for a reaction from me as he clicked his little fingernail.

My heart dropped further as worry swept in. I looked at my sisters and Yao who were looking at me, their faces stricken with horror. I couldn't bear to look at First Uncle; I couldn't figure out why he would take such trouble or delight in giving us the bad news. I was angry with him- it was none of his business- but more than that, I was angry with my father and hated what he had done to my mother. I was angry that he didn't come to tell me what had happened instead of letting me hear it from First Uncle. Their room was still in darkness which meant that he was still asleep. Where was Mother? Why didn't he go look for her and bring her back? Most of all I hated the fact that First Uncle was gloating.

I didn't respond to him; instead I quickly ushered the girls and Yao to the kitchen to get away from him.

'Quick, go brush your teeth and wash your face or we will be late,' I said.

Mei Lin had already got the enamel mugs with the toothbrushes down from the top of our cupboard in the hall. Once out of First Uncle's hearing and trying to hide my own anxiety, I said to them, 'Don't worry, I'm sure Ma is alright. Let's get ready quickly.'

171

We brushed our teeth and washed our faces in silence, each preoccupied with our own thoughts. Then while we were eating the sliced bread and coconut curd that Mother had prepared for us the night before, Yao spoke up; there were tears in his eyes.

'Will Ma come back to us?'

'Yes, of course, Ma would never leave us,' said Mei Chin. I could see that she was being brave and fighting back her tears.

'But why did she go away? Is she angry with us?' asked Mei Choon. She looked at me for the answers.

'Where is she?' asked Yao. 'Why didn't Papa go and find her?'

'I don't know,' I said.

'I'm sure Ma is not far away,' said Mei Lin, her eyes moist.

'What if she doesn't come back?' said Mei Choon.

'I will go and find her myself,' said Yao pulling his chest up and sticking his lips out.

'Ma will come home soon, but you mustn't be late home, we don't want any more trouble. Let's go to school and see what happens when we come back,' I said finally.

I wanted to wake Chung Lin up to ask if she knew where Mother was but I knew I couldn't disturb her or her sisters at that time of the morning. I would have to contain my worry and anger.

That afternoon I was the first home from school. I raced up the stairs. Relief quickly displaced my worry when I heard the sound of her sewing machine. I dashed into the room and there she was sitting at her machine, engrossed in her sewing. She looked up.

'Ma! Are you alright?' I searched her face for hints of what she was going through, what she was thinking and how she was feeling. Her eyes looked puffy and I knew she had been crying.

'Yes, yes,' she said.

'Where were you last night, Ma?'

'I was in Aunt Ai Chien's house... I couldn't go far from you,' said Mother. 'Now go and eat your lunch.'

She smiled at me as if to convince me she was really fine and there was no need to fuss. Then we heard Mei Lin come up the stairs. She rushed into the room, breathless. Her face lit up when she saw Mother and she reached out to touch her arm.

'Ma,' she said as she searched mother's face.

'Good girl. Now both of you, go and eat your lunch,' said Mother.

We did as we were told knowing that we would never know what she and father rowed about but were just glad that she was alright.

Later that evening when I was trying to concentrate on my homework in my room, Mother came in with a stack of folded clothes. She put them on the bed and as she did so I got up and walked to her and sat on the bed beside the clothes to look up at her.

'Ma,' I started and then swallowed before saying, 'leave Papa, go away from here. Go anywhere where you will be happy. I will look after my sisters and brother, you won't have to worry about us.'

The words rushed out like a machine gun firing. I had it all planned in my head. After all, I was already shopping, cooking and washing for us since I was twelve. Every morning Mother gave me two dollars to buy the fresh food required for the seven of us. I was considered proficient especially since I could fry fish without it sticking to the wok. She had made sure my sisters and I knew what to do; we all had our chores set out for us from a young age. We each had different jobs. Mei Lin's was to sweep the floor and dust the rooms and help me with washing the clothes while Mei Chin's to wash the dishes. I reckoned we could manage without her, or at least we could function so that she could be free and happy.

Mother looked surprised but she was not angry. 'Don't be silly,' she said. 'How can I leave you all?'

'You can, Ma. I hate seeing you so unhappy, I hate Papa for being so awful to you.'

'Don't talk like that. Last night's argument was my fault.' She placed her cool hand on mine as she sat down beside me. I leant against her, feeling the softness of her arm against mine and rested my head on her shoulder. 'Now, don't you worry, everything is alright. Grown-ups do this sort of thing; it's not nice but it happens.'

I lifted my head and turned to look at her; I couldn't believe it was her fault. Mother was a happy, gentle and kind person. Everybody liked her; everywhere she went she made friends easily. She got on with all sorts of people even the shopkeepers and market traders and especially the fishmonger whom she impressed with her knowledge of fish-she knew her red snapper from her red mullet although she could only afford the small *ikan kuning*. She would always have a game of verbal ping-pong with them. It was never boring going to the market with her; she would show me how to tell if a fish was fresh or she would point out the vegetables that were good for us. 'This prevents cancer,' she would say, pointing to some watercress and show me how to select the best. She always had a ready smile for us.

I hesitated then I blurted out, 'Did Papa hit you?'

I dreaded the answer as soon the words tumbled out.

'Papa wouldn't hit me.' She looked at me as if the idea was preposterous, a slight frown appearing.

I had never seen him strike her but I reasoned that if he could hit me, my sisters and brother, why would my mother be exempt? It would be so easy to reach out and strike Mother when he was inflamed. I dreaded it when my sisters were late coming home from their friends'; if Father's mood was foul, being late for dinner was punishable by caning. I would worry as I cooked, willing them to fly home in time to help set the table or at the very least be present, preferably seated at the table, when he came down for his meal.

Once, Mei Choon came home late from visiting a friend. Father had already sat down at the table. As she

174

walked in from the shop entrance, I could see the anxiety on her face; she was breathless as she approached the table. Mother looked tense; none of us spoke - not that we children were ever allowed to talk during our meal. Father got up, his face taut with anger. He had brought his cane down from his room and laid it on the floor at his feet.

'She is home now, isn't she?' said Mother, trying to placate him.

Without answering he picked up the cane, turned to Mei Choon who looked terrified by now and he struck out at her legs. Her hands stretched out to defend herself but to no avail. The tears came but no screams.

'I won't be late again, Papa, I'm sorry,' was all she could say.

One more strike and I became so incensed and upset at seeing her in pain and yelling that I got up and stood in front of her.

'Papa, enough,' I said calmly.

To my surprise he stopped, his arm dropped to his side and then he sat down at the table. I helped Mei Choon sit down to eat. She was sobbing and feeling thoroughly miserable.

We were only ever late once. The only way to get away without a beating was a legitimate excuse which usually had to do with after-school activities: netball for Mei Chin, hockey and badminton for me, Debating Society for Mei Lin.

I don't remember if I believed it when Mother said Father would not hit her. All I wished was that she could be free and happy.

Chapter 18

My sisters and I were studying when we heard a piercing scream from Third Aunt's room which was next to ours. I charged out of our room and into hers with Mei Chin immediately behind me. Third Aunt was writhing on the bed, her face white and sweaty, her eyes closed, her breathing shallow and rapid as she drew her knees up to her lean body.

I turned to Mei Chin. 'Quick, go and get Ma,' I said, and then went to Third Aunt's side and took her hand. 'Third Aunt, what's the matter? Are you in pain?'

'Yes,' her voice was barely audible, as if she was one her last breath.

'Ma is coming.' Her hand felt cold as she squeezed mine. She opened her eyes and looked straight at me.

'Go fetch your Third Uncle… hurry.'

Before I could move Mother was in the room. She took one look at Third Aunt and said to me, 'Tell Papa to phone for an ambulance then go and fetch Third Uncle.'

On my way down the corridor I met Kin striding towards me, his shoulders raised. He was tall, a head taller than me; his furrowed brow above a face peppered with red spots made him look menacing; It seemed as if he was about to walk through me, although I wasn't sure if that was partly due to the embarrassment of knowing that I had seen his father hitting him the day before.

'What's happening? What's wrong with my mother?' he barked.

We rarely exchanged words although once, quite unexpectedly, we found ourselves on the five-foot way after I had just said goodbye to Soo Yin. He had cycled up and stopped. We acknowledged each other and before I knew it we were discussing religion or more precisely, Christianity, and he ridiculed my attending church.

'She's in a lot of pain,' I answered as I continued walking past him. 'We need to call the ambulance quickly. I'm going to ask my father to do that. You'd better go in and see her.' He pushed past me without another word.

Father was at the top of the stairs. As soon as I had told him the situation, he ran downstairs and headed to Lam's shop to use his telephone.

I ran as fast as I could to the tailor shop on Jalan Idrus where Third Uncle had been working for a long time. He was surprised to see me and as I started to tell him what had happened, his face turned pale. He dropped his sewing and ran out of the shop without a word. I ran after him, keeping a couple steps behind all the way back to the shophouse.

When we arrived Uncle Yew was already in Third Aunt's room with a wicker chair taken from the landing to help carry her downstairs. She was still writhing and now groaning. Mother and Chung Lin moved away to let Third Uncle in beside her. He grabbed her hands.

'We're taking you to the hospital,' he said softly,' you'll be alright.' She nodded.

Kin and his sister Yen were standing in the corner, he was still wearing the scowl while she was sobbing with both hands over her mouth. A wave of pity for them came over me and, at the same time, regret that as cousins we were so far apart even though we lived under the same roof. Yen, who was about the same age as Mei Choon, could be friendly and chatty when she chose to be but was mostly frosty to Mei Choon. She was spoilt, and knew how to whine until her parents gave her what she wanted. Although I wished for us all to be friends, I had little time for her.

'The ambulance is here!' someone shouted from the landing where my curious sisters and cousins were waiting and watching.

Third Uncle and Yew stepped back to let Mother and Chung Lin lift Third Aunt out of the bed and into the chair. Once in, the men lifted the chair and carried her as gently as they could out of the room to the landing with us following behind. My sisters stood aside to let them pass, their hands clasped over their mouths when they saw Third Aunt's white face. Balancing the chair between them as Yew and Third Uncle started to negotiate the stairs, the girls dashed to look through the peepholes in the floor.

I touched Yen's arm. 'Your mother will be alright,' I said.

She didn't respond but kept walking. After she had watched her mother being carried into the ambulance with her father by her side, she and Kin then went back upstairs into their room.

With all the commotion outside in the street, several of the neighbours including Ai Chien had come out on to the five-foot way to see what was going on. Mother had to give a rundown of what had happened to Ai Chien before we went back into the shophouse.

Father was sitting in his chair when we walked into his room, the corners of his mouth turned down. He looked up at us.

'I hope she will be alright,' Mother said as she welled up. 'I feel sorry for the children.' She sat down by the sewing machine. 'She said....she said that if she were to die....I was to make sure that Yen went to live with her sister in Singapore.' She shook her head as she wiped the tears from her eyes.

Father looked sorry but said nothing.

I felt my eyes welling up too. 'I am sure she will be alright,' I said. 'I wonder what caused the pain, what's wrong.'

I couldn't wait to find out; the human body and its workings had become my favourite subject in school. But more than that, I was hoping that this incident, our inadvertent involvement which had been unthinkable until now, would somehow change things between our two families. I couldn't see my father and his brother speaking to each other as if there had never been animosity between them, but I could see us cousins becoming friends. I wanted this wall of ice between us to disappear. The fact that Third

Aunt had actually spoken to Mother, given her the responsibility of her daughter's welfare, seemed to me that the melting of the icy barrier might have begun. We could only wait. Wait to hear if Third Aunt would recover, wait to see if this was indeed the watershed I was wishing for and the mark of a new beginning in our relationship.

Later I went to see Kin and Yen in their room to ask if they would like some dinner. They were sitting at the table doing their homework.

'I'm hungry, yes,' said Yen nodding, her large eyes fixed on me as if she wasn't sure she should accept my offer.

'Come on then, we'll go down and eat. What about you?' I turned to Kin. Although his face had relaxed a little he didn't look at me; he looked at Yen.

'No.' A pause and then to Yen, 'You go and eat if you want.'

Yen nodded again and seemed relieved that her brother had given permission.

I took her hand and led her downstairs. When Mei Lin saw us she got up from the table to get her a bowl of rice.

'Come and eat,' said Mother reaching her hand out to Yen.

It was late that night when Third Uncle came home. Unusually for him, his shirt was creased, his face drawn. Uncle Heng was in the shop when he walked in.

'Ah, Soong, how is Yin Li?' he asked as he rose from his stool.

'The doctor is operating on her now,' he replied.

'That's serious,' Uncle Heng said, looking solemn. 'At least she is being treated now.'

Uncle Heng didn't ask nor did Third Uncle explain what the problem was. When he saw Mother, Chung Lin and me on the landing waiting for news he said quietly,

'The doctor said she was pregnant.' Looking embarrassed he continued, 'The foetus got lodged in the tube instead of the womb. They are operating on her now.'

Mother nodded and at that moment Kin and Yen had come up to him. He turned to them.

'Your mother will be alright. You can see her tomorrow morning.'

'That is good…Have you eaten yet?' asked Mother.

'No. I don't want anything,' he replied as he walked away with his children to their room.

Third Aunt returned home a few days later. When we heard her coming into the shop we ran out to meet her, pleased that she was well again. Mother had brewed some chrysanthemum tea and made me take her a mug. She was sitting on the edge of her bed leaning against the headboard looking tired although her cheeks had a healthy colour compared to the last time I saw her there.

'Third Aunt, Mother said to give this to you,' I said, both hands holding the mug to her. She took it from me.

'Thank you,' she said and started to sip it.

I waited. I was hoping that she would say something to me, anything, to indicate that we were on new footing. She put the mug on the table by the bed and shut her eyes as if dismissing me. I waited another minute or so. Realising that nothing was forthcoming I walked out of the room and went to my mother in her room. She looked up from her sewing machine.

'I don't think anything's changed, Ma,' I said.

She knew what I meant.

'Hmmm.' She gave me a look that said she was not surprised. My face must have shown my disappointment. 'Never mind,' she continued and then carried on with her sewing, the sound of the machine drowning the whirring noise of the new table fan that Father had bought.

'What are you making now?' I touched the fabric she was stitching. It was cerise pink cotton which felt soft and light.

'A skirt, a layered skirt,' she said as she stopped machining, pulled the fabric away from the footer and then cut the thread. She lifted it up to show me and then put it against my waist even though it was too small for me 'It is bias cut and there are two layers to make the skirt fuller. What do you think?'

I looked down at it. '*Wah,* I like it! Ma, can you make me one like it?'

She smiled, took the skirt and placed it on the machine again. 'When I have time,' she said. 'Now I have to finish this and see whether other people like it or not.'

'They will definitely like it,' I said. I was sure of that.

Mother had been working very hard and never seemed to have any time off. There was never enough time for her to go to the cinema like she used to when we were younger, but she didn't seem to mind or complain. It was this work and the sale of her dresses that enabled her and Father to pay off their debts.

The debts had been particularly hard for Father to bear.

One afternoon he called Mei Chin into his room. He was sitting in his chair and holding a creased bit of paper in his hand. She immediately recognised it as the note she had scrunched up earlier. She realised that she must have dropped it outside his room and he had picked it up when he came home. She became afraid of what he was going to say or do. He had opened it and read what was written on it,

Pay me back my money. Joo Lee.

'What is this about?' he asked, his voice was calm.

Mother looked at her.

'I…I was hungry during recess and borrowed ten cents from her to buy something else to eat,' said Mei Chin. Her face was as solemn as Father's; she was regretting eating the cake she didn't really need after the bowl of noodles she had bought with her lunch money and was now dreading the consequences.

'If you ever need more money for anything ask me or your mother. You don't have to borrow from your friends, do you hear?' His voice was controlled, barely concealing the anger running through him. He dipped his hand into his trouser pocket and brought out a ten cents coin. 'Pay your friend first thing tomorrow morning.'

Mei Chin knew she had got off lightly and as she walked away from the room she heard him explode, saying to Mother,

'Don't we give her enough money? Start borrowing now, where will it lead? Don't you know what your daughter is doing?'

The orders for Mother's dresses kept coming from Wei and they tripled when Chinese New Year or the Malay *Hari Raya* was approaching. When I mentioned to Mother that she was working too hard, she said, 'My worry is that there won't be enough work. Hard work won't kill me.'

She continued machining, the noise of the machine stopped me speaking and when she paused, I quickly said, 'I'm sorry I can't help you, I mean really help, apart from sewing the odd button or sweeping the floor after you.'

'Your help is to study hard and keep an eye on your sisters and brother.'

She started machining again and then stopped to look at me.

'I've been thinking that I might recruit Chung Lin. Teach her to stitch, yes, she can sew but she needs to know how to do it properly and neatly. We can double the output that way, if not more. Papa thinks it's a good idea.'

Chung Lin's laundry business had kept her fully occupied with her younger sister Fah helping her. The two of them had built up a large clientele but she wasn't satisfied. She wanted to be able to do something less backbreaking and had once hinted to Mother that she would like to learn to sew properly. Mother had not taken her seriously then but now she was considering recruiting her.

Twenty-two years old was approaching the marry-by date according to the matchmakers. Although Chung Lin was sometimes depressed by her belief that she was doomed to be a spinster she had somehow come to terms with it. She knew she didn't have to worry about the older siblings. Lee was a great cook and housekeeper and had been snapped up as a housekeeper-cum-cook for the wealthy manager of the Overseas Chinese Banking Corporation on Jalan Rahmat. Koo had decided he wanted to be a goldsmith and took up an apprenticeship with the jeweller at the corner of Hakka Street and Jalan Rahmat. To Chung Lin's relief his boss fed him in the shop so there was one mouth less to feed.

It was Fook she worried about. He was still so young but not in school because he hated it. He and Yao would play together with their fighting fishes or fly their kites in the field nearby. Other than that he did very much what he wanted and as long as she had him to look after, her chances of marriage were slim. She had hoped that the new woman in her father's life, now that it had come out in the open, would offer to take some responsibility but there was no such luck.

I recall the day he brought the woman home without any warning.

Chung Lin was all set to start on her ironing marathon- the two baskets of washing next to the table where she had laid out the thick covering, the new electric iron that she had invested in was poised ready for use and the transistor tuned to receive the afternoon story at two o'clock. The window was opened wide to catch what little breeze there was. I was sitting in front of the window watching Mei Choon engrossed in a new piece of work at her drawing table. Chung Lin had just started ironing when we heard Fah calling as she ran up the stairs,

'Big Sister, *Pak* is here! He's got a woman with him!' She tried to keep her voice down. 'They are coming up the alley!'

When she got to the landing she tossed her plait behind her shoulder and then started waving her hands to beckon Chung Lin to go downstairs.

Chung Lin had already switched off the iron.

'What are you talking about?' she asked.

'It's *Pak*, he's brought a woman here. You better go downstairs.'

183

Chung Lin, frowning, walked slowly to the top of the stairs as if still taking in what Fah had said, then peered down before descending.

In the meantime Mei Choon and I had dived down onto the floor and stuck our eyes over the holes. When Chung Lin got to the bottom of the stairs and had just put on her clogs, she saw her father and the woman entering the hall. I waited until all I could see was the tops of their heads. Then I tiptoed to my mother's room.

'Ma, they're here,' I whispered knowing she would have heard Fah earlier.

'You're nosey,' she said as she got up from her stool and walked out of the room to the top of the stairs.

'I want to know what she is like.'

We were all curious – the whole household had been wondering and wanted to know who this woman was and what she looked like. Having heard it confirmed that she had something to do with a coffee shop, I had imagined her with a coat of skin-coloured foundation painted on her face like a geisha girl and bright red lips. I was surprised at what I saw.

When we got downstairs, we heard her say, 'You must be Chung Lin,' as she smiled at Chung Lin.

Her voice was kind and soft. Her face was without make-up except for a touch of pale pink lipstick; there was a sprinkle of freckles over her cheeks. Her almond-shaped eyes radiated warmth, they seemed to implore us not to judge her. She was petite and had short wavy hair. She wore a blue floral shift with a matching blue bag and brown high-heeled shoes; a thick gold necklace and sapphire earrings were all the jewellery she wore.

'Yes,' answered Chung Lin, looking disconcerted. She had immediately felt self-conscious knowing that she looked dishevelled in her *samfoo* in contrast to the immaculate woman before her. She had wanted to hate the woman who had taken her father away from his family but facing her now she couldn't help feeling disarmed by her genuine smile.

By the time the stranger was introduced to Mother, and the rest of us she was accepted by the entire household and her position as 'Younger Aunt', in deference to First Aunt, was secured. We were enamoured by her charming manners; she had turned out to be quite different from what we expected. Despite the fact that she did work in one of the coffee shops she was homely and down-to-earth, not the frivolous empty-headed man-eater we had expected. Mother liked her instantly and the two of them got on right away.

After that unexpected introduction First Uncle moved out to live with Younger Aunt and only came to the shophouse during the day.

Chapter 19

Hockey practice over, Soo Yin and I got ready to go home. I might have been butter-fingers when it came to netball but put a badminton racket or a hockey stick in my hands and I was a different animal: a tiger. In hockey I played the left half position in the school team while Soo Yin who was fast on her feet played right wing. We'd had a good workout and I was feeling exhilarated.

We pushed our bikes up the slope from school and on to the roundabout. It had been extremely dry for weeks and there was a faint whiff of orange fragrance from the yellow flowers of the Angsana, most of which had started to drop like confetti under the canopy of the giant tree. Then side by side we free-wheeled down the main street. I felt happy and free as we cut through the air which cooled our skin, aiming at the wobbly yolk of the sinking sun beyond the river.

'You want to go to Youth Fellowship tonight?' Soo Yin called out above the sound of the traffic, her long black hair swirling in the wind behind her. How I envied her hair, naturally wavy and glossy while mine was dead straight and shoulder length.We had been best friends since Kindergarten and we often did things together after school like sharing a coco-cola float at the new milk-bar when I could afford it. We confided in each other about most things. Although she was tough on the hockey field, off the field she was lady-like, much more so than I was. I always thought we were like chilli and chive, so different –she was elegant, pretty and graceful while I was plain and a tomboy; she often seemed to have her head in the clouds while my feet were clamped to the earth - and yet we got on very well.

'Not sure,' I shouted back.

I was mindful of the remark that Third Aunty had made to Chung Lin within my hearing, 'This western religion…who will keep up praying to your grandfather and grandmother?'

They were not my gods, nor were they my idols. It was clear in my mind that I could and would continue to talk to Grandfather Chun Hong. I was more afraid of approaching my father to ask for permission to go to church although he hadn't objected the very first time I asked after our classmate, Bee, had pestered us to go saying that she would pick us up in her father's chauffeur-driven car.

A bus was waiting at the bus stop. I moved to its right but it pulled out without indicating and as I was already speeding I found myself racing with it. The driver hooted at me and when I had passed him I stuck my tongue out at him.

'What about you? You going?' I asked.

'Yes. Come, *lah.*'

'I have to ask my father.'

'Good. As long as you are not seeing *that fellow*,' she said making a face.

I grinned and shook my head.

We said goodbye and parted ways at the junction with Jalan Ismail. When I got home I parked my bike on the five-foot way and locked it. Mr Ting was putting away a pair of half-finished football boots on his shelf, Leng was tidying the worktable while Uncle Heng, standing at his sewing machine, was scraping the bottom of his starch bowl. I caught a whiff of the sour smell from it as I walked into the shop.

'Time to make a new bowl of starch, Uncle Heng,' I said.

He looked up at me and smiled. 'So, did you win this time?' he asked.

'Yes, we won, of course,' I replied.

'Good. There is a prize waiting for you inside,' he tilted his head towards the hall.

'What prize?'

'Can't you smell it?'

I sniffed at the air but detected nothing until I stepped inside the hall. I gasped when I saw a large basket of

187

durian, my favourite fruit, sitting on the floor by the dining table where Father, the girls and Yao were still eating their dinner. Yew was standing over the basket.

'*Wah*, this is from good stock. Smells really good,' he said. There was at least a dozen of the hard spiky fruit.

Mother saw me as she walked in from the kitchen with a bowl of steaming soup in her hands.

'*Aiyahh*,' she said, 'Ah Leong just dropped this off a few minutes ago. *Aiyahh*, really, I wish his father wouldn't do this. I can't afford to reciprocate.' She laid the bowl down in the centre of the table.

'I hope he doesn't think we are starving,' said Father.

'It's a lot of fruit,' I said. We could never have afforded anything like that. One fruit shared between us all was a luxury.

'Ah Leong said it was from his father's plantation.' Lian turned to Jung. 'His father's got an ulterior motive, to do with Chiew and his son.' She shook her head. 'It's premature. *Aiyahh*, this man didn't get where he is today without knowing how to shower people with gifts. I don't feel comfortable taking his gifts.'

I burst out laughing. The girls giggled; I saw the glee on their faces as they eyed the durian.

'Ma, we're just friends and it's only food. Let's eat,' I said. I leant my hockey stick against the wall and bent down to inhale the heavenly aroma of the fruit which sent all my senses tingling and my salivary glands into overdrive.

'You don't know, it's a sort of bribe,' said Mother, shaking her head.

'Can I skip dinner and eat this instead, Ma?'

'No, eat your dinner. There's chilli bean curd, go get yourself a bowl of rice.' She was convinced that accepting the gift would be misconstrued as collusion. 'Yew, you take one, give one to Mr Ting and ask Uncle Heng to come in to eat.' As an afterthought to me, she added, 'Don't eat too much, it is hot food and you don't want to get sick.'

Ah Leong's father had a formidable reputation. It was said that he was subservient to the Japanese during the Occupation that he did more than bow to them although no one could say what it was that he did and was rewarded for it. It was said that this was how he had made his fortune. He owned three goldsmith shops in Hakka Street, one in Kuala Lumpur and three motorcars that we knew of. Not just an astute businessman he also made sure his workers were trustworthy. One story told about him was that he would deliberately leave a dollar note on the floor before a new worker started sweeping to see their response. We knew of his three wives, each of whom had a house in different parts of Batu Pahat and there was a rumour that there was a fourth one in another town.

According to Mother his second wife had told her, when they met in the market, that having seen me a couple of times he approved of me. He had gone so far as to say that I would make a good match for Ah Leong. I knew Ah Leong through his sister, Ai Ming, who was in my class. Older than us, he was good-looking, charming and friendly, a great catch. Who wouldn't be flattered if he was interested in them? We had talked about school and sports but I wasn't romantically inclined towards him, at least not initially. I didn't think too much about his father's gifts or intentions, after all at sixteen I was too young, marriage hadn't appeared on my radar yet. I had just passed my Lower Certificate of Education exams and was now aiming to do well for my Cambridge School Certificate.

Later that evening I was in my room when I heard Chung Lin calling from downstairs,

'Chiew, your friend is here!'

Mei Chin and Mei Choon who had been combing each other's hair stopped what they were doing and scrambled out of the room, started tip-toeing when they got to the landing and then crawling to the peep-holes. Yao who had been watching his blue fighting fish was not far behind. He was very protective towards me when male friends came to visit. I stood quietly in the corridor, waiting for them to

189

tell me who had come to see me downstairs. Mei Chin crept quietly towards me.

'It's Ah Leong,' she whispered in English. 'What you want to do?'

'Go tell him I'm not here, I've gone to see a friend,' I whispered back.

'Tell him to go away,' Yao mimicked us whispering.

Mei Chin nodded and with a big grin pulled her shoulders up to her ears, dashed to the top of the stairs and then straightened up before shouting in Hakka, 'She is not at home.' She could see Ah Leong standing at the entrance behind Chung Lin.

I waited to hear what Mei Chin had to report, not daring to make a sound and hoping that Chung Lin would not give the game away. Mei Choon was glued to the hole.

'That's alright, I'll call another time,' I heard Ah Leong say and then Mei Chin came running to me.

'Did you hear that? He will call another time,' she said.

I nodded. 'I'll deal with that when it happens. Better not go out now.'

She then tip-toed back and pushed Yao away from the hole so she could check that Ah Leong had gone.

'You don't like him, *ah*?' asked Mei Choon when we were back in our room. Mei Lin looked up from her book.

'I also don't like him,' Yao chipped in as he returned to his fish bowl on the table.

I screwed my nose and shrugged. 'He's nice. *Ya*, I know I should thank him for the durian and all that, but I can do that another time.'

'My friends think he is very handsome,' said Mei Chin watching my face to see my reaction. She and Mei Choon repositioned themselves on the bed and then she picked up her comb from the bed to comb Mei Choon's hair.

'How come they know?' I asked.

'In his father's shop, they saw him.'

'And how come they know who he is?'

'O.K. I tell them,' said Mei Chin, feigning guilt.

'*Told* – past tense. Not *tell.*'

'O.K. I *told* them,' Mei Chin said with a grin.

'Handsome isn't everything, you know,' I said.

'Ya, it is! I don't want to be with someone who got a face like a pig.'

We laughed.

'No,' I said and then turning to Mei Lin, 'He wants to be a businessman, like his father. He's not interested in Shakespeare or any of the books I told him about.'

Mei Lin pulled a face. 'So what do you talk about?'

'He can talk a lot, maybe that's the trouble. He talks like he knows everything. And he has this habit of making this irritating sound at the back of his throat, like….'

'Like a turkey coughing..' said Mei Choon

'Like a pig snorting..'said Yao.

We all giggled.

'Ugh!' said Mei Lin. 'You should just thank him for the durians, maybe he will bring some more.'

'Ya!' Mei Chin and Mei Choon shouted in unison.

I felt I was caught in a fast-moving current; everything around me seemed to be changing, the worst of which was what was being done to my playground.

There had been a mushrooming of buildings in town and the playground was clearly a prime location for shops. We - the children who had outgrown the playground and the younger ones who came after us - were devastated that it was going to be concreted over.

'Where are we to play when it is gone?' the younger ones looked at each other and asked, dismay written all over their little faces.

Each family had had to clear away their stacks of firewood in readiness for the building and without any warning the diggers came one morning. We stood in the alley, as if in mourning, and watched.

Had I known earlier I would have gone to pick that last hibiscus flower. Instead I watched silently as one of the

191

diggers yanked the tree out of the earth and threw it with its roots dangling into the skip. I was cross that it was treated with no regard but I stood by, helpless. I felt like a friend had been ripped away from me. I wanted to cry but was afraid that the others would laugh at me. The tree was still holding out one flower.

Then an army of male and female workers, wearing straw hats and well covered against the sun, descended on the ground with their cement mixers, hoes and yokes and baskets. Not long after, a box-shaped building materialised housing a car showroom and a restaurant with full air-conditioning. Our playground was now relegated to history.

But as one playground closed, another opened up for me. As soon as my uncle Tian qualified he was posted to Kota Tinggi, a small town on the east coast, just a short distance from Johore Bahru. He was to teach English and geography in the secondary school and this was where he had carved out a new life for himself. Father remarked how lucky he was not to be posted to some far flung, mosquito-infested village in the jungle in the north.

Kota Tinggi was divided by a river with Tian's school on the side that had only recently been cleared of the jungle for building. The rented house where he lived was also on this side, just on the edge of the school field. On the other side of the river, accessed by a concrete bridge, was the built up town area of shops. Everyone seemed to know everyone here and the teachers including Tian were well respected by the community.

A few months after he had started teaching, he came back to Hakka Street, causing a stir when he arrived in his new Beetle. All of us children rushed out to cheer him where his car was parked on the street while the grown-ups looked on calmly. Heng was all smiles and nodded his head in approval. Father was also beaming although he couldn't help wondering what his cousin in China would say if he knew of Tian's new acquisition.

'*Wahh*, you've done well,' said Heng still nodding his head. 'This is an achievement.'

Everyone had crowded around to look at the pale blue car and touch it.

'Uncle Heng, how are you?' said Tian, smiling.

'Good, good....What make is it?'

'Volkswagen. It's made in Germany.'

'*Wok-ss-wa-gong,*' Heng repeated softly.

'*Wahh*, Tian, beautiful car!' Jung was stroking the bonnet.

'Look inside, Second Brother.' Tian opened the driver's door to show off the smart upholstered seats. Yao squeezed in between them and tried to push his way into the car.

'I want to drive, show me how, Uncle,' he said.

Tian laughed and rubbed Yao's head. 'You have to wait till you are older.'

After lunch, Tian gave out presents to everyone. When he came to me, he handed me a brown paper bag. I looked inside and let out a squeal.

'It's just what I wanted!'

It was a brown handbag. All my friends had one and now I too had one. It didn't matter that it was mock leather; I was jumping up and down with joy.

Tian smiled. 'You can all come and visit me during your holidays,' he said. 'I can come for you and also drive you back.'

We jumped at the chance and so began my and Mei Choon's regular visits to Kota Tinggi during the school holidays. Here we made friends with Tian's students who invited us to join them on their outings including hillwalking in the jungle. But the best thing was being at the waterfall at Lombong, about half an hour's drive away from Tian's house.

This was my new playground where I swam and dreamt, rested and then swam and dreamt again to the sound of water falling into the pool. Unlike my previous playground, there was not a smidgen of concrete around me.

193

I'd dive from a rock ledge into the cool water which reflected the green jungle and blue sky or float face up and watch the dragonflies and butterflies as they flitted between the scented flowers borne on the tall trees bordering the pool. I'd drift on my back, marvelling at the beauty around me, soaking up the peace and calm until the noisy hordes of day-trippers descended on the place at the weekends with their rubber floats and baskets packed with chicken curry, *nasi goreng* and *mee siam*.

Our holidays with Tian gave me a taste of the kind of life which until then I could only look in from the outside. Driving about in his spanking new Beetle, eating out instead of sweating over a hot stove, never worrying about being short of anything, it was sublime. It certainly beat rinsing out sauce bottles to sell to the scrap merchant for a few cents to supplement my pocket money. Best of all I got to shop at *C.K. Tang's* and *Robinson's* departmental stores in Singapore, shops that my friends frequently boasted about but until now were places I could only dream of going to. Before that the only thing that I could boast about was being able to take my friends to the movies for free, which was how we got to see Elvis Presley in *Blue Hawaii* and *Kid Galahad* and Cliff Richard in *Summer Holiday*.

My friends' interest in fashion and clothes had its use: it nudged my mother's creativity in the direction that she'd been wanting to explore for some time. Making clothes for me and my sisters as we got older provided her with the challenge of getting not just the style right but more importantly the fit over the curves perfect. When my friends started asking Mother if she would make dresses for them too, she was delighted.

The landing became a tailor's workshop with Chung Lin working at her own machine which she brought up from the shop, now competent in sewing and boasting that she made the most perfect buttonholes. Instead of just frocks for little girls, now Bermuda shorts, bell-bottoms, miniskirts, A-line dresses and halter-neck dresses came off the production line, each with Mother's own variation of the fashion to suit the fabric and the client.

Sitting in his chair in his room, Father would look out and watch the buzz of activities on the landing. Then one day he said to Mother,

'I think we should take over First Brother's half of the shopfloor.'

Chapter 20

Knowing that Younger Aunt had a big sway over First Uncle, Father waited until she was present before he put his proposal to use his half of the shop for Mother's business. Younger Aunt enthused about the plan and commended Mother on her efforts. First Uncle didn't have much choice but to agree then quickly demanded a rent of a hundred dollars per month. It was agreed that Uncle Heng would continue working in the shop as he had a stream of regular customers.

Father immediately took charge of the redecorating guided by Mother's instructions. First Uncle stayed away and for once, all of the rest of our two families were united and worked together. Everyone including the youngest boys, Fook and Yao, helped to clear, wash, clean and scrub. We polished the glass cabinets that stank of mothballs and the sewing machines wrapped in dust and cobwebs then white-washed the walls. The sewing machine in Mother's room and the landing were brought down into the shop again. Mother had insisted on having a small cubicle with a tall mirror as a changing room, so a carpenter had to be called in to build it.

It was when Father was polishing the original signboard with the shop name which Grandfather Chun Hong had put up that he became emotional. Mother noticed his tear and suggested that they should retain the name but have a smaller sign with the name *Lotus Dressmaking* in English as well as Chinese under it. It was the name that Father had suggested when he decided that Mother's clothes should have a label; it was after Mother whose name means *Lotus* in Mandarin.

Once the display window, cabinets and the worktop were re-fitted the place was transformed. The dull grey, brown and blue of the men's fabric were now replaced with the bright rainbow colours of women's dresses which Mother hung in the window. Her scissors, tape measures, pencils and a new ledger were neatly arranged on one side of the worktop.

On the day that we put the finishing touches to the shop, there were curious stares from passers-by on the five-foot way, some stopping to enquire when the shop was opening. In the other half of the shop Mr Ting finished hammering the last nail into a boot that he was working on and looked up to see what we had achieved.

'You will be wanting my half of the shop next,' he said to Mother, grinning.

'Not likely,' replied Mother. 'But why don't you make ladies' shoes? That way we can complement one another. I fit the customers with dresses and you fit them with shoes.'

Mr Ting laughed then shook his head as he rubbed the boot on his lap. 'I'll have to start all over again and learn to make them. No, no, I'll stick with these.'

Heng who for days had been watching the transformation now stood back to survey the new cabinets and the display window. His eyes glistened as he gently nodded his head.

'*Ahh*, takes me back,' he said softly. 'Chun Hong would have approved.'

The next day, opening day, all of us who had helped were in the shop to share in the excitement and anticipation of the new venture. Just before the opening Mother took a dozen bottles of *Brand's Essence of Chicken* and a box of cake to Wei to say thank you for her encouragement while Father burnt joss sticks at Grandfather and Grandmother's shrine.

When she returned to the shop Mother had insisted on putting out sweets and cookies on the work top.

'Come every one, come, let's drink and eat,' she called out to us all.

It was truly a day of celebration as all of the neighbours including Ai Chien came to congratulate Mother and Father. I'd never seen Chung Lin so happy, smiling so much, dressed not in her usual *samfoo* but in a red floral frock which she had made herself. Shoppers stopped to admire the display of Mother's handiwork and asked about costs. Then to her delight a woman wanted a blouse made to order and started to tell her what she had in mind.

The best surprise of all was when my maternal grandparents and uncles turned up.

'So, all that struggle and fighting with the sewing was worth it,' Grandfather Shao said to Mother, a big smile on his face and holding a cheroot between his fingers ready to put in his mouth. He was thinking of the time when he was teaching her as a little girl to sew and she would cry whenever she had to unpick. 'Here, this is to help you add up all the money that comes in.'

He handed Mother a new abacus. 'Every business should have one.'

Poh, Mother's second brother who was a salesman for a tyre company in Singapore, had been fascinated and interested in what she had done; he had wandered around the shop feeling the fabric and admiring her handiwork.

'This is good quality stuff,' he said to Mother. 'I'm sure that it will sell very well in Singapore. Perhaps you ought to explore having an outlet there.'

'I'm glad you think it is good,' replied Mother, looking pleased. 'One step at a time. Let's see how this works out here first.'

'Think about it. I've contacts there. I can easily put you in touch with someone.' Poh stopped suddenly and looked like inspiration had struck him. He became excited. 'Better still, I could be your partner.'

Mother smiled. 'Let's wait and see.'

In that same year, 1968, my classmates and I were to sit the Cambridge School Certificate examination.

It was recess. My good friend and classmate Suriati and I had just finished our duty as Prefects checking that the school grounds were litter-free after sending out groups of students to pick up rubbish. We walked over to join a group of our classmates under the Flame-of-the-Forest tree at the edge of the school field. I loosened the collar and necktie that was part of our Prefects' uniform, glad to be in the shade at last. A gentle gust of breeze swept through as I wiped the perspiration from my forehead.

There'd been animated discussions in the group. The talk had got round to our plans for the future, we'd not long started our last year in school.

'…I'm going to do nursing in England,' said one.

'*Wah*, you want to go so far,' said another.

'*Ya*, the English training is the best, accepted all over the world. I can then go to Canada or Australia to work if I want.'

'I just wanna get married and have lots of children!' someone else said, spreading her arms out and giggling which made the others giggle too.

'You have to find a boyfriend first.'

'Ah, I don't say anymore.'

'I think I want to be teacher. Like Mrs Lim…' said Maznah. We laughed as she mimicked Mrs Lim, our Head mistress, balancing on her high wedge shoes and peering over her spectacles.

'I am going to Australia to do matriculation,' someone else piped up.

'What? What's matriculation?'

'You're alright, you're good at your studies.'

'What about you two?' Bee asked looking at me and Suriati.

'I'm going to Sixth Form in Johore Bahru,' replied Suriati without hesitation.

'*Wah*, so sure, *ah*.'

'You, Chiew?'

I hesitated and then I said, 'I want to go to university.'

'That means Sixth Form for you, *lah*,' someone pointed out.

'Me too,' said Maznah, her voice serious now. 'I don't know what I want to be yet but I know I also want to go to university.'

'Hey, Chiew what about your boyfriend?' asked Nona who had said she wanted to be secretary.

'What boyfriend?' asked Yeoh. 'Nobody told me about it.'

'Ai Ming's brother, *lah*. Hey, he's very handsome,' replied Nona, smiling teasingly at me.

'No, *lah*,' I quickly denied it. 'He is only a friend.'

I looked at Ai Ming who was also smiling at me.

'He likes you very much and I don't mind you for a sister-in-law,' she said.

At that all the girls laughed but when I looked at Soo Yin, she wasn't smiling. She'd told me before that she didn't think Ah Leong was good enough for me.

'He's just a friend,' I repeated.

'*Alamak*, don't be shy, *lah*.'

'You know, I think you'll be the first one to get married and have lots of children,' Yeoh said thoughtfully.

'Why?' I was surprised why anyone would say that.

'Because you're so homely, you cook and do everything a housewife should do. Make a good wife, *lah*.' She chuckled as the others nodded their agreement.

Later on the way home from school I thought about what Yeoh had said. It seemed so unfair. Just because I didn't go partying and gallivanting like they did didn't mean I was going to be the first to settle down. If I could, I too would have gone down to Singapore to shop with them and even go and meet up with American 'red-haired devils' in Sembawang.

I had hesitated about saying that I too wanted to go to Sixth Form. It would mean going to study in Muar, a town an hour's journey along the coast north of Batu Pahat. It was the nearest town where there was a Sixth Form college but it would mean a huge amount of money that my parents would have to pay each month if I were to study there. I knew it wasn't feasible, unaffordable when there were five of us needing school fees. Mother's business had started well but I wasn't sure that it could stand the cost of my studying in Muar. There'd been talk of co-ed Sixth Form classes starting in the boys' High School in Batu Pahat which would be my only hope of ever taking the next step to university.

Earlier in class everyone had been excited at the prospect of the major change of stepping into the adult world. Some of our Malay friends who had travelled miles from the villages around had said they would leave school at the end of the year, get married and have children. Others had said they would go to college; they would have no trouble as MARA - the Council created by the government for the development of the indigenous people which excluded the non-Malays- was there ready to assist them in whatever they wanted to do. As we discussed our choices of careers and ambitions, the divide and the inequality between the Malays and non-Malays were now becoming obvious and real to us although we didn't talk about them.

For the adults it was different.

The government's language and educational policies had stirred up old feelings that didn't lie too deeply beneath the veneer of social harmony. There were plans not only to install Malay as the medium of instruction but eventually to conduct the Cambridge School Certificate and Higher School Certificate exams in Malay.

'But what is the point?' said Jung, a note of exasperation nailed to his voice.

The shops had not long closed and he, Heng, Mr Ting and Lam had brought their stools outside to have coffee on the five-foot way.

'This language is of no use outside Malaysia,' he continued. 'Our children can't communicate with foreigners in Malay. Their Malay certificates will be useless abroad. It's so short–sighted of the government.'

'Look at what they want to do to the Chinese High School!' said Lam, the vein in his neck bulged. 'Close it down. Then what is going to happen to our language? Good thing my Big Dog and Big Head have graduated. As for Little Dog….*ahh*,' he shook his head, 'we'll have to wait and see.'

'What else are they going to throw at us? They can't submerge us Chinese or throw us out!' said Mr Ting.

'*That's* just it!' said Heng. 'They *are* throwing us out. Many people are leaving. Take that doctor Lim on the next street. He's going to close his practice and emigrate to Australia. They are chasing away our clever people, the doctors and teachers.' He took a deep breath before continuing. 'That chap who owns the hardware shop on the main road, his son is also going to Australia. Can't get there fast enough. He said there was no future here for his children.'

'I suppose Australia is better than here. I heard they don't allow Chinese into the 'whites only' toilets,' said Lam, slapping his arm where a mosquito had just landed. 'I also read in today's paper that a Chinese businessman converted to Islam, changed his name to a Malay name and guess what? He has all the help and incentives he wants from the government!' He flicked the flattened insect off his arm.

'It's all right if you've got the money to emigrate,' said Jung.

'Ah, pigs! What do they know? Lazy lot and they have everything handed to them!' said Mr Ting.

'They want us to give them a generation to catch up with us Chinese. As if they could!' said Lam.

'Our Chinese party isn't doing very much for us,' said Mr Ting. 'They're useless! Giving in to the Malays as usual. It makes you want to vote for the communist party.'

'Maybe we should vote for the new party this time,' said Lam clenching his lips as if he had decided.

'Yes, this new party, *Gerakan*, sounds promising,' said Jung. 'They say they're fighting for equal rights, equal opportunities no matter what the colour of your skin. We've heard it all before but maybe this one will deliver.'

202

'What is the use of voting for them? The Alliance will still win, you'll see,' said Mr Ting shaking his head as he picked up his cup of coffee.

'I agree,' said Lam. 'What's the point of voting? The Malay pigs will get what they want as always.'

Jung gulped his drink. 'No, we must vote! Vote for the *Gerakan* and see if it makes any difference.'

'So far Tungku Abdul Rahman has been fair and reasonable but he'll surely give in to the more extremist in his party. What else can he do but give in to their demands, more rights for the Malays, *again*,' said Heng. He picked up the coffee pot and topped up everyone's cup.

'We're being pushed out, that's for sure.' Lam nodded vigorously.

'I still think that we should give the *Gerakan* a chance,' said Jung.

As the men sipped their coffee there was a sense of expectancy born of a wish to see change but there was also a strong conviction that they would be disappointed.

There was a great deal of excitement over Mei Choon and Yao's award of a bursary from the Shaw Brothers, the owners of the cinema where Father worked, for the under-twelve children of their employees who had done well in their end of year exam. We were overjoyed. Father and Mother were immensely proud although they never said so but it showed on their faces. The bursary was a hundred dollars for each child plus lots of goodies like books.

'*Wah*, Papa, that is *a lot* of money,' said Yao, his eyes rounder than ever.

Father nodded. 'Yes.'

'You can have it all, Papa.'

Father smiled. 'I will keep it for your school fees, that's what it is for.'

'Maybe I can have a toy car?' Yao searched Father's face. 'Just a tiny one?' He brought his hands close together to show Father the size he had in mind.

'All right. We can look for one when we are in Kuala Lumpur.'

Yao jumped up in the air, throwing his arms about. 'Thank you, Papa!'

'Papa, I don't want anything,' said Mei Choon. 'Maybe I'll buy Ma something.'

The presentation of the awards was to be held in Kuala Lumpur. We'd been there once before, years ago when Mei Lin, Mei Chin and I had won the award. It'd been a wonderful trip then, all of us bundled in a taxi, arriving in the dusty capital then staying in a hotel. That was the time Father bought me the Japanese doll, the very same doll that I cherish to this day.

This time it was just Father, Mei Choon and Yao who would travel to Kuala Lumpur as the rest of us had exams to study for and Mother was too busy with her new shop.

The year ended with the CSC examination and when the results were announced, all of my friends and I jumped up and down with joy. When we finally came down to the ground and stood still, we realised that the time for dreaming was over and that we had to decide on the next move.

I knew what I wanted to do but when I heard that Joo Eng and Bee were going to apply to do nurse training in England I lost sight of my aim, seduced by the idea of joining my friends on their adventure. After all, I'd long dreamt of going to England, being totally besotted with the country - spiritual home of Jane Austen, Shakespeare and Agatha Christie but more than that, home of great minds like William Harvey and Charles Darwin. More importantly, this option would solve the problem of finding money for Sixth Form. Even better than that, I'd actually be paid during the training. The idea of travelling with my friends and training in the same hospital with them grabbed me and the sound of the names of the potential hospitals - *Chase Farm, Lister* and *St. Mary's* - was simply too beguiling.

We rushed to ask Mrs Lim for a testimonial.

As soon as we entered her office we blurted out our plans, each of us chipping in with ideas of what we wanted to do. She didn't stop us but merely looked up at us from behind her desk by the window with its venetian blind pulled down. She sat there peering over her spectacles, amused by our excited outpouring of why, where and when we were going. She listened. When we'd finished, she looked at us one by one and then said slowly,

'It's good to hear you know what you want to do.... Yes, of course, I will give you a testimonial and good luck with your application.'

She stood up. I thought we were being dismissed, instead she leant towards me. She took off her spectacles with one hand and stared into my face. She didn't speak right away. Then she said softly,

'You, Chiew...You can be a doctor. Not a nurse.'

I was stumped. This was the woman who didn't want me to be her Head Prefect because she said I was headstrong and had made me her Assistant Head Prefect instead, this was someone who I thought didn't like me at all. My head had started to spin.

I looked past her and through the gaps between the slats of the blind, momentarily fixing my gaze on the scarlet crown of the Flame-of-the-Forest tree as if to steady myself.

'I'm not giving you your testimonial yet,' she said.

'*Oh*,' was all I could say.

Sixth Form classes for Arts and Science were scheduled to start in High School a little later than the usual start of the academic year. But it didn't matter that it was late. I was proudly among the first intake for the Science subjects and I was as happy as a child with two giant clouds of candyfloss at the fairground.

The other person who was just as happy and proud was my father who was gratified that I made it to the school he had wanted to attend all those years ago.

Chapter 21

It had flitted across my mind once, maybe twice, that marrying Ah Leong would ensure I had a comfortable life, perhaps even a life of luxury. I wouldn't have to worry too much about getting a job; my future would be secure and I could enjoy all the trimmings that came with being the wife of a rich businessman.

One evening, a week after I had started at High School, we sat in his car in our favourite spot by the river to watch the sun gathering in its last amber rays on the opposite bank to the accompaniment of buzzing mosquitoes. Turning to me, he reached for my hand and placed a little velvet box into my palm.

'Open it,' he said. A tentative smile spread across his face as I raised my eyebrows.

I was curious as to what I would find. A brooch? Earrings? I had never been given jewellery before; I felt my cheeks warming as I opened the box. When I saw the gold ring with its sparkling blood red stone - the size of my thumbnail - I gasped. My jaw dropped.

'What's this for?' I asked.

'For you. I want you to have it.'

I pictured him browsing the showcases in his father's shop and then picking the one he liked, or thought that I might like.

'It was my mother's. Put it on,' he continued.

He leant towards me to take the ring out but I put my hand up against his chest. I shook my head, closed the box and pushed it back into his hand.

'No, I can't take it,' I said.

The meaning and the weight of the gesture was too much for me. I wasn't ready to be tied down. I was very fond of him; he was a good man, someone most mothers would welcome as a son-in-law, even if I sensed my own mother had some reservations. As for my father, I had no idea what his thoughts were.

Confronted with the ring, I realised that things were more serious than I had thought and that Mother's concern was justified. I saw the disappointment on Ah Leong's face as he held the closed box and seemed unsure what to do with it.

'Maybe it's a bit too soon. I can wait,' he said quietly, looking ahead.

'No, don't wait.'

'Why?' His brow furrowed.

'Because...I'm not sure...and I want to continue studying.'

He spun round to look at me. 'So how long will you be studying?'

I noticed his hands tightening his grip on the wheel.

'Five, six years.'

'That's not a problem. I can wait.'

Before I could say anything, he pushed the box into his pocket and turned the ignition key. 'Let's go and get some supper.'

When I got home Mei Lin who was doing her homework in our bedroom looked up from her books when I came into the room. 'Had a good time then?'

I giggled.'You'll never guess what Ah Leong wanted to give me.'

'No. What?'

'A ruby ring! The stone was this size!' I pointed to my thumbnail.

Her eyes widened. 'You didn't take it, did you?'

'Of course not.'

'*Phew*, that's a relief.'

'Pity,' I said holding my hand out and spreading my fingers. 'I'd quite like a ruby ring, in fact, any ring.'

'You can buy yourself one when you can afford it. Don't have to wait for a man to give you one.'

She returned to her books leaving me to think about what she'd just said.

'I never thought it would come to this! This is amazing!' said Heng; his eyes sparkled as he leant his grey head close to the transistor on his sewing machine.

It'd been a long day of waiting for the results of the General Election.

'Completely unexpected,' said Jung, shaking his head in disbelief as he rearranged the rolls of fabric leaning against the cabinet behind where Heng was sitting in the shop. Lian was cutting a piece of cloth at the worktop while Chung Lin was at her sewing machine in front of Heng's. Mr Ting was leaning over the counter, holding a shoe in his hand and pointing out the details of the stitching to a Chinese customer.

'It just shows that the non-Malays are really fed up with the establishment and actually standing up to be counted,' continued Heng.

'The Gerakan Party has won more seats than they'd dared hope and the other opposition parties also did well,' said Jung, the look of surprise still pasted on his face. 'Certainly enough to put a brake on the Alliance's moves.'

Lam burst into the shop, his face flushed with excitement and grinning.

'Have you heard?' he shouted. 'The opposition parties won a total of thirty-seven seats.' He pulled a stool from the back of the shop and sat down next to Heng.

'Yes, listening to it now,' replied Heng as he made space for him near the radio.

'That should choke the Alliance,' said Lam.

'Yes, they might have the majority of seats but I think they need at least two-thirds majority to walk over the other parties,' said Jung.

'Maybe now they will listen to us for a change,' said Lam.

'Yes, maybe now we can have a say, have an equal share in everything. We can hope. And the way things have turned out, maybe we can expect things to change from now on,' said Heng.

13th May 1969

The supporters of the Gerakan Party and DAP in Kuala Lumpur were jubilant over their victory. They took to the streets to celebrate their victory, cheering, shouting and singing their joy at what they had managed to achieve.

Ah Leong's father had sent him to Petaling Jaya, not far from Kuala Lumpur, to sort out some problems in the shop there. He'd been there for a couple of days and was just making his way back to Batu Pahat after his mission was accomplished. He knew his way around Petaling Jaya and always took the same route to get back to Batu Pahat. How he ended up in Puchong which was completely out of the way was a mystery to his father.

It was getting dark and the streets in Puchong were busy. Hawkers were setting up their food stalls and hanging up their gas-lit lamps over them for the evening. As he took a left turn to head out of Puchong, he suddenly saw smoke in the distance and a crowd of mainly Chinese men on the road, shouting and screaming. They were coming his way. Some were brandishing sticks and lead pipes; others were wildly throwing stones and bottles and shouting.

Realising he was heading into an angry mob, he knew he'd have to turn back, and quickly. He started to do a U-turn but before he could go any further he saw in his wing mirror a group of Malays coming from behind, hurling stones and bricks and charging towards the Chinese crowd. He was caught in the middle. The engine stalled; he couldn't start it again. He tried once more but the engine refused to start. He looked up to find that he was engulfed by an dangerous cocktail of distrust, bitterness and rage that ironically had been sparked off by the glimmer of hope of equality for the non-Malays. The last thing he saw were angry faces distorted by hatred and seeking revenge.

The discontent and anger at the injustice and inequality perceived by both the Malays and Chinese had finally erupted. Like a long deep cut into a swollen abdomen, the riots laid bare the festering tensions between the two groups. The distrust between them was now out in the open but no one had expected it to come to this bloody violence, this carnage.

It took four days for order to be restored to the capital, but elsewhere in the country the racial violence and fighting persisted. The whole country was stunned by the intensity of the bitterness and anger felt by both sides. Newspapers reported that around two hundred people had been killed.

The reverberations of the riots might have bypassed Batu Pahat if it were not for the senseless and tragic death of Ah Leong, an innocent bystander caught in the middle of a bloody clash. The news shocked the residents and brought home to them the reality of the divide between the two ethnic groups. A group of half a dozen or so young Chinese men, in a fit of revenge, set upon two Malay youths who were caught unawares as they cycled into town. Fortunately for the two boys, a vigilant police patrol intervened in time to put an end to what could have developed into another mindless bloody fight.

The funeral of Ah Leong was subdued but grand as befitted the son of Mr Chong, a pillar of society. Huge numbers of people turned out to pay their respects although, due to the circumstances of his death, some stayed away for fear of more trouble. An uneasy peace hung over the town during the procession. Malays stayed away while the predominantly Malay police force was on full alert.

Away from the funeral, an awkward silence prevailed amongst colleagues, workmates, classmates and friends. Everyone was deeply affected yet no one wanted to talk about the tragic and unfortunate death in case they stirred up more ill feelings. The communities of Batu Pahat were on edge and suspicious of one another but they knew that they had to get over the tragedy and move on.

I hadn't told Mother about the ring. I knew she wanted more than just marriage for me and a few days later I told her and Father about my plan for my future.

It was late in the evening. Mother had packed up in the shop and we were in their room with Father sitting in his chair, sweat trickling down his brow even though the table fan was blasting away.

'Ma, Papa, I've applied to the Malayan University to study.'

I waited to see their reaction. They looked at me.

'Is that so? That's good,' said Mother, her face lit up.

'And don't worry,' I quickly added, seeing the concern on Father's face, 'I've also applied to a couple of charities for a scholarship including the Hakka Association.'

'*Hmm*...What are you going to study?' he said as he wiped the beads of sweat from his forehead with the back of his hand.

'Medicine. I want to become a doctor.'

Father's face softened and he nodded. 'You said the same thing when you were small, when we were walking to the kindergarten.'

'Did I?'

I didn't remember that, but I did remember him holding my hand in one hand while pushing his bike with the other as we walked, passing the shops bursting into life on the way to Charlton Kindergarten every morning.

'Yes, we'd seen a boy who'd fallen off his bike.' He had a far-away look in his eyes. 'He'd cut his leg and was bleeding. You said then that you wanted to become a doctor so you could make people better.'

'It's a good choice,' said Mother.

I was pleased that both of them approved of my choice.

Ah Leong's death devastated me. I'd lost a good friend in the most unthinkable and horrific way. Saddened by his death, it also woke me up to the reality of the

211

circumstances my country was in and with it the seeds of restlessness were sown.

Chapter 22

I was washing up in the kitchen when Mei Lin came rushing in waving a brown envelope.

'It's here! It's here!' she shouted.

It was the letter from the University of Malaya that I'd been waiting for. It was going to open the way to an exciting future. Drying my hands quickly I grabbed the envelope from her. My hands started trembling as I tore it open.

'I can't bear it,' I said. 'What if I don't get in?'

'You'll get in,' Mei Lin said.

I read the first line. Then I read it again.

'No!' I screamed. 'It can't be!'

Tears gushed like a hose pipe turned on. Hand over my mouth, I pushed the letter into Mei Lin's hand and ran out of the kitchen past Third Aunt and my cousins who stopped eating their lunch and looked up at me nonplussed. I ran upstairs, past my parents' door, dived into my room and collapsed into a howling heap on the bed.

The university had rejected me.

I couldn't make sense of it. Why? How could it be? I had three A's in the Science subjects. There had to be a mistake although something told me it wasn't a mistake. I couldn't believe it. I was shattered. The rejection ripped me up like a private tsunami, smashing my hopes and plans to smithereens, then scattering them like debris in the aftermath. I wanted to die. Yet I found myself fighting for breath as the sobs rushed from the bottom of my being, crushing my lungs.

I heard my mother come into the room with Mei Lin. She sat down beside me on the edge of the bed and stroked my back; Mei Lin knelt on the floor by my head as she rubbed my arm. They said nothing for a long while as my body shook with painful sobs.

Then in a soft voice, Mother said, 'It's alright. It's not the end of the world. Don't cry anymore.'

I couldn't stop.

'Your papa can't bear to see you cry like this.'

Father hadn't come to see me; I didn't expect him to. He was sitting in his room, hurting because I was hurting. Knowing that he couldn't bear to see me cry was a small consolation.

'What am I going to do, Ma?' I said when I eventually stopped sobbing and got my breath. 'I don't know what I should do.'

I lifted my head and through the curtain of hair glued to my sodden face, I saw Mother's eyes wet with tears, filled with pain. I felt I had disappointed her; I was on the verge of believing that what my grandmother had said about me was true. *Fit only to be married off to another family, keep house and procreate.* Then the memory of Ah Leong came hurtling back, and with it more tears.

'There are other things you can do,' said Mother.

'You can teach,' said Mei Lin who had been quietly crying with me.

'But I don't want to teach, or work in a bank.'

The next day, Father sat me down in his room. The fan was clattering more loudly than usual, but did nothing to dispel the smell of fish frying that had wafted through the window from the kitchen below. I was nervous, thinking that he was about to scold me although his face, flushed with heat, was relaxed and not stern.

'You have to understand that your rejection is not your fault,' he said. 'The government is trying to appease the Malays by giving them a bigger share, more control in everything after May 13th.'

'I know. It's not fair,' I almost shouted. 'They're pushing us Chinese out. We built this country, laid the railway lines, tapped the rubber, mined the tin. That's why this country is prosperous.'

214

'Yes, the Malays say it's not fair too. They were here first. So now, they get help to improve their lot in business, education....They want to get as many Malays as possible into university, they have asked us to give them a generation to catch up with us. So that means less Chinese can get in... You did your best and you did very well.'

'And they get in whatever their results,' I said feeling the anger pounding against my chest at the injustice and unfairness of it: why me? I thought. Why was I the unlucky one to be rejected?

Father nodded.

'Papa, I don't know what to do.'

Studying abroad wasn't an option. From friends whose older siblings were studying in England I'd found out that the exchange rate was prohibitive, at eight dollars to a pound. And scholarships didn't extend to studies overseas. In fact I didn't even know if Father could have afforded sending me to Malayan University if I had been accepted. As it was, school fees for the five of us took a great chunk out of their income. Even if he could afford my university fees, my sisters after me would have to sacrifice their opportunities.

'We've got to make the best of the situation,' he said in a calm and steady voice. 'There're jobs in private companies owned by Chinese. You can try them.'

I was just relieved that he wasn't angry with me.

As I watched Soo Yin pack her things into her suitcase in her bedroom I felt as if my guts were being wrung. I was going to miss her like crazy. I couldn't believe that just a few months earlier when her boyfriend had broken her heart she'd refused to eat. As she lay on her bed, like *Sleeping Beauty* with her beautiful black hair spread out like a fan on her pillow, I'd had to coax her to eat and then actually fed her spoon by spoon while her mother was grumbling away.

'Will you come back during the holiday?' I asked, trying to keep my voice light in an effort to hide my disappointment.

'*Ya,* of course. You can come to P.J. to visit me at the uni.' She looked at me, her eyes told me she understood what I was feeling and going through. 'Something will come up. It's just unlucky you have to wait.'

I nodded and watched in silence as she put the last of her things in the case.

'Hey, you must write to me and tell me what life is like there.' I tried to sound cheerful. 'Make sure you write, promise? I'll be waiting for your letters and I might go and see you.'

'Yes, I will, I promise.'

I knew she would but I wasn't sure that I would go and visit. I needed every cent I could get, I needed to get a job, and it was urgent I did so.

When I got home that night, Uncle Heng was still working at his sewing machine.

'Uncle Heng, have you not been for your walk yet?' I said as I leant my bike against one of the other machines and then locked it.

'In a little while,' he replied. 'Got to finish this for tomorrow. So, tell me, what are you planning to do now?'

I sat down on the stool in front of his machine. I didn't answer right away. I looked down at the floor in front of my feet. Then I looked up at him. It struck me then that he looked tired. His tanned face had barely creased despite his age; he was still the lean man that he had always been although his hair had turned quite silvery and I noticed that the hairs from the mole on his chin had gone the same colour.

'Are you alright?' I asked.

'Yes,' he answered brightly. 'Never felt better. So, I asked what you are planning to do.'

'I'll find a job. Not much else I can do.'

I felt sorry for myself then and my eyes welled up. My future seemed as black as if the sun had been totally eclipsed and would never shine on me again.

'You'll be fine. I know you will not sit like a braised chicken in a wok waiting for something to happen. You're

216

the sort who will always do well,' he said looking into my eyes, as if willing me to shake off my despondency.

'Then why am I here instead of going off to university with my friends?' I gulped a sob that had snatched at my throat. What made my rejection harder to bear was the fact that Third Aunt hadn't stopped boasting about her son Kin who a year earlier had been awarded a scholarship from some company in Kuala Lumpur to study Chemistry in Malayan University.

Heng picked up the trousers he was stitching and gave them a good shake. He smiled, then said, 'If you hadn't been educated, if your father had not had the foresight to send you to school you would very likely marry some rich man, like the boss of a successful noodle factory. Boss's wife,' he said, leaning toward me for emphasis, 'nothing less. But you have set your eyes on higher things and knowing you, you'll get there.'

I forced a laugh at the thought of me being the boss lady of a noodle factory.

'You will get there, wherever you want to be,' he continued. 'It will take a bit longer than you hope, that's all.'

'I hope so. I really hope so,' I said.

Later that night, Mei Lin and I lay talking for a while on our bed.

'So what do you think you will do now?' she asked, watching closely my tear-stained face.

'I'm not sure yet.'

'I know you'll think of something.'

'All I know is that I can't stay here.'

'You mean *here* as in *this house*?' she frowned.

'No, I mean *this country*. There's no future for me here. I can't speak my mind freely, I feel like a fugitive in my own country. I can't stay here.'

'Where will you go?'

I took a deep breath.

'I don't know yet. I just know I can't stay. Soo Yin is off to M.U. tomorrow.'

I was choking with envy at the thought of my friends going on to do as they had planned. A couple were going to Australia, others to Penang or Malayan University. My future looked very bleak.

'England? Nursing?' said Mei Lin, raising her brows.

I looked at her, surprised, as the thought had crossed my mind.

'Maybe, but I need to find the fare for the flight and you know it's very expensive. Three, maybe four thousand dollars. Where am I going to find this money?'

'You need to get a job then,' said Mei Lin.

I was lucky as not long after that, a friend's older brother who was teaching in a secondary school in Mersing, on the east coast, told me about a vacancy for a relief teacher to teach Biology. The new head teacher there was previously one of the Arts teachers in Sixth Form in High School; I knew him and felt I stood a good chance. I wasted no time; like a half-starved tiger sprinting after its meal I went for the job and got it.

Father travelled with me to Mersing. He and I said little to each other throughout the four hours' taxi ride across the southern part of the peninsula, along a winding road flanked by lush palm oil plantations most of the way. But I was glad he went with me.

We arrived at the school reception in a white single-storey building set in a well-groomed lawn when lessons were still going on and it was quiet. The assistant head teacher Mr Ho, a middle-aged man, met us and assured my father that he'd look after me. Unfortunately Father couldn't stop to look around as he had to take the long journey back home again in the same taxi. After he'd helped me take my bags out of the boot, he looked at me for a moment without saying a word. I could feel that he was reluctant to let me go.

'Look after yourself,' he said. 'Write and let us know how you get on…. Don't forget.'

I nodded. I was both anxious and nervous but I knew that he was even more anxious than I was about me as he'd kept reminding me to look after myself and to be careful before we left Batu Pahat. He and Mother were worried about my accommodation which hadn't been sorted out yet. I waved to him as the taxi drove off, feeling more nervous than before, and quickly wiped my tear away before picking up my bags and following Mr Ho into the building.

The job was a means to an end but I didn't regret my time in the school. It offered me not just independence but also opened my eyes to the beauty of the beach and the uninhabited islands off the coast. Mr Ho, a keen scuba diver, would often hire a fishing boat to take me and the students to the islands to swim and dive. Although the older students were more like friends while the younger ones looked up to me like my sisters did, I felt it was a huge responsibility being their teacher. The good times there as well as enjoying the teaching didn't dim my vision of the reason for my being there. The only thing I didn't like was the tearful goodbyes to my family every time after a weekend at home to return to school. I loved the place including the little room I had above a grocery shop and made a note that I would return one day, one day when I had achieved what I wanted to do. I couldn't wait to embark on the next stage of my plan.

The year at the school went quickly.

Back in Hakka Street during the holidays, I decided that I would tell my mother what I'd planned to do. But when I went to her room the door was locked as she was getting changed to go out to the cinema with Wei. I hovered for a bit before I spoke up.

'Ma, I've decided to go to England to do nursing.'

I could hear her moving inside but there was no response from her.

'Ma, did you hear what…'

'You can't go!' Mother shouted, her voice bordering on a shrill, as if I had said I was going to throw myself in

219

front of a car. 'It's too far away! What if your sisters and brother follow you and do the same? No, you can't!'

'Ma, I have to. There's nothing here for me. At least I will get a qualification and work. I will be paid.'

What I didn't say was that I'd already bought my ticket to London and all the necessary documents - my work visa, the letter of acceptance from the Lister Hospital- were ready.

'No, no. We'll talk more when I come home.' She didn't disguise the panic in her voice.

I didn't see her again until the next morning. Both she and Father were in their room having just got ready for work, Mother was sitting on the edge of her bed while Father was in his usual chair. I perched on the stool that was there and faced them. Before I could say a word, Father said, 'Your mother has told me what you said last night.' His tone was soft.

I waited; my pulse was racing as I wondered what his response would be. I looked at his face then at Mother's, but I couldn't tell what they were thinking. Then a look of approval, delight and relief and pride all rolled into one spread across them. Mother's nose reddened as the tears started to roll. She reached for her handkerchief in her dress pocket.

'Is that really what you want to do?' Father continued.

I nodded looking from one to the other.

'It's just that it is so far away,' said Mother as she wiped a tear away.

Father started rubbing the arms of his chair as he continued to look at me. 'We think it's a very good idea,' he said. 'It's just that England is very far away... We won't see you for a long time, it's not as if you can pop home easily.' His voice then lifted. 'But there will be more opportunities there for you I'm sure and we're very happy for you.' He sounded as if he couldn't believe this was happening. As he slowly took a deep breath he turned and stared out of the window.

220

Chapter 23

London, September 1972

Like a bottle of champagne, shaken, and ready to burst, I was filled with excitement and anticipation. I was also dizzy but that wasn't due to jetlag after flying from the other side of the world. I hadn't just travelled more than the six thousand miles from Singapore; I was about to savour something that couldn't be more different to what I'd had much earlier in Singapore. Only forty-eight hours ago I was sitting at the roadside in Newton Circus, sweltering in the Singaporean heat and eating with my family a farewell meal which Mother's brother, Poh, had insisted on paying for.

Now, catapulted from innocence to a den of iniquity - I could hear Pastor Jenkins's warning of fire and brimstone in one ear - I was sitting in the restaurant of the Playboy Club in Park Lane. I was with my new friends and fellow travellers Ann Lim and two brothers, Peter and David Tan who were complete strangers to us until we sat down next to them in the plane. Like me, Ann was going to do nursing but in Grantham. Peter was a businessman while David was studying somewhere else in England.

'I never dreamt I'd be doing this! Not in a million years!' I gasped and was trying not to let my jaw drop. I wasn't looking at a Bunny logo, or a picture of a Bunny girl. I was looking- no, staring- at a live voluptuous Bunny gliding gracefully towards our table. She was a Marilyn Monroe look-alike, who seemed too perfect to be real, complete with the Bunny ears and bow-tie. At once I felt inadequate and self-conscious. I was wearing my new *cheongsam* with side slits that Soo Yin had insisted should be high enough to show off my legs. *What legs?* I asked myself now. The Bunny before me had legs that seemed to go on forever; I thought she would need binoculars to see her

221

feet. Her black satin costume with a tuft of cotton-tail showed off every soft curve of her body, reminding me of the plastic dolls in some of the shops in Hakka Street –tiny waist, pointed breasts, eternally long legs, glassy blue eyes and shimmering blonde hair.

Hours earlier, around about the time we were flying over Paris, Peter the older of the two Chinese brothers had casually leaned over to ask Ann and me,

'If you are not doing anything tonight would you like to have dinner with us at the Playboy Club?' Peter, it turned out, was a member of the Club and obviously liked Ann.

Would Cinderella like to go to the ball?

How often did a chance like that come up? Of course, we didn't have any plans. Big Ben and Buckingham Palace could wait, I thought.

Now, in an elegant room surrounded by beautiful and sophisticated people and food that I had never eaten before, I knew I was in a different world, especially when I saw the number of shiny pieces of cutlery neatly arranged on the white damask-covered table with sparkling glasses and candle-light. I'd had to look around to see how the natives were using them.

Marilyn Monroe approached us, smiling sweetly even pouting slightly as she made eye contact with each of us in turn. By now I'd drawn up my jaw and even managed to smile in return and I resisted the urge to hide my self-consciousness by taking another sip of the Chardonnay that Peter had ordered.

'Good evening, ladies and gentlemen,' she said, revealing her beautiful white teeth. 'It's a buffet dinner and here are your keys to the food over there,' she held out four cardboard keys the length of a fork in one hand and, with the other, pointed to a long table laden with mountains of food. 'The key entitles you to one helping. You can pile on as much as you can on your plate.' She sounded as sweet as the chocolate pudding on the table.

Peter took the keys from her and she beamed at us again.

'Enjoy your meal,' Marilyn said and then waltzed away, her little white tufty tail wiggling.

I also felt a stab of guilt. Guilt, because I had been elated about flying off leaving my family behind while they were tearful about my going.

Everyone had been excited about coming to the airport to see me off. I was embarrassed at the fuss but nothing would keep Uncles Heng, Tian and Poh away. Uncle Heng thought the airport was extraordinary. He had dressed in his best white shirt and brown trousers matched with shiny leather shoes; I'd never seen him dressed so smartly before.

'*Wah*, I had to wait till I'm this old to come to an airport,' he said, shaking his head as he looked around the terminal and then stood in front of a huge glass window, mesmerised by the planes on the apron and the size of them. 'If not for you, Chiew, I might never have seen all this.'

Father didn't say much. His face, flush with heat in spite of the air-conditioning, was full of words, words that he could not articulate to me. His eyes told me he was sad to see me go, that I would be too far away from home. A few days earlier, in his room, he had said quietly to me, 'I wonder when we will see you again, how long we will have to wait.'

'I don't know, but I'll save hard so I can come home soon,' I had said.

All the way to the airport he'd been fidgety and irritable in the taxi. Once or twice he'd snapped at Mother when she spoke to him and that in turn had annoyed me.

It was my sisters and brother who made me laugh, all talking at the same time clamouring for my attention.

'You are not going to change into an English person, are you?'

'Just think- you're going to become so fair like the English people!'

223

'What if you marry one of them?'

'You won't forget your own language, will you?'

'Will you send me some nice make-up?'

'Send us lots of photos so we can see what it is like, where you are going!'

I knew I would miss Mother most and I couldn't help feeling anxious about not being there with her when Father flew into one of his bad tempers. Of my siblings, Yao was the one I hated leaving most. He had just started secondary school.

'You study hard, O.K? Then one day you can become anybody you want to be, a doctor, engineer, anybody,' I had said to him as I rubbed his head which came up to my shoulder. He looked fresh and clean in his white shirt and navy shorts, his eyes bright and happy.

He looked at me and gave me one of his heart-warming smiles.

'Yup, I will,' he said, squeezing my arm. 'I wish I could go with you.'

I squeezed him back. 'You can, one day.'

The prospect of a new venture, a better future for me, was cause for celebration and I had to admit I was ecstatic and shaking with excitement at the thought of leaving. I wanted to laugh for joy and to cry at the same time. It felt as if I'd sprouted wings and there was no limit to where I could go; England beckoned, I succumbed gladly and willingly.

It hadn't taken my mother long to get over the shock of my decision to come to England despite her worry that my siblings would follow in my footstep. She saw the wisdom and all the benefits of my choice. Once converted to the idea, she became very excited and although she lamented about the distance, she was enthusiastic about my taking such a huge step and breaking free from all the constraints of my homeland. Not even Third Aunt's snide remark could dampen her enthusiasm.

'What's there to boast about?' she had said, her mouth full of rice, loud enough for all in the house to hear.

We were near the landing. '*Aiyahh*, she is only going to wash other people's bottoms!'

Mother didn't rise to the bait, while I resisted the temptation to sweep the floor directly above where she was eating to sprinkle some dirt through the peepholes onto her food. We heard Uncle Heng come into the hall and say,

'How can you say that? She is going to be doing a very worthwhile job, looking after sick people.'

Ai Chien, who had come bearing a plate of steamed cakes for us, said in her usual loud voice,

'*Ha*, Lian has every reason to boast. Only a clever girl like her daughter can go to England to study.'

'Exactly,' said Heng.

Third Aunt said nothing more.

Mother jumped into a frenzy of making clothes for me.

'You will need warm dresses and a coat,' she said. 'We need to make you the best dresses. It will also save you money since everything is so expensive in England.'

'I'll be the best dressed nurse in England, Ma,' I laughed.

'What's wrong with that?' She looked away and then said, 'Three years...it's a long time. I wonder when I will see you again after you've gone.'

'I'll be back as soon as I've saved enough for a flight.' It was a promise I meant to keep.

When it was finally time for me to head for the departure lounge I looked over at Mother. Her eyes had welled up and her nose turned red. She reached for her handkerchief in the handbag that she had treated herself to for the occasion. Despite the red nose I thought to myself how lovely and youthful she looked in her floral-patterned shift dress, her sweet face framed by her short wavy hair, her lips coloured a shade redder than normal.

'Goodbye, Ma, take care of yourself,' I said. I wanted to throw my arms around her and give her the biggest hug but instead I just put my arm round her shoulders.

225

'You take care of yourself,' she said as she grabbed my free hand.

I looked at Father; his face was crumpled with sadness. I didn't know what to do, to shake his hand or what? 'I'm going now, Papa,' I said. 'Take care of yourself.'

He nodded as he reached out to touch my arm with one hand and took my hand with the other. 'Be careful,' he said quietly. His hand felt firm and warm.

Earlier we'd talked about the IRA bombs in London and I had assured him that I wasn't going to be anywhere near or in London.

'Write as soon as you arrive.' His eyes, still fixed on me, looked like they were about to fill up with tears.

'Yes, I will,' I replied. At that moment I felt sorry that I had been angry with him. I quickly turned to Uncle Heng and the rest of the family and waved, 'I'm going now!'

They all shouted goodbye and waved back.

As I walked away through the departure gate, I couldn't stop smiling as the excitement and sense of anticipation tingled through me. I was embarking on my new adventure. I turned back one last time to see Mother and Father drying their eyes.

The morning after our night at the Playboy Club, both Ann and I rushed out of the Bed-and-Breakfast in Nottinghill Gate and we struggled to push our luggage into a black cab for King's Cross station. We were still laughing at having to pay a one-pound fine to the landlady for coming back after eleven o'clock.

At King's Cross Station we said goodbye, not knowing whether we would see each other again but were grateful that in the short time we had been together we'd had such fun. Her train came first and I was left alone in the vast foyer, standing under the huge clock and surrounded by hundreds of alien-looking people whizzing past. Suddenly I felt the chill in the air; a shiver went through me. For the first time since I left Batu Pahat I felt nervous and unsure of myself.

I counted my luggage again to make sure I hadn't left anything behind. I had two large suitcases at my feet, a guitar slung across my back, my mock-leather handbag over my shoulder, a transistor in one hand and an umbrella in the other. I was wearing the navy bell-bottoms Mother had made for me, a white T-shirt and a red jacket, and my hair was braided in two plaits. I looked at the huge board in front of me searching for which platform the train to Stevenage was leaving from.

'Are you alright, luv?' a voice said to my right as I felt a gentle tap on my shoulder.

Surprised, I turned to look up at the face of a tall elderly man wearing a flat cap.

'Yes,' I replied. 'Thank you' and I ventured a half smile.

'That's good. It's just that you looked so lost then.' The man smiled at me. 'I'll just go back and join my wife in the queue.' He pointed to a long line of passengers in front of the ticket office. I spotted a grey-haired woman in a tweed suit, smiling in our direction.

'Thank you,' I mumbled as I watched him walk away. At that moment I felt my confidence return. I could understand what the man had said; his accent didn't confound me. Reassured, I quickly headed for the platform I wanted half dragging and half kicking my suitcases along.

Once in the train, I put my suitcases on the shelves by the door and sat down on the seat facing them so I could see them as I hugged my guitar, handbag and transistor on my lap. The heated compartment started to fill up making it even warmer and when the train began to move, its chugging sound and the rocking motion of the train set off the jetlag which combined with the effects of the late night, rushed at me making me feel sleepy. But not knowing when the train would stop at Stevenage I willed every fibre of my body to fight sleep, afraid that I'd miss my stop if I gave in.

I suddenly realised I hadn't had time to stop and look at this race of people that I was going to be living amongst for the next three years. As I scanned the passengers around me I thought I would keep myself awake by studying them. Some of them had nodded off, some were reading while others stared out of the windows at the landscape flying past. I noted the colour of their hair and was amazed at the variety of shades; I didn't know there could be so many variations of brown and blonde, unlike the black that I was accustomed to. And the eyes! Their colours brought to mind colours of precious gemstones- sapphire, amber and emerald. Seeing them in pictures was one thing, but seeing them in three dimensions was something else. They were set so deep and close, and separated by such a high bridge that I wondered if the right eye could see what was on the left without having to move the head. Did the nose get in the way of the cup when drinking? My friends and I had asked each other that before behind Pastor Jenkins's back. Surreptitiously I looked at the eyes of the woman sitting opposite me and noticed they were almost emerald, a stunning green which took my breath away.

What worried me most was whether or not I would be able to tell these faces apart and whether or not I would recognise them when I saw them again.

When I'd finished with my musings - the natives' appearances, what my family were doing, the whole experience at the Playboy Club, the weather, whether I should stick to my Chinese name or use my baptism name – I realised I was the odd one out in the compartment like an anorexic in a crowd of Sumo wrestlers. I stared out at the flat green landscape, wondering what I could expect to find in Stevenage and if I could ever adapt to my new surroundings. The thing was, when I first stepped out of the plane at Heathrow the strangest feeling came over me: I felt as if I had been here before.

An hour later we arrived at Stevenage and I managed to drag my luggage out onto the street to find a taxi.

I was just about to say the destination when the driver said,

'Lister Hospital?'

228

'Yes, please,' I replied, puzzled at first then quickly remembered that many of my compatriots had been coming over here to train. I wondered then how he felt about that but didn't dare ask.

We drove in silence. I looked out of the window, absorbing everything I saw although it was mostly concrete buildings at first but when I saw the half-timbered houses on the main street of the old town, my heart started racing and my imagination spinning. I half expected to see Shakespeare in full costume but wearing trainers coming out of the pub with a jug of beer in hand and Jane Eyre, with a rucksack on her back, window shopping. Right away I knew that I'd have no trouble adjusting to my new environment.

After we emerged from the streets of the town and had driven along a tree-lined avenue, the driver took a turning and pointed to a large building like a neat stack of white shoe boxes jutting above the tree tops in the distance.

'There's the new hospital,' he said. 'You'll want the nurses' home. Which building do you want?'

'*Er*.. Beech House please,' I replied.

I craned my neck to get a better view of the hospital but only caught glimpses of the tinted glass windows as we turned into a narrow lane leading to the nurses' home. When we eventually stopped outside Beech House, I quickly got out my purse for my fare mindful of the ten per cent tip that my travel guidebook had recommended.

'That'll be one pound twenty,' he said.

He got out and took my luggage out of the boot while I quickly worked out the ten per cent. When he'd put down the last piece of luggage on the ground I handed him a note and coins.

'Thank you,' I said.

He took the money and then to my surprise he picked out twelve pence and pushed the coins into my hand.

'It's alright, love,' he said and winked at me. 'Thanks and good luck.'

Ten minutes later one of my English flatmates opened the front door for me and welcomed me with the biggest and warmest smile. The last of my worries was completely banished. I knew for sure that I would settle very happily in my new home.

Chapter 24

Miss Mary Cunningham, the Principal Nursing Tutor, finished off the tour of the hospital with a smug look as if she had designed the hospital herself and was waiting for us to applaud. Petite in her smart green suit, she stood with her hands behind her back pursing her lips as she looked at us. We - fifteen fresh-faced young student nurses in our new pale blue uniforms and black clumpy shoes, hair tied back neatly under plain white hats to indicate our novice status - were suitably impressed. I was awe-struck.

Each of the floors of the hospital was H-shaped with the wards located in the arms while the link was the concourse where the lifts were situated. The ward was designed so that the beds were located at the ends of the floor with a long corridor in between. We were standing in the corridor. A hint of irritation had crept into her high-pitched sing-song voice when she pointed to the entire length of the corridor and said,

'You'd be right if you thought that nurses were not consulted in the design of the ward. Well, at least you'll never get DVT with all the walking you'll have to do.' She frowned to emphasise her annoyance.

The hospital was the state of the art in hospital design. It was rated the best in Europe in terms of the design, layout and the equipment according to many experts like Miss Cunningham who had seen other hospitals and were in a position to compare. The eleven storey square building was modern with neat, unfussy lines.

The interior was open plan giving it an airy bright look and feel, full of light compared to the dull, formidable looking and unwelcoming older hospitals. It was strikingly clean with just a faint smell of disinfectant. On the concourse, a couple of cheese plants softened the clinical look. The wards had been carefully designed to maximise comfort and privacy for the patients and to minimise cross-infection. The new beds were adjustable to suit the height of the nurses to prevent back strain. Orange and cream striped curtains hung between the beds.

It was the equipment that gave the place a futuristic feel. Above the head of each bed, piped oxygen emerged from the wall. Next to it was a mercury sphygmomanometer and cuff accessible for routine or emergency use and next to that a suction hose with a clean receiver and a fitted sterile nozzle stood to attention ready to clear an airway.

The treatment room was immaculate; the emphasis was on the prevention of infection and cross infection backed by strict adherence to the aseptic technique which the nursing tutors and the sisters preached relentlessly and an efficient Central Sterilising Unit in the basement.

The disposal of dirty linen, dressings and excreta was carried out in an ultra-modern sluice room installed with the most up-to-date disposal units in the wall and stocked with disposable urinals and bedpan liners. Nurses or auxiliary nurses were no longer required to hand-wash those receptacles, freeing them to attend to the more important needs of the patients.

A cosy day-room in the link with comfortable armchairs and a brand new television afforded patients a change in scenery, the double-glazed windows provided a staggering view of the woodland surrounding the hospital. Like an artist's watercolours blotting the paper, splashes of red, gold and yellow were just spreading through the green of the trees as summer had begun to ease into autumn. Later, when winter set in the trees would turn into fans of bronze filigree against the grey sky.

The environment, the cold, and even the new cuisine were easy for me to adjust to. My bedroom was new and modern, furnished with a comfortable single bed, wardrobe, desk and washbasin. Crawling out of bed to go to work in the dark and returning home in the dark was depressing but bearable. Some nights I would wake up confused as to where I was:

was I in 22 Hakka Street or was I in Beech House? I would half expect to hear the familiar vendor's clanging of the wok echoing from across the street. Now I woke to birdsongs instead of the rattling of the stalls. Although I missed my mother's cooking and stuffed bean curd terribly I was eager to try out the English cuisine.

What proved to be more challenging were people and accents.

My three flatmates, Gabby, Fiona and Vicky, all freshies like me, were lovely. It was Vicky who had opened the door to me when I first arrived and she didn't show any sign of surprise at the sight of a foreign-looking girl. I immediately warmed to her lightly freckled face with pale blue eyes, and her hair, bushed out like a can-can skirt, was the most fiery red that I'd ever set eyes on. Her smile was like an invitation to sit by the fire on a chilly night. I felt right away that she and I would get along.

'Hello, I'm Vicky,' she'd said, holding the door wide open.

I introduced myself, looking like a one-man band with all of my worldly possessions strapped to me. She, on the other hand, looked elegant and very slim in a turquoise T-shirt and a short brown skirt. I was a little surprised when she said, 'Come in, we've been waiting for you, the others are already here. Here let me help you with your bag.'

She bent down to pick up one of my suitcases and led me into a bright kitchen with the smell of burnt toast coming from the *Baby Belling* oven on the worktop in front of a large window. Fiona and Gabby were sitting at a Formica-topped table where there was a teapot, three identical blue mugs and half eaten toast on three plates. They both gave me huge smiles and stood up when they saw me, towering above me in their platform sandals. I smiled up at them as I put my transistor, umbrella and handbag down on the table and then wriggled under the strap to take the guitar off my back.

Fiona's Scottish lilt intrigued me right away. Her long hair was what she later told me she called *mousey* which she hated.

Gabby was from Liverpool; her accent threw me completely and I almost squinted at her dazzling blonde hair.

Within minutes, we were talking like old friends curious and interested about one another and where we had come from- four strangers from different corners of the earth, even if my corner was a little further away than theirs, thrown together in a small flat. I'd never felt so at ease in the company of new friends as I did just then.

But I didn't feel as comfortable with all of the other girls in my group. I was conscious of the fact that I was the only foreign girl, both in appearance and in origin. My discomfort was soon justified when Susan from Yorkshire told me, using expletives that made my cousin Hock look tame, that I was abrupt and rude. It happened when we were practising lifting patients together in the classroom and I was telling her what to do.

In my defence the local girls' voices were at least two octaves higher than mine; compared to their gentle and soft tone, mine was harsh and my speech staccato and came across as direct and snappy. I was upset and embarrassed by the criticism. I knew it was imperative that I bend and soften my tongue so that I didn't sound so hard; it wouldn't do to leave a trail of disgruntled people behind me.

But it wasn't just that I had to make myself understood; I had to understand them as well so it was a case of quickly re-tuning my ears to the different accents. The girls could talk and when they started talking all at once they sounded like blackbirds arguing with magpies making it even harder for foreign ears like mine which were more accustomed to the tongue-curling twang of Hollywood.

I decided that if I was going to make all of this effort, then they could learn to say my Chinese name without my making it easy for them by using my baptism name, Christine. Besides, I felt a strong need to hang on to my identity and my culture.

What I loved most was the freedom of speech. This was what I had longed for and to actually experience it gave me a sense of liberation, of having wings and being able to fly, of being able to fill my lungs to the full. Here in England I didn't have to look over my shoulders if I wanted to disagree with the government. I couldn't get over the fact that the natives could criticise their Queen and government openly without fear of reprisal. For this I happily put up with the man who, on spotting me and my flatmates arriving at the disco in the *Mecca* in old Stevenage, pulled down the corners of his eyes and laughed at me. And the porter who called me a 'chink' and even the English paediatric consultant who said in his lecture, 'To know what a child with Mongolism looks like, look at a Chinese person.'

Almost a year into my training, I was assigned to work on the medical ward where I was to have the privilege of working with Sister O'Brien, one of the finest nurses who set very high standards of nursing care and was very eager to teach them to us. Unfortunately for me, her strong Irish accent made her difficult to understand at times. My problem became a joke amongst the other staff but she was always patient and would say with a twinkle in her eyes, after I had interrupted her for the third time,

'Nurse Chiang, if you keep asking me to repeat what I've said, we'll get pressure sores by the time I finish this report.'

It was on her ward that I first came face to face with the death of a patient.

The call bell in one of the side rooms had gone off.

'I think it's Mrs Young's,' I said to Staff Nurse Johnson. 'Shall I go and see what she wants?'

'Yes, love,' she replied.

With Miss Cunningham's mantra humming in my ears, *Never run on the ward except in an emergency*, I walked briskly down the long corridor.

I'd got to know Mrs Young, a fifty- four year old housewife who loved doing tapestry and was involved with the *Save the Children* charity. She had been admitted a few days earlier for an investigation of the cause of her chest pain. Like all the other women on the ward she was perfectly charming and appreciative of what we nurses were doing. In fact she was positively motherly and encouraging towards me knowing that I was only a student a long way from home.

The door of her room was half open and I'd walked in expecting to see her sitting up in her bed. Instead I found her lying on the bed with her head flopped to one side. Her eyes were shut and her hand still gripping the call bell.

'Mrs Young!' I called out, my heart thumping against my chest wall.

I grabbed her wrist to feel for her pulse but couldn't find it. I yelled for Staff Nurse.

Before I knew it, I was sucked into a drama that even though I'd been taught what to do, I never thought I would encounter so early in my training. The cardiac arrest team seemed to appear out of nowhere with their trolley as soon as Staff Nurse and I pulled the pillow from under Mrs Young's head, laid her flat and started cardiac massage. It was only when Sister O'Brien pulled me away from her chest that I realised that I had been frantically shouting, 'Come on, Mrs Young! Come on!'

As I moved aside to allow the cardiac arrest team to take over, I was overcome with sadness. The whole episode was over in minutes. Then they pronounced her dead but her limp lifeless body, her face drained of colour kept coming back to me. My thoughts flew to my mother - what if it had been her?

That night as I lay in bed, Third Aunt's deprecating remark about my job - *she is only washing other people's bottoms* - came rushing back to me adding to my wretchedness. Then Mrs Lim's small voice, *'You can be a doctor'*, which depressed me even more. I'd had enough of bed-making, bedpans and bed baths, and was feeling as if I had been shunted into a traffic lane I wasn't meant to be in and there was no way I could get out of it.

I had learnt so much in such a short time: I had seen how quickly the skin could break down on my *pressure areas* rounds, pushing my stainless steel trolley laden with talcum, a basin of water, soap, a bottle of oil and a gallipot of egg-white. The egg-white was Sister O'Brien's trick; it was to be applied to the broken skin and then dried with oxygen from a small cylinder on the side of the trolley. 'But, of course, prevention is the best,' she would say, 'and to achieve that you turn the bed-ridden patients frequently and you *rub* the pressure areas.' In her view pressure sores were synonymous with bad nursing care.

I could move patients with the Australian lift, perform catheterisation, insert and care for a naso-gastric tube and give hypodermic injections. Latin- and Greek-derived words and words ending in *–ectomy, -itis* or *–ology* had become my staple vocabulary and topics of conversation. I had nursed patients with *salpingitis* and *bronchiectasis*. I had cared for post-*cholecystectomy* and *–nephrectomy* patients. *Cardiology* fascinated me. I had witnessed what could go wrong with the human body and the consequences and had even started diagnosing strangers I saw on the street. But the more I got into nursing, the more I realised that what I was doing wasn't enough. I knew that I cared about people and I wanted something more.

The hierarchy in nursing also irritated me no end. Miss Cunningham had told us that in her day they weren't allowed to speak to their seniors until they were spoken to. That wouldn't have gone down well with me although I was being careful not to upset anyone with my outspokenness. Fortunately it wasn't as bad for us as the senior nurses were more approachable and we co-existed happily.

I hadn't counted on missing my family so much, especially on Chinese New Year's day. Some of my compatriots in the hospital who'd been in the hospital a lot longer invited me to join them for the celebration, which helped ease my misery. Even though Father had installed a telephone in the shop, I couldn't phone them. A three-minute call would have cost me almost half of my month's pay of

237

forty-four pounds and I couldn't afford that kind of extravagance. I was saving to travel to Europe now that I had been to London with Vicky to see Big Ben, Buckingham Palace, Chinatown and Oxford Street. Luckily my sisters wrote regularly which kept me informed of what was happening at home.

The best news I received was when Mei Lin told me she had been accepted by Malayan University to read Economics. Paradoxically she was rejected for nursing at the same university. In casting her net wide she had also applied to do nursing as well. When she and her friend were called for an interview, they had eagerly dashed off to Kuala Lumpur and returned to Batu Pahat confident that they would get a place. The next day they read in the paper that only those with a pass in the Malay language, *Bahasa Melayu*, need apply which effectively precluded non-Malays as that was never an option for them in school.

But she was delighted about her acceptance by the university and the bursary of five hundred dollars each from the Johore government and the Lee Foundation. I was overjoyed for her, pleased that at last one of us was going to university and for that at least, Malayan University was exonerated.

Even Father wrote to me although he was always very brief and always started and ended his letters the same way.

Dear Chiew,
How are you? We are well and hope you are in good health.
We are very glad that you are doing well……
Your father

His cursive writing was always immaculate, perfectly executed like printed calligraphy. I could just see him sitting at his desk with his Sheaffer pen poised in his hand as he pondered what to write. Mei Chin told me he missed me and that my letters were important to him. She

238

told me how he would eagerly look out for the postman when he thought a reply was due.

Seeing illness everyday made me worry about my family even more: what if they became ill? Mrs Young's premature death made me even more melancholy and magnified how much I missed my mother. I felt as if I had a big hole in my chest. Burying my face in my pillow so that my flatmates couldn't hear me, I cried myself to sleep.

I stretch my arm as far as I can to reach it. I can't see what it is that I am reaching for but I know I want it, yearn for it. It is a matter of life or death. Every fibre in my body aches as they stretch to grab the object which is tantalisingly close, but just as I almost touch it it edges away from my fingertips. In my frustration I try harder and then suddenly whatever it is, is gone, and I am left gasping.

Chapter 25

It was only a small wooden house with two bedrooms and a tin roof but it was surrounded by a large garden covered with lallang grass grown to its full height and morning glory that crept along the edge of the drain around the house. It stood apart from the other houses along the red-earth path on the edge of town, near the church on Jalan Mohamed Akhir.

Jung and I often walked past this house, in the early days, not long after we were married. We never saw the people who lived in the house although some evenings we would see a man spraying insecticide around it to control the mosquitoes but we never saw anyone cutting the lallang grass. Secretly I dreamt about living in it, the peace and privacy, especially when it got noisy in No.22 but it was Jung who saw its potential and worth.

'That house is sitting on a prime site,' he told me. 'One day the land will be worth a lot.'

In those days I didn't see further than the tip of my nose. But I never forgot what he said and he was right because the town grew.

We never lost sight of that wooden house. As soon as it was put up for sale we grabbed it, bought it outright. The land all around it was larger than we thought. Three quarter acre. Imagine. And it was cheap, cheap as pig's dung. Wah, we were so excited, so nervous as well. We could not believe it, at last, our own property.

The business in the shop was doing well. My brother Poh had made good his prediction: he gave me large orders for sale in Singapore. I employed two more helpers to do the machining in the shop.

The plan was to gradually move into the new house but keep the business running in the shop, sleep in the new house but work in the shop, and eat there as well. Jung would still get to work easily on his bicycle. It was a good fifteen, twenty, minutes' walk to the shop for me.

For the children it would be much better, more room and quiet to study, also convenient to get to school.

Standing in the evening shade in the alley, Lian was telling Ai Chien her plans for the house when she became distracted and broke off. Yao was coming up the alley towards the house, looking dishevelled, his schoolbag slung over his shoulder, his head hanging down, oblivious to the people he was passing. She called out to him as he made for the door.

'Yao, where have you been?' She turned to Ai Chien. 'I must see what he has been up to.' She rushed to catch up with him as he continued to walk into the house, ignoring her.

When she caught up with him in the kitchen, she grabbed his arm to turn him towards her. He had grown a lot in the last year and he was now a head taller than her but he looked thin and haggard, and there was a dull look in his eyes. He was sullen and reticent. He looked down at Lian but said nothing.

'Where have you been?' she repeated. 'School finished four hours ago and you didn't come back for dinner. Your papa asked where you were, and I told him you were probably still at school or with friends.'

Until a few months ago, he was happy and content and would do as he was told. Then he started coming home late and even missed his meals but Jung didn't lose his temper like he did with the girls before.

'Yes, I was at school,' he replied looking around in the kitchen. 'Is there any food left?' He opened then shut a cupboard, deliberately avoiding looking at Lian.

'Yes,' said Lian.

241

She went to the cupboard and took out the bowl of cold rice, fried spinach and tofu that she had saved for him. 'Now tell me, what were you doing in school?'

He sat down at the table but instead of answering her, he picked up the bowl and started to eat. Lian sat down beside him.

'What's the hurry?' she asked. 'So, what were you doing in school?'

Yao gulped his food, still avoiding looking at her.

'The usual,' he said. 'Nothing exciting, talking with friends.'

Lian studied his face. She was alarmed at how tired he looked, his eyes were bleary, their usual sparkle was missing. There was something wrong but she didn't know what it was. He'd been sullen and distant for some time. She had put it down to growing up, but lately, she was afraid that there would be more to it than that. His schoolwork was suffering badly. From being consistently at the top of his class he had sunk to the bottom. His latest school report had shown his work had deteriorated drastically and Jung's chastisement seemed to have no impact on him at all.

Although Lian and Jung didn't know, Yao had become aggressive in school. Worse than that, the teachers couldn't control him. One day, something one of them said sparked him off causing him to throw an almighty punch at the blackboard. He hit it so hard that his fist went through the material and ripped it. There was an uproar and he was sent to the headmaster who took the cane to him.

Just as Yao swallowed the last mouthful of rice, Jung came down the stairs ready to go back to work. He had changed from his day work clothes into a crisp white shirt and brown trousers. His colleague, Ahmad the usher, was sick and the manager had asked him to stand in for him. Jung's face, glum as usual, softened when he saw Yao.

'Why were you home so late?' he asked.

'I was with friends in school... we played football,' replied Yao flatly, staring down at his empty bowl.

242

Frowning, Jung walked over to the table and looked at him. 'You look tired. Are you alright?'

Yao nodded.

'Make sure you do your homework.' Turning to Lian, he said, 'Maybe a brew of some herbs is what he needs, as well as a good sleep.'

As soon as he'd left, Yao stood up and walked upstairs, leaving Lian sitting at the table, despondent at not being able to reach him.

Upstairs, in their room, Mei Chin and Mei Choon were engrossed in their homework and studies in their room. Mei Chin was sitting on the bed with her books laid out in front of her while Mei Choon was at the desk. They looked up when Yao walked in.

'You look terrible! Like a zombie! What's the matter? Didn't you sleep last night? I heard you creep in last night,' said Mei Choon.

Yao had chosen to sleep on a camp bed in the corridor when he felt he was too old to be sharing a room with his sisters.

'*Shuddup* and mind your own business!' he snapped and threw his bag on the floor.

'That's not nice, Yao,' said Mei Lin who managed not to raise her voice as she knew it would only antagonise him. Neither did she want to confront him with her suspicion that he had taken her money from her purse, something she discovered before she set off for school that morning.

'You know it's Moon Cake festival today, don't you?' asked Mei Choon.

She and Yao had always been close and shared secrets but now she sensed that he was shutting her out.

Yao didn't respond. He grabbed a clean shirt from the wardrobe and turned to walk out of the room.

'I'm going out.' His voice which had broken not long ago was now hoarse. 'If Ma asks, just say I've gone to see my friend.'

243

'I hope you'll be back for moon cakes!' Mei Choon shouted after him and then turned to Mei Chin with a puzzled look.

The resplendent full moon took centre stage against the dark and cloudless sky and seemed to be smiling down at the children playing on a traffic-free Hakka Street. The shops were closed and the street had turned into a nocturnal playground. The children were showing off their glowing colourful lanterns as they paraded up and down the street laughing and shouting against a backdrop of the clanging of the ladle and wok from the vendor frying noodles.

'I can't see the lady on the moon!' a little boy shouted as he stared up at the moon. 'My grandmother said I should see her there.' The other children around him laughed.

'Come on, silly. There is no lady up there. It's just a story,' said an older girl as she adjusted the candle in the lantern he was holding.

On the five-foot way, a couple of tables had been laid out with moon cake neatly cut into small pieces, melon seeds, peeled pomelo and tea. Knowing that this was going to be her last time celebrating with the neighbours Lian had bought a few boxes more than usual.

Heng and Chung Lin were sitting at the table enjoying the cool breeze, sipping tea and cracking melon seeds. Jung was still at work. At Mei Chin's insistence Lian had left her sewing to come out on to the five-foot way to watch the children and look at the moon. Mei Chin and Mei Choon had also come out and as they watched the younger children playing in the street they were wishing that they had a lantern too.

'Ma, what about some noodles later?' asked Mei Lin, her appetite whetted by the aroma coming from the food stall across the street.

'Didn't you eat enough earlier?' said Lian.

'Of course she did. She's just gutsy!' said Mei Chin, but the aroma had tempted her too.

'If you are hungry we'll get some. Mei Chin, you go upstairs and bring my purse down,' she said then changed her mind. 'No, I'll go myself. You wait here.'

It was quiet inside the shophouse. She hadn't seen Yao anywhere and hoped that he was in his sisters' room doing his homework. She passed Yew coming out of the hall.

'Have you seen Yao?' she asked.

'No, but I heard someone going upstairs earlier,' he answered and carried on walking.

As Lian climbed up the stairs an uneasy feeling came over her. On the landing, instead of going into her room for her purse, she turned and walked quietly down the corridor.

The door to Mei Chin and Mei Choon's room was shut but seeing the door to Chung Lin's sisters' room ajar she walked in quietly. Against the wall separating the two rooms was a table. She looked around and found a stool, picked it up and gently placed it on the table. Her heart had started racing; she wasn't sure what she would find but whatever it was, she knew she had to see for herself. She climbed up on to the table and then carefully stepped on to the stool. She looked over the top of the wall.

Fear gripped her like a sheet of ice wrapped around her heart.

Yao was hunched over the desk, his hands shaking, he was holding a piece of crumpled silver foil with some white powder on it over a lit candle and he was sniffing the vapour like it was his last gasp of air.

She felt something inside her snap and let out a heart-piercing cry.

Mei Choon heard it from the bottom of the stairs. Impatient for her noodles she had decided that she would follow Lian to chase her up. She came charging up the stairs and met Lian, looking frightened, heading for her room.

'Ma, what's wrong?' she asked.

'Go, get Mei Chin to bring your father home. Tell him to come quickly!'

245

'Open the door, Yao!' shouted Lian. She banged on the door. There was no response from him, no sound from the room. She banged again. Then she heard the door being unbolted and when it opened Yao stood before her looking half-dazed like he had been dragged out of a deep sleep. 'Why? Yao, why?' she cried.

'What?' said Yao.

Lian grabbed him by his arms and looked into his eyes. They were dull and bloodshot. They were not the eyes of the son she knew and the sad sight of him tore at her heart.

'You can't deny that you were smoking that white powder!' She felt herself shaking.

'That was nothing, Ma.'

'Nothing? See what it has done to you!'

She had heard of this 'white powder', the new curse that had infiltrated the town. She had heard stories of its disastrous and tragic effects on the youngsters – the lying and stealing and, worse, how lives were being ruined. When Yao had noticeably changed before her eyes, she had worried that he'd fallen victim to it but she couldn't face up to it. She had made all sorts of excuses for his change. She just didn't believe it could happen to her son and neither did Jung. She had seen the effects of opium smoking – she had seen her own father smoke it in a licensed joint in Pontian and seen how it numbed the pain in his jaw and calmed him - but that was nothing like the effects she was seeing in Yao.

The moment Jung heard Mei Chin say he was to go home right away, he knew that his worst fear had come to pass. He knew right away it had something to do with Yao. Like Lian he hadn't wanted to face the possibility that Yao could be entangled with drugs. It was inconceivable to him – Yao was a good boy and not only that, he was sensible and intelligent too. How could he have fallen prey to this? He felt a surge of rage mixed with a fear of losing his son.

How Jung got home in one piece he wasn't sure. He couldn't even remember cycling back to the house after Mei

Chin had turned around on her bicycle to go home. He felt as if he was adrift on the high seas, waves whipping mercilessly around him. It was the darkest moment of his life.

Chapter 26

When Inspector Ahmad who had arrested Yao offered to take charge of him, Jung and Lian needed no second invitation. They were at their wits' end and were grateful that someone understood their desperation and anguish. The Inspector had explained that the drug, the 'white powder', was heroin and that Yao was another unfortunate young victim.

Underneath his tough exterior, the Inspector was filled with compassion born of having been through the same hell that Jung and Lian were in. When his own son had become addicted as a teenager, his successful rehabilitation had taken several attempts. Inspector Ahmad's mission now was to help other drug addicts he arrested for petty thefts. In Yao's case he was willing to overlook the theft.

'It has to be *cold turkey*,' he had said, hitting one fist into his palm. 'Otherwise *tak boleh*. It's the only way to break the addiction. That was what my son went through. *Susah.*' He shook his head, remembering how tough it had been, 'but *sekarang dia* okay after that. Not very nice, very hard, but I can try help your son.'

Jung applied the last touch of red paint to the sword and then stood back from the canvas on the floor to view his handiwork. The ancient Chinese warrior –*The One-armed Swordsman* -poised with his blood-stained sword in his right hand, stared back at him, looking as angry and intense as Jung had pictured him in his mind. He was the hero of another of the martial arts movies churned out by the Shaw Brothers. Satisfied with what he had achieved he proceeded to add the title in bold black characters. As he did so he couldn't help wishing that he could slay the demon that had captured his son the way the *One-armed Swordsman* dealt with his enemies.

Backstage, behind the huge screen, cut off from the rest of the cinema with hardly any sound of traffic from the main street, it was here that he felt a semblance of peace within him. It was the only time he felt calm, surrounded by a company of paint-pots, brushes, the smell of turpentine, old and new canvases and his own imagination.

Apart from his Malay colleague, Hamid, whom he'd known since he started working at the cinema, no one else came here. Hamid who did everything from cleaning the cinema hall to ushering, faithfully brought him a mug of coffee every morning, knowing that he couldn't leave his painting. He would put the mug of black coffee on the paint-covered table next to Jung and say, 'Hey, *minum*,' then stand for a minute or two looking at Jung's painting, tilting his head this way and that way, then turn and walk out. Initially Jung had been too ashamed to tell him about Yao's addiction; although some of the neighbours on Hakka Street knew about it, word hadn't spread to the cinema. Since telling him he had felt better and appreciated the fact that Hamid respected his silences when he didn't feel like talking. This morning it was the same. Right on the dot, at eleven o'clock, he appeared with the coffee.

'Hey, *kopi sini*.' He put the mug down on the table.

'*Terima kaseh,*' Jung thanked him.

Hamid took a step closer to the poster. He nodded. '*Wah, mata dia garang,*' he said, pointing to the warrior's eyes.

Jung smiled his appreciation, pleased that his first critic thought the eyes looked fierce too.

Hamid turned to pick up some scrap paper from the floor, scrunching them into a ball as he walked out leaving him to continue. It was only then that Jung realised it was the first time he had smiled in a long while.

He wondered, as he'd been doing for the past four days, how Yao was doing since Inspector Ahmad took him in. Was he winning his fight? It had taken all of his willpower to refrain from running to the police station on the main street, only ten minutes' walk away.

Taking Yao into the police station with the Inspector and Lian, he was pierced by the memory of his own time in prison but Yao's needs left no room for any of the old memories to distract him. But now he couldn't shake off the memory of Yao's face twisted with fear and shame, tears streaming down, as Inspector Ahmad led him away to the cell.

He hadn't been able to sleep; dark rims had appeared under his eyes and Hamid had remarked that he had lost weight. If it weren't for his painting he would have gone crazy; even in these peaceful surroundings where his troubles usually shrank to a surmountable size, the problem with Yao was larger than he could ever imagine it would become. He had consoled himself that no news was a good sign and quietly willed Yao to break his habit. All he could do now was hope and wait.

Floundering at first in fear and anguish, he had ranted and blamed Lian for the state that Yao was in.

'You should have been looking after him! You're here whereas I'm away at the cinema. It's always your clothes, damn clothes,' he had shouted at her.

But he knew that it wasn't her fault. It had started so innocently, just an experiment with some boys after school - a tentative try of the new 'smoke'.

When Jung had eventually calmed down he then started to reproach himself; questions and doubts stabbed at him. What did I do wrong? he had asked himself. How did I not see it? The signs were there. Would moving into the new house sooner have prevented this happening? Had he been too easy on Yao? How could he not have noticed it himself when it all started? If he had then he might have been able to stop it or not let it get this far. His frustration at his impotence in helping his own son only exacerbated his impatience and anger.

The last year had been the worst he had known. The pain was sometimes unbearable seeing Yao slip in and out of stupor and deny that he had taken anything. The worst of it was the blankness that he saw in his eyes. Sometimes, Yao appeared like a stranger to him. Where had his real child gone, the son that he knew? The fear of having lost Yao ripped him up so much that he wanted to scream and shout until it all went away. He hadn't wanted to live his life through his son. To him Yao was a bed of the best seeds sown which had germinated. He had been watering it, tending it, but maybe he hadn't done enough. He hadn't believed it when he realised how bright Yao was as soon as he was able to walk and talk, and he was proud, so proud that his chest stuck out, so far out that sometimes he thought there would surely be a price to pay. Was this the price? Yao being poisoned?

All he wanted now was for his son to become well again and to get his young life together.

Jung knew that it was Lian who had held the family together; she was the tower of strength that he was not. Her business had kept them afloat as Yao's numerous trips to the rehabilitation centres had eaten into their savings. The journeys exhausted them physically and sapped them so much emotionally that they felt hollow. They would have done anything to get Yao off the drug. There had been moments when he felt as if he was at the edge of an abyss and wished he could jump in and be free of the worries. But always he would pull back so that he could be there for Yao. He didn't doubt that if he had to endure prison again so that Yao could be free and clean he would have willingly done it for him.

They had started by taking him to a centre in Tampoi then another in Klang. They had put so much trust in the centre and pinned so much hope on the staff to wean him off the drug only to be disappointed. After a week's stay Yao would leave no better than when he went in.

They soon found out why. The centres were not drug-free; Yao had unwittingly let slip that heroin could be bought in the centre. Someone would supply it as and when needed, only, no one was willing to tell, leaving the authorities utterly helpless. All the anxiety and all the hopes that accompanied each trip came to nothing.

The last four days of waiting and not seeing Yao had been heart-breaking. He and Lian drew some comfort and strength from the support of their new friend, Mrs Kang, who visited them regularly. A devout Christian, she told them that she was praying for Yao and also invited them to the church near their new house. For Jung church was the last thing on his mind. They had declined the invitation at first but as time went by Lian started attending the church. When Inspector Ahmad came on the scene it was like an answer to their prayers. Now they waited to see and hear the outcome of the treatment.

The room was spinning around him as Yao opened his eyes. The smell of stale vomit hit his nostrils. Lying on the hard wooden plank that served as a bed he was conscious of his body aching, an ache that had nothing to do with the hard surface he was lying on. It was from a craving; his body was railing against being so abruptly deprived of what it needed. His mouth felt like the inside of a cement mixer; he licked his lips. He put his hand to his face and felt it moist with sweat. He wanted to sit up but his head felt as if it had been stamped on by a herd of bullocks.

For a long while he couldn't work out where he was. Gradually as his brain stopped reeling he realised that the stench was from his own vomit and the events leading to the present came back to him, like a swelling wave which he couldn't hold back, stirring up the pain and shame in him. The hard bed and the sight of the bars in front of him reminded him that he was in a police cell and confirmed that it was no nightmare, that he had really gone through the most harrowing experience, both physically and mentally.

It had all begun four days ago in the market. He and his friend Ah Tee were scanning the place waiting for the right moment to pounce on their victim. The street was crowded; the stalls were surrounded by housewives browsing and laden with their purchases and looking for more to buy. Yao was very nervous at first although he had done this once before. He had picked the purse of a woman

252

at a night market and got away with it. Ah Tee, a couple of years older than he and hooked on heroin for years told him he'd done it many times and had never been caught. It had surprised Yao that he had to resort to stealing when his father was a rich businessman but Ah Tee had boasted saying how easy it was to steal, especially if they chose the right target.

That morning he reiterated how easy it was, nudging him with his elbow and pointing out an old woman carrying an open basket with her money purse in it. Yao could see the purse which was screaming to be taken. Encouraged by Ah Tee's confidence in him, he decided he would do it, and besides, he had no choice; he could feel the claws of his craving scratching at him and he knew he needed to get the money quickly for another fix.

They followed the old woman as she wandered from one vendor to the next. Lifting her purse was easy and they would have made a clean get-away but for the fact that some woman nearby who saw Yao in the act of picking the purse, yelled out and pointed to him. The two boys were startled by the shouts and ran, pushing their way through the crowd, directly towards the policeman who was standing outside a coffee shop.

It was all over very quickly. The policeman, who had not expected any change to his routine of making sure that no vendors' stalls blocked the traffic, was jolted out of his serene mood. He saw Yao, charged towards him and in a split second he grabbed him and was quickly assisted by a fellow officer. Ah Tee disappeared into the crowd leaving Yao shaking in the hands of the policemen.

The shame of being caught, of being made a spectacle of and then being taken to the police station was nothing compared to the shame of facing his parents when they came to see him. Although he couldn't remember much of the conversation, he could never forget the worry and pain etched on his parents' faces. And he remembered feeling utterly wretched for disappointing them.

Everything after that was very hazy. He vaguely remembered the officer coming into the cell to talk with him. He'd explained what would happen if he agreed to go *cold turkey*. Yao had heard of it but hadn't had the courage or strength to go through it knowing it would be tough.

'No drug from now, *faham tak?*' said the Inspector, looking earnestly at him.

Yao nodded.

'*Cold turkey*. That means you fight the craving, never mind how tough,' he'd said as he pushed his fist into the air. 'It will be painful. Very painful. You want more drug but you can't. I will be here to help you through it,' he'd nodded, looking very serious.

Then the Inspector had sat back and waited. Waited patiently for him to decide whether to accept his offer or not. It had been plain to Yao that he had no option but to accept. Somewhere in his moth-eaten mind he'd known that he wanted out of this mire and misery, if not for himself then for his parents.

The agony of the withdrawal was like nothing he had ever experienced before. As the symptoms of the withdrawal gradually heightened, his body felt as if it was being methodically and mercilessly clawed by demons. At times he felt he could tear his hair out, his body ached. His head felt as if it was swelling and waiting to explode. He screamed as he writhed. He cried. He threw himself about, kicking and yelling as the pain tore through his body. Throughout it all, he felt the strong arms of Inspector Ahmad holding him down. Inspector Ahmad was a tall, lean man and very strong for his age; in this struggle Yao would have easily overcome a lesser man. When he eventually calmed down, the Inspector wiped his brow, sat with him and patiently encouraged him.

Yao didn't know how long it had lasted. All he knew was that he'd wanted it to end quickly. Then gradually the agony started to ease and as it did it left him feeling washed out.

The torture seemed so distant now. He lay quietly. How did he get to such a state? How did he allow himself to go so far? A mixture of emotions overcame him – shame, remorse and gratitude. He thought of his parents, the worry he had caused them. He was thankful that they had stood by him and that they hadn't seen him in the depths of his struggle during the withdrawal. Relief came rushing in when it dawned on him that he had won the fight, broken the hold of the effects of the drug. He resolved never to touch the powder again.

Suddenly hunger pangs struck him and as he tried to sit up he realised how weak he was and noticed that his shirt was soaked with sweat. Just at that moment he heard footsteps, the clomping of leather heels against the bare concrete floor of the corridor. He turned to look through the bars.

'Ah, you are awake,' said Inspector Ahmad cheerfully. 'Good. *Makan* time.' He was carrying a tray. He opened the gate, walked into the cell and placed the tray down on the bench by his side. 'You must *makan* now,' he said.

'How long have I been sleeping?' Yao rasped, his throat felt dry.

'One day.' Inspector Ahmad's voice bore no anger or irritation.

Yao felt a deep sense of gratitude and respect for the man standing in front of him. He'd half expected Inspector Ahmad to scold him but he only said,

'*Makan*.' He was pointing to the tray which had a plate of boiled rice with sambal and a glass of water. 'You need to get strong now.'

Chapter 27

It was Nick's voice that attracted me to him.

I was cutting a piece of toast into soldiers for six-year-old Trisha who was propped up in her bed when I heard him. We were in the ten-bedded bay opposite where Sister's office was and from where Trisha was she could see people coming from the corridor before turning right to enter the office. I had my back to it when he walked in and all I heard was, 'Good morning Sister, I'm Dr Ross, your new houseman.'

His voice exuded confidence without the arrogance that some of the other young doctors came packed with; its deep tone sent a soft wave of warmth through me like drinking hot chocolate on a chilly night. There was a hint of a burr which, I discovered later, was an Inverness strain of the Scottish accent. I thought then that I wouldn't mind having a doctor with a voice like that; I couldn't resist turning round to look at him.

There he was, in his white coat with his stethoscope hanging round his neck, standing at the door to the office, not so tall that his head could touch the top of the doorway, but his shoulders were broad enough to block the way. Trisha, who had been watching us, looked up at me when I turned back to her toast; in her little voice she said, 'He's got a nice face.'

He wasn't what I would call handsome, not a Robert Redford or Sean Connery and his wild brown hair looked like he had only run his fingers through it when he got up that morning.

It had turned out to be a busy morning as the ward was almost full and we were one nurse short. I didn't see him again until later that afternoon when he was dealing

256

with a very apprehensive four-year-old, Jonathan, who had just been admitted with intermittent abdominal pain.

Sitting on the edge of the bed Nick fished out a coin from a pocket in his white coat and held it up between his fingers in front of Jonathan.

'See this coin here?' he said.

Jonathan nodded.

'Good. Now watch carefully because I'm going to make it disappear.' He closed his fingers over the coin, rubbed his hands together and then opened his palms.

Jonathan's face lit up. 'It's gone,' he said softly.

'I wonder where it's gone.' Nick lifted the cover from Jonathan's chest and bent down to peep. 'Nope, not there.' Then he frowned. 'I wonder where it could be....*Ah*..look, it's here!' With a sweep of his hand he touched Jonathan's ear lobe, pretending to pull the coin out of it and then held it up in front of his face.

'Magic!' said Jonathan.

'I'll do you another one after I've had a look at your tummy, alright?'

Jonathan was playdough in Nick's hands.

I was disappointed that our paths didn't cross again and as luck would have it, it was my second last day on the ward before moving on to the geriatric ward in Hitchin.

Two weeks later, after finishing our early shift Vicky, Gabby, Fiona and I sat in the kitchen, utterly exhausted, drinking our tea as we moaned about work and staff. We exchanged notes on the most interesting diseases, treatments or procedures that we had observed on the ward. Suddenly Vicky looked down at her fob watch and then turned to me.

'We've got badminton. I've booked it for seven and it's almost half six. Colin's bringing his friend. Finish your tea, we've got to get ready,' she said.

Colin was the new doctor that she had been seeing for a few weeks. We leapt out of our seats to get changed and then ran to the gym in the hospital.

The sound of racket hitting shuttlecock echoed in the large high-ceilinged gym when I opened the door. As soon as I saw Colin's friend on the court I spun round to look at Vicky. She was looking straight ahead, smiling at Colin as she started to take her coat off. I turned back to see him waving after he had delivered a thundering smash. When I looked at his friend again I felt my heart starting to beat faster.

Putting my hand on Vicky's arm I opened my mouth to speak but nothing came out.

'What?' said Vicky now trying to look straight-faced.

I raised my brow. She said nothing, and then she smiled.

'Nick said he wanted to meet you, and I didn't want it to look like I was fixing you up.'

'*Ohh..*' I was stumped and could feel my heart thumping even faster.

'C'mon, let's join them.' Vicky walked on and I followed taking my coat off at the same time. We threw our coats on the bench by the wall.

Colin and Nick stopped playing.

'Hi girls!' Colin called out. 'Chiew,' he said pointing his racket at Nick, 'this is Nick.'

Nick strode up to me with a big grin on his face and clasped my hand. His grip was firm yet gentle but I felt I was grasping a mini-lightning bolt in my palm as a warm pleasant charge shot through me making me blush. I looked up into his face and thought, *You were right Trisha, he has got a nice face.* His smoky brown eyes smiled at me and I felt my knees wobble.

'Hi,' he said, 'how are you?'

'Good, thanks.'

'Will you partner me against those two?' He tilted his head to Vicky who had joined Colin on the other side of the net.

'Sure,' I said.

'Warm up first?'

'Yes.' I'd never been so lost for words before.

As the game progressed I became less self-conscious. I was impressed with Nick's skill, how light he was on his feet and I was amazed at how easily we complemented each other as partners. After an hour or so of very competitive play and sweating enough to avert a hose-pipe ban, Colin suggested we freshen up and then go to *The Three Hammers* pub for drinks.

We walked together across the car park to the staff's accommodation. The doctors' blocks of flats were separated from the nurses' flats by a large swathe of lawn with concrete paths linking them. Colin and Vicky walked ahead, hand in hand, leaving me and Nick to fall in behind. As Nick rubbed his forehead with his towel then his hands and the handle of his racket he asked,

'So, how do you spell your name?'

I told him.

'Hmm, mine is just boring N-I-C-K.'

'It could be spelt *K*-N-I-C-K, if you wanted to be different.'

He chuckled. 'You were working on the children's ward, weren't you?'

I nodded.

'I thought I'd frightened you off. You left pretty sharpish after I'd arrived.'

'I didn't even notice you'd arrived,' I lied.

He smiled.

'So is this your first job as a houseman?' I asked.

'Yup. Does it show?'

'I thought you were good with the children,' I said looking up at him.

'*There*, you did notice me!'

We burst out laughing.

'I'm working in the geriatric ward in Hitchin now. Compared to this new hospital it's a dump of a place. The walls are like a sieve against the cold draughts,' I said.

'Yes, many of the old Victorian hospitals are like that,' he said.

'Did you and Colin go to the same medical school in Edinburgh?'

'Yes, but he is a Sassenach,' he said with a smile.

Although I didn't know what a Sassenach was, I could see they were very close.

In the low-ceilinged, smoke-filled room of the *Three Hammers*, Vicky and I sat facing Colin and Nick across a round table beside an open fire which was throwing off a scent of cherry wood. We joked about the hospital canteen's sweet curry with raisins and made fun of grey-faced Sister Bennett who had a reputation of being a man-hater. We discussed the merits of *The Clockwork Orange* after we had covered rugby and football. We told tales from our travels; Vicky and I had been to Athens in the summer while the two men had just come back from skiing in Alpbach in Austria. When I told them about the Malaysian beaches on the east coast Nick was fascinated and said he would love to go there one day.

We talked and laughed until the landlord called closing time.

Nick helped me with my coat and as soon as we stepped into the cold night air and just out of Vicky and Colin's range of hearing he asked,

'Can I see you again?'

'Yes,' I said, hardly able to contain myself and conscious that I couldn't help the big smile across my face.

'Oh, good. I'm off tomorrow. So, tomorrow?'

'I'm on an early shift, so that'd be okay.'

'Great! I'll pick you up at seven,' he said. 'I've really had a good time tonight.'

'Me too.'

When we arrived at the entrance to our block we turned to face each other.

'Good night then,' I said.

'Good night,' he said and then bent to kiss me on the cheek.

When Vicky and I got back to our flat she couldn't stop teasing me.

'You two certainly got on very well. Noticed him looking at you a few times,' she said. I hoped she didn't see me looking at him when he wasn't looking at me.

'He's nice,' I said without hesitation, 'and guess what? I'm seeing him again tomorrow night.'

I was tingling with a bevy of butterflies jiving in my belly and I thought to myself that if I had to choose someone to revisit the Malaysian islands with, Nick was definitely high up on my list of possibilities. Without a doubt I would share with, or even give him, my last piece of stuffed bean curd. I liked his face; a fall off his horse when he was a teenager had caused an ever-so-slight kink in his nose in an otherwise symmetrical face down to the cleft, like a potter's mark, in his chin. And when he smiled at me it was as if I was the only one in his sphere of vision and I was special.

The next evening couldn't come fast enough for me.

At eight the next morning after a trudge through the icy air in the dark from the flat to the bus stop, followed by a slow bus ride, I was in the geriatric ward in Hitchin.

The first bit of bad news that greeted me and the other two student nurses was that the fourth nurse was off sick. The second was that the boiler had broken down and we were told to do what we could to keep the old ladies warm. The irony was that the coal miners' strikes that had been crippling the country and reducing the working week to three days had not affected the hospital keeping warm, but now the broken boiler was threatening to freeze us all.

When we walked into the ward the smell of stale urine dangling in the cold air assaulted us. Between us we had to get the thirty ladies out of bed, help them to the bathroom or onto a commode, then get washed and dressed in time for breakfast. It was busier than in Billingsgate fish market as we flew like spinning tops between commodes, the dirty-laundry bin, the mountain of clean bed linen and the women in their beds or on commodes shouting for attention. Sodden bedclothes were yanked off the beds as soon as we got the women out. I had just helped Mrs Jones with the moustache to her chair at the breakfast table when the Nursing officer, Mrs Roberts came into the ward.

'Nurse Chiang, I would like a word with you in the office as soon as you've finished with Mrs Jones,' she said.

Surprised by her summons, I quickly washed my hands while she waited, then followed her to Sister's office. She stood aside to let me in before shutting the door. Standing very straight in her stiff navy blue uniform and with an equally stiff white hat edged with lace perched on top of her head, she went straight to the point.

'Now, Nurse Chiang, you know full well that you *do not* wear your cardigan when you are working on the ward. You've been told that at the very start of your training.'

I was stunned. Then I said, 'But it's freezing. The boiler's broken down.'

'I know about the boiler. This,' she pointed to my attire, 'is not the uniform on the ward. Now take the cardigan off, and go back to work.'

It wasn't just the tone, the condescension, but the absurdity of it that irked me.

'There're more important things to worry about than my blessed uniform.' Too late to pull back the words, they'd leapt out of my mouth and she had caught them. Her face turned rigid.

I walked away and started to take off my cardigan as I headed for the nurses' locker room then returned to the ward just in time to see Mrs Henley throw her bowl of porridge on to the floor in a tantrum, defying her imaginary friend who was forcing her to eat it. I wanted to scream and run out.

But I didn't.

Nick turned up at the flat that evening looking very smart in his tan leather jacket and corduroy trousers. When I opened the door to him, he was holding a potted pink and white azalea plant in his hands and smiling. He pushed it towards to me.

'For you,' he said. 'I saw it in the florist's shop this morning and thought you might like it.'

I was flabbergasted, happy and self-conscious as I took it from him and thanked him.

When he led me to his maroon *MGB-GT* parked near the front door of the block, I did a mental flip while at the same time fighting the jaw-dropping reflex. He opened the passenger door open for me and as I sank into the seat he said,

'I thought we might go to the *Cromwell* restaurant in old town. The food's quite good. What do you think?'

'That'd be fine I'm sure,' I said trying to sound casual.

The evening turned out to be just what I had expected. Facing each other across the table, we talked and talked and laughed like two kids bouncing on the trampoline together oblivious to the others in the busy restaurant.

He told me about his growing up in Inverness; his father was a butcher and mother, a bank clerk. How he loved sailing and fishing and how the smell of the sea always filled him with a feeling of being wrapped in a warm duvet while savouring his favourite vanilla ice-cream. Then he made me laugh when he told me about the time when he was twelve and the prank that he and his cousin Jimmy played on an unsuspecting drunkard on the eve of Hogmanay.

The victim was a man who would sway, stagger and sing all the way past Nick's parents' house at the same time every night on his way home from the pub. Nick had put a flat whisky bottle, tied with a piece of cotton and half filled with tea, on the pavement and then holding the other end of the cotton they hid behind the hedge and waited for him to appear. And just as they had hoped, the man appeared, spotted the bottle and eagerly staggered forward to bend down to pick it up, at which point Nick gently tugged the bottle away. Each time the man tottered forward to reach for it, Nick would pull it away while Jimmy rolled about in silent laughter. I could just picture the whole moon-lit scene and see the hapless man stumbling towards the bottle that kept creeping away from him.

I asked him about his training in Edinburgh and I was fascinated as I listened to him. I loved his sense of fun and honest mischief. By the end of the evening I had an inkling that he was the man I wanted to spend the rest of my life with, although I didn't tell him that until much, much later.

The next day I was summoned to see the Principal Nursing Officer.

Miss Carter, middle-aged, with her auburn hair piled neatly on her head and her stiff suit spelling out 'no nonsense' sat behind an imposing desk. I had only seen her once before during my induction week. Her tall and angular stature commanded attention but I was determined not to be intimidated by her. She took off her spectacles and eyed me as I walked in and then motioned to the chair opposite her.

'Hello, Nurse Chiang. How are you?' Her voice was firm; the corners of her mouth lifted like an invisible string attached to them had been pulled.

'I'm well, thank you.'

'Now, I understand you were rude to Mrs Roberts yesterday.'

'I didn't think I was.'

'Now, tell me what happened then.' She still had the smile pasted on her face.

I started to explain. '....This was the first time I wore my cardigan at work but it was for a good reason. It seemed to me petty to worry about the cardigan. There were more important things to worry about, like looking after the thirty dependent patients. '

Miss Carter stiffened, the smile vanished. Before she spoke the corners of her mouth lifted up again. 'I hear what you are saying, Nurse Chiang. It was unfortunate that the boiler was not working. I'm sure you must have felt the cold more than anybody else, not being used to this weather. We'll forget about this incident but you must remember that we have to maintain strict uniform code. Is that alright?'

If Nick hadn't come into my life then I might have rushed into packing my bags. Meeting him was like arriving at an oasis in the middle of a desert.

When I got back to the flat and told Fiona what had happened, she simply said, '*Och*, you should go *bell her heed*.'

I didn't boil Miss Carter's head. Instead, I apologised and promised I wouldn't do it again. Knowing full well that I needed the qualification, I was going to focus on revising for the exams. I knew what I had to do next.

Chapter 28

Batu Pahat
April 1976

I didn't recognise Yao when he came striding towards me, out of the sea of bobbing faces at the *Arrivals* gate in Singapore Airport. I saw a lanky teenage boy with a cheeky grin showing off his white teeth, close-cut hair and wearing shirt sleeves and trousers. It was only when he called out, 'Hi, sis,' stretching one arm towards me that I realised who he was.

'Yao!' I called out grabbing his arm. '*Wah*, you've grown so tall!'

I had no idea then of the hell he had gone through in the months before. He looked so well, his eyes bright and clear. As he took my trolley from me I held on to his arm and looked up at him brimming with sisterly pride and affection.

'So how are you?' I asked.

'Good,' he said. 'You look different, fairer.'

I laughed and turning to look for the rest of the welcoming party I quickly spotted my family waving furiously at me. Mei Lin and Mei Chin were there as promised as they were on their second semester break. Then I saw Mother's smiling face. I had been seized with a need to hug her, had been longing for it and at the same time wondering how I would react to Father when I saw him. I knew I couldn't hug him even if I wanted to; it just wasn't the done thing, but on seeing Mother, I burst through the seams of my ingrained reserve and threw my arms around her.

'Ma, it's so good to see you,' I said. The relief that she was well and the joy of holding her swept over me. I could feel her happiness with her arms around me; I felt like her little girl again.

'So glad you've come back safely,' she said as she pushed back to look at me. 'You look well.'

We held each other for a little longer while my sisters looked on, showering me with smiles of welcome, laughing and talking at the same time. I turned to see Father who was standing beside us and smiling at me. His eyes told me he was glad to see me. I gently let go of Mother and took his outstretched hand.

'Papa, are you well?' I said.

'I've been waiting so long for this day,' he said, both his hands over mine.

'It's so good to be home,' I said, feeling I could burst with joy.

His bronze face was a picture of health, his hair still black and shiny with *Brylcreem*. I had missed him and I wanted us to get on during my three weeks at home. Seeing his happy face I was now sure that we would get on very well.

'Papa, you've got a gold tooth!' I said. One of his upper right teeth had been capped.

He chuckled. 'Yes, had to have it done last month.'

'You've lost weight.'

He nodded. 'Yes, it's better for me. Healthier.'

Coming home was as easy as falling into a large bean bag; it was like fitting into an old jigsaw and I blended into the crowd instead of sticking out like a scarecrow in a field. It was so good to slip back into speaking Hakka again. Being there was like stepping into my comfortable slippers, in spite of feeling like I had landed in a steam bath fully clothed. I had forgotten how hot the tropical heat was. I was excited and happy to be back in spite of missing Nick and wishing he was with me. It had been hard leaving him behind and I couldn't wait to tell my sisters about him.

Nothing prepared me for what my parents told me about Yao and his addiction and the agonies of the rehabilitation. I felt like a tidal wave had hit me, leaving me prostrate and gasping for breath. Once the fright and horror of it sunk in I started to blame myself. Would he have succumbed to it had I been around to keep an eye on him instead of being so far away? We'd been so close and I would surely have noticed the signs, or at least he might have talked to me about it.

'We didn't want to tell you before. You would have worried and we didn't want you distracted from your studies,' said Father. He was right; I would have pulled my hair out with worry.

'Thank God he's fine now, that's what matters,' said Mother. 'He's very careful not to mix with the wrong crowd again. Comes straight home from school and buries his head in his books.'

Father sighed. '*Ah*, Yao is basically a good boy. Just led astray, that's all. He'll grow out of it, this wanting to experiment everything. I don't think it has left any permanent damage. At least I hope not. He's clean now.' He then allowed a smile to appear as he looked at me. 'Tell me what it has been like the last three years.'

I told them all about the adjustments to the people, the weather and the training and when I had finished he said, 'You've done well to finish your training. What will you do now?'

'You mean, am I coming home to work?'

'Of course your ma and I would like you to be nearer home, but it's entirely your choice. The truth is, even if there's a great demand for nurses trained overseas you'll need to speak fluent Malay.' He shook his head. 'They're making it *so* tough for non-Malays to get jobs.'

Both he and Mother watched me closely, waiting for my answer.

'I'm thinking of going to medical school.'

Mother's eyes widened. 'But you've just finished training,' she said. 'You mean you can change just like that?'

268

'Yes, but it's not going to be easy. First, I have to get accepted by a university,' I said and explained what had happened.

Before my friends and I finished our training we were told that jobs were in short supply and advised to look elsewhere for work. I was lucky to get a position in the Metabolic Ward at St Mary's Hospital in Paddington and moved to London as soon as the results of the exams came through.

'Life in England sounds good, so many opportunities,' said Father. 'You must do what you think is best.'

I now looked at Mother and Father with eyes of admiration for their tenacity and most of all their love in their fight for Yao and marvelled at how they had coped with the ordeal. I couldn't imagine the anguish or pain and at times the hopelessness that they had been through. Mother looked so serene and at peace, a testament to her new found faith. Father seemed like a man who had been whipped a few times, then got up and steeled himself against anything else that might come his way.

I resolved to be more understanding and patient myself and not to jump up in anger when he displayed his impatience towards Mother.

Suddenly the pictures and drawings I had seen earlier in Yao's room fell into place. He'd been showing me his room when I'd noticed his dog-eared drawing pad on the table. I had picked it up to look inside. The pencil and charcoal sketches were of human forms with distorted faces dripping with pain and screaming. They had made me jerk my head up to look at him. But seeing how well and relaxed he was, although a little skinny, I had no reason to suspect anything was wrong or that they reflected his own demons. When he'd told me he was studying hard for his exams I was reassured that he was on the right track.

I became very watchful over him now. The more I looked at him the more I admired his focus on his studies and his will-power in staying away from the so-called friend who had got him hooked in the first place. I could only pray that he would continue to be strong and remain focussed on his studies.

Mother and Father's new house was like a monastery compared to the menagerie on Hakka Street. Blissfully peaceful, it was surrounded by a well-trimmed lawn edged with banana trees to provide shade that Father worked on tirelessly. He was fussy about not leaving stagnant water around which would breed mosquitoes. To the side of the house where his gleaming bike was leaning against the wall, he showed me the potted orchid plants hanging from a pergola that he had built. On the new veranda at the front of the house there were pots of pink and red roses that Mother liked. The red path in front led to the Chinese church as Mother reminded me.

'It is just five minutes' walk from here so I have no excuse not to attend,' she'd said.

Walking around barefooted on the cool smooth concrete floor and with a constant breeze flowing through the house I could see why the house was ideal for Father. In the front room his desk stood at the window with its familiar paraphernalia of paint brushes, pencils and pens neatly arranged. Four rattan armchairs and a low table marked out the sitting area which was separated from the kitchen by a small room for Yao while Mei Chin and Mei Choon shared the second bedroom upstairs. Mother proudly showed me the gas ring she'd had installed and the large water tank in the bathroom where we could bathe with no fear of being told off. I was struck by a deep sense of gratitude seeing how content she and Father were.

One of the highlights of my time back home was sitting with my sisters and Yao in the front room like five hungry fledglings in a nest pushing and shoving to share our news.

After I had filled them in on my life in England to '*oohs*' and '*aahs*', Mei Choon piped up,

'This secretarial course I've told you about in my letter, it's Pitman's, the best. I can do shorthand now and touch type too. Can do almost fifty words per minute which is *very* fast, but not fast enough yet.'

Her course was at a private school on Rangoon Road in Singapore. She was living with Mother's brother Poh and his family to keep the cost down. Still very keen on painting, she had ambitions of having an exhibition of her work one day but in the meantime she knew she had to earn her living.

Mei Lin was finishing her accountancy course at University while Mei Chin was in her second year at the same Malayan Teachers' College that Uncle Tian had attended. As I listened to them telling me about their courses I glowed with pride at how well they were doing and was so pleased that their future seemed secure. Yao's turn would soon be next; he seemed very at ease sprawled on the floor beside me.

They brought me up to speed with all the changes that had taken place such as the legal requirement that Mother employ a Malay girl in the shop. It was the first step to greater integration between the ethnic groups. Sadly the Cambridge School Certificate exam had been replaced by the Malaysian Certificate of Education with even greater marginalisation of English.

'The Malays are learning to speak Hokkien now. They are doing very well,' said Mei Chin.

'Chung Lin is getting married!' shouted Mei Choon, 'and I'm going to be her bridesmaid. It's a pity you'll be back in England. She's getting married in two months' time.'

'Oh, good! Who to? She deserves someone good,' I said, feeling really happy for her.

'He's a carpenter, got his own business in Jalan Kluang. It was *so* sweet. He saw Chung Lin in the shop one day and asked his aunt to match make for him, through Mother,' said Mei Choon.

'You know since we moved out of the shophouse, Hock has taken over Papa and Ma's room and also got married,' said Mei Chin. 'His wife is a lot younger than him and very pretty.'

'What about First Uncle?' I asked.

'Don't see much of him. He has two children now, two boys. He brings them to the shop sometimes, usually in the afternoon,' said Yao.

'I'll avoid going in the afternoon then.'

'I go there sometimes to see Fook and play on his drums. He's very good, y'know,' he nodded, 'definitely got talent. Sometimes we play together, me on my guitar and he his drums.' He had shown me the classical guitar that Father had bought him, a reward for being good.

'Is he working?' I asked.

'Yes, in the new supermarket that's just opened near the bus station. But he really wants to be a musician,' said Yao.

'Oh, I forgot this, this is big news,' said Mei Choon as she screwed her nose, 'Third Aunty, Uncle and Jin have moved out. Gone to live with Kin in P.J. or somewhere there I heard. Nobody is sure, you know how secretive Third Aunt can be.'

'So the house is practically empty! What about Uncle Heng? How is he?' I said.

'He's well, still walks a lot. Ma and Papa asked him to come and live with us but he prefers it there. Says he's too old to move. He asked to see you soon,' said Mei Chin.

'How's Papa been?' I wanted to know how he had been towards Mother especially under the shadow of Yao's problems.

'Much the same,' said Mei Choon. She dropped her shoulders. 'He can be so grumpy sometimes. Sometimes he blames Ma and takes it out on her. Then he's always checking on Yao. If Yao's late coming home he worries. Don't blame him though.'

Mei Choon was right; Father hadn't changed. During the time I was home I had heard him muttering and

272

grumbling at Mother but not a sound from her. I had to resist the urge to barge into their room and tell him to stop. But I didn't say a word as I crushed the shoots of anger and walked away, feeling sorry for Mother. How could I be angry with him when clearly he was pleased that I was home? Whenever he could he would buy an assortment of *nonya* cakes on his way home from the cinema because he knew I loved and missed them. The delight on his face, his smile, each time he handed me them was enough to wash away any irritation I might have felt. Besides I had promised myself that I would be more patient.

The first morning that I went to the shophouse with Mother we left Father tending his plants before going off to work at the cinema. Mother suggested that we take a trishaw which I was reluctant to do as it had always filled me with guilt whenever I saw how hard the trishaw-man had to pedal. So we walked instead. As soon as I stepped outside the house I strained my neck to look everywhere like a first-time tourist absorbing the atmosphere; I soaked it up as if there were molecules of Chinese-ness in the air. It was as if my Chinese-ness had been diluted through being away for so long and living amongst the British.

The air felt different; it was heavy with moisture and thick with the aromas that I had missed. I had been told about the new Food Court at the riverside and couldn't wait till the evening to pay a visit. We walked past a group of stalls opposite my old kindergarten where a crowd already gathered to buy their breakfasts. My nose twitched like a mouse on the hunt, savouring the smells of fresh mangoes and banana fritters, steamed dumplings amidst spicy curry bubbling and the frying of noodles. A man was unloading his mountain of water-melon from the back of his lorry.

The streets bustled with shoppers haggling, motorcar horns hooting, bicycle bells ringing and the latest Chinese pop-music blaring from some shops. Walking along the five-foot way we weaved between baskets of papayas and mangosteens, a table of the daily Chinese, Malay and English newspapers, a cobbler's box, a man sharpening knives, a *satay*-man tending skewers of meat over a coal fire, an old man selling *toto*-lottery tickets, and gunny sacks of dried mushrooms, dried fish, rice and lentils.

We stopped at the herbalist's shop on Jalan Jenang where Mother bought some ginseng.

'I'll brew this for you when we get home, it's a good restorative,' she said.

Mother knew a lot of people so we had to pause every so often to greet someone and then she would introduce me as her daughter who had come home from England. It was lovely to observe her as she exchanged news and chatted with the people she'd met. She looked pretty in her printed dress, her short wavy hair suited her and she had lost none of her youthfulness. She looked fresh and cool, as if she was in an invisible air-conditioned bubble, while I looked like I had just emerged from the shower, beads of sweat cascading down my forehead and my T-shirt sticking to my damp skin.

When we eventually came to the main road I noticed that there were distinctly more cars now, driven by drivers who seemed to have no regard for street signs doing as they pleased, nor did the pedestrians care as they stepped out slowly in front of them. The cyclists were the same although there seemed to be fewer of them.

As we turned into Hakka Street my heart leapt at the thought of seeing Uncle Heng, Chung Lin and everybody else.

Chung Lin, Uncle Heng, Mr Ting and his son Leng, Uncle Yew, Hock and his new wife and Fook came out into the shop to greet me like a victorious soldier coming home.

'Welcome!' they shouted, smiling and looking at me closely to see if I had changed and seemed surprised I could still speak my mother tongue.

In the midst of the familiar scents of leather, polish, fabric and Uncle Heng's starch, I filled them in on what life was like in England: the people and their curious ways, the plain food and the spectacular changing seasons.

'*Wah*, the snow must be very, very cold,' said Chung Lin, looking very much like the bride-in-waiting, her cheeks aglow and her eyes vivid with anticipation of her big day.

'Not sure I like their kind of food. It must be tough for you going without noodles and your mother's stuffed bean curd,' said Uncle Yew.

When I told them how much a plate of noodles cost Uncle Heng looked amazed.

'*Wah*,' he said, 'twelve dollars for a plate that cost only thirty cents here. That would feed a family for a day!' He shook his head. 'I'm sure it's not as delicious as what you get here.'

When I asked him if he would ever go back to his village in China to live, he said that Malaysia was now his home. He had been away far too long; besides, life in the old village would be very different to what he had been used to since coming here.

Ai Chien, hearing that I was in the shop, came to the shop to welcome me home. Her welcome was quickly followed by her lamenting the fact that her sons, Big Head and Long Head, hadn't been able to get a good job with their degrees from Taiwan and were working in their father's business.

'You got the right idea going to England,' she said. 'Your mother won't need to work anymore when all you girls are working.'

Mother's half of the shop looked good with piles of cut fabric waiting to be stitched on her worktop, next to a register bulging with orders and strips of fabric like an extended accordion. Apart from Chung Lin, there were now three other women, one of whom was Malay, working at the sewing machines which stood in a line at the back of the shop. The orders from Singapore were still coming in; the *Lotus* brand was spreading far and wide.

I wished then that Nick could have been there to meet my family and Uncle Heng at the same time as I wondered how he would have reacted to the house and its inhabitants if he was. Would he run a mile if he saw all this? I had already told Mother about him and she wasn't disappointed or upset by it.

'I suppose that's inevitable, living amongst them. As long as you're happy, it doesn't matter what colour the skin,' she'd said.

I had been afraid that both my parents would be repulsed by and object to the idea of my going out with a *red-haired devil.* Even if they didn't, would the fear of what others might think, of being stigmatised, prevent them from accepting Nick?

I was relieved when Mother didn't disapprove. I presumed that she would have told Father and since I hadn't heard any objections, it was safe to assume he wasn't opposed to it either. My sisters and Yao on the other hand were thrilled.

I decided to go upstairs to see my old room, but first I paused at Grandfather and Grandmother's shrine to pay my respects. Taking a bunch of joss-sticks from a packet lying by the side of the shrine I lit them and then stood them in the urn. The smoke of the incense trailed behind me as I kicked off my sandals and mounted the stairs. Looking down I noticed that the air-well was now devoid of the tanks of fish.

It was quiet when I got to the landing. Father and Mother's old room - now used by Hock and his wife - was open. I looked inside. The new furniture was arranged differently but the familiar stuffiness still hung in the air. I turned to face the corridor and smiled at the sight of the peep holes on the warm wooden floor which sent a tingle up through my bare feet as the surge of memories hit me. The afternoon sun was oozing through the skylight; my twinkling column of dust greeted me.

A strange feeling came over me. It was a sense of disbelief that I had finally broken free from here, yet, cutting right through it was an awareness that this 'home' had in many ways moulded me. I was aware that here there was no room for pretences or airs; all my flaws, weaknesses and strengths were laid bare. Any delusions I had of myself melted away. I had been moved to believe in myself and to aspire to better things, to rise like the dancing dust in my column of sunshine. If walking through the streets concentrated my sense of Chinese-ness, here in this menagerie I was stripped bare of my mask and forced to rediscover myself. A question popped up: *what did Nick see in me*?

As I moved quietly down the corridor passing the rooms on my right, I fancied I could hear children laughing and shouting. I stopped at my old room. A set of drums stood in the middle of it. The column of dancing dust was anchored right next to the drums. I did what I always did; my eyes traced the path of the sunshine from the linoleum-covered floor right up to the skylight.

**

I stretch my arm as far as I can to reach it. I can't see what it is I am reaching for but I know I want it, yearn for it. It is a matter of life or death. Every fibre in my body aches as they stretch to grab the object which is tantalisingly close, but just as I almost touch it it edges away from my fingertips. In my frustration I try harder and then suddenly the object is gone, and I am left gasping.

I'd hoped that once I had qualified as a nurse the dream would disappear but it insisted on haunting me, coming more frequently and I would wake up feeling restless.

Fired by the knowledge that Alexander Fleming discovered penicillin in the very same hospital where I was working and meeting Roger Bannister, the four-minute-mile

277

man I'd admired as a girl and now a neurologist, when he came to see a patient on the ward, I'd applied to University College, London. A tremor of nervousness coursed through my body when I was filling in the forms; my hopes had been catapulted sky high and I was dazzled by the possibility of my getting into medical school so much so that the thought of failure was too much to bear.

I had worked out the finances. I realised that I could do agency work at the weekends to supplement the grant that I was hoping I would get. There was a demand for nurses – State Registered Nurses or SRNs - at the private hospitals in London which catered for wealthy British and Arabs, where I'd worked before. For that I was grateful I'd finished my training. The pay they offered was good and I was prepared to put up with pampering the rich sick and an ugly pot-bellied Arab flashing his gold rings and trying to entice me to dinner at his hotel.

Reassured that Mother and Father could support my sisters and my brother I was more excited than ever at the thought of moving closer to my target. All I had to do now was wait.

Chapter 29

Summer, 1976

On the morning of Chung Lin's wedding, as the hairdresser was putting the finishing touches to her hair in her room, Lian walked in with Mei Choon behind her carrying a bouquet of red roses. Chung Lin's black shoulder-length hair had been swept up into a chignon at the top of her head changing her appearance completely. Mei Choon, who had come home for the weekend especially for the occasion, let out a gasp.

'It suits you, this hair style, it really does. You look beautiful,' she said touching Chung Lin's hand.

Chung Lin smiled shyly. Her face was lightly made up; her lips were a bright red in contrast to her fair complexion.

'Wait till she puts on her gown,' said Lian as she turned to thank the hairdresser who was packing to leave.

The moment the white lace gown was on Chung Lin, all Mei Choon could do was squeal, '*Wah*, so beautiful... so beautiful.'

'You think so?' Chung Lin's eyes sparkled as she looked into the mirror, a flash of surprise crossed her face. Turning to Lian she said, 'Thank you, Second Aunty.' Her eyes started to well up.

'Don't go and spoil your make-up,' Lian answered quickly as she wiped her own tears away. She was feeling very pleased that it was she who had made the wedding gown for her.

Mei Choon suddenly remembered the flowers in her hands. 'These roses are for you,' she said holding them out to Chung Lin.

'Everything is just perfect,' Chung Lin said softly, looking at the roses as she took them from Mei Choon. 'I never thought this day would come.'

After the wedding ceremony, Kau had insisted that, as well as a dowry, a lavish dinner for family and friends was given by the groom in a riverside restaurant. The *Sea View* restaurant was chosen as, out of the many restaurants popping up in town, it was one of the better ones with air-conditioning. The ten-course meal was a surprisingly noisy and happy occasion; all disagreements were buried for the time being as the relatives and guests caught up with the latest happenings in their lives. Kau was being agreeable and relaxed, content to let his wife do the talking while he fussed over their two sons.

Beer and then later, VSOP cognac were served to the men. Feeling generous and happy for Chung Lin, Jung had bought the two bottles of cognac for the bride and bridegroom to drink a toast with their guests. The newly-weds went from table to table serving the brandy to shouts of 'Yum Seng!'

Lian had noticed that Hock had been drinking freely resulting in his face looking as if he'd been sunburnt. By the end of the dinner he was talking loudly and incoherently, so much so that Jung had decided to step in to stop him making a fool of himself. With Yew's help he got Hock on his feet and walked him home.

A little while later and thinking nothing more of the incident, Lian decided that she and Mei Choon should stroll back to the shophouse to pick Jung up. When they got into the shop, they were surprised that only half the lights were on. They could see Jung sitting at one of the sewing machines staring ahead of him, both his fists clenched on top of the machine, his face black like the sky just before the monsoon rain.

'What's the matter?' Lian asked feeling a lump expanding in her chest.

Jung tightened his fists even more as if to divert the rage from his voice. 'I just found out who informed the police,' he said.

It took Lian a few moments to realise what he was talking about and when she did she was shocked. The lottery incident and the price he paid had never been mentioned again after he came home from prison.

'Who?' she asked, frowning. How was it possible that between the restaurant and the shop he could discover who the culprit was when for years they had been unable to?

Jung didn't answer right away. He took a deep breath but it didn't stem the outpouring of fire through his veins as the years of suppressed indignation erupted.

'That son of a tortoise! It was Kau.' He spat his name out like it was poison.

'But how? How did you find out?'

'Young Hock.' He said pointing to Hock who was flat out on his back in the camp bed in the hall as he couldn't make it upstairs and was completely dead to the explosion he had caused. 'The alcohol didn't just loosen his tongue, it stirred his conscience too. He told me, us - me and Yew- that he was there when his father told the policeman. He couldn't say anything to me then because he was afraid of what his father would do to him.'

He slammed his fists on the wooden apron of the sewing machine.

Panic struck Lian. 'What are you going to do? You're not going to confront him now, are you? Not today, not now. It's Chung Lin's day. You mustn't spoil it for her.'

She knew that Kau was still in the restaurant and she had visions of Jung dashing off to confront him in front of the guests.

At that moment Yew walked in from the hall shaking his head and saying, 'How could First Brother do such a thing?' He looked at Mei Choon first and then sank onto the stool near Lian. 'I knew he was bad,' he continued, 'but to do something like that to your own brother is unforgiveable. What would our father think if he were alive?'

Neither Lian nor Jung answered him. Mei Choon, utterly bewildered, was looking from one to the other and wondering what they were talking about.

Jung suddenly leapt up to his feet and stormed towards the entrance of the shop.

Lian called out, 'Jung, don't do anything rash. Don't do anything you will regret. I know you're angry, but it happened so long ago and now everything is alright. You won't achieve anything by confronting him now. He'll deny it and then what? What can you do? Hit him? Don't give him the satisfaction of knowing you know but aren't being able to do a thing about it. And don't go and spoil Chung Lin's day, please. She deserves to have her wedding day unblemished.'

'I can't stand it here anymore.' Jung's voice was gruff and he didn't look back.

'I'll come with you.' Lian gathered up her things and hurried to catch up with him as she beckoned Mei Choon to follow her.

Jung had charged out of the shophouse like a bull with a headache while Lian was trying to rein him in. His eyes glazed with fury, he stomped up the street, turned right and kept walking until he came to the main road. He turned right again and marched down the street towards Rex Cinema, unaware that Lian and Mei Choon were running behind him. Thoughts ricocheted in his head. All of the years he'd wasted on his suspicion and wariness. All these years he had been so sure that it was one of his work mates who had betrayed him when all the time it was his own brother who had done the dastardly deed. He strode on and as the cinema came into view he wondered how he was going to make it up to them.

Lian was relieved that they were heading away from the riverside and were not likely to bump into Kau if he had left the restaurant. When she eventually caught up with him she said, 'Think this through before you do anything.'

'That's what I'm doing,' said Jung.

'Where are you going?'

'I don't know. All I know is that I can't bear to be in that house again.'

Mei Choon looked more confused than ever but refrained from asking any questions.

'Can we slow down?' asked Lian, struggling to keep up with him in her new shoes.

Jung stopped in front of the cinema and looked at it for a moment. The camp bed by the entrance was empty and he wondered where Avatar the night watchman was. Then he saw the big bearded man in his long white shirt which matched his turban and baggy trousers coming from the side of the building. Avatar saw him, smiled and waved. Jung walked up to him and as his face eased into a smile, a sense of liberation flooded through him.

'Hey, not asleep yet?' he said.

'Sleep?' Avatar shook his head. 'No *lah*. What are you doing here?' He looked at his watch. 'So late already.'

'Had to walk off the big dinner and brandy.'

'Ah, the wedding!'

'It's late. I'll see you tomorrow,' said Jung, turning away to rejoin Lian and Mei Choon. 'Let's go home,' he said to them.

As they walked away, Jung felt that some of the steam within him had been let off. But more than that, he was glad that he could look at his colleague without the finger of caution poking at him.

By the time they got to their own house, his head was very clear and he knew what they should do. Less than two weeks later he found an empty shop to rent in Jalan Rahmat and moved Lian's entire business there.

**

It was our day off work and Nick had driven all the way from Leicester where he had his second houseman job at the Royal Infirmary to be with me in London. He had decided to take me to see *Madam Butterfly* at the Royal Opera House giving me my first taste of opera. It was a ploy to distract me from my worry about *the* letter from the university and it worked.

I was still buzzing with the music and the voices of the singers ringing in my ears as we walked hand in hand through Covent Garden. We passed *Café Bellini* where we had earlier had lunch and come upon a little boy howling beside an equally distraught mother on the Piazza. The boy's pinched face was red and wet with tears as he stared at his balloon spiralling up to the blue sky. Nick had walked over to him and pointing up to the balloon, he'd asked, 'Is that your balloon?'

The boy stopped crying and nodded.

'How did you make it go so high?' Nick continued. 'I wish I could do that!'

We watched the boy's face change - pride replaced despair- as his mother mouthed a 'thank you' to Nick.

Now I was walking on air, on the hot air that had shrouded London and the rest of the country. There was no sign of any let-up in the boiling temperature and no stirring of the air to provide some respite from the heat. But it didn't diminish my exhilaration.

'That was *so* fantastic!' I said still hearing the music in my head.

'Glad you liked it,' said Nick, his pleasure and smugness at the success of his scheme written all over his face.

'There's so much to see and do here in London isn't there?' I sighed at the thought of the thousand and one things I could do like visiting the museums, art galleries and the theatres. 'The thing about London is that I don't feel I stand out like a foreigner, because it's so cosmopolitan here.'

'You're not a foreigner anymore, you've got your Permanent Residence and you're as good as a citizen.'

'I know that, but sometimes I can't help feeling self-conscious. Okay, there are lots of foreigners here too but take the French or even Spanish, they have the advantage of being indistinguishable from the natives, they blend. I mean, just looking at them you wouldn't think they were foreigners. The thing is I don't feel so conspicuous here in London as I did in Stevenage,' I said.

'But you *do* stand out, darling. You stand out like a dazzling star in a dark sky,' he raised his hand to the sky, 'like a flame torch in a dark cave. I'd pick you out anywhere.' He was trying to keep a straight face as he squeezed my hand.

'Now you're taking the mickey.' I screwed up my brow pretending to be cross.

We took the tube to Bayswater. We knew we were in the right place as when we emerged from the station, the aroma of doner kebab struck our nostrils. Vertical spits of roasting meat were visible in the restaurant windows as we walked along the busy road before turning into Moscow Road and then into Palace Court. This was the leafy salubrious part of town where the nurses' home was, with rows of grand red brick Victorian buildings with steps leading to the front door where I expected *Mary Poppins* to appear with her charges at any moment and burst into a song.

St Mary's nurses' home was the most dowdy-looking one of all the buildings with three floors of rooms overseen by the warden Mrs Goodman who strictly prohibited overnight visitors. We pushed open the heavy door at the top of the steps and sneaked past her office more out of habit than necessity as Mrs Goodman would have gone home. Giggling, we crept up the stairs to the second floor. Two flights of tattered carpet and the dark polished mahogany banister of what in all likelihood was once a grand stairway.

As I opened the door to my room I heard the sound of paper dragging across the carpet at the bottom of the door. I saw a brown envelope. My heart started to accelerate.

'This must have come in the late post,' I said as I bent down to pick it up. The blue post mark read *University College London*. My pulse was racing so fast that my head felt light. 'It's here.' I turned to Nick.

I could feel the shiver in my hands as they held the envelope.

'Go on, open it,' he said.

Please God, let it be good, I prayed silently as I took a deep breath and started to tear back the flap. Slowly I pulled out the letter and unfolded it. I read it and read it again, then looked up at Nick with his brows raised, waiting for me to say something.

'I got it, I'm in,' I said quietly, 'UCL's accepted me.'

'Well done!' he said, wrapping his arms around me.

I clung to him as tears came rolling down my cheeks.

Chapter 30

Autumn 1979

Inspector Ahmad heaved a sigh as he stood up. He had seen too many relapses; Yao was just another but it had cut him up more than he had expected. There was something special about Yao and he had been so proud and pleased when he pulled through the *cold turkey* treatment.

Jung and Heng stood up to see him out.

'Thank you for all you have done for my son,' said Jung.

'Leave him there till he is clean,' Inspector Ahmad said, as he held out his hand, first to Jung and then to Heng. He didn't say it, but to his mind, the fact that the centre in Singapore was run by the church would ensure that it was really was drug-free. 'Let me know how he gets on.'

Jung could only nod. He walked with the Inspector to the verandah and waited until he got on his bicycle and cycled off. His heart weighed a ton. All he wanted now to do was to get Yao to the centre as quickly as possible. He walked back to the front room and sank into the chair next to Heng without a word.

In Yao's room, Lian and Mei Choon had finished packing Yao's bag while he sat hunched, both hands gripping tightly the edge of the bed as he stared at the floor. His hair still wet after his shower was neatly combed. He had thrown on a white T-shirt and shorts.

'Are you sure you won't eat something before we go?' Lian asked.

Yao shook his head.

'Pastor Ang will be here soon.' Without looking at the clock, Lian knew exactly what time it was. She'd been looking every ten minutes or so since nine o'clock and Pastor Ang was coming for them at ten. 'Maybe we should wait in the front room. Is there anything else you want in your bag?' she asked. She had already packed some steamed dumplings.

Yao shook his head again. When he didn't move, she sat down beside him. Mei Choon moved quietly to sit on the other side of him and rubbed his arm. He remained still.

'We're very lucky that Pastor Ang is so kind,' said Lian.

Lian couldn't believe that she was reliving the nightmare of Yao's addiction. It had happened so insidiously. Like a mugger lurking round the corner, the drug habit waited to pounce on its victim.

Yao had always known that his friends who smoked cigarettes would sometimes use something stronger and so he had conscientiously avoided hanging out with them. One day, not long after his exams, a friend approached him and suggested to him about playing his guitar at a nightclub in town. It had appealed to his vanity having long harboured an ambition to play publicly. Without hesitation, he went to find out more and was instantly given the job.

Lian and Jung were horrified but unable to stop him. They hadn't seen him so alive, so enthusiastic and cheerful for a long time, and he was confident of his will power in the face of any temptation. Besides, he reasoned, it was only one night a week.

For months there were no signs of trouble, until that Sunday night, exactly three days ago. Lian remembered clearly when it happened, for earlier that morning, they had received a call from Mei Chin to say that she and her fiancé Albert had booked a trip to Perth. Mei Chin had sounded so very excited about it. Both Lian and Jung were very happy for them as they liked Albert. They found him very respectful and hardworking, but more importantly, it was obvious that he cared very deeply for Mei Chin.

Later that evening, Yao, happy and smiling, waved goodbye as he cycled off with his guitar across his back and headed for the nightclub. Lian and Jung stood watching him go with doubts gnawing at them but there was little they could do to stop him. As usual they waited up, worrying and wondering how he was getting on and regretting that they had let him go.

It was well after one o'clock in the morning, much later than normal, when he came home. Jung dashed downstairs as soon as he heard him come in. He instantly realised that Yao had been drinking, and worse, he had been smoking. Disappointment, fear and anger came at him like a high-speed train out of control. It was all too much for him. He snatched the guitar from Yao and slammed it against the banister.

Yao had yelled at him as he watched his prized guitar being destroyed. He then dashed out of the house cursing.

Lian ran after him and eventually caught up with him at the end of the road. She pleaded with him to go home but he refused saying that Jung had no right to destroy his guitar. Then like a firework that had burnt out, he became quiet, turned around and walked home with her.

The very next day Pastor Ang came to see them and told them about the Changi rehabilitation centre in Singapore. It was owned and run by a church and had an encouraging success rate. He then offered to drive Yao there himself.

In the meantime Mei Choon had heard the news and rushed back home from college to be with them.

Yao turned and looked at Lian. His eyes were bloodshot but it was the ghostly vacant look in them that sent a shard of ice through her chest. She wondered if he'd had a sniff of the white powder even though he had assured her that he hadn't. She put her hand on his hand and gently squeezed it. 'It will be alright. They will look after you there.'

'I am sorry, Ma.' Tears tumbled down his cheeks, then his thin frame shook as the sobs hit him.

Lian put her arm around his shoulders. 'I know,' she said dabbing her eyes as she suppressed her own urge to cry. 'Just stick with the treatment. You will get better.'

'Yes, you will get better,' echoed Mei Choon, wiping her tears away.

Then they heard Jung call, 'Pastor is here!'

Pastor Ang was standing next to Jung when they emerged from Yao's room. Looking ten years younger than his forty-three years, his fresh looking face beamed at them.

'Ah, good morning,' he said first in Mandarin to Lian and then in English to Mei Choon and Yao. Then pointedly at Yao in a soft tone he said, 'You are going to be fine.'

Yao grunted and turned his eyes to the floor.

'Got your passports?' asked Pastor Ang.

'Yes, I have them,' said Jung.

'Let's go then,' said the pastor as he led the way to his car.

Jung and Lian followed him with Yao carrying his bag, Heng and Mei Choon right behind them. Jung got into the front passenger seat while Lian climbed into the back. Heng opened the door for Yao and just before he climbed in behind the driver's seat he put his hand on Yao's arm.

'You're very lucky you have so many people who care about you,' he said. 'It won't be easy but you will get through it.'

Yao nodded; he stepped into the car and Heng helped shut the door. Mei Choon reached in through the window to squeeze his arm. 'Bye, Yao,' she said.

Yao looked at her briefly and then turned to face the front.

Mei Choon stepped away from the car. Through a torrent of tears she watched the car move off.

An hour and a half later, Pastor Ang and his passengers arrived at the start of the Causeway linking Malaysia and Singapore. The lanes were packed with snaking lines of traffic slithering then converging at the immigration check-points.

290

'This traffic would be far worse if it was the weekend,' he said, shifting in his seat to ease his stiff back. 'Can I have your passports?'

Jung, who had the passports ready in his hands, passed them to him. In the time it had taken them to get there his respect for the man sitting next to him had grown. Pastor Ang had a reputation for his stirring sermons – small, at five-foot four, but packed with an explosive energy that was electric he had been nicknamed *chilli padi*. He told them about his time spent in Taiwan and Indonesia as a missionary for six years before coming to Batu Pahat and said he felt called to move on again, this time to Hong Kong, but where exactly, he wasn't sure. Jung was struck by his faith and impressed by the great works he had done especially drawing so many people to Grace Church. Unlike Lian who had been going there regularly, he remained outside the fold of believers but for Yao's sake he would grab with both hands any help offered to him.

As they waited in the queue, Yao, who had slept most of the way, woke up and started to rub his arms as if he was cold.

'Is the air-con too cold for you?' asked Lian.

He didn't answer; instead he looked around him as if searching for something.

'What is it?' asked Lian. Both Jung and Pastor Ang turned round to look at him.

'Nothing!' Yao snapped and then became still.

Relieved, everyone sat back although Lian's eyes remained glued to him.

One by one the cars in front of them inched forward edging closer to the window from where the immigration officer would lean out to scrutinise each passenger. When their turn came, Pastor Ang greeted the stony-faced officer '*Selamat pagi*' and handed their passports to him.

Lian started praying silently, worried that the officer would somehow spot that Yao was a heroin addict and arrest him. She placed her hand on Yao's to reassure and calm him and watched as the officer carefully inspected each passport in turn. To her relief, the officer gathered them all up in a bundle and handed them back to Pastor Ang then waved them on.

There was still the Singaporean immigration to face at the other end of the Causeway. They drove on in silence across the Straits of Johore. The morning sun had burned up the haze over the waters and on the horizon a tanker was just coming into view. Yao didn't appear interested in his whereabouts when normally he would be curious and ask questions endlessly, but it was a relief to Lian that he was quiet.

The traffic slowed down as they approached the Singaporean Immigration checkpoint. This time as it came to their turn she felt calmer, ready to face the ordeal of the check. Nobody spoke while the officer looked through their documents. Then without any question, he returned the passports.

'Thank God,' whispered Lian.

'The worst is over now!' said Pastor Ang brightly as they drove away from the checkpoint. 'We are approaching Woodlands. This is where you buy duty-free fruit. We will do that on our way back.'

'That would be nice,' said Lian. Any other time and she would have been excited about the prospects of browsing the rows of stalls with oranges, apples, pears and other fruit imported from Australia.

Pastor Ang took a left turn towards Changi on the east coast of the island. The road was bounded on either side by masses of casuarina, banana, Flame-of-the-Forest and bougainvillea trees, giving it a manicured feel quite distinct from the jungle that they had left behind in Malaysia. The dual carriageway was busy, but traffic was moving fast and smoothly in both lanes. He glanced at his watch and estimated that it would take another half hour to get to the centre.

A sense of trepidation filled both Lian and Jung, although neither gave any hint of it. Both had derived some strength from the pastor who had been calm and upbeat throughout the journey. Yao started to fidget again, shifting his feet and then shaking his shoulders. Lian thought nothing of it at first, but a few minutes later, as they approached a built up area where there were some shops, he became more agitated; he jerked then swung his head to the left and then to the right.

'What is wrong? Jung, I don't like this,' she said; she could feel her own nerves twitching.

Jung reached out to grab Yao's hand but he shook him off. Yao groaned and started shaking as if he was in a trance.

'What is it?' asked Lian, her voice trembling.

The groans became louder. He twisted and turned as if he was shaking something off. His eyes rolled. 'I must get out! I must go!' he shouted.

'We're not there yet!' Lian was now frightened. She tried to take his hand, but he was pushed her away and started waving his arms about hitting Lian's face once.

With all the commotion in the back seat it was impossible to drive on and Pastor Ang slowed down, hoping to pull up as soon as possible. Ignoring the angry hooting from the car behind him, he swerved sharply onto the verge. The car immediately behind whizzed past on the right. Behind it was a heavily loaded lorry moving at an equally fast speed. Before they knew what was happening, Yao threw open the door and leapt out of the car.

Neither Lian nor Jung nor Pastor Ang heard their own screams. All they heard were screeching brakes and a heart-stopping thud as the lorry flashed past them.

Chapter 31

It was during my second year at UCL, I was walking along the corridor in the Cruciform Building when I suddenly realised that I was no longer haunted by the dream. The dream in which I was reaching out for something as if my life depended on it. It had been as if the black clouds had been blown away leaving a clear sunny sky. I was happy. I was on the road to my ambition, the way ahead looked clear and the final destination certain. My sleep had been restful and dreamless until one night I had another dream, a different one.

The sky is clear blue. The warm sunshine on my skin lights up a curiosity within me. The woods in front beckon me; a soft carpet of bluebells hugs the earth beneath the green canopy of the trees. I am on my own and I want to see what's in or beyond the woods. As I start to run towards the woods I feel light like I'm being carried on a cushion of air beneath my feet. As I get nearer to the edge of the trees I start to feel a dense weight upon my being.

I enter the woods. It turns dark briefly and then I come out into the light again on the other side. Suddenly I'm at the edge of a cliff. There's scaffolding along it and the sea turns into a man-made pond. The sky is still blue and clear.

Still feeling as if I'm floating, I look down below at the water. I see a dark object floating in it. I screw up my eyes. The object comes into focus suddenly. It's a body bobbing up and down in the water. Something tells me it is lifeless. I strain to look at the face and see that it is that of Yao's. I feel as if a dagger has been pushed through my heart; I scream and scream.....

The screams seared through my body snapping me out of my sleep; my heart was thumping away, my breathing shallow and audible.

I wondered what triggered the nightmare. Perhaps it was the experience at Marble Arch underground station when someone had spotted an unattended bag on a platform and the alarm bells went off. Vicky and I and everybody else belted out of there as fast as we could. I was convinced that that was what prompted the dream, but why Yao? The image of his dead body was still vivid, sending an icy tingling down my spine.

I didn't believe in premonitions. When I calmed down and told Nick about my dream he said that he'd heard someone say that if you told somebody about the dream, whatever it was, it would never happen. We both laughed.

The grief of losing my little brother was a physical pain that sat in my heart and wouldn't go away. I blamed myself for his waywardness. If I had stayed at home instead of coming to England perhaps I might have noticed the signs and put a stop to the addiction before its tentacles wrapped so tightly around him. Or he might never have been tempted to experiment in the first place.

If I thought the sky had collapsed on my world and blacked it out after Yao died, then what my father and mother felt must have been a thousand times worse. For a long time afterwards Father retreated into his workshop, pulling up the drawbridge so that not even Mother was allowed to come near him. He painted and painted. In fact no one in the family had any idea how much he had painted until many years later. After he had retired, a reporter from the national Chinese newspaper, *Sin Chew Jit Poh*, interviewed him. The result was a one-and-a-half pages article about his paintings and the work he was doing with young children who were interested in drawing and painting.

He never talked to me about Yao. The first time he took me to visit his grave I was inconsolable. If I had never doubted the existence of God before I did then. How could He let a bright light like Yao be snuffed out so suddenly, and so prematurely? I watched Father sweep the leaves off the tiled surface of the grave, lost in his own world, and then lean over to tenderly caress Yao's smiling face in the oval photo on the headstone.

Yao was the son who was to pass on his name. Did Father ever imagine what it would have been like if Yao had lived? What it would have been like to watch him grow into a fine man and become an engineer, a doctor or lawyer? Did he dream that he and Yao would design and build together the house that he and mother were living in now? Did he have hopes that one day, when he was an old man, Yao would look after him?

Mother was a tower of faith and grace, a flashing beacon for all of us as we tossed about in our sorrow. It wasn't that her pain was any less; it was that she believed that it was all part of God's will although she couldn't see why or how. Like Father she immersed herself in her work and drew solace from the company of her Christian friends. Unlike him, she could talk about Yao and reminisce about various times like how he came home after a day out on a school trip clutching a piece of drift wood that he had picked up on the beach. He thought she would like it. For days after school he would sand it and polish it until finally he mounted it on plinth so that the foot long piece of wood stood upright like 'an upside down octopus dancing, swinging its legs in the air'. When she was cooking pig's trotters she would say, 'This was Yao's favourite. He loved it with lots of chilli.'

Years later when my first daughter was born, I had a tiny glimpse of what he and Mother must have gone through. It was three in the morning and the labour had been mercilessly long. When she finally emerged I was completely exhausted feeling like I had moved Earth to the moon and back again. So tired was I that all I wanted was to close my eyes and go to sleep but the desire to see and hold my child was stronger. As I held her in my arms all I could think was that I couldn't possibly love the next child as much as I loved her. I guessed that when the object of such a love was taken away it left an ever-expanding pain in its place.

Father once told Mother that his daughters had proved to him how short-sighted sex prejudice was. Perhaps the only consolation for him now was the knowledge that his daughters were as good as, if not better than sons.

Mei Lin became a chartered accountant and worked for a big firm in Kuala Lumpur. She later married Peng who was the manager of a branch of Overseas Chinese Banking Corporation in the same city and they had two boys and a girl.

Mei Chin met Albert when she was teaching in a secondary school in Singapore. Albert, a Chemistry graduate, was the first person in our family to actually use his western name instead of his Chinese one. Both of them had had ideas of emigrating to Australia which set off alarm bells again for Mother but fortunately they decided to settle down in Singapore and start up a business in the water purification system that Albert had designed. That meant that they and their two children were able to visit Mother and Father quite regularly.

My youngest sister Mei Choon who never thought she would live too far away from Batu Pahat uprooted one day and struck out to work in Melbourne as Personal Assistant to the MD of a pharmaceutical company. She went on to marry an Australian by the name of Peter and had two daughters and a son.

Wherever we were in the world, we daughters always returned to Batu Pahat to visit and make sure that Mother and Father were well, not just out of filial duty but out of love.

Father was very proud to have Nick as his son-in-law which made me wonder why I ever worried about his accepting him. He never noticed Nick's colour at all, neither did Mother who adored him and said she couldn't wish for a better match for me. I discovered later that it was his Uncle

Wong who was disgusted by my marrying Nick. 'Why can't she find someone of her own kind? Our own Hakka people,' he had said, to which Father had told him it was my choice, my life.

My daughters were the most precious of gifts to him. I remember the day he and Mother turned up at our flat in Highgate a few days before Emma was due. Nick had arranged the surprise trip, flying them over and then on the evening before they turned up at the flat he told me that Vicky and Collin were going to call in on their way to the theatre. I was sitting with my cup of tea in the living room when the doorbell rang. Nick went to open the door and when I looked up and saw my parents I was overjoyed.

When Father first saw Emma in the cot his face was filled with joy and amazement; it wasn't big enough for his smile, the smile that always sent a glow through me. The same smile that had swayed my mother into marrying him.

He was always smiling or laughing when he was with them. He couldn't do enough for them and the girls in turn loved him. *Koon Koon* was the best, they had said. He took pleasure in showing them things, whether it was how to mix paints and colours or explaining Chinese customs and the origin of the various festivals. He folded birds and animals out of coloured paper while the girls were rapt in wonder. As soon as they could speak, he taught them Mandarin and Malay. Mandarin was a must, he had insisted, so that they could communicate with *Poh Poh*, their Chinese grandmother, and because it was the up-and-coming language as China was opening its doors. Malay, so they could understand what was being said around them when they were in Malaysia. One day as the girls were watching Mother stuff mincemeat in bean curd at the kitchen table, Father said, 'In Hakka, this dish is called *yong tofu*, your mummy's favourite food.' The girls repeated the Hakka name after him, and Mother gave them each a piece of bean curd to play with.

He didn't hide his pride in his bright and beautiful Eurasian granddaughters, who drew attention wherever they went in town. If he could have blown a trumpet to announce their arrival he would have. He was quick to introduce Nick and the girls whenever he bumped into any one he knew and he loved telling Emma and Sarah about the time that their father first arrived in Batu Pahat.

It was the summer of 1977. I had been worried about Yao and after the end of first year at UCL I decided to go home to see for myself how he was. Nick couldn't come with me as he had to present a paper at a conference in Dublin.

I was relieved that Yao was fine physically although I was disappointed that he had decided that he didn't want to study anymore. He told me he wanted to go into music, write songs and sing. He seemed happy enough although sometimes I thought he was like a boat bobbing in the open sea without a rudder.

'Don't worry about me, sis,' he'd said, throwing me one of his disarming smiles. 'I'll be okay. Hey, when I'm famous and have lots of money, I can come and see you in England.'

No matter what I'd said I couldn't change his mind and there was nothing else I could do. All I could do was to sit on the floor with him and listen as he strummed his guitar.

A week into my stay I received a telegram from Nick. It read: *Wait end of Jln Rahmat. 7 p.m. Wed. Love. Nick.*

Father would say to the girls, 'Once your mummy realised what it meant, we couldn't believe it. Your daddy was coming to BP to see her!'

Guessing that Nick meant I was to wait for him at the Food Court end of the main road at seven o'clock Mother, Father and I walked to exactly that spot and waited. We were excited and curious wondering if he would really appear. Then true to form, he did. After peering at dozens of cars coming towards us we saw a car slowing as it approached us then the hooting and head lights flashing.

'It's Nick! He's here!' I shouted, barely able to refrain from jumping up and down.

When he pulled up we were all laughing. Father grabbed Nick's hand as soon as he climbed out of his hired car. He was delighted to meet him. We were aware that lots of passers-by were staring at us, at the strange *red-haired* man in the middle of the road.

'Welcome, welcome,' said Father beaming, then turning to me he said, '*Wah*, he's done very well to find his way here, all the way from Singapore airport, all by himself.'

Nick grinned. He hadn't been warned about the suicidal chickens flying at cars from the side of the winding road or the potholes or the cyclists who would cycle into him out of nowhere.

Father took great delight in taking Nick around town and showing him the town at the same time as showing him off. He also took him to have coffee in the Hainanese coffee shop near Rex Cinema and then to another in the market place for an Indian *roti prata* breakfast. There Nick would have his first taste of *teh tarek*. Open-mouthed, he watched the tea being *tarek* or 'pulled' as the tea-maker, after starting to pour it into a mug, dragged the stream of the tea away forming an arc from the mug to the spout of the teapot to as high as his arm would allow. Father watched with pleasure as Nick lapped up everything he showed him, but then Nick was enjoying the attention he was getting as people wanted to shake the hands of the strange visitor.

I took him to 22 Hakka Street. I had to let him see where I grew up. Mr Ting the shoemaker had expanded his business to take over the whole shop. Hock and Yew still worked for him. Nick charmed everyone by talking to them while I translated for him. Uncle Heng was favourably impressed; he thought that Nick was not only respectful and polite but that there was a solid quality about him. I then showed him my grandparents' shrine and explained how we venerated them. He then asked,

'May I show my respects by lighting a few joss-sticks?'

300

'Of course,' I replied, surprised.

He took a handful of joss sticks from a pack lying on the ledge, proceeded to light them and then pushed them into the sand in the urn.

Uncle Heng who was watching nodded his approval.

Nick was fascinated by the art of shoe-making and wanted to try cutting a piece of hide for the sole which Hock offered to show him how. To my surprise he then announced that he would like a pair of boots made; there and then he kicked his sandals off to have his feet measured by Hock before choosing the leather.

That trip home was the last time I saw Yao and it was after this that I had the dream.

1986

Heng moved out of 22 Hakka Street in 1984 but not without much persuasion from Jung and Lian.

'You must let us look after you,' Jung had said. 'Climbing those stairs is not safe.' Despite his silver hair, his lightly creased face belied his eighty–six years. Although his stiff joints made climbing difficult he could still out-walk many half his age.

'What about the children when they come home? asked Heng.

'There're too many rooms here. Besides, they're so seldom all home at the same time. Don't you worry about them. If necessary they can stay at one of the hotels,' said Jung.

Their new detached brick house in Taman Bunga had four bedrooms. It was airy and bright with a large garden. Taman Bunga was a new estate located a little further away from town which meant that Lian had to take a trishaw ride to the shop. The business, now with six machinists, was mostly run by Chung Lin although Lian managed it and would still cut and sew when she and Jung weren't travelling.

When Heng finally acknowledged that it would be best for him, he moved in with them, but it didn't stop him doing what he enjoyed most, which was walking to the town, wandering through the market and visiting 22 Hakka Street or dropping in at Mother's shop for a chat and coffee. Sometimes he would call in at the cinema to watch Jung work and then have lunch with him at one of the stalls nearby. At home he would help tend Jung's plants.

The day before he died he had gone about his business as usual. In the morning he'd seen some sweet potato leaves at the market and bought a bunch to cook. In the afternoon he visited Lian's shop, chatted over coffee and admired the new fabric that had arrived. In the evening he and Jung walked together to the Food Court for some supper. He had his Hakka noodles as usual, savouring every bit of it. Then they went home and after listening to the news on the television he went to bed.

The next morning as Lian got ready to go to the shop, she became concerned when she didn't hear him moving about. Normally he would be up and pottering about in the garden, watering the orchids, sweeping up the leaves or simply savouring the roses and their perfume before the sun got too ferocious. She went out to look for him and when she didn't see him decided to knock on his bedroom door. When there was no reply she opened the door.

Heng had died in his sleep. It just seemed his style; an unassuming man, he came quietly and went quietly without any fuss, without drawing attention to himself. He would have been shocked if we had told him that he had left a big mark on our lives. With his passing he left a huge gap in mine. I felt I had been cheated; I had so desperately wanted my children to meet and know him. I wanted him to tell them stories of my grandfather, how they met and what they did together and how they had built the tailoring business in 22 Hakka Street. Now they would never hear those stories from him and it was up to me to tell them what I knew of him and repeat the stories he told me when I was a little girl.

Chapter 32

I'd told Nick and Father that I wanted to see an old friend before I dropped them with Emma and Sarah at the new shopping mall on the same side of town as Mother and Father's house. Now, five miles away from the old town of Batu Pahat, I stood alone looking at Uncle Heng's grave.

The sun was creeping up the clear blue sky. Despite my umbrella the heat and humidity were unbearable, but on the gentle slope of the baked hillside I found the peace and stillness a balm to my soul. I'd wanted to escape, to be alone; it had been a hectic holiday since we'd arrived from London almost two weeks ago. Like typical teenage girls, Emma and Sarah never seemed to tire of shopping after the sight-seeing. Bowled over by the Twin Towers, dazzled and mesmerised by shops in Suria KLCC in Kuala Lumpur, they still found the shops in Batu Pahat just as interesting. The new shops in the air-conditioned shopping malls had sucked the life out of the town I knew and grew up in, leaving it a lame appendage of a chaotic conurbation without a heart or soul. No longer the bicycle town it once was, cars now outnumbered people and it was not unusual to see cars triple-parked on the streets.

The town had grown beyond recognition. There was a marked increase in the number of Malays involved in businesses, running stalls and shops. Not only were they more visible in town, especially in Kuala Lumpur, they seemed to outnumber the non-Malays. The country was irrevocably a Malay and Muslim one now and its economy had developed faster than that of any of the other Far Eastern countries.

The cemetery looked like a miniature city of high-rise blocks on the hill slope with each grave a rectangular box-shaped mound covered in tiles of shades of grey, blue or white. I'd had no trouble finding Uncle Heng's grave; his headstone was plain and on it his name, his date of birth and the date he died were engraved in gold.

I started to clear away the dry leaves and pulled out a small sapling that had grown close to the headstone. Apart from Mother and Father no one else came to visit Uncle Heng's grave on *Ching Ming*, All Souls Day, when Grandfather and Grandmother's graves would be visited and cleaned. Whenever I came home, I often made this journey to the cemetery on my own.

Nearby, where the jungle bordered the cemetery, there was rustling of leaves in the trees and some monkeys made their presence known, chattering, playing and swinging from tree to tree. I placed one of my two bunches of chrysanthemums on Uncle Heng's grave, then said goodbye before moving to look for Yao's.

Time would heal, I had heard it said so many times, but it didn't for me. I could still remember vividly that bitterly cold and dark evening when the telegram arrived for me telling me to phone home. Then the shock of hearing about Yao's death. In spite of the passage of the years, visiting his grave was always painful. Time certainly hadn't diminished my sense of guilt either.

The ground between the closely packed graves was bare, the red soil was dry and crumbly. A breeze sighed past me as I picked my way between the rows of the tiled mounds. When I arrived at Yao's grave it looked as if it had been cleared recently. I looked at the oval-shaped photo on the headstone and his big smile instantly hit the pain and guilt buttons turning on the tears. The protective sister in me still scolded him and asked, 'Why, why?' Why, to so many things. Why did he try it? Why did he not tell me or his other sisters? I, of all people, would have listened and helped. Or was I too busy, too absorbed in my own career to give him the time he needed? Why did he succumb again when all was going so well? What was going through his mind? There were no answers to the questions. Instead, they just left me with a deeper sense of failure after the guilt.

As I knelt to place the flowers before the headstone, I noticed that the plot next to his grave was still empty. I swept away the dry leaves with my hand then sat on the edge of the mound and looked across the cemetery, down the slope of the hillside toward the road where my car was parked. Beyond the road and as far as my eyes could see, it was green and lush, thick with tropical jungle. This view hadn't changed in all the years I had been coming here. This was one part of the land that had not yet been plundered and it afforded a strange sense of calm and stability.

A few cars drove by along the road but they were too far away from me to disturb the peace. This was the one place on earth where I was in touch with myself. This was where I was most honest with myself. Any sense of self-importance was quickly discarded the moment I set foot here. This was where I regained some equilibrium in my hectic life.

I had plenty to be thankful for: Nick and our daughters, Mother and Father's good health and especially now that they had retired and were living a comfortable life. I thought of Mei Lin whom I had seen the day before and was so pleased that she was looking well. Her long painful journey through the treatment for non-Hodgkin's lymphoma was now a dim memory.

Age had not mellowed Father. A few days after we'd arrived at Batu Pahat, I happened to return to the house earlier than planned having left Nick, Emma and Sarah with Mei Lin and her girls in town. As I walked up the drive to the house, through the iron gate of the main door I could hear his raised voice in the kitchen. He sounded angry but I couldn't make out what he was saying. My heart dropped like a free-falling lift. I had so hoped that his temper had evaporated over the years and that he would show Mother the respect she deserved. Anger rose within me as I walked up to the verandah. I didn't want to hear any more so I'd quickly called out to Mother through the gate.

And yet when she'd complained about her tired legs I had seen him rubbing her calves like two old lovebirds. She

305

said her calves often felt like they were dead after a lot of walking and when she sat down she would rest her legs on a footstool. Father would sit on a lower chair next to her legs so that he could massage her calves while they watched the telly. The sight of them like that had always warmed me towards him and made me feel I had misjudged him.

Earlier that morning Mother heard me arguing with Nick because he'd kept me waiting and I had exploded in his face. Before I left the house, she took me aside and said how like Father I was in temperament. 'Give in a little and don't be so headstrong,' she'd said. I admitted I was at fault and said no more. My excuse for my irritability was the heat and the exhaustion from visiting relatives.

My eyes strayed in the direction of Grandmother and Grandfather's graves. I had sometimes wondered what Grandmother would have said about my two daughters, while I was certain that Grandfather would have embraced them. Somewhere in the cemetery lay First Uncle as well. Mother told me a long time ago that he had died. For Chung Lin's sake she'd gone to his funeral. Hardly anyone else attended apart from his wife and children. I'd felt a tiny pinch of pity for him then but no sadness or sense of loss.

A loud screech from one of the monkeys in the trees behind me jolted me out of my reverie. I looked at my watch and realised that I had to move quickly. Nick would start to worry if I was late getting back to pick them up from the shopping mall. I could just imagine both of the girls laden with bags and still wanting more. We couldn't be late as Mei Chin and her family were coming from Singapore and the girls always looked forward to seeing their cousins, James and Kelly.

'I saw this amazing top in *Fajar*! It was so gorgeous but they didn't have my size,' said Emma. She was sitting on the sitting room floor with Sarah, Kelly and James in and surrounded by her shopping bags. 'But, look at this!' She held up a red Ted Baker T-shirt against herself. 'This was *sooo* cheap!'

306

'*Aww*, cool,' said Kelly, 'it looks great. I like the colour!' Kelly was a year older than Emma and the image of Mei Chin down to her smile, looking every inch the fashion-conscious teenager in her pink cropped top and a short stripey turquoise and white skirt with her hair bunched in a ponytail.

'You girls are always shopping,' muttered James shaking his head.

'So you don't like shopping, James?' asked Nick standing nearby with a glass of cold beer in his hand. James looked up, bright-eyed and was about to speak when Kelly butted in.

'You've got your head stuck in the computer all the time. I keep telling him, there is life outside that computer of his, Uncle Nick, but he won't listen,' she said.

'I like building things and there is this brilliant programme…'

'There he goes again!' said Kelly pointing at him with a smile.

'Try this,' said Emma, holding out a skirt to Kelly. 'If you like it, it's yours.'

'Got something for you too, James,' said Sarah as she rummaged through her bags. James momentarily had nothing against shopping and was eager to see what she had got him.

'Oh, Dad, I got a tablecloth for Grandma Helen!' called out Emma holding up a large piece of batik cloth.

'That's nice,' said Nick, fingering the fabric before moving away to join me, Mei Chin, Albert and Father at the table in the dining room where Yao's driftwood stood on the side table. 'Well, James is outnumbered, I'm afraid,' he said.

Albert chuckled. 'He's alright. He was very excited about seeing Emma and Sarah.'

'It's good to see the children get on so well,' said Nick. 'So, how is business?'

'Not bad. Can't complain,' replied Albert. 'The orders are coming in, so that's good.'

'We've just been saying, maybe, next year we'll go to England,' said Mei Chin.

'That'd be so good, don't you think?' I said turning to Nick.

'Yes, absolutely! Will you come too, Dad?' Nick turned to Father.

'I have no plans. See what your mother thinks,' Father smiled and looked at me.

'Where's Mum?' asked Nick.

'She is in the kitchen preparing something for us to eat,' said Father. 'I will go and see how she is doing.' He got up and walked to the kitchen.

We carried on talking, discussing what we could do and the possibility of having Mother and Father coming along when we heard a loud smash, the sound of breaking plate, in the kitchen. I rushed into the kitchen.

The fridge door was wide open. Next to it, Mother was bending over to clear up the broken plate while Father stood over her rubbing his elbow, his face angry. It looked like Mother had accidentally swung the fridge door open and hit him and I'd just caught him saying, '....Are you blind?'

His tone stung me. I had heard it too often. Something inside me, the string that had been holding down the lid on my anger, snapped.

'Why are you always so horrible to Ma?'

I was aware I had raised my voice. I saw Father's face change to surprise as I turned around to walk out of the kitchen, afraid that I would say more than I should. I walked into Mei Chin who looked puzzled.

'What happened?' she asked.

'I don't know why I bother coming home!'

After that outburst the wall between us reappeared. I didn't want to speak to him and although we were polite to each other he kept his distance. Three days later when we arrived back in London I was so remorseful that I couldn't wait to phone them. I shouldn't have allowed the anger to fester within me, I should have overlooked it, forgiven him instead

308

of letting the incident blind me to the uneasiness I had created between my mother and father by being cross. What I had done was reprehensible especially as my mother was left to pick up the pieces.

I waited while the phone rang until it was picked up. On hearing Father's voice I said, 'Hello, Papa, we've arrived home safely.'

'Good..good. Was the flight alright?' Father's voice was light and happy. I felt relieved. I pictured him smiling, showing his gold-capped tooth, happy that we were safe and sound. I knew he hated us leaving; he had shed a tear when we were saying goodbye at the airport. 'Have Emma and Sarah gone to bed then? They must be exhausted after the long journey.'

'Yes, they've crashed into bed. It's been a long flight. Luckily I managed to sleep.' A pause. 'Are you alright?'

'Yes.' Silence. 'Uncle Yew...he phoned earlier to say he was sorry that he missed you before you left. He's coming to visit us tomorrow.'

'That's good. Tell him from me that I'm sorry too. Have you eaten?'

'Yes, just had dinner'

'Can I speak to Ma?'

'Yes. You take care,' he said. I cursed myself then for being so intolerant.

'Ma, we're home. How are you?'

'*Aiyah*, this house feels so empty now,' said Mother. 'It was so odd cooking for just your papa and me. I miss the girls. How are they? Gone to sleep, have they?'

I'd felt better after the phone call; it was as if I had deleted everything from the screen and could start afresh. What animosity I'd felt had dissipated by the time I got back to London and now after hearing Father and talking with him as if nothing had happened merely confirmed my opinion that we got on better with some distance between us. Whenever I went home we would get on for the first couple of days. We'd get so far talking about different things and then we'd pull back, as if we had come to the edge of a cliff, afraid to open up to each other.

A few weeks later:
It is not any old bed; the bed frame is white metal, one I recognise as a hospital bed, similar to the ones I had seen in the hospital in Batu Pahat as a child. The man lying in it is an old man. His face is serene, his eyes are shut. I recognise him. It is Father. There is a strange silence, almost eerie, there is no one else around. It is as if we are suspended in milky white space. I am sitting at the bedside, holding his left hand. The gesture itself is weird for I am conscious that I've never held his hand as an adult. His thin hand feels cold in mine while I am burning with questions which I can't bring myself to ask him. Suddenly he opens his eyes. He looks at peace. He turns to face me; his eyes which have lost their fire are beseeching me- to do what, I'm not sure. Then he says, 'It is alright. Everything is fine.'
I burst into tears.

I woke up sobbing, gripped with fright and felt warm tears running down my cheek. I quickly swept the image aside, ramming the whole nightmare into the bowels of my consciousness and chiding myself for being silly. It wasn't difficult to figure out the reason for the dream: I was anxious to reconcile with him and then live happily ever after. And it was a wake-up call to me to close this rift between me and my father.

I'd thought that I had time, time to have that heart-to-heart talk with my father to tell him that all the ructions we've had were like loose fragments I had wiped off, that underneath them was the precious stone of our bond. I had planned that on his and Mother's next visit to us I'd engineer an opportunity to talk with him. Instead I had been robbed of the chance to do that. He had ended up lying in a hospital bed as in my dream. Except he was in a coma, and not only was I not there beside him, I wouldn't get to hear what he might have wanted to say to me.

Chapter 33

April 2005

By the time I'd cleared customs, just after nine a.m., Albert was waiting at the *Arrivals* gate for me. He looked sombre, gave me a brief smile as we greeted each other and then took my trolley from me.

'Are you hungry? We can have something to eat before we go,' he said.

'No, I'm not.'

'Good, then we go right away,' he said.

He directed me towards the car park. We walked for a bit before he spoke again.

'The funeral is at Grace Church. Normally the burial takes place very soon after death but they've delayed it until you get here.' It'd been three days since Father died. 'All your sisters are already there. Mei Choon arrived yesterday morning. Peter and the children can't come as there's school.'

I nodded. 'How is Ma?'

'She's coping,' replied Albert, 'very calm.'

I was in no mood to talk further; luckily I was able to plead jetlag and my fitful sleep on the plane. Albert nodded as he lifted my cases into the boot of his car. Once we got into his car I closed my eyes. The reality of Father's death was slowly sinking in as we sped down the Express Highway to where he was lying, waiting for me to say farewell to him. I fought back my tears.

In the turmoil of emotions, the afternoon at Whipsnade Zoo wandered into my head. It was the summer of 1998, Mother and Father's second visit to England. I had decided to take them and the girls to the zoo. The weather forecast had promised a warm and sunny afternoon. Instead it turned chilly when we got there. We were sitting at a picnic table by a pond watching some swans when a cool breeze swept past. Wearing only shorts and a T-shirt, I shivered and drew my arms around me.

Father who was sitting next to me on the bench noticed; he reached out and stroked my arm. 'You are cold,' he said.

His gesture took me by surprise and I'd pulled away without meaning to. I felt awkward and was cross with myself for embarrassing him.

'I should be used to this unpredictable change in the weather,' I quickly said. 'Should've brought a cardigan.'

Now I wished I had hugged him or at least held his hand and not recoiled like I did. Did he die of a broken heart, grieving because I'd always shown so much anger toward him? Had I said something that upset him when we last spoke? Did he know that, no matter what I might have said, I had always loved him? If he didn't, it was too late now to do anything. I felt another stab at my heart.

The mixture of sleep deprivation, jet lag and grief was potent and I succumbed to its numbing effects until we arrived at the church about three hours later. As we pulled up in the drive way someone shouted, 'She is here!' Adjacent to the church was the funeral parlour, a large lean-to where a huge crowd of people had already gathered at the entrance. I knew that Father would be lying in his coffin, just beyond where those people were. My heart started thumping. Then I saw my three sisters all dressed in white T-shirts and black pants coming out of the crowd towards me.

As I jumped out of the car Mei Lin grabbed and hugged me tightly. 'I can't believe papa's gone,' she said through her tears. Mei Chin and Mei Choon wrapped their arms round us, their tears flowing as freely as mine. Over Mei Lin's shoulders I saw Mother coming towards me. She was wearing a black cotton trouser suit.

'Ma!' I cried. My sisters released me to go to her and as I hugged her my tears came again like a waterfall. When the sobs had ebbed I looked at her face which was dry but drawn like she hadn't slept for days. There was a lost look in her eyes.

'Go and see your papa.' Her voice was gentle.

I nodded, dried my face and took her hand. We walked into the parlour towards the coffin which stood in the middle of the floor in the back half of the parlour that now looked like a makeshift church with rows of benches facing the coffin. I was aware of my uncles and aunts and many other familiar faces around; I heard someone call my name but my eyes were fixed on Father's photograph. I placed my hand over my mouth, dread mounting as I approached the coffin. I took a deep breath before I looked inside.

When I saw his face I felt my heart would burst as yet another searing pain went through it. I'd seen death often enough but it didn't prepare me for seeing my father like that. The corners of his mouth weren't curled down; he looked serene, almost mask-like. I'd expected to smell *Brylcreem* but I didn't although his grey hair was neatly pressed down. Instead all I could smell was the satin lining of the coffin. I couldn't believe that he couldn't reach out to touch my hand and tell me that everything was alright. When I eventually accepted it I felt I was transfixed while everything that was going on around went past me like a carousel in slow motion.

The funeral service was surreal.

Mother had insisted that we children should wear black and white, in keeping with our Chinese custom. Someone had handed me a white T-shirt and black pants to change into. I was sitting next to Mother in the front row along with my sisters and their families. I was aware of people filing in and sitting down. Papa would be pleased at the huge turnout, I thought. Relatives I hadn't seen for years and relatives I hadn't met before were there. My uncles Keow, Kok, Tian and Yew and their families were there. I had seen Chung Lin earlier and there were dozens of faces I didn't recognise, friends of Mother and Father's.

315

A young Chinese pastor conducted the service in Mandarin. When the singing started with a Mandarin version of *Nearer my God to Thee*, a woman's loud voice stuck out – out of tune and sounding like a blackbird with a sore throat. I couldn't help thinking that it would annoy Father. Mentally I smiled. Then it struck me: I was my father's daughter. We *were* alike in many ways, something I wouldn't admit to before, despite my sisters and my mother constantly telling me. I'd seen glimpses of him in me but had refused to admit to it. A part of him was in me - his temper and impatience as well as his fastidious streak. Perhaps, it was these similarities that kept us apart just as like poles of magnets repel.

Throughout the service I kept a watchful eye on Mother. Her face bore marks of the past few days' strain, dark rims round her eyes from which the sparkle had flown. While my sisters and I cried unashamedly, I hadn't seen her cry. Her composure worried me. She hadn't cried at all, not even when we were looking at Father in his coffin. 'Papa looks so peaceful. I'm glad he's wearing a suit. Always fussy about how he dressed,' was all she had said. Perhaps she'd cried herself dry, I thought, or perhaps the shock hadn't sunk in yet.

The weather changed as the cortege made its way through the cemetery. It'd started to drizzle. Someone was holding an umbrella over us as I held Mother's arm to help her up the slope. I was vaguely aware of the crowd of people around us as we were guided to Father's final resting spot. When the pallbearers came to a stop, Mother let out a cry. We'd stopped next to Yao's grave, his face smiling at us from the headstone. My arm shot out to wrap round Mother at the same time as Mei Choon's did. I'd had no idea that Father had bought the plot next to Yao's grave. Mother's sobs were barely audible. In a soft voice she said, 'He's next to his son at last.'

That evening in Mother's house my sisters and I sat with her in the sitting room after Peng and Albert had discreetly moved to join the children on the verandah.

316

'This is the first time all you sisters are together,' said Mother as she looked at us. 'The men in this family are gone now...Papa would have been so proud to see you all and your families. He was very proud of you all, even if he didn't say it. He said you were all so precious.'

No one said a word as we started crying quietly. Mei Chin got out of her chair and went to sit on the floor by Mother and rubbed her hand on her lap.

I couldn't help but admire my mother as I watched her. Right to the end she was loyal to Father. I couldn't fathom her emotions or what she was thinking.

She continued, her voice calm and controlled. 'It happened so quickly, so suddenly. The day before he died, he was very relaxed, much happier than I had seen him in a long time. He helped me peel the prawns. I cooked while he tended to the orchids. We had a lovely lunch. I'd also cooked pig's trotters. He loved it.' She paused as if she was lost in her thoughts. 'He was looking forward to your Uncle Tian coming to see us.' She looked at me with her weary eyes. 'You phoned later that evening...he was so happy you phoned...We went to town next morning. We were walking along Jalan Rahmat when he collapsed, outside the coffee shop.' She shook her head in disbelief. 'Someone called for the ambulance....I never thought he would go like that, so suddenly, so quickly.' She sighed, then looked at the gold watch on her wrist and fingered it. 'He gave me this for my birthday.'

None of us spoke; we could hear the children talking outside in the garden. Then Mei Choon said softly, 'At least Papa didn't suffer.'

We all nodded.

'Ma, it was a good way to go,' said Mei Lin. 'I don't think he would have coped if he was in any way incapacitated and had to depend on you or anyone. No, I can't imagine him an invalid.'

I looked at Mother; she seemed to agree with Mei Lin. I too agreed but said nothing. Her life would be hell on earth, I thought.

317

The evening went on with tales and reminiscing of Father; tears mingling with laughter. Finally, when everyone else decided to go to bed, Mother and I held back and remained in the sitting room. There was an air of peaceful resignation about her. Then, as if she knew what was going through my mind, she looked at me and said,

'You remember when you were younger, much much younger, about thirteen, you said I should leave your papa?'

I nodded.

'He was my husband, I had to stay by him regardless,' she continued. 'Papa loved you best. He always said you were the best thing that happened to him.' She looked at me as if she was appealing to me to believe her.

'I know,' I said. What else could I say? That I thought she only said that to appease me, to stop me feeling angry with him?

'How do you feel, Ma?' I said, watching her face and hoping she would open her heart to me. She looked worn out, the fine lines under her eyes had deepened.

'I'm alright. Will you sort Papa's things, his papers in his desk, tomorrow?'

'Yes. Let's get some sleep now.' I got up and went to put my arms around her.

Early next morning I decided I would embark on my task before the rest of the family got up. The sun was just rising; only a cock's crow in the distance interrupted the silence and the air was cool. It was my favourite time of the day. It always made me feel as if I was imbued with fresh inspiration, standing before a blank canvas, ready to create a masterpiece.

Father's old wooden desk, still in good condition and highly polished, was by the side window in the sitting room looking out on to the garden that he had loved and tended. The soft, gentle rays of the sun lit up his handiwork, revealing a neat and carefully landscaped garden with pink bougainvillea, groups of red, yellow and orange canna lilies and a tall straight hibiscus tree densely dotted with delicate red flowers. I took a deep breath and sat down at his desk. I felt I was trespassing and at the same time the knowledge that he'd never ever sit at the desk again sliced through me like a sharp razor.

The top of the desk was as just he had left it - a large jar of paintbrushes that had been carefully washed and dried sat on the left corner and on the right, a letter pad and a pen-holder with his favourite Sheaffer fountain pen and pencils. I pulled out a drawer on the left. The contents had been ordered into variously coloured folders, neatly stacked up according to size. I took out a folder full of receipts for almost all of the items in the house, then another of personal documents including his and Mother's birth certificates and passports. I opened his passport; immediately the sight of his photograph shattered my resolve not to cry.

I picked up the next folder, placed it on the desk and proceeded to open it. The first thing I saw was instantly recognisable. It was a reprint of my first paper published in the Lancet way back in nineteen eighty-six. I remembered sending it home, eager to show it to my parents. I was surprised that Father had kept it all those years.

Curious, I looked to see what else was in the folder. A postcard from London that I'd sent when I first arrived. Another, from Greece - my first holiday in Europe. Then I saw a yellowed black and white photograph of Father as a young man, smiling and showing off the baby in his arms. The baby was me.

I lifted the photograph to find a small envelope made out of a lined page neatly cut from an exercise book. It had turned brown but was still uncreased as if it had been kept pressed in a book for a long time. I stared at it. The memory of it came like a figure slowly emerging from a thick fog. My heart started to gallop; my hands shook. I took another deep breath. I then opened the envelope and gently pulled out a folded note with a child's spidery handwriting across it.

Dear Father

How are you? I miss you.
Please come home soon,

Chiew

Epilogue

Batu Pahat
A year later

I had returned to Malaysia to spend some time with Mother. Against all advice from her friends she'd chosen to live on her own. When she took me to visit her old friends Ai Chien and Wei in Hakka Street, we sat on the five-foot way in front of Wei's shop drinking coffee. Ai Chien, rubbing her arthritic knees, said in her usual loud voice, '*Aiyah,* we old people shouldn't live alone.'

'I agree,' said Wei who had got up to refill the mugs. 'You should go live with one of your children, in England or Australia.'

'Too cold,' Mother said. 'Also I can't speak English. I'd be a prisoner in their home, not able to go anywhere and when I like. My own home is best.'

'But the house is too big for you,' Ai Chien said.

'Won't be when they all come home to visit,' said Mother looking at me.

When I suggested a live-in housekeeper, she looked at me as if I'd insulted her, her brow wrinkled.

'I'm not old yet. I can still look after myself, but when the time comes and I feel I need help I will consider it,' she said.

After we'd said good bye to Ai Chien and Wei and were just about to cross the street, Mother pulled on my arm and turned to me with a twinkle in her eyes.

'Let's go and see the old shophouse,' she said.

I frowned. 'Why do you want to go there?'

'I thought you might like to see it once more,' she said.

I took a long hard look at the old shophouse across Hakka Street. It looked shabby. The awning was down to keep the afternoon sun out of the five-foot way. The upstairs window shutters were closed. A strange feeling came over me, as if I was about to visit an old friend I had neglected and who was now dying.

We crossed the street, ducked under the awning and stepped onto the five-footway of the shophouse. The air was hot despite the awning but I was more concerned about what I was facing. I stood still for a moment and slowly drew in a deep breath while Mother greeted the two young women sitting like glum buddhas in the shop. On the left were racks of mock-leather shoes and plastic sandals. On the right, more racks. I thought I could smell fabric, lots of fabric. I felt a tingling down my arms, my heart started racing. I was on the threshold of facing my childhood. Conscious of both a longing to return to it and a dread of what I might find, I headed for the back, for the door to the living area where I expected to find my grandparents' shrine overlooking the entrance. I stopped suddenly.

'Where's the door?' I shouted, my voice quivering.

In front of me, where the door should have been, was a brick wall. For a moment I was confused. I felt as if I'd been slapped; tears sprung to my eyes. I stared at the wall then turned to Mother.

'The back half must be unsafe, that's why they've filled it in,' she said softly as she took my arm.

I wanted to scream. It was as if the wall had declared my past null and void, that my childhood was of no consequence or worse, it didn't exist or happen. Behind the wall I could hear a little girl chanting happily '*A man, a pan, a man and a pan…*', her first clutch at English. Like darts, scenes of my father and uncle quarrelling, Grandmother's bowl of wriggling baby mice and Mother crying came at me. Then I felt the anguish and despair of a teenage girl who couldn't wait to leave the shophouse.

**

Today we went to a garden centre. When we were in Mother's garden yesterday admiring the plants, she remembered that Father loved the Bird-of-Paradise plant but couldn't find one to buy. 'He was amazed at the structure of the flower, thought it looked so majestic,' she said.

We found the plant in a garden centre in Ayer Hitam and were thrilled. It was in bloom with orange and purple flowers. We rushed home with it and took it into the garden.

'I think we should plant it about here.' Mother pointed to the spot by the group of canna lilies in the circular bed. 'He loved looking out from his desk.' She turned to look at the window by where his desk was.

'I can start digging then,' I said. The sun had moved round so the spot was in the shade of the hibiscus tree.

'Good,' she said and walked back into the house.

When I'd finished planting, I sat down on the bench under the hibiscus tree to cool down, wiping the perspiration from my forehead. This was where Father would sit on cool evenings. I looked up at the red hibiscus flowers and thought how beautiful they were. Then I looked at the new plant and studied the flowers which did look like birds with orange crowns and I was sure he would have liked them. As I sat there, I recalled the dream that I had of him. He was smiling at me although he didn't say a word. His smile said it all, 'Don't worry, it's alright.' This time he placed his hand on mine and it felt right.

I saw Mother coming towards me with a tray of drinks. She smiled when she saw the plant. 'That's nice. I think Papa would have approved,' she said as she set the tray down on the bench and sat down herself. 'Yes,' she nodded, 'it looks perfect there.'

From out of nowhere a quiet calm descended on me. I felt my spirits starting to lift. I felt that at last I could begin to let go of my regrets.

Lightning Source UK Ltd.
Milton Keynes UK
UKOW041949210513

211049UK00001B/8/P